KELLY IS UNBREAKABLE

By Jackson Keller

Copyright © 2021 Jackson Keller

Paperback ISBN: 9798719588216

First Paperback Edition April 2021

Edited by Alex Lehto-Clark
Cover by ArTrOcItY
Layout by Damonza

Printed by Amazon

www.jacksonjkeller.com

For Sam, whose adventures never fail to inspire.

I ran away from home when I was nine years old. Didn't make it very far, but not because I chickened out or got picked up by a concerned adult. I saw something in the woods that I shouldn't have.

Footprints, disappearing beneath a March blizzard, littered the forest. They led me to a clearing, to a person wearing nothing but a t-shirt and gym shorts in the storm, their face buried against a tree. Snow piled on top of ratty blonde hair that twisted to their waist. I cowered behind another tree and studied this person. This girl? She looked young, but she was tall. Very tall. Way too tall. And skinny, like someone stretched a child's skin over a Halloween skeleton. The way her hair and clothes whipped around almost convinced me she was a banshee haunting the forest. But she couldn't be a ghost. Her light blue shirt and pitch-black shorts shined in the white-out. Snow melted against her warm body. A ghost wouldn't be so damp.

She stumbled back, her gangly legs like a baby giraffe taking her first steps, and screamed. Oh god, she screamed. Her shriek knocked me over. I curled into a ball, slammed my hands over my ears in a futile attempt to block the sound stabbing through.

She lurched and flung her arm back, winding up a punch aimed at the mighty oak tree she leaned on seconds before.

Nothing could've prepared me for what happened when that punch connected.

Her fist tore through the bark, splintering off massive parts of the tree with her touch. Gravity shifted as the tree began its final descent. The girl just stood there.

If I were going to wake up from the nightmare, surely it would've been when the tree hit the ground. Surely it would've been after the exploding flurry of snow and branches. Surely the earthquake that rocked my body would've jolted my head from my pillow.

None of that happened. I was wide awake. This monster was real.

She took a deep breath and stood up a little straighter. Then, she noticed me in her peripheral vision and locked eyes with me.

Her irises glowed a deep, bloody red.

CHAPTER 1
CHRIS

KELLY'S ICY EYES stared down at me when I woke up. A weak smile crept across her face as I sat up and rubbed the sore side of my head. Christ, they must've intentionally designed these desks to give sleeping students migraines.

Besides her, and Patterson hacking away at some poor bastard's essay with red ink, the classroom was empty, silent except for a ticking clock that freed everyone about five minutes ago. Students were always in a hurry to leave their classes, but none ran as quickly as the unfortunate souls in Mr. Patterson's sixth period. Being in the room with him was punishing enough, but when you knew that in just an hour and a half you'd be on your way home, listening to him prattle on made you want to pound nails in your ears.

"How long have I been out?" I asked Kelly, not particularly caring if the teacher heard me. This wasn't the first time I'd fallen asleep in his class, nor would it be the last. If he didn't notice during lecture, he sure did when Kelly and

I sat here like morons five minutes past the bell. Would it really kill her to shake my shoulder and wake me up?

"Pretty much the whole class," she said, brushing a tangle of blonde hair off her face, "Don't worry, I took notes."

"Appreciate it," I said, though I was less concerned about whatever tripe Patterson was talking about that day and more about the splinters I'd have to pick out of my hair. You could actually see "Class of 1973" carved into the top of my desk, obscured by fissures and cracks. I was surprised I didn't get detention for falling asleep this time. Usually, Patterson slips that telltale pink sheet under my elbow and doesn't even bother waking me up. If he was feeling merciful today, then I needed to get the hell out of dodge before he changed his mind.

I sprang up and Kelly flinched so hard she nearly tumbled over her seat. I tried not to look like I was running for the door.

"And where do you think you're going?" Mr. Patterson's smug, droning voice echoed.

I gritted my teeth and tightened my grip on the doorknob. Really, what could he do if I just ignored him and bounced?

I didn't leave, but I refused to turn around. Kelly's shadow wiggled against the door as she fidgeted, "Um, we were just going home. Class is over, isn't it Mr. Patterson?"

"Miss Hatfield, you know perfectly well I'm not talking to you. You're free to go. There's something I need to speak with your little friend about."

Just had to add "little" there, didn't he? I finally turned around. Patterson hadn't even looked up from his desk.

Kelly closed her eyes for just a brief moment and opened them again. We've been friends since we were kids; you'd think their color wouldn't phase me anymore, but I was taken aback by that pale blue every time her gaze met mine. They looked like they belonged on a husky, or maybe a ghost.

I let go of the doorknob and shuffled out of her way. She shot me a non-verbal "good luck" and sidled out to the freedom of the hallway. The door creaked shut until it clicked, sealing me in.

"Have a nice nap, Mr. Underwood?" he said, sliding a pink slip to me without even looking up.

Asshole. He was enjoying this. I pawed at the detention sheet and said, "What do you want?"

I had to stifle a laugh as he put his grading pen down and steepled his fingers with a scowl. Leroy High exclusively employed self-important bozos, but even by those illustrious standards, Mr. Patterson was a real piece of work. His rumpled brown suit and crusty goatee were clearly modeled after a college professor he once had, but he always looked more like a Confederate general to me. Surely the principal hired him to teach the Civil War because he fought in it.

"Tell me Chris, do you know what I'm doing here?"

Indulging him would be the quickest way out of the room. "Grading papers."

"Very good," he flipped through the stack of essays, "Yours seems to be missing. Care to explain why that may be?"

"Forgot about it," I said with a shrug.

He glared at me over his glasses, "You are aware that this essay was worth fifteen percent of your grade?

3

I nodded.

"You are also aware that you need to pass this class to graduate?"

I nodded.

My silence struck a nerve. "Do you think you deserve special treatment? That you're somehow exempt from doing work because you're a senior?"

I shook my head.

"Good, because you aren't getting any. You know I don't give out extra credit."

I nodded.

He stood up and leaned forward on his desk to look down at me, probably feeling real big because I was one of the only guys in the senior class he was taller than, "I think we would both prefer if you didn't have to repeat this course, don't you? So how about you leave your attitude at the door and do your work for once, hm?"

I nodded.

"I'm glad we understand each other," he said, as if that conversation was remotely productive, "Now get out."

I rushed out of the room and made my way toward the senior hallway, pushing against the wave of underclassmen scrambling to the buses. A thin coating of pale, snotty yellow, our school color, covered the lockers and most of the walls. Green flyers with lions, monkeys, and palm trees on them announced the theme for the upcoming prom: Jungle Fever. Jesus. I couldn't believe they let the student council get away with that. When you're from the city, that kind of over the top small-town racism never stops surprising you.

The senior hallway was packed as usual. Everyone took

their sweet time since we didn't have buses to catch. I hoped that my brother had left already, but no, Thomas and a pair of his meathead henchmen lumbered around a few lockers down from mine. They either didn't notice or didn't care that I'd finally shown up.

Meanwhile, Kelly sat against my locker, already deep in her sketchbook. Everyone seemed content to pretend she wasn't there. This worked to her benefit, because she was a lot worse at making herself inconspicuous than she thought she was. Although she saved the baggy anime t-shirts and gym shorts for home, her unofficial school uniform of solid-color hoodies and sweat pants did little to obscure her peculiarities. Her hair still twisted down to her waist in a pale blonde jungle, and she kept growing and growing until she hit a truly colossal 6'4, the tallest student at Leroy High and maybe the tallest person in town, period. I was one of the shortest guys in the class, just barely maxing out at 5'5, so together we were quite the sight to behold. This might not be such a big deal if Kelly had filled out a little with age, but she wasn't exactly proportional for her height, with lanky limbs that matched her flowing hair, something she did her best to hide with those puffy hoodies and sweats I mentioned earlier. I don't know why she bothered trying to blend in. Every peanut brained yokel here was going to treat us like trash no matter what we did.

"Hey!" she said, casting a shadow over me as she sprung up, "How'd it go?"

I presented the pink slip without comment. Kelly frowned, also not having to read it to know what it meant.

"Oh."

"Yeah."

She stayed silent for a moment, looking at me with the caution you'd give a sleeping bear. I cocked my head at her. Detention was nothing out of the ordinary.

"What?" I said.

Twisting her hair into knots between her fingers, Kelly's mouth hung on the cusp of saying something. Whatever it was though, she let it fall by the wayside and stopped herself with a small smile, "Nothing. I was just worried we wouldn't be able to hang out, but I forgot that it's Friday. We'll have plenty of time after detention, right?"

"Guess so."

"So, what's the plan, captain?"

I shrugged, "Haven't given it much thought."

This response obviously dissatisfied her. Her smile faltered for the briefest of moments, and she recovered with a fake sounding laugh, "I don't believe it. Chris Underwood doesn't have some scheme planned for the weekend?"

"We could go back to your place and have a movie night or something."

Kelly bit her lip, "I mean sure, but we can have a movie night any time we want. It's the first day of spring! Don't you wanna go somewhere?"

"It's 35 degrees."

"Okay, it doesn't have to be *outside*. I dunno, I don't really wanna sit around the house today."

"Alright, alright, I'll come up with a plan. Give me something to do for the next three hours."

Kelly nodded. "At least detention's better than dealing with Rich, right?"

That little comment woke me right up. "Oh shit," I

shook my head back and forth, yanking on my hair, "Shit, shit, *shit.*"

Kelly's voice went soft, almost fearful, "Hey, calm down. I thought skipping play practice was a good thing!"

"No. That fat fuck's going to use this as an excuse to back out of our deal. Well, he's a dead man if he tries. He knows how much I need this!"

"He wouldn't have asked you in the first place if he didn't really need you, right? I don't think he's gonna kick you out."

Unable to come up with any response, I kept shaking my head and went for my locker, forcing Kelly aside. But when I entered my combination and pulled on the door, it wouldn't open. I never kept enough clutter in my locker for it to jam, but Leroy High was falling apart at the seams, so it wasn't much of a shock. As I kept fiddling with it, the last remnants of Kelly's fake smile evaporated.

I stopped and looked back at her, "What? Spit it out."

She hesitated again, but eventually came out and said it, "Chris, have you been feeling okay?"

The question felt like a sneak attack. I tried to look and sound authoritative, "Of course I'm okay. Why do you ask?"

"It's just…" she bit the inside of her cheek, "You haven't seemed like yourself recently."

I wondered if throwing her a bone would get her to back off. "I'm fine," I said, "Just tired. Probably need to stop staying up so late."

Didn't work. She looked increasingly concerned as she leaned in to whisper, and her voice carried farther than

I would have liked, "You're not having nightmares again, are you?"

I scanned the area to make sure nobody heard her. Most people kept me and Kelly at a good distance, but my brother and his boys were close enough to hear what we were talking about. Everyone thought Thomas was my older brother, but he's actually my fraternal twin. Hard to blame them since he had like five inches on me and was built like a rhinoceros. Only our faces shared a resemblance. The same brown eyes. He kept his hair buzzed down, but it was the same black color as my shaggy mop. Honestly, looking at the two of us side by side was like witnessing the results an experiment dedicated to turning one clone into a glorious Adonis and another into a vampire.

Thomas and one of his linemen tended to their phones while the scrawniest of the three tried to stuff his overflowing locker shut. The lineman smacked Thomas on the arm, "Bro," he said, "Look at this shit."

Shock and disbelief slowly dawned in Thomas's eyes as he scrolled through his "bro's" phone. He wandered to the middle of the hallway, not paying attention to where he was going and forcing people to dart around him while he focused on whatever he was reading, "Jesus. That's only half an hour from here."

The scrawny kid grunted as a few papers slid from his locker to the ground. "The fuck are you guys talking about?"

"Some asshole at Willow High shot fifteen people," Thomas said.

Certain the only people who could have heard us didn't, I leaned back in to answer Kelly's question, "People have nightmares all the time. There's nothing unusual about it."

Something in Kelly's eyes pleaded with me, like she was holding back what she really wanted to say, "Chris, it's not the same for you."

"Yes, it is. Now drop it."

Kelly looked hurt, but drop it she did. Wanting to fill the silence before she had the chance to ask more questions about my sleeping habits, I said, "You're cutting it close if you want to catch the bus."

"It's okay. I've got time to see you off."

She had a car with no license, and I had a license with no car, so normally I drove both of us home in her baby blue station wagon. Technically, the car Thomas drove was for me to use as well, but since he was always out and about, I stopped arguing for my right to it long ago. Meanwhile, Kelly had a garishly ugly, but perfectly functional vehicle she could drive whenever she pleased. Or, she would, if she hadn't failed her driving test every time she took it. Something about being behind the wheel made her lose her grip. Some of the stories are actually pretty funny, not that I dared laugh about them in front of her. On her very first attempt, she hit the accelerator too hard and plowed through every single cone on the maneuverability test, crashing into the DMV's back wall for the grand finale. Most recently, she made it all the way to the end of her exam without a single point against her, and in joyous celebration, Kelly smacked the car's dashboard, and gigantic chunks of her grandpa's old clunker poured out of the bottom. The instructor promptly failed her. After that, she decided she was perfectly happy having me as her personal chauffeur, which worked out fine until I inevitably got slapped down with a detention.

Anyway, I felt a little bad trying to send her away like that, but I wasn't in the mood for chitchat. I guess Kelly didn't have much to say either, so I struggled to get my locker open in awkward silence, save for Thomas and his friends bellowing behind me. As much as I couldn't stand the guy, it was the kind of conversation that turned heads, so I couldn't help but listen in.

Finally slamming his own locker shut, the skinny guy leaned in with a giggling half-whisper, "You ever wonder if someone's planning to shoot this place up?"

Without missing a beat, the burlier goon said, "You know that sophomore they caught jerkin' it in the library? I heard he's got a list."

Thomas rolled his eyes, "I'll believe it when I see it. You'd have to be one dumb motherfucker to actually write out your hit list."

I tugged on my locker again and searched the edge for a place to slide my fingers in, thinking maybe I could pry it open from the inside. It stayed shut. Putting both hands on the handle and my foot on an adjacent locker for leverage, I yanked back as hard as I could. It still didn't budge. A few of the other students in the hall were staring now, and that was the point where I officially started getting frustrated. I took a step back and ran both my hands through my hair.

My feeble strength clearly wasn't going to be enough, so I turned to Kelly. "Can you—"

I cut myself off when I realized what I was about to do. "What?" she said, "What is it?"

I ran through all the possible consequences of asking her to open it for me. On the surface, it was an innocent enough request, but there was always the chance she'd see it as a violation of Rule One. The last time I broke Rule One, she refused to speak to me for a week. Better not risk it.

"Nothing," I said, returning to the locker, "Don't worry about it."

Rule One. The secret sauce that allowed our friendship to function, that allowed Kelly's life to function. I was never, under any circumstances, allowed to talk about Kelly's "condition" with anyone, herself included. As far as Kelly was concerned, she was completely normal; an ordinary teen girl with absolutely nothing unusual about her. To her credit, she held up her end of the bargain very well. I don't even remember what her last major incident was, but that just made Rule One all the more infuriating.

Still, I didn't dare break it. She could live her life how she wanted, and it really only bothered me in times like this. She could rip the door off its hinges in less than a second and nobody would suspect a thing.

Kelly creeped over my shoulder and started sizing the locker up. A rush of excitement came over me. Maybe she'd pull it off on her own.

"Do you want me to find the janitor?" she said.

I tried not to frown and kept jiggling the handle, "No, I've got it."

I tried prying the locker open again, and the door crushed my fingers when I moved my hand the wrong way. I pulled them out and kicked the locker as hard as I could.

"*Fucking piece of shit!*"

Everyone in the hall silenced at my outburst. Hitting the locker actually did the trick, and a tidal wave of my stuff flooded out as it popped open. Kelly kept her head glued to the floor, scooping up a few of my books and pretending like nothing embarrassing happened. I did my best not to look at Thomas's minions when they started to giggle. Slowly, everyone murmured to each other and returned to their business, while Kelly rose and handed me my stuff.

"Thanks," I said.

"Don't mention it."

Another awkward silence filled the air between us while I reorganized my things. At that point, I wanted nothing more than to pack my shit up and go serve my sentence, but without any conversation with Kelly to distract me, my attention kept wandering over to Thomas. His skinny henchman was sizing me up, like a chimp trying to solve a Rubik's cube in a research lab. Something broke through his pea brain in a fit of laughter as he nudged my brother and not so discreetly tilted his head in my direction.

"What?" Thomas said.

"Dude," he whispered with another obvious gesture, "Your brother."

Thomas glanced at me while his buddy cackled. It took him a minute, but once he caught on, Thomas smacked the guy, "Fucking dumbass."

"Nah, Trevor's right," the other football player said, "Just look at him."

Unlike the other two, Thomas made no effort to control his volume, "I have to live with the guy. You seriously think I wouldn't catch on if he was planning to shoot this place up? Besides, he doesn't have the balls. Half the time when I get up for a midnight piss I hear him crying in his room. He's too much of a pussy."

I slammed my locker shut.

"Chris, don't…" Kelly whispered.

I paid her no attention as I strode towards them.

Thomas's goons started laughing and muttering to one another, but my brother stood his ground, cocking an annoyed eyebrow at me, "The hell is your problem?"

I lobbed a punch at him, but he was prepared for it, putting one arm up to block and using the other to casually shove me away. I lunged again, this time grabbing his scalp and pulling down while I kneed him in the stomach. He gasped in surprise, but I lacked the power to seriously affect him. He snarled and broke free from my grasp, sending his fist directly into my face. It felt like my skull fissured in a hundred spider-web cracks. The force sent me flying back, tripping over my own feet. The back of my head slammed on the hard floor. The other students, now crowded in a half-circle around us, gasped. A waterfall of blood flowed out of my nose and down the side of my face.

My vision went fuzzy as pain took over all my senses. It wasn't something I simply felt, it was something I heard, saw, even tasted. The initial stab faded into a dull, constant thud as I groaned and attempted to prop myself up, but I was too frazzled to make it on my own. Nobody came to help me up, so I stayed down and craned my neck to search the crowd, blinking as the lights now seemed exceptionally bright against the white walls. There were murmurs and whispers. Unease crept into Thomas's expression as he fretted over whether or not he just scrambled my brain. I frowned when I didn't see Kelly among the crowd.

My spirits lifted as the crowd began to part. I hoped it was Kelly, coming to throw a concrete-shattering counter-attack in Thomas's face.

Mr. Patterson's voice echoed from the other end of the hall. "All right, break it up! Out of the way!"

Patterson muscled between the two people in front, narrowing his eyes at us, "Why am I not surprised?" He kneeled down and offered his hand, but I refused it, wobbling to my feet on my own. Patterson sighed and turned to Thomas, "Go to the office. The principal will speak to you first," he turned to me and grabbed my arm, nearly spitting with contempt, "As for you, you're going to the nurse. But don't worry, you'll get your turn. Now walk."

I kept hoping I'd spot Kelly as he dragged me through the crowd, but she was nowhere to be found as it dispersed. She had a real knack for disappearing at the worst times.

"Can't go ten minutes without causing trouble, can you Underwood?" But I ignored him and kept glancing over my shoulder, hoping that Kelly would show herself.

She didn't.

CHAPTER 2

KELLY

I LEFT THE second Chris threw that punch. Every fight he picked with Thomas ended the same way. I didn't need to watch.

Instead, I went to an empty bathroom and checked my eyes in the mirror. Still blue, thank goodness. I was probably okay to leave, but just to be safe, I waited a little so the crowd in the senior hall could clear out. After a few seconds, I rubbed my face a few times, rapidly blinked to make sure that my eyes were okay.

I turned to leave and almost ran right into two of the popular girls, one just tall enough to look like a model who was tiny compared to me, and the other short and cute with a stylish pixie cut. I stood frozen and felt all the blood in my body rush to my head. How long had they been staring at me? Too long. They had these mean little grins on their faces. They didn't even try to hide it.

I lowered my head and stepped around them, moving

maybe a little too quickly. I could hear them laughing behind me. I'm pretty sure one of them said, "All the makeup in the world won't help her," but I might've imagined it, too.

With nowhere else to go, I wandered the halls with no end point in mind.

Way to go, Chris. Way to go. That morning I thought maybe I'd convince him to skip play practice so we'd have more time to hang out, but he was stuck at school for at least the next three hours. And, to make things even worse, he was gonna get suspended, which meant his mom was gonna kill him, which meant I wasn't gonna see him for at least a week. It made me wanna shake him by the shoulders and yell, *"Take your stupid medicine!"*

I could tell he wasn't. I could always tell. Without his medicine, all the things that made him fun to be around, his intensity, his curiosity, his adventurousness, all got sucked out of him and left a zombie shuffling around in his skin. At least until a mood swing kicked in. Then he'd get mad and do something stupid. Usually picking a fight he had no chance of winning.

Oh well. If Chris wasn't gonna be himself, I'd have to do it for him. I'd think of something fun for us to do and it'd make him feel a lot better. Then, when we finally went home, his mom would catch on to what was going on and drag him back to his therapist and everything would go back to normal. That's what always happened. There was no need to make a big deal out of it. He kept perfectly quiet about my condition, so I had no right to bug him about his. Everything would be okay.

That just left the question of what to do until he

finished talking to the principal or going to detention or whatever ended up happening to him. I stopped in front of the hallway leading to the stage, and thought maybe I should go to play practice. Even though I wasn't really part of the play, I'd get bored and follow Chris there instead of going home, so I kinda helped the stage crew unofficially. It'd give me the chance to talk to Rich and smooth things over a little, because if Chris got kicked out, that'd just make him even grumpier, and that was the last thing I wanted. Sure, play practice might've been boring, and all the underclassmen stared at me and whispered mean things when they thought I couldn't hear them, and whenever I read lines for the people who were absent Rich would yell at me for saying it wrong even though it wasn't my part, and the crew all called me Jack Skellington because they couldn't remember my name, but… but at least…

I kept walking. Rich never would've asked Chris to join if he wasn't really needed, and Chris knew his lines. It'd be okay to skip. There was no need for me to talk to Rich. There was no way he'd kick Chris out.

And even if he did, it's not like their stupid deal made any sense in the first place. See, the play Rich was directing apparently needed more boys than the drama club had, so he offered to do Chris's final history essay if he played a part. Rich was an honors student, and Chris had a good semester if his report card came back without any D's, so I guess it seemed like a good deal. But Chris wasted so much more time going to practice almost every day than it would've taken to just do the essay himself. I know he was worried about failing, but I could've read it over for him if he asked me. I mean yeah, I wasn't as smart as Rich, but if I helped out it'd at least be good enough to pass.

With no real reason to wait inside the school, I went out the main doors and found a dry spot on the curb to sit and draw on. A gentle wind brushed my hair in my eyes as I bent down to grab the sketchbook in my bag. I thought about taking off my hoodie to cool down a little, but I was pretty sure that the Sailor Moon t-shirt underneath would draw attention to me if anybody walked by, so I forced myself to wait until I wasn't on school grounds.

It was always hard for me to appreciate the first day of spring. I barely noticed the change of weather, and the flowers hadn't started to bloom yet. Misty skies blocked out the sun, and globs of melting snow were a reminder that winter could come back whenever it felt like it. Ohio spring was mucky and gross and grey.

No, you didn't forget today because of the weather. You forgot what today was because you're horrible and stupid and selfish and awful. You're not allowed to forget today.

With some paper and something to draw with, I could keep myself occupied for hours. Ever since I got accepted to art school, I'd been trying to branch out into more realistic stuff, sketching cool things in my line of sight, but if I didn't have a specific thing in mind I always ended up doing some kind of goofy fan art. It's weird, until it was time to apply for college I'd never really thought of drawing as something to make a career out of or anything. I drew just to draw. I guess you could call it a compulsion, something to keep my hands busy. You need finesse and control to be a good artist. So, I thought maybe if I drew enough, it'd give me the deft touch needed to not break the pencil or whatever. It was something Grandma taught me to do when I first moved in with her, when she found out what I was. She liked to paint, and always told me that whenever she was upset, painting helped her calm down. It didn't matter if the final picture was any good. The act of making it was what really mattered.

Grandma spent the whole morning crying, and you had the nerve to ask her what was wrong. She doesn't even know. She does all these nice things for you and she doesn't even know you're the one who ruined her life. How are you able to look her in the eye, let alone live in her house?

A harsh buzz from my bag broke my concentration. I took a deep breath and ignored it, not even bothering to check who it was. Grandpa was the only person who ever called me. My grip on my pencil loosened, and my work started getting sloppier. You never really realize how long a phone goes on for until you're trying to ignore it.

What would Grandpa do if he ever found out the truth? He's a pretty old school guy, he'd probably want to take you to the proper authorities. I'm kinda surprised he never figured it out. He's smart, and he has everything he needs to piece together what really happened. He probably figured it out a long time ago and just doesn't want to believe it.

I put my pencil down and looked at my finished drawing. Horrible, just horrible. I must've drawn over a thousand stupid Pikachu in my life and suddenly I couldn't draw one without it looking like a lumpy potato. You'd think I'd never drawn a straight line. What garbage. Why did I waste my time on these stupid cartoons anyway? They looked like crap and they didn't do anyone any good.

My insides were on fire, and my eyes burned. I worked

to keep my breathing calm, and tried my best to gently slide my hand into my bag. I don't know why I bothered going for my pocket mirror. My eyes were obviously glowing, and my panic at that thought only made them burn harsher. Then, while I rooted around in there, the phone went off again, and I tore my hand out like it was going to bite me.

Quickly running out of options, I hugged my sketchbook and clenched my eyes shut, not caring about how silly I must've looked to anyone walking by. Everyone knew I was a weirdo already, so that didn't matter. What mattered was keeping my condition hidden. It got so bad that I started talking to myself.

"Calm down. Calm down. Everything's gonna be fine," I took another deep breath, and kept talking out loud, like saying it with conviction would make it true, "Everything's gonna be fine. You're gonna wait here for Chris. You're gonna take him on some kinda adventure, and you're gonna have a great time. You've got it under control."

The phone rang again. I reached in and shut it off with one quick motion.

"You've got it under control."

NINE YEARS AGO

I'll never understand why Chris didn't run. You'd think he'd lose it as soon as he saw me knock down that tree, but he just sat there, looking at me.

I almost laughed in pure shock. All that worrying over anyone finding out about me, all that work to keep my condition a secret, totally ruined in one stupid, stupid moment. He must've been trying to come up with some sort of explanation for what he just saw, but there was no explanation. There was no point in trying to get him to understand when I didn't even understand.

I walked away without looking back, knowing I'd start crying again if I did. I didn't bother asking him not to tell anybody. Nobody would believe him, and it wouldn't matter if they did. No one would ever find me anyway.

Ice and water slid down my legs and into my socks. On most kids, the snow would've come all the way up to their knees, but it only came a few inches above my ankles. I focused on moving one foot at a time and tried to stop thinking about Chris spotting me.

Come on Kelly, it won't be so bad. You always wanted to go

on an adventure. You just need to find the right place. Like…
like Alaska! Sure, it's a pretty long way, but once you're there,
you don't have to worry about anything anymore. You can do
whatever you want there. You won't have to go to school and
you can explore the wilderness and play in the snow and live
with the animals and you won't have to worry about anyone
getting hurt and—

I couldn't hold my tears back. Dad was right. If I just stayed in the house the way he wanted me to, everything would've been fine.

I remember the first time I asked him about going outside, when I was really little. The cartoon reruns were getting boring, so I spent a lot of time looking out the windows, waiting the whole summer for the school bus to come back. Every day I imagined it stopping at our house. Every day I imagined getting on to have all sorts of wacky adventures and make all kinds of friends. But that morning, watching the bus didn't make me happy the way it usually did. I tore away from the window and went down to our kitchen table while Dad made breakfast. He stayed behind the counter and sliced up an apple, not greeting me with hugs or kisses. Dad always kept his distance. It was safer that way.

"What's wrong, sweet pea? You look sad," he said.

My question wasn't unreasonable, I don't think, and I tried to say it in a way that wouldn't make him mad.

"Um, Daddy? Why don't I go to school like all the other kids?"

Nearly dropping the knife in his hand, Dad hid his surprise by turning to grab a plate out of the cupboard,

"Because you're safer with Daddy than you are with some teacher who doesn't know nothing."

"But the other kids are safe there."

Dad cracked an egg over a skillet, keeping his back to me as he talked, "You're not like the other kids. Why are you asking about school anyway? You not happy here?"

"No, I'm happy. But I get kinda lonely 'cause you gotta work all the time."

He said nothing, letting the egg cook a little before coming back to the counter, his stern gaze digging into me, "Kelly, what do you think will happen if I let you get on that school bus?"

"I dunno—"

"Well I do. You're gonna spend all day surrounded by strangers in a place where I can't look out for you. You're gonna have to spend every minute of every day making sure nobody can see what's wrong with you. It's too much for you to handle."

Energy bubbled inside me, but I fought to push it back. Losing control in front of Dad was the fastest way to get punished, "But I've been really good lately—"

"All it takes is one mistake, Kelly. One mistake and everyone in the whole world knows about you. You wanna risk that because you've gone a few months without breaking my furniture?" He paused and waited for my answer, but I couldn't keep looking him in the eye, "Well? Do you?"

"No…"

"No, you don't. Because not a single one of those kids'll be able to look at you the same way if you mess up. They'll think you're some kinda monster, Kelly. You won't have even one friend. And that's if you're lucky. If you end up on the news, there's gonna be cops and soldiers breaking down our door to take you away from me. That what you want?"

"No!"

"Good. Then I don't wanna hear no more about school. You have everything you could ever want right here."

Dad went back to making breakfast, taking the eggs out of the pan and slicing up the last of the fruit. My eyes started burning and I drew my arms to my chest and locked them up tight and put my head down. I should've left the room and found a place to calm down, but I was afraid if I made any sudden moves, I'd make everything worse. So, I stayed still, hoping I could cry quietly enough for it to pass.

Dad stopped what he was doing when I sniffled just a little too loudly. His voice was thick with icy anger. "You better not be crying."

I shook my head back and forth, shutting my eyes so hard they started to hurt.

Dad's knife thudded against the counter when he put it down, "Because you know what happens when you do that. I think you better let me take a look at your eyes."

But I didn't listen, keeping myself withdrawn like a turtle. Each one of his footsteps sent a tremor of fear through me.

"I'm not fooling, Kelly. Let me see your eyes, right now."

I should've just shown him. I was gonna get punished either way, but fear took over my brain. When he got close, I sprang up to run for it, putting my hand on the table to keep my balance.

The table cracked and buckled in a flurry of splinters and dust, and I crashed on the floor between both halves.

"Goddammit Kelly!"

Dad yanked me up by my hair, pushing my face toward the pile of broken wood like a puppy who just ruined the carpet, "You see? You see what I'm talking about? This is why I can't let you outside!" With another yank, he dragged me over to the basement door, shoving me down the stairs because he knew the impact couldn't actually hurt me. The lock clicked into place behind me as I tumbled down every single creaky step before slamming against the concrete bottom. I scrambled to my feet. The walls of that window-less, cramped hole in the ground felt like they were closing in on me. There weren't any lights, and Dad purposefully had all the furniture taken out so there'd be an empty space where I wouldn't wreck anything.

I ran up the stairs to stand right behind the door, stopping just short of banging against it because I didn't wanna break it and make him even angrier.

"Daddy! Daddy let me out!" I squealed.

His voice already sounded distant, "You break the rules, you get punished! That's how it goes!"

"I'll never do it again, I promise! Please, I don't wanna be down here!"

"You wanna go to school? You wanna leave me? Then get this under control! 'Cause I'm not letting you out until you're *normal.*"

I screamed and cried as his footsteps echoed away, but he didn't come back. The punishment lasted until the next morning. They always lasted until the next morning.

Sure, it was harsh, but I finally understood what Dad always knew. Everyone would be better off if I disappeared.

So that's what I had to do.

A gust of snowflakes drenched my clothes, melting on

my body. My condition had a lot of downsides, but it was like it was made for running away. A weird side effect let me stay warm even in the blizzard, and I could walk for hours without feeling tired. If any ten-year-old had a chance of making it to Alaska on foot, it was me. The only tricky part would be food. I really liked food, but I wasn't sure that I actually needed to eat. Hunting and stealing both seemed bad, but I couldn't think of any other options.

The coldness of the snow wasn't a problem, but the weather still made me nervous. The wind muffled all sound. I'd already blown my cover by letting one person sneak up on me, and although I'd managed to stop crying, I had no idea if my eyes were still red. If only I'd been thinking straight and brought my pocket mirror, but the only thing I remembered to take with me was...

My blood went cold. My sketchbook. The one comfort I had for the road, and it was gone. I must've dropped it without even realizing. I immediately dropped to my knees and started digging through the snow. Stupid, stupid, *stupid.*

Then, to make things even worse, a voice rose over the blizzard.

"WAIT!"

Footsteps crunched behind me. I didn't turn around.

"You forgot this."

I blinked, batting snowflakes from my eyes, and glanced over my shoulder. Chris reached into his coat and pulled out my sketchpad, offering it to me with a shaky arm.

"It got a little wet. Sorry."

Huffing and puffing from chasing me, he steeled himself when I stood up, gulped before clenching his free hand into a fist. Even though he was obviously scared silly, he did his best to not look that way. I took the notebook from him tenderly, like he was handing me a sleeping baby, and tucked it under my arm after dusting snow off the cover.

"Um… thanks."

We awkwardly stared at each other for a little while before I started on my way again.

"Wait." He stopped me. Something in his brown puppy dog eyes looked almost hopeful. "Where are you going?"

I hesitated for just a moment, "I'm running away. You're not gonna tell anyone about me, are you?"

"No. But…" He took a deep breath and paused, like even he wasn't sure what he wanted to say, "Do you think maybe I could come with you?"

It was a joke, right? It had to be.

But his voice and his eyes were so sincere, so innocent. For a second it didn't seem like such a terrible idea. He already knew my secret, so there shouldn't be any issue. Then, the little voice in my head spoke up, *No Kelly, You can't take him with you. He's only gonna get hurt if you do.*

Still, I didn't say no right away.

"Why?" I asked.

He hesitated, like he wasn't sure he should tell the truth, "I don't know, you'll be pretty lonely all by yourself."

"Aren't you scared of me?"

"Not really," I must've looked pretty skeptical, because he quickly added, "Okay, a little bit, but I mostly think you're cool. Your drawings are awesome."

I thought I was going to throw up. He looked at it. It didn't make me feel good knowing he liked them; nobody was supposed to look at my drawings.

He continued, "And I don't know, you're like a super-hero or something."

The little voice of reason was right. He had no idea what he was dealing with.

He tried to say something else, but I cut him off before he could.

"My grandma and grandpa were fighting when I woke up. I know it's wrong for me to listen without them knowing, but I couldn't help it. I guess they'd been talking to a friend of theirs whose grandkids got in a fight at school."

I knew they were talking about the fist fight him and his brother had at recess the other day. I didn't say that part, but I think he figured it out, anyway. Actually, fight is maybe the wrong word. It was more like his older brother pinned him against the ground and beat the stuffing out of him.

Somehow the guilt on his face made it much harder to tell the story. I took a moment to calm myself before I could keep going, "And that made Grandpa really scared. He was saying that he didn't want me in school anymore if the teachers weren't looking after us properly, because if something happened with me someone was gonna get seriously hurt."

All the energy brewing in me made me sick, and holding everything in became impossible. I had to sit down in the snow and tear up a little before I could finish. "He doesn't trust me, and the worst thing is that I know he's right. I shouldn't be in school. I never should've been in school."

I buried my face in my hands and soon I was a mess of tears and snot. Chris took a seat next to me, but I scooted away to keep my distance. He didn't try to come any closer. He didn't try to calm me down. Even though he had no way to know what being in school meant to me, he didn't try to convince me everything would be okay. He just let me cry.

And he didn't run.

I'm not really sure how much time we passed just sitting there. Fifteen or twenty minutes, maybe even longer than that. When I finally calmed down a little, he unzipped his coat and handed it to me, telling me to wrap my notebook in it so it wouldn't get wet. Feeling how soggy my drawings were already, and not even considering the fact that normal people couldn't handle the winter with just a t-shirt on like I can, I bundled it up. Then he stood, and I cocked my head at him as he packed some snow into a ball.

"Come on, let's make a snowman," he said. He kept packing snow together and rolling it around, only stopping when he noticed I wasn't moving. "It's easier to forget the bad stuff if you're not just sitting around."

He made another snowball, leaving it at my feet before going back to his. I didn't really see how making a snowman would make anything okay, but I put his bundled coat on a log and helped. Weirdly enough, he was right. Rolling the snowball around numbed me. I wouldn't say it made me feel better, but watching the ball get bigger and bigger, leaving a long trail of grass and mud behind it, gave me something meaningless to focus on. It helped me push my sadness away, at least for a little bit.

We spent a good amount of time making that snowman. I actually forgot Chris was with me until he rolled back into view, struggling with a snowball about half his size. He did a double take at mine, which was almost twice as big. We'd packed all the snow in the area into the two unbalanced parts of our snowman. He bent down and tried to lift his, but he could only get it about an inch off the ground without dropping it. Placing my hands gently around it, I took the snowball from him and plopped it on top of the snowman's bottom half. His face flared red as we both stepped back to check our finished work. It was a pretty disappointing snowman, a shrunken head lost in a huge body.

"He's kind of a porker, isn't he?" Chris said.

I nodded, pressing my pointer finger on my lip, wondering if there was any way to fix him. Inspiration hit me when a few big rocks on the ground caught my eye. I gathered them up until I found two about equal size. I grabbed the snowman's head and put it back on the ground, pushing it against what used to be his body. Then, after pressing my rocks into the bigger snowball, I grabbed a few twigs and stuck them at the top. We both started giggling when I stepped away to reveal the finished product: a big snow head with a bulbous snow nose, rocks for eyes, and spindly twigs mimicking a few stray hairs. Definitely an improvement. I don't even know what was so funny about it, but we kept laughing, and seeing each other's reactions just made us laugh harder.

Chris caught his breath and wiped a tear away, "Well, I've made up my mind."

"About what?"

He grabbed his bundled jacket and handed it back to me, "I'm not letting you run off alone. I'm coming with you, whether you want me to or not."

I smiled and nodded, "Let's go." For once, the little voice didn't object.

We walked side by side for a little while, but having to slow my pace so he could keep up made me a little embarrassed; my legs had never felt so long before. We hadn't gone far when he awkwardly rubbed the back of his neck and said, "Hey, I think you're in my class, but I don't think I know your name."

I stared at him in disbelief, and suddenly I was cracking up again.

Chris took on a defensive tone, "What's so funny?"

"You wanna run away with me and you don't even know my name?"

He stared at the ground, too embarrassed to respond.

A goofy grin stuck to my face, "It's Kelly. You're Chris, right?"

"Yeah. How'd you know?"

Guessing he didn't wanna hear the actual answer, I said, "You're the new kid. The teacher introduced you in front of class, remember?"

The truth was, everyone knew Chris's name, although I'd been keeping a close watch on him even before that. Him and his brother arrived in the middle of the school year, just like I did the year before. Nobody really noticed him until one day, during quiet reading time, the screechy tornado siren went off. The teachers didn't want anyone to know it was coming so we'd act like it was a real emergency. We were all a little surprised, and most of us covered our ears as we lined up for the hallway. That's probably why it took everyone so long to realize Chris was screaming. He hadn't gotten up from his seat until the teacher went over to calm him down, but when she tried to get him to move, he swatted her away and ran out the door to the playground. The class started laughing, crowding around the windows as the teacher ran out to chase him. The gym coach ended up having to leave his class to pull Chris off the jungle gym, and he got sent to the principal's office for the rest of the day.

The other kids started making things up as soon as it was over. The ones sitting near him when he started screaming said he peed himself. Another kid said that while the teacher was trying to get him to come back, he punched her hard enough to leave bruises she had to cover up the rest of the week. From there the rumors got more intense, to the point where everyone thought he was some kinda psycho. The one I remembered most was that he had to leave his old school because he stabbed a girl with a pen. Those rumors only got worse with his latest incident, when his brother pinned him to the blacktop and started whaling on him, screaming, "It's all your fault! It should've been you!" It was hard to miss all the conversations, from our class and others, about what exactly Thomas meant by that.

Either way, they started making fun of Chris all the time; first behind his back, then to his face. Nobody even gave him a chance.

But I sat behind him, and I thought he seemed like fun. He always brought his Game Boy and played it under his desk when class got especially boring, which was good for me because I was tall and could watch over his shoulder. Actually, I was sorta impressed. If I was allowed to have something expensive like a Game Boy, I'd never bring it where a teacher could take it away, but he didn't care. He was willing to risk it. And besides, I knew what it felt like being the new kid. I knew what it felt like to be excited to make all sorts of friends until, slowly, you realize that nobody likes you because you're weird and ugly.

I started thinking about maybe talking to him, but whenever I tried to lean forward and do it, a little voice in my head would say, *No Kelly, that's a terrible idea. What are you gonna do? Play tag with him at recess? Yeah, right. You wouldn't be able to do anything normal friends do, and you could never, ever tell him why. Why would he want a friend like that? He's better off without you in his life.* Then I'd realize the little voice was right and sink back into my seat, ignoring the new boy while he faded into the rest of the class.

Now I knew for sure I should've just talked to him. Maybe none of this would've happened if I had.

"Where did you move from?" I said, trying to fill a big pause.

He stayed quiet, like he didn't wanna tell me. Eventually he mumbled, "Brooklyn."

"Oh. Where's that?"

"New York."

My eyes went wide. He may as well have said he was from the future, "New York? Like New York City?"

"Yeah."

"Wow. Did you like it there?"

Something about his eyes didn't entirely look right. I don't exactly know how to explain it. They were kinda glassy and glazed over, like someone flipped his brain's off switch.

"It was okay. Is Squirtle your favorite?" he said almost in one breath.

I blinked a few times, "Huh?" He pointed at my chest, where the cheerful Pokémon's face beamed from my t-shirt. The change in subject was about as smooth as sandpaper, but I got the hint that his memories of New York weren't really happy ones, and knew better than to push him.

Besides, Pokémon! I'd been waiting my whole life for someone to ask me that, "Yup! Isn't he cute? I like those little sunglasses he always has."

"Charizard's the strongest though."

"Maybe, but I don't really care about which one is the best or anything. I just like watching the show. I've never even played the games," I tried to laugh, "If I had a Game Boy, I'd probably just break it."

"You can play mine, if you want."

"That's okay. I'd feel really bad if I did something to it." I hesitated. Would he think it was weird that I'd been watching him play during class? Better not mention it. "But I wouldn't mind watching over your shoulder. Do you have it with you?"

He frowned, "No. My mom took it away when I got suspended. Besides, I didn't think I'd be running away from home today."

We said nothing as we both caught the first sign that this was a pretty stupid idea.

Not wanting the conversation to die, I dug my sketchbook out of his coat and bit the inside of my cheek. I'd never shown my drawings to anyone but Grandma before—not on purpose, anyway—but he'd already seen some of them. If he liked Pokémon, he might actually think they were cool. I flipped through a few pages until I found my favorite drawing and held it out, careful to keep from accidentally touching him. I wanted to say something about what he was about to see, but it all sounded stupid again, so I did the awkward thing and kept my big mouth shut.

My arm snapped back to my side the second he grabbed the notebook and I looked away, nervous that he'd think it was lame, but desperately trying to remind myself that he liked what he already saw.

The picture I gave him was a fully colored scene of all the starter Pokémon running together. It was definitely my best work. Not to say that it was a perfect drawing or that my lines were straight all the time or my perspective wasn't a little bit wonky or… oh okay, it wasn't really that great, but you have to start somewhere, right? I thought I was actually pretty good for my age. Art is the one thing I could always be proud of.

Finally, he said, "You're a really good drawer."

It surprised me. Not his compliment, really, but his face. Like a fire lit behind his eyes, gave the sad looking boy some life as he smiled. I couldn't remember the last time someone said something that nice to me. I dunno, something about his smile told me he wasn't just saying that. He really meant it. That made me blush.

"I'm not as good when I'm not copying something," I said, "But I didn't trace it or anything like that."

He admired the picture for a little while longer before putting his finger on the edge of the page. I had to stop myself from yelping as he flipped to the next drawing.

Don't make it weird. He likes them.

He was about to make another comment when he stared at me in surprise.

"What?" I asked, suddenly afraid of what he had to say.

"Your eyes. They're blue now."

They are? I ran my hand against my face. Without my mirror I had no way to tell for sure, but I felt normal.

We kept walking and talking as he flipped through the rest of my notebook. I dunno if we talked about anything other than cartoons, but that was okay! It made me feel like a normal kid; I never had a conversation like that with anybody.

I don't know how much time we wasted talking about nothing, but we only stopped when we reached the edge of the forest. A white blanket of snow spread out forever in front of us. A car cut through the distance in a straight line, but the road itself was invisible.

"So, what now?" he said.

"I, um, I don't really know. I was thinking it'd be best if I went to Alaska."

"Alaska? We're walking all the way to Alaska?"

It sounded stupider and stupider the more I explained it, "Yeah... except I don't know if we're even going north."

Chris peered in the distance at another car inching through the snow. He tilted his head back toward the woods, "Let's stay away from the road so nobody sees us. We can walk by the trees while we figure out where we're going."

We kept moving near the edge of the woods. Slowly, it became obvious that something was wrong with Chris. The cold turned his tan skin almost purple, and it took him twice as long to talk because he kept stuttering over his chattering teeth. It took me way too long to realize he was freezing without his coat. I was still holding it.

He shook his head when I tried handing it back to him. "Your drawings will get ruined."

"That's my fault for not bringing a backpack. Take it."

Reluctantly, he slipped the coat back on, but since it'd been soaked by so much snow, it might've made things worse. He was pretty much putting on a wet towel.

Watching him slowly get frostbite was the last straw. This was never going to work. I was a real idiot for thinking everything would be fine if I just ran away.

"Maybe we should go back," I said.

Chris stopped in shock, "What? Why?"

"I'm starting to think this is kind of a stupid idea. We're not really ready for this."

His sudden glare made my heart sink. What did I say? He sped up, forcing me to chase him, "Hey, wait!"

He continued walking without looking at me, "You go home. I'm not going back."

What had gotten into him? He picked up his pace and kept his head down, making it hard for me to get a good look at his face. Sobs started coming with his shivers.

"Hey," I said, finally stopping him, "What's the matter?"

"I'm not going back," he repeated.

"Come on, you're gonna freeze to death out here."

"Good," he completely broke down, crying his eyes out while marching forward. His words made him go faster. "I'd be better off that way. I hate it here. Nobody likes me and my brother is mean to me all the time and I don't know why and Mom doesn't care at all and..." He trailed off, the overwhelming emotion making him lose his focus.

"I like you."

He stopped again. There was some shock in his eyes, and a little bit of hope. I surprised myself by going on, talking without running my words through any kind of filter, "I had fun with you today. You're really nice. You made me feel better when I was sad, and you didn't freak out when I…" I stumbled a little just thinking about my big mistake, "Well, you know. I wanna be your friend, but I can't be if you run away by yourself, and I definitely can't be if you freeze to death."

For a second I thought he was gonna keep going without me. I didn't know what I'd do if he did.

When he finally answered, it was so quiet that I could barely hear him, "Do you really mean it?" he said.

"Really." I tried to think of something else to say to make him feel better, "You know, I always kept to myself 'cause I was afraid that if I made friends, they'd find out I wasn't normal. But you already know, so that doesn't really matter, right?"

"I still don't see why that's such a big deal," Chris said, wiping his eyes, "I think it's cool that you have powers."

Hearing someone talk about my condition made me uneasy. Even Grandma and Grandpa danced around it whenever they could. I was happy he didn't think I was a monster, but still, I couldn't help but panic hearing him talk so frankly about it.

Maybe it was just the word he used.

Powers.

"It's hard to explain. I just don't want anyone to know."

"Okay," he sniffled, "Your secret is safe with me."

If it wouldn't have broken every bone in his body, I

would've hugged him. Wanting to show how thankful I was, I tore that first Pokémon drawing out of my sketchbook and handed it to him. He didn't take it at first, giving me a confused look, and I felt silly, because giving him the picture made sense in my head.

"I, um, I dunno," I said, "I thought it'd make us being friends more official, or something."

All his tears dried with a smile as he neatly folded the drawing and stuck it in the pocket of his coat, "So now that we're officially friends, what do you wanna do?"

"I think we should go home," I said, "We've been gone a long time. Grandma and Grandpa are probably real worried about me."

He hesitated, "Maybe we should stay out a little longer."

"Oh." I frowned, "You mean you still wanna run away?"

"No... not really... but I'm gonna be in pretty big trouble when I get back. I probably won't see you again until my suspension is up, and..." his face reddened, "I just don't want the day we became friends to end with me crying like a baby. Let's do something fun."

I smiled, "Okay. What were you thinking?"

"Let's go finish our snowman. I bet with your super strength we could make the biggest one ever," he started running back the way we came and waved for me to follow, "Come on! Let's go find him!"

Energized by his returning enthusiasm, the two of us ran side by side. It was a reckless thing for me to do, but I was too excited to care. How lucky was it that we just happened to stumble into each other? It made me wonder...

"Hey!" I said, "Where do you live?"

Chris pointed off in the distance, "Just outside the woods that way, I think."

"Wait," I twisted around, not watching where I was running as I tried to judge how far we were from my house. Grandma told me a few weeks earlier that two boys my age had moved in next door, but I never went over and introduced myself the way she wanted me to.

"The one with the green roof and the puppy statue on the front porch?"

"Yeah, that's it."

"I live next door!"

"What? We're neighbors?"

"We're neighbors!"

"You know what that means, right? We gotta hang out all the time!"

"And we can sit next to each other on the bus!"

"And we can walk over to each other's houses whenever we're bored!"

We kept going like that all the way back to our silly snow head, and then immediately got to work. We spread out to any area we didn't clear of snow earlier, making all sorts of snowballs of different shapes and sizes. Keeping the big nose was our unspoken objective for the finished snowman, but since the nose was a separate snowball, we couldn't find a good way to keep it attached to the head; it was so heavy that it kept falling to the ground. We tried making all kinds of bodies, even a four-legged snow sphinx, but we couldn't get it to look right.

When I spotted a log with a sturdy looking branch jutting out the top, I had an idea. Chris watched in awe as I dragged the log over and skewered the snow head like a shish kebab. Then, I stuck the nose snugly on the end of a branch, hoping it would hold its weight.

I hoisted the fallen tree, with our creation on the end of it, into the air. I wanted our goofy head to sit at the top of the upright log like a totem pole, but when I tried lifting it up, both snowballs fell apart and rained down on my head.

Chris started laughing, and that made me laugh, and before we knew it neither of us could stop.

CHAPTER 3

CHRIS

THE GOOD NEWS was that I didn't have to serve my detention. The bad news was that I got suspended again. After the nurse made sure my concussion wasn't serious enough to warrant a hospital visit, she sent me down to the office. I didn't waste any time trying to explain myself, having been down this road enough times to know precisely how it ended. Sure enough, they gave me three days out-of-school suspension for instigating the fight, while Thomas just got a detention because he "acted in self-defense," as if there was a pint of his blood splattered at the back end of the senior hallway. I got used to the fact that we were never going to get equal punishment for the same crime. As the football team's star quarterback, the staff did everything in their power to make sure he benefited from as many loopholes as possible. The principal avoided calls from angry dads so long as my brother stayed in the game, so his record showed a star student instead of a complete degenerate. Of course, Thomas had long since played his last game for the

Leroy Lions, so that didn't even matter for this particular incident. Principal must have been acting out of habit.

Thomas had to serve his time that very evening, so the secretary escorted him to the library while the principal dragged me through the school's side door like he was taking the trash out. He told me I'd better not be seen on school property until next Thursday and slammed the door behind him, as if I'd ever stick around a second longer than I absolutely needed to. I pulled out my phone to text Kelly the score. About an hour had passed since my fight with Thomas, so she'd be long gone. My phone greeted me with six new texts from Rich, the director of the school play I'd been roped into. He averaged one about every three minutes.

Der Führer

Remember there's practice today

Hey how late you running?
We're starting with your death scene
so you need to get here

What the fuck? Everyone's saying you
started another fight

Please tell me you aren't suspended

There are only two weeks until the show.
What am I gonna do without you?

You know what I don't care. You're out.
Have fun writing that paper by yourself

I swore under my breath and kicked a hunk of ice on the sidewalk, almost breaking my big toe since it was much sturdier than it looked. Gritting my teeth, I shuffled towards the main lot, pretending I wasn't in pain even though nobody was watching. Normally, I wouldn't care about being kicked out of some bullshit school play, but I'd just blown a pretty sweet deal, and the easy last weeks of my final semester were gone. I'd have to work my ass off to scrape by in History, and even then, a passing grade was far from a guarantee. Suddenly, another year at Leroy High seemed like a real possibility. If it came to that, I'd just drop out. It's not like I was going to college either way.

Parking spaces were determined by the social pecking order, so naturally we got stuck with the juniors in the back corner, far from the main entrance. I got inside the car, started it up, and cranked the heat as high as it would go to counter the March wind. When I leaned back into the seat, a searing pain shot through my body and clouded my vision. A ringing echoed in my ears. Must've hit my head harder than I thought.

The pain didn't go away. The ringing amplified the longer I sat there. Hot air pumped through the vents and smothered me until my clothes clung to my skin with a thick coating of sweat. The ringing drowned out all other sound, and I couldn't breathe. I reached for the door to try and escape the car, but the handle kept slipping out of my trembling, sweaty palms. The door swung open after what felt like an eternity of fumbling and I nearly fell out. Stepping back into the cool outdoors made breathing easier, but the ringing persisted, and my stomach lurched. I hovered over the concrete, stabilizing myself with a shaking hand on the hood of the car. At any moment I expected to vomit, but nothing happened. However slowly, it seemed like things were returning to normal. My stomach stopped hurting, my hands stopped shaking, and my hearing returned.

I got back in the car and slammed the door, tears welling up in my eyes as I screamed and laid into the horn.

All the way by the main entrance, a blonde figure on the curb perked up at the sound and looked over in my direction. I froze. They were so far away that I hadn't even noticed them. How much of that shameful little freakout did they witness? I squinted through the dirt-smudged windshield to get a better look.

…Kelly? As if to confirm my thought, she slung her bag over her shoulder and bounded toward me. Why was she still hanging around? Perhaps she missed the bus, or tried going to practice and got kicked out? But those weren't good reasons to stay at school; she could have called her grandpa and gone home any time.

Before she got too close, I twisted the rearview mirror around to get a better view of my face, frantically wiping my eyes. They were still a little red, but since my nose had swollen so much, I didn't think she'd notice I'd been crying. No one had seen me cry since I was nine years old, and I'd be damned if I broke that streak on top of all the other shit that happened.

The passenger door opened and Kelly bounced in with a smile on her face, "You could've swung around and picked me up, you know."

I rolled with it. "Feeling lazy."

Kelly buckled in as I put the car in drive, "How'd you manage to sneak by me?"

"Principal shoved me out by the dumpsters."

Her face drooped, and she let out a heavy sigh.

I nodded. "And Rich kicked me out of his little side-show when he found out."

"Oh." For some reason, she looked guilty, "I'm sorry."

"It's not your fault."

An awkward silence hung in the air as I pulled out of the parking lot and started down the highway. Nothing summed up the experience of living in Leroy, Ohio quite like driving home. It was almost a completely straight shot back to our street. No stores, no restaurants, not even any hills. You keep going and going and going through corn-field after cornfield, but you're never going anywhere.

After a few minutes of driving, Kelly's sullen expression eased up, "At least you'll have the afternoons to yourself again. Once your suspension is done, I mean."

I was barely paying attention to her, feeling like I was going to fall asleep at the wheel, waking up and overcorrect-ing when the car subtly veered into the next lane, "Doesn't change the fact that I'm totally fucked."

"It can't be that bad. Just work extra hard on your paper."

"It won't matter. I need an A on this to pass and my best essay for Patterson got a B minus. Dude's a Nazi with a red pen. Say what you want about Rich, at least he wasn't grading me."

She considered this for a moment, "I do pretty good in his class. I can help you, if you want."

I didn't hesitate for a second, "It's fine. I'll figure some-thing out."

When Rich came to me with his proposal, I had something he needed, and he had something I needed. It was an even trade. Taking Kelly's help for nothing in return was just charity. I'd rather work at it and fail on my own terms than have my dead weight dragged across the finish line.

At my rejection of her offer, Kelly went quiet. The empty plots of farmland rolled and repeated on the windows like a Flintstones backdrop. With no conversation being made, or really any thoughts going through my head, the monotony of it all started lulling me to sleep again. It made me so drowsy I nearly missed the road leading back to our neighborhood, but all my systems jolted back on while I was crossing under the green light by the gas station. The tires squealed as the car spun at a right angle without dropping speed. Kelly yelped and clutched the side of her seat. I kept speeding straight for a few minutes until the car bounced like it was about to leave the ground for good. I panicked because I thought I hit something, but settled when I checked the rearview mirror and saw the railroad track marking the halfway point between my house and the school. The tracks around town didn't have warning lights or barriers. Usually I remembered to take that intersection a little slower. Usually.

With the car finally settled, Kelly looked around, and a visible unease crossed her face.

"So did you decide what you wanna do? Are we going somewhere?" she said.

"Home."

Kelly said nothing at first. The still air betrayed her heavy breathing, "But we were gonna hang out."

My fingers rapped on the steering wheel, and I tried

to not sound too annoyed, "Look, it's been a long day. I'm about to pass out and I want to take a nap before my mom gets home and murders me."

Right as I said it, my phone buzzed. Speak of the devil and she shall appear. I let the car glide to a stop at the edge of the road. Since we were no longer on the highway, I didn't have to worry about holding up any kind of traffic. I pulled my phone out and imagined Mom's stone stare on the other end of the line. There was no bluster with Mom. Her scolding was done with surgical precision.

When my thumb hovered over the answer button, Kelly said, "Can't you call her back later?"

"Are you crazy? I'm a dead man if I don't deal with this right now."

"But you're gonna get in trouble anyway, right? We can go somewhere and you can act like you didn't see it."

I narrowed my eyes at her, "She won't buy that for one second and you know it. We'll hang out some other time."

"Come on," she pleaded, "It's gonna be a whole week before I get to see you again. Chris, I know you're having a bad day, but we can make it better! We can make tonight the last hurrah before a long, boring week. It'll be fun, I promise!"

The phone kept going as I stared at her, studied the quiet desperation in her eyes. There was something she wasn't telling me. There was always something she wasn't telling me. Kelly fidgeted in her seat, like she'd crack at any minute.

When the phone stopped, I sighed and shut it off. Since I didn't pick up on her first call, my fate was sealed.

"Where do you want to go?"

Kelly's face lit up, "I'm getting kinda hungry. Wanna grab a pizza at Harry's?"

"Fuck it," I said, "Harry's it is."

I took the car out of park and did a U-turn in the middle of the road. It was a twenty-minute drive to Harry's, and Kelly's renewed enthusiasm made her talk the whole way, but I can't remember anything she said.

CHAPTER 4

KELLY

HARRY HORSE'S IS what you probably think it is: Chuck E. Cheese with horses instead of mice. Chris always claimed the place was a front for a drug ring because we never saw anyone else in there, but he said that about any place that was even a little run down. Other than the dust, and the dim lights, and all the broken games hogging space on the floor, it wasn't really that bad. Sure, maybe it was a little weird that it had no employees other than the two scary looking guys who owned it and shouted at each other in Italian. And yeah, maybe it was kind of creepy that one of the animatronics didn't move anymore, so it hung there like a dead body while the others sang and danced to the three kiddy country songs that played over and over again, but...

Okay, Harry Horse's was pretty shady. I have no idea how Chris found it, but when he first got his driver's license, he followed a couple of backroads and pulled into the cracked, vine-covered parking lot, saying he wanted to check it out. I only followed him inside because I was worried about him getting stabbed or something, but I ended up kinda liking it. The games that still worked were pretty cool, the pizza was good, and Lorenzo was friendly even if his English wasn't so great. Maybe we were lame or weird for going there all the time, but I didn't care. It was fun.

Chris and I got a large pizza to split and sat at our usual table by a broken pinball machine, behind a wall where the animatronics couldn't see us. Well, I say we got one to split, but I ate most of it. Chris had maybe one slice. I didn't even notice I was being such a pig until I grabbed the last piece. That really embarrassed me, but Chris was too busy dozing off to notice.

I'd kinda hoped he would get some of his energy back when we got there, but I still didn't let his tiredness bother me. Once he had the chance to rest up, he'd start acting more like his normal self. I stood to go find something to do in the meantime, stretching and feeling the cool air on my bare arms and legs. I got so hot in the clothes that I wore to school that I always kept a spare anime tee and pair of shorts in my bag so I could change the second I got done with school. Even if I'd gotten used to the discomfort, it never stopped being a relief when I could finally change. When I first started going to public school, I learned the hard way that showing up with Goku and Sailor Moon on my clothing and wearing shorts in freezing weather was a good way to get a lot of weird looks I didn't want.

The cool thing about Harry's was that it had real games, not like a Chuck E. Cheese. The place had been in business for a long time, maybe since the eighties. That's why most of the games didn't work anymore: Francesco didn't wanna pay to get them fixed, and without anyone taking care of them, they all fell apart over the years. But that also meant there was plenty of old, cool stuff you don't see anywhere else. I smiled and bounded out to the main floor.

It turned out that most of those games weren't really much fun by yourself. Most of the better single player games were broken, so I had to make do with the racing games and beat 'em ups and all the other stuff meant for at least two people. An orange tint glimmered off the windows as the sun got lower and lower, but time crawled by so slowly while I hit nearly every working game, looking back at Chris every once in a while. He never stirred, asleep face down on the table.

Come on. Give it up. Neither of you should be here.

But I ignored my brain and moved on to the next game, Pac-Man. I grinned and put my first quarter in. I could waste hours on Pac-Man.

You're unbelievable. That's how you're spending today? Pac-Man? What kind of daughter are you?

Games where you had to mash a lot of buttons made me nervous. I was always worried about getting carried away and breaking the machine by putting too much pressure on them, but I got really good at Pac-Man because all you needed was the joystick. The high score above the maze was mine, and whenever it changed, I made sure to beat it even if it took the rest of my quarters.

Yup, the world's so much better with Kelly Hatfield in it. She's so great at Pac-Man.

I only managed to clear two boards when I got my first game over. Some practice was probably needed. I hadn't come back to this game too much since Chris's silly challenge ended, so it made sense that I'd be a little rusty. Ready to start again, I plunked another quarter in.

See, Chris wasn't so great at this game, but he got pretty good at Donkey Kong. The summer we first started coming here, Chris gave me a challenge. He was always making some sort of pointless bet. Since both games crashed when you got far enough in them, he declared that whoever reached the kill screen of their game first would get one favor from the loser, anything they wanted within reason. That summer, we spent a lot of time at Harry's trying to beat each other. Whenever I had a good run, Chris would come watch and make loud noises at tense moments to throw me off, but that was okay, because whenever he did really well, I'd walk by and gently hum "It's a Small World After All" to annoy him until he cracked.

Neither of us ever reached the kill screen because the Donkey Kong cabinet started leaking some weird goop and wouldn't run anymore. But thinking about it, the challenge never really ended. Maybe I could get to the kill screen right now and use my favor to force Chris to stop being such a baby.

No, shut up Kelly. It's not that simple. He's got a serious condition and it's not his fault. Stop acting like you know anything about his problems.

Dead again, and I hadn't even gotten much farther than before. I groaned and rustled the coins in my pocket. I was going to run out of money at this rate, but I put another one in and started again.

Yeah, but if I had medicine that made me normal, I wouldn't ever miss a dose.

Francesco's voice boomed from the kitchen and startled me, making me lose a life almost instantly. Lorenzo started shouting back, but I managed to ignore the argument raging in the background and got my flow going again. They argued so often and we could never understand a word of it. Chris thought they were doing it on purpose to hide sketchy mob connections. I just think they preferred to talk to each other in their first language.

Pac-Man's repetitive waka-waka started to grate on my nerves Francesco and Lorenzo's argument escalated over all the clashing noises in the arcade. One of the older games next to me eeked out a constant whine, and the dying screen flickered in the corner of my eye. The rusty joints of the animatronics thumped and creaked, and the crackling speakers made the energetic banjo music barely audible. Gurgling zombies and a machine gun roared from a game all the way by the entrance. I died again, grumbling as I reached for another quarter. Was Harry's always so noisy? Would it really cost so much to fix some of their stupid equipment? It sounded like everything was about to fall apart.

Ten years. It's really been ten years.

I died again and put in another quarter.

Spring is ruined forever for you, isn't it Grandma? You can't watch the flowers bloom without thinking about him. It's horrible.

Dead. Another quarter.

Thank goodness I never told you about the punishments. It'd ruin the good memories you have left. You wouldn't understand that he was doing the right thing.

Dead.

I forgot. I forgot about him and it's all my fault.
SNAP.

It echoed through the entire arcade, overpowering every other noise, or at least it seemed like it. When I unclasped my hand, a thin steel bar slid onto the machine, along with the crumbled remains of the big plastic ball topping the joystick. With no more controller to guide him, Pac-Man kept running into a wall until one of the ghosts swooped in and gobbled him up.

My eyes flitted all around the arcade, to the empty counter, to the entrance, over to Chris. He still had his head down on the table. When I realized the coast was clear, I closed my eyes and took a deep breath.

I couldn't believe the noise didn't wake him up. Holding the pieces of the broken joystick in my hand, I tried to look relaxed as I walked over to the trash can, like I needed to throw away a napkin or something innocent like that. Would it be more suspicious to look at Chris or to keep my head up when I passed him? Before I could make a decision, my eyes wandered over to the windows, and I almost yelped when I saw it was dark out. When did the sun set? We hadn't been there *that* long... had we?

I passed Chris without looking at him, glancing towards the kitchen to make sure the owners weren't around before tossing the joystick in the trash. For good measure, I grabbed a ton of napkins and pretended to wipe my nose before dropping them all in a big glob to cover it up. There. Nobody would know it was me.

I spun around and immediately froze. Chris's big brown eyes stared directly at me, his head still on the table.

Oh god, how much did he see? I had my hand pretty

much wrapped around the joystick, and he was kinda far away, but he might've caught a glimpse of it when I threw it out. If it were anyone else, I probably could've convinced them that nothing was weird, that the joystick broke from old age like all the other games, but Chris knew better. When it came to my condition, he knew I held both of us to the same standard of absolute perfection. If I wanted him to not talk about it, I couldn't give him anything to talk about. So if he saw me—

Wait.

He was awake?

He was *awake?* For how long? He hadn't just been sitting there while I ran around the arcade by myself, had he? If he'd been up for a while, he would've come and found me, right? Right?

I walked closer to him, really studying his face, trying to figure out if he was just waking up, but nope, he'd been wide awake for a while, just staring at the walls. I don't think he even noticed me walking up to him. He really was going to sit there and mope the whole night. You know, I get that he was tired, I get that he had a bad day, but I couldn't believe he'd rather sit and stare at a freaking blank white wall than play a game with me, or even *talk* to me. Where was the Chris who was ready to drop everything and run all the way to Alaska with a girl he didn't even know, just because she was lonely? I wanted that boy back. This other jerk could wallow someplace where he wouldn't bring everyone else down.

Suddenly, Chris made eye contact, and when he did, he sat up straighter, cocking his head and narrowing his eyes at me. Why was he giving me such a funny look? Unless...

Oh. Oh no. My eyes. I needed to check. A busted arcade cabinet with a blank screen reflected the parlor behind me, and I tilted my head to try and catch a glimpse of my reflection, but the angle was wrong. We weren't little kids anymore. If he saw my eyes now, they'd terrify him.

Thinking quickly, I put on a big fake smile, "Hey! You're up!" I said, trying to sound enthusiastic. A few coins jingled as I shoved my hand in my pocket, but I didn't have nearly as many as I thought I did. Counting out half, I dropped a few on the table and waved toward the maze of games, "Let's play something!"

I bounded off again, glancing over my shoulder to see if he was actually going to follow me. Thankfully, he did, and all the suspicion left his face. Sure, he was still acting pouty, but this was a good start. I could get him to play a few games and then he'd wake up and then he'd start acting more like Chris. It occurred to me that we never really played the shooting game near the front counter, so I made my way over to it.

"Ooo, how about this one?" I said, putting one of my last quarters in.

Chris rubbed his neck while I pulled the gun out of the holster, "I think I'll just watch."

Really? He couldn't bring himself to play one stupid game with me?

"Come on, please? It's not as fun by yourself."

He took a deep breath, fishing through his pockets for a coin and hesitating before putting it in. Even after he hit the start button, his hand hovered over the plastic gun like it was going to attack him, and he lunged for it a little too quickly. Chris got himself killed almost instantly. Once his continue prompt started counting down, he threw the gun in the rack and stepped away from the machine. I glared at him, but he didn't see me because he had turned away.

Fine. I could have fun without him. My character kept marching forward through the mansion. Things were going okay, zombies stumbled towards me in a big mob on the right side of the screen and I managed to keep them from getting close by mashing the trigger. Out of the corner of my eye, an air duct rumbled and a swarm of bugs poured out and rushed me. I shot all of them down, but while I was taking care of the bugs, the zombies I was keeping at bay pounced and slashed off half my health. It would've been nice if I had a second player to cover me. It was nearly impossible to win by myself, not without a huge pile of quarters to buy more lives with. To make things even worse, the gun's trigger started sticking.

Wait. Gun. Oh duh, stupid, stupid, stupid, what were you thinking? Of course he doesn't want to play the gun game. You might as well be asking him to go back in time and shoot his dad himself.

It's just a game! It isn't a real gun! Like seriously, the guy who has no problem picking fights with football players can't handle holding a plastic gun?

That's not fair and you know it! You've been friends for years; you should know better by now. This is your fault.

It's not my fault he doesn't take his medicine!

Look at him. He's about to fall asleep again. A good friend would've let him go home and rest, but no, you had to drag him out here because you can't bring yourself to face Grandma and Grandpa. You're not just annoying, you're a coward.

I'm trying! Is that so much to ask? That he tries?

Chris's eyes widened, "Kelly!"

"*WHAT?*"

A zombie popped up and slashed off the last part of my health bar. The game let out an evil laugh as the continue screen counted down numbers dripping with blood. My grip on the light gun tightened, and the plastic cracked apart in my hand as I kicked the machine.

From the sound you'd think someone set off a bomb. With nothing blocking its path, the cabinet screeched like a car burning out as it rocketed several yards across the floor, toppling over when it crashed into the front counter. Glass shattered and wood cracked. Coins clanked on the linoleum floor as they drizzled from the hole my foot created. The game screen exploded into shards. Screws shot off in multiple directions as the back of the machine cracked in half, and a mess of dangling wires slithered onto the floor.

The arguing in the kitchen stopped. Chris had his hands slammed over his ears, and after a few tentative blinks he put them down, looking back and forth from me to the sparking game.

"I didn't," I stammered, "I didn't mean to—"

Chris's last bit of drowsiness went away as he reached for me. I jumped back when it looked like he was gonna try and grab my wrist. He must've remembered that breaking Rule Two would be a good way to get his arm ripped off, because he stopped and used his outstretched hand to pull his hoodie up.

"Run!" he whispered.

He vaulted over the ruined arcade machine blocking the way to the exit and burst out the double doors. I stood frozen in place. Maybe I could explain everything to Lorenzo and Francesco. That had to be better than just leaving it for them to find. Everything would be fine, there had to be a way I could explain everything.

I gave up on that idea when I started hearing footsteps, and their arguing got louder. Every hair on my body stood on end as I rushed for the entrance. I didn't dare try anything fancy the way Chris did, so I slowly sidled in the space between the machine and the wall, constantly keeping an eye on the hallway that led to the back.

Right as the shadow of a stocky guy made its way forward, I pushed the glass door open. A weak bell dinged as it flung off its hinges, and it shattered when it smashed against the concrete. I yanked on my hair with both hands. *No no no no no no, this isn't happening, this isn't happening, this isn't happening...*

"Hurry up!"

Chris's voice echoed from the parking lot. There were no streetlights to guide me, so I had to squint until I found a dark blob. The car's headlights blasted on. Some glass crunched under my feet as I made a beeline for it. I stopped when I reached the passenger door. Taking a few deep breaths, I tried to keep calm as I gently slipped my fingers around the handle, praying I wouldn't rip the door off. To my relief, it clicked open like it would for any normal person, and I slid in as Francesco's silhouette burst from Harry's entrance.

Chris didn't even give me a chance to buckle my seat belt. I barely closed the door when he stomped on the gas and tore out of the parking lot. For about two miles, we flew down the road as fast as the hunk of junk would take us. We were lucky there weren't any other cars or animals around, or else there would've been an accident. Chris made a hard left down one of Leroy's many backroads and slowed down, putting the warning lights on so people would know to go around.

We sat there for a long time. Chris stared at me, trying to find the right words while I quietly lost my mind.

They know. We were the only ones in there; they know it's me. They know and they're gonna call the police and it's all over.

Chris sighed, and finally said, "Alright. Tell me what's wrong."

"Nothing," I said, "Nothing's wrong."

They probably have security cameras in there. They probably have video proof for the whole world to see. I tried so hard to be normal but I screwed it all up and now the whole world is gonna know about me.

"Kelly."

"Seriously, I'm okay," I said, "My foot slipped, that's all."

It's just like you said, Dad. The government is gonna take me away in the middle of the night and they're gonna experiment on me and then when they're done they're gonna lock me up forever and I'm never gonna see Grandma or Grandpa or Chris ever again. Are they even safe? Are they gonna take them for knowing about me? Chris can't even deny it because he's on the video too. Oh god, I'm so sorry Chris, I knew you never should've been friends with me.

His jaw dropped, "Your *foot* slipped? You seriously expect me to believe the first time you've used your powers since we were—"

I instinctively cut him off at the p-word, "Rule One, Chris."

His face hardened, and his grip on the steering wheel tightened, "Alright. I give up. I should have gone home hours ago."

A chill went down my spine as I thought about coming home to a crying Grandma and a furious Grandpa, "*No! Please, don't! I don't wanna go home!*"

"You're out of your mind if you think I'm going to sit here and let you shovel bullshit down my throat."

"Then we don't have to talk! Just drive! I don't care where we go!"

Shaking his head, he took the car out of park and it sped off with a rough jerk, like it was reacting to Chris's frustration. When I was sure that we weren't headed for home, I curled up in my seat and stared out the window as we turned down shady backroads and got on unfamiliar highways. My glowing red eyes reflected back at me from the window, and it hit me all at once: that's what Chris was trying to tell me before I kicked the machine. I was losing it.

I stole a glance at him. He stewed in silent anger and focused on the road. I guess it would be pretty frustrating, not having any idea what was going on. Nothing at Harry's would've made any sense to him. But even so… he saw my monster eyes and didn't freak out. It made me wanna tell him everything, to blurt out every last detail so he knew exactly what was going on. So I didn't have to feel so alone.

No. He can't know the truth. He'd never look at you the same way again.

CHAPTER 5

CHRIS

I TURNED DOWN random intersections, rolling by dark field after dark field, and within minutes I had no idea where I was. The wet runoff from melted snow sludge gurgled over the muddy road, and a sickening slurp rose from the ground as my tires glided over the muck. For an instant the back of the car lurched towards the ditch on our right side, but a quick correction with the steering wheel kept us from slipping too far.

I tried not to glare at Kelly. Her foot slipped. Give me a fucking break. Her glowing eyes and that kick were the first glimpses of her power I'd seen in almost a decade. You'd think that'd give me the right to say *something*, but no. Apparently, the absolute lunacy of Rule One only applied to me. She can blow up a kiddie arcade all she wants, but I'm the bad guy for even beginning to ask about what's on her mind. If she didn't want to tell me, fine. That wasn't anything new. But the least she could do is say so and not treat me like a goddamn moron.

And it's not like her slip up was even serious. Harry Horse's is down another game and we stop going there for a while, big deal. Nobody saw her, and even if they called the cops, there wasn't a shred of evidence putting us there. Francesco and Lorenzo hadn't come out front to check on us once, there was no way in hell they could afford security cameras, and they couldn't have seen it was us in the dark parking lot. Besides, short of a homemade bomb, how would two normal teenagers wreck that thing the way Kelly did? The police would take one look at that dump and assume the machine blew up because Francesco didn't properly maintain it or something. We were completely in the clear, but go ahead Kelly, go ahead and use your fucking rules to shut me out.

Literally the only thing keeping me from going straight home was the looming threat of my mother. I was at the point of no return with her. So much time had passed since she first tried to call me that her anger had to hit terminal velocity by now. Since things couldn't get any worse, it'd be best to delay the inevitable and squeeze my last bit of free time from the day. Tiresome as Kelly's bullshit may have been, I'd take it over the evisceration Mom had in store for me.

We rolled forward into flat nothingness. All of Leroy's blemishes, the decay of barns barely held up by rotting wood and the rusty tractors left in yards with tattered "For Sale" signs tacked on, were obscured by shadow, and we seemed to be on the only stretch of road in Ohio not littered with bloated raccoons and decomposing deer. The cloud cover dissipated, and a window to the universe opened above me, revealing a sea of stars and the glow of the full moon to light my way.

The soothing scenery and rhythmic clicking of the old station wagon eventually cooled me down.

I took another look at Kelly, who hadn't moved from her place at the window. Moonlight made a translucent outline over her already pale skin, and from the way she was sucking on her lower lip, I picked up on a huge red flag. Kelly was a little claustrophobic, and being in the car for too long made her uncomfortable. She could tolerate it if we had a destination, but she never wanted to just go for a joyride, especially at night.

I rolled down her window, and let the biting air blow in. Kelly jolted back and looked at me. Her eyes had returned to their normal pale blue. I kept pressing the window down as she tried to put it back up.

"You're gonna get cold," she said.

"It's alright. I could use some fresh air."

She slowly leaned her head right against the window's edge, letting strands of her hair billow out. After searching my face for any sign that I was downplaying discomfort, she seemed assured enough to look away.

Strained silence hovered between us. I tried to think of a way to start making things better, but I kept brushing against the boundaries laid by Rule One. If there was nothing I could say, then at least I could get her out of this stuffy car. I tried to think of somewhere to go for a distraction, but Leroy was enough of a wasteland during the day, let alone the middle of the night.

Pathetically, the best I could think of was the truck stop. "I'm getting hungry. You mind if we stop somewhere?"

"Do you ever think about cemeteries?"

That got my eyes off the road and back on her. "Uh, not really. Why?"

She hesitated, "I just think they're kinda interesting, you know? Whenever I pass one, I always start thinking about the people buried there. Like, who they were and stuff. Is that weird?"

I had no idea what she wanted to do at the graveyard, but I got the hint, and took a turn down the first road on my right, hoping I'd eventually end up someplace familiar. With enough lucky guesses, I found myself back on the highway before too long. I didn't ask any questions, but did wonder if she planned on elaborating.

She didn't, of course, and the silence weighed on us again.

A sign indicated the graveyard was on my next left, and we crossed under the rusty entrance arch within minutes. The top of a single mausoleum loomed on the crest of a hill, and I parked the car near a fountain so cracked it must have been dry for the past decade. The headstones visible in the headlights were so weathered and worn down it looked like they'd crumble if you leaned on them. Hills rose and fell all around us, like they only chose this plot of land because it wasn't suitable for farming, and it was much larger than you'd expect for a town so small, with headstones and crosses stretched on hilltops for a mile or two in nearly every direction. Leroy's an old town, established sometime in the 1830's. The dead probably outnumbered the living a hundred-fold. If Leroy had one thing in abundance, it was space for bodies.

The chill in the graveyard made me wish for a winter jacket, and the moisture in the air made my hoodie feel damp. Kelly wandered off toward a random hill. I probably should have stayed in the car, but the promise of some explanation for what happened today enticed me. I kept my distance as she meandered around. Occasionally, she'd stop to admire some flowers or read a headstone. Since she didn't give me any signal to back off, I came a little closer when she lingered longer than usual at a cross with fresh white lilies.

Crouching down to get a better look, she pointed at the dates, "This girl died back in the sixties, but someone's still bringing her flowers." She seemed to be talking mostly to herself, "She was only seven years old. I wonder what she wanted to be when she grew up."

Kelly drifted all over the cemetery, stopping at all kinds of graves. There was no rhyme or reason to it; some she'd give no more than a brief glance while others she'd stay at for several minutes. Some had flowers, some didn't. Some were marked with rounded headstones, others with crosses. Some memorialized those who passed within the last decade, while others had been gone for several lifetimes.

I didn't expect her to try and strike up a conversation with me, not after I acted like a total dick earlier, but while examining a particularly weathered grave she turned to me and said, "Hey, you know what we should do? We should come back and put flowers on all the graves that don't have any. It's sad seeing so many of these people get forgotten."

The man underneath us died in 1864. I deliberated

over my words very carefully, trying to avoid upsetting her, "That'd be a nice gesture, but I think flowers are more for the sake of the living. Nobody's left to remember a lot of these people."

"You don't think they can see us?"

The question gave me pause. It had been quite some time since I last thought about that kind of thing. Unable to come to a satisfactory answer for myself, I said, "Sure hope not."

We continued on a good while longer. I knew Kelly found what she was looking for when she did a double take at an unassuming bronze plate with a few small sunflowers sticking out of the vase. Kelly took a seat in the grass, brushing the back of her hand against it. She shifted her gaze from the grave to the sky, holding her knees against her chest. I sat next to her, trying to not make my attempt at reading the plate too obvious. The grave belonged to "Beloved Father and Son, Lucas Hatfield." The day of death? March 20th, exactly a decade ago.

Oh, Kelly. Why didn't you just say something?

It explained so much and yet nothing at all. Ten years is a long time. The anniversary of her Dad's death by itself wouldn't be enough to make her break such a long streak of keeping her powers hidden. Or would it? I had no idea. Honestly, it was easy to forget she even had parents for all she mentioned them. I wasn't certain that her mom actually existed, and the only thing I knew about her dad is that he died in an accident. Perhaps her grandparents said something to her, or her mom was trying to wiggle her way back into Kelly's life, or maybe she just saw something on TV that reminded her of him. There were hundreds of different explanations to choose from, and all seemed equally plausible.

Never had I wanted to hug her so badly, but that was out of the question. Rule Two was the only one I hadn't once considered breaking. It forbade physical contact of any kind. Getting too close made Kelly squirm, so I could only imagine the kind of disaster that would unfold if I actually touched her. There had to be something I could say to show her I cared. She was my best friend! It should have been easy, but it felt like trying to comfort a stranger.

There was just so much we didn't talk about.

She startled me with a sudden movement, leaning forward and plucking a flower out of the vase. "Grandma must've put these here today," she said. A few petals fell off as she rolled the stem between her fingers, "That's supposed to be my job, isn't it?"

"It's not supposed to be a job. Like I said, it's supposed to be for the living. For you," I nudged my head toward the ground, "Not him. If you don't feel like you need to, you don't have to."

Petals drifted down and covered the plaque. The flower wasn't going to hold out much longer the way she was playing with it, so she gently placed it back in the vase, frowning when it disturbed the others. "Sometimes I wish I could just forget about him, erase him from my brain or something like that, but I know that's wrong."

I hesitated. That hit too close to home. "You aren't a bad person for wanting the pain to go away."

She sighed and shook her head before I had the chance to say anything else, "I'm sorry, forget I said anything. You wouldn't understand."

Wow.

Yeah Kelly, no way I'd know shit about having a dead dad.

She didn't budge when I sprang up, didn't protest when I stormed off in the car's vague direction. Every time I glanced back she hadn't moved, and the farther away I got, the more it looked like she belonged there, a stone monument in a sea of them. When she completely disappeared over the hill, I picked up my pace, not caring how disrespectful it was to trample over resting souls. When I finally found the parking lot, I wasted no time getting in the car to turn on the heat and radio.

That was it, then. She didn't trust me.

My eyes started to sting, and a hint of water crested their surface.

I clenched my fists, pounded on the dashboard, and took a deep breath. No. Don't cry. Yeah, it sucked that my best friend didn't trust me. But she was still my best friend. I could fix this, not by crying, but by seeing tonight as the wakeup call it was. By getting off my ass and doing something about it.

But what? Kelly was an impenetrable fortress, all her secrets kept under lock and key by a brave face. I'd never get in so long as Rule One was there to stand watchful guard. Its shadow loomed over our every word; its roots entangled themselves in Kelly's every action. When such a core element of her being was off the table, there was no way to connect. So long as it lived, we'd always be strangers.

No, thinking about it more, Kelly wasn't a fortress. The arcade cabinet proved that. She was a tower of Jenga blocks. Carefully constructed, but always under the threat of coming apart with just one wrong move. Pull out Rule One, and all that awkwardness and distance would fall away.

Plus, it's not like it served any real purpose. The fact of the matter was that I knew what she really was like, so there was no point in ignoring it. You would think she'd appreciate having someone to confide in. Hell, with no Rule One, she might even learn to enjoy having powers.

The question of course, was this: How exactly do you get rid of Rule One when you've lived under its reign for nearly ten years?

That's when I had an idea. A dumb idea. A ridiculous idea. Kelly would never go for it. She might even stop speaking to me all together.

But that was a risk I had to take. The writing was on the wall. If I did nothing, we'd keep puttering along like this until the fall, when she went off to college and I'd be trapped in Leroy. We'd text and video chat for a little while until she found some new friends, and the gulf of life experience between us would keep growing until we finally stopped talking to each other.

I wouldn't allow that to happen. Rule One would crumble by the night's end, it was just a matter of whether our friendship would survive the blow. But, if our friendship had to die, I didn't want it to waste away in a hospital bed, a husk of its former self.

I wanted it to go out in a blaze of glory.

CHAPTER 6

KELLY

I'D NEVER ACTUALLY seen Dad's headstone before. I didn't go to his funeral. Not because I wanted to get back at him or anything. I was a little too young to have thoughts like that. I just couldn't bring myself to look into his grave the way I stared into the basement the night he died. Grandma and Grandpa fought and screamed and cried and begged me to go, but in the end there was nothing they could do to force me. Looking at it now, I was surprised to see how small and plain it was. I guess we didn't have any money to get him something nicer.

Dad never really had money. A lot of his paycheck went to me in some way or another. If it wasn't food or other kid supplies, it was to repair or replace something I'd broken, and when my mom… No, not my mom. I've never even met this woman. I don't have a mom. When his ex-wife divorced him, she took a lot of the savings and stuff. He used to complain about it every once in a while, usually when I asked him if he'd buy some sort of toy I saw on TV. Thinking about it, I never really knew much about Dad. Most of what I know about his life Grandma told me, that he never really left town, he had a job at the garbage disposal plant and married his high school sweetheart, they tried to have a baby together and it didn't work out, and then they divorced and at some point he adopted me, but they never went into specifics.

Whenever I thought about Dad, my mind would wander and try to fill the gaps of his story. I imagined a young, happy couple with a bright future ahead of them. They don't have college degrees or great jobs, but they have each other, and that's what matters. Besides, what they really want is a family. With both of them working full time they're able to buy a small house not far from town square that has enough room for a few extra tiny people running around. What happens next changes every time I think about it. Sometimes it's a visit to a doctor, where a man in a white coat tells Dad that he won't ever be able to have kids. Sometimes in my mind, they succeed, but his pregnant wife loses the baby before it's even born. Sometimes they have a beautiful baby girl, but something goes wrong and sickness takes her away from them before she's even had a chance to live, although thinking about it more, there'd be a second headstone in front of me if that were true. Either way, the family they want doesn't happen. It stays just the two of them, and whether through grief or frustration, their once happy marriage starts to fall apart, but they manage to keep their relationship together for a little while.

But then one day, Dad's out on the job. He's emptying a dumpster somewhere when he hears a baby's cry. Or maybe he's working in some office when one of the men working for him brings the abandoned baby to his attention. I don't actually know what Dad did at the trash plant, but either way, Dad sees this as a sign from God, a way for him and his wife to have the family they always wanted.

He brings the baby home, but his wife is furious. How dare he try to replace what they lost with this monster he picked out of the garbage? No, this baby isn't hers, it could never be hers. But Dad is insistent. The baby girl needs a family as badly as they do. This is the last straw. This is what finally breaks their marriage. His wife leaves him, and then Leroy. Dad raises that baby girl all alone.

But what if they didn't lose their first baby? What if Dad's wife carried her all the way to term? What if the doctor found a way to help them have one? That little girl would be Kelly Hatfield. She'd be normal and pretty and there'd be no reason to keep her in the house because there wasn't a chance that she'd ever hurt anyone. She'd go to school and make lots of friends and be the best big sister there ever was to her multiple siblings. Her parents never would've divorced, and her dad would be alive.

And me? I'd have another name. I'd be somewhere else. Probably in an underground lab somewhere in Nevada, once the government found out what I was. They'd raise me away from everyone else, and occasionally they'd run some tests on me, but mostly they'd just make sure that I was safe. That everyone was safe.

Maybe I had the right idea when I was little, maybe the Alaskan wilderness is the only safe place for someone like me. But that still carried a certain amount of risk. There really wasn't anywhere I could run and hide forever. Somebody would find me eventually.

Maybe... maybe there was a more permanent solution.

A chill ran down my spine. It always did, every time I thought about dying. Not because I was afraid of it, but because I was afraid I couldn't. All those times Dad threw me down the stairs, all those times smacking against the hard concrete of the basement floor, and I never broke a bone, never scratched or scraped my skin. What if nothing can actually hurt me?

Don't be stupid. You're a freak of nature, not a god. It's probably easier than you think. Just get Grandpa's hunting rifle, bring your energy to its lowest point, and then just...

After everything that happened that day, this thought is what brought me to tears. Like killing myself was inevitable and I should go home and get it over with already. I sat in front of Dad's grave and cried for a long, long time.

...No.

Stop it, Kelly. Stop feeling sorry for yourself. You're going to keep going because you have to. Yeah, you screwed up pretty bad today, but he only died in vain if you let yourself give up like that. Everything he did, he did because he wanted you to have a normal life. All those punishments were to help you control yourself. They were temporary. He wanted you to go out in the world and be normal, not hide away forever. So stop crying, and stop moping. Tomorrow, you're going to get up, you're going to have a normal Saturday, and you're going to pretend today never happened.

I stood up, suddenly aware that I was alone. Getting so lost in my own head made me completely forget about Chris, and I retraced my steps to find him. He wasted a lot of his time putting up with me. On his last free day, too. I owed him an apology.

Since I had done so much wandering around, finding my way back was harder than I thought, and I hoped Chris hadn't gotten lost himself. Eventually though, the parking lot appeared. The car was already running. He must've been keeping his eye out for me, because he turned it around so the passenger side faced me as I carefully shuffled down a hill.

"Hey," I said, opening the door.

"How you feeling?" he asked.

I buckled up and used the rearview mirror to check my eyes. Blue. "I'll be fine."

"You sure?"

"Yeah."

He didn't say anything else, but it was weird, something about his face seemed off, somehow. He rolled out of the cemetery way faster than you'd expect him to. Even weirder, when we came to the road on our right that led home, Chris turned left.

I watched the way home disappear in the rearview mirror, "Where're we going?"

I finally figured out what was weird about his face. He was trying to hide a grin.

"You'll see."

CHAPTER 7
CHRIS

KELLY RAISED AN eyebrow when the metal clown came into view, barely visible beneath foliage and rust, "Leroy's Landing?"

Our car bounced over roots and potholes in the desolate parking lot. The clown, whose colors rusted away decades ago, pointed a crooked finger at a blank sign above the padlocked gates. Vandals detached and stole the letters that once spelled "Leroy's Landing!" almost immediately after the place closed. The exclamation point had an extended stay in my home, somewhere in Thomas's room. From what I understood, it served as an heirloom for the football team, bouncing between each senior house before getting passed to the next generation at the end of the year.

Leroy's Landing was an amusement park that opened in the late forties, when some optimistic young fool hedged his bets on Leroy's population exploding after the war, which, needless to say, didn't happen. Regardless, the park became a beloved landmark for Leroy and other towns in broader Northeast Ohio. Supposedly, it was quite charming in its heyday, but charm alone can't sustain a business. With Cedar Point only an hour drive north, Leroy's Landing kept losing business until it was forced to close during the economic recession of the early eighties, leaving it to rot and decay as teenagers and drug dealers actively defiled the memories of Leroy's older citizens. The town went into an uproar when someone purchased the land and announced that they were going to demolish the park to put up a sub-division, but all the complaining to the town council in the world couldn't stop the inevitable, and demolition was set to begin right around graduation.

We seemed to be the only ones there, but an empty lot didn't necessarily indicate an empty park. The place tended to attract methheads after dark, so we'd need to do a thorough sweep of the interior and pray the cops didn't show up before we could get my plan underway. The park was nestled at the end of a dirt road in an overgrown forest, and I would've preferred to have more escape options. I'd thought about parking the car far away from the site, so we could run into the forest and wait out trouble if need be, but then realized it'd be difficult enough convincing Kelly to go in without a mile long walk.

When I opened the door, Kelly said, "We're not going in there, are we?"

I paused. Like everyone else in town, we'd been there during the day a few times, but knew better than to come at night. The abundance of wiry structures and shadowy clown faces, not to mention the possibility of getting shivved by one of Leroy's jumpier denizens, made an after dark outing an exercise in nightmare fetishism. I had no idea how to make that sound remotely appealing.

Then, I realized I didn't have to.

I closed the door and walked up to the gate. A chill ran through me when I put my hands on the rusty bars, but I sucked it up—thankful I had all my shots—and clambered over it. When the headlights flipped back on with the pop of a car door, I climbed faster.

"Wait!" Kelly said.

I didn't answer her until I had dropped on the other side, and even then I kept it short so she wouldn't have a chance to argue. So long as I kept going farther in, she would chase me. "Come on!" I waved her over before heading for the old ticketing pavilion.

My plan was to stride forth with unassailable confidence, not stopping for anything until I had Kelly in the heart of the park, but I stopped dead in my tracks before I had even formally entered. A dark figure loomed in the distance, his features distorted by shadow. Sweat started soaking through my clothes.

Suddenly, I was in the New York apartment again.

What is he doing here where's Dad I can't see Dad please leave us alone take whatever you want just please don't shoot oh Jesus please don't shoot

A snapping twig made me spin around. It was only Kelly. I jerked my head back towards the park, expecting the man to lunge at us, but he stayed still.

I held out a hand, keeping my eyes on the shadow, "Give me your phone."

"What?"

"Just do it!"

Kelly dug around in her pockets, and upon grasping the phone I immediately fumbled for the flashlight function. My arm quivered as the light waved around the figure.

Kelly yelped as she doubled back. My heart rate skyrocketed for a moment, but came down almost immediately. The light revealed the shadow's true form, a seven-foot-tall statue of Lenny, the park's monstrous clown mascot. Wear and tear over the years chipped the paint away, making him look less like a cheerful entertainer and more like a melting homunculus. We said nothing to each other, stepping forward to get a closer look. The only human feature recognizable from the splotches of color and cracked concrete was his jagged grin.

"Oh, brrrrrrrr," Kelly hugged herself and rocked back and forth, "Can we go home now? We really shouldn't be here."

"No," I said, steadying my breath. "There's something I want you to see." I cut her off when she opened her mouth to protest, "And it has to be tonight. I don't know when we'll get another chance to come back."

Kelly shivered as Lenny caught her eye again, "Okay, but can we make it quick? What is it that's so important, anyway?"

I moved past the statue, entreating her to follow, "I told you, you'll see."

Both of us jumped as another crack echoed further in the park. Kelly jogged forward to stay next to me, "I don't think I'm in the mood for surprises."

"You'll love it. Now come on, we need to make sure nobody else is around first."

"It's not a body, is it?"

I cocked my head at her, "What?"

"The thing you wanna show me, it better not be a dead body or I'm gonna freak out."

I sighed. "It's not a dead body. How twisted do you think I am?"

Kelly averted her gaze as she played with her hair.

I couldn't keep from grinning. "Smartass."

A small smile creeped across her face.

We walked, with some trepidation, into the maze of stands that used to house games and concessions. Over thirty years of graffiti covered each head to toe, ranging from the generic ("Class of '89 Rules"), to the pretentious ("Capital is dead labor, which, vampire-like, lives only by sucking living labor, and lives the more, the more labor it sucks." No way someone didn't copy *that* off Reddit) but regardless of their individual quirks, every single stand had at least one dick drawn on it. The structures on the edge of the compound tended to be overrun by ivy as the forest reclaimed its territory. Conversely, black soot marked the remains of those closer to the park's center. Lots of them burned down in the fire that destroyed the arcade. I could think of a few kids who might've been responsible for that, the kind of people who liked to come out here and set off explosives. These smaller structures bore the brunt of vandal activity because nobody wanted to be the asshole who accidentally burned the roller coaster down.

The center of the park lowered into a circular amphi-theater, and as I passed the ashen remains of the arcade to check it out, I noticed that somewhere along the way Kelly stopped following me. Doubling back, I found her at the remains of a lemonade stand, leaning over a heart carved into the wood, complete with initials. I made sure my footsteps were good and loud so she wasn't startled as I approached.

"Did I ever tell you my grandpa proposed to my grandma here?" she asked.

"No," I said, feeling nervous, "Did he really?"

She nodded, pointing to the Ferris wheel looming over the trees, "He gave her the ring at the top of the Ferris wheel. They tell me the view was amazing," she paused, "You know, now that we're actually inside, I think this place is more sad than scary."

"Yeah?"

She nodded, "People made so many nice memories here, and now it's all just falling apart. Like none of it mattered." She stared at a broken beer bottle on the ground and stuck her hands in her pockets, "Seeing all this trash makes me kinda mad."

The plan seemed less likely to work with every word that came out of her mouth. I walked away with the intention of getting her to follow me to the amphitheater, "If it's scary you want, I'm sure there are more clowns up ahead."

That got her to smile, "Why'd they make their mascot a clown, anyway? Does anybody actually like them?"

"Afraid of them, are we?"

She tapped her finger to her lips, thinking it over. "Not really," she finally said, "But I don't *like* them either."

"The fifties were a more innocent time."

We wandered around the amphitheater for a bit until I saw the tracks from the old kiddie train snaking away. Our best course of action would be to follow them. They looped all the way around the park, so by sticking to them, we'd hit all the major structures, and I could decide which best suited the plan.

The first thing we found following the track was the resting place of both the carousel and the funhouse. The carousel's broken mirrors reflected the bug-eyed faces of screaming animals, but it looked positively inviting compared to the funhouse, a psychedelic plastic nightmare that required you to stroll into Lenny's gaping maw to enter. Neither seemed like particularly good places to start.

For fun, I reached into my wallet and checked how much cash I had, counting out a wad of bills while the spooky scenery had Kelly distracted.

"Twenty bucks if you go through the funhouse," I said.

"No."

"What happened to this place being more sad than scary?"

"Okay, fine. This place is sad *and* scary."

I grinned and put the money back in my pocket.

The next group of attractions we crossed were the big ones. We passed the kiddie train, derailed just before it reached the station, its cars toppled in all different directions to block our path on the tracks. From there, it was a short walk to the two tallest structures in Leroy: the Ferris wheel and StarLight, the roller coaster. With its jagged edges and moonlit silhouette, the wheel looked like a torture device for titans. It was harder to see the wooden coaster's blemishes at a distance, but the tattered caution tape wrapped around the entrance said it all. Teens had taken to climbing it back in the day; the peak of the highest hill was apparently a hot make-out spot, at least until a board cracked underneath a young couple and sent them falling to their deaths. To my knowledge, nobody else was ballsy enough to try climbing it again.

I considered both as options. They certainly would make a statement, though I doubted Kelly would be too keen on the Ferris wheel, considering it held some significance for her. The coaster, maybe.

We pressed onward and passed a few unremarkable sights. Bathrooms, maintenance buildings, an algae infested pond complete with fountain, the like. We were running out of park to explore when Kelly spoke up again.

"Hey, Chris?"

"What's up?"

"I'm sorry. You know, for earlier."

"Don't be. You have nothing to apologize for."

"I dunno, I feel bad. Because I see what you're trying to do."

"Oh?" I said, trying not to give anything away, "And what am I doing exactly?"

"I've been annoying you all day about going out somewhere when all you wanted to do was go home and rest, but after I made you stop at the graveyard, you started worrying, so you wanted to take me on some kind of adventure to cheer me up. Don't get me wrong, I really appreciate it, but I'm okay Chris, really. If you wanna go home, we can go home."

Relieved she hadn't actually caught on to what was happening, I leaned closer to her with a mischievous grin, "So you *are* glad we came out here."

A smile creeped across her face, "Yeah. This place is cool, once you get used to it. It's actually kinda pretty, in a weird way. Even with all the clowns and graffiti, it feels kind of like we're—" She cut herself off, staring in disbelief at the barn coming into view, "Oh, seriously? Come on!"

The last stop on the tour was the petting zoo, because no country carnival would be complete without some smelly goats for the kids to rub their filthy hands all over. The goats themselves were long gone, of course, but their humble abode still stood proud and tall. In fact, of all the attractions left, the barn was in the best shape. Probably not a coincidence, since a group of scrappy individuals banded together to deface it with a big, brazen Confederate flag on the rooftop. Crass as it may have been, I had to admire the tenacity behind it. Any court jester can spray a penis on a building; it takes a lunatic to dedicate an entire week to coating every inch of the roof with their racism.

Kelly shot me a glare and crossed her arms, "What are you smiling about? It's not funny."

It wasn't, but Kelly's visceral disgust confirmed exactly what I was thinking: this was perfect.

"We're almost there," I said. "Let's make sure nobody's inside."

Due to the rusted hinges, the barn doors took some force to open. I strained and put my back into it as Kelly watched, and after some effort it swung open with a creak. Without thinking, I stepped inside and ran face first into a dangling spider-web. I screamed and stumbled backward, using one hand to brush off my body and the other to pull strands out of my hair. I spat when the web clung to my lips. Kelly laughed the whole time.

"Shut up," I mumbled, wiping my hands on the door frame. Though my fingers were still sticky, I dug Kelly's phone out of my pocket, and as I clicked the flashlight app back on, I realized how fortunate it was that I never gave it back. It made my plan a thousand times easier. She wouldn't dare try to take it by force, meaning she couldn't call and ask someone to pick her up. I held all the cards.

Sweeping the room with the beam of light, seeing it relatively empty surprised me. Being the only sizable structure in the park in anything approaching decent condition, I assumed the barn would be a drug lab, but apparently, I was wrong. Careful to duck under the dangling spider web, I strode forth.

"I think I'm gonna wait out here," Kelly said.

"That's fine," I replied, leaning over the rail and shining the light in the first pen. An animal musk still lingered in the air, not of horses and goats like in its heyday, but of stale mouse shit. It could've been my imagination, but I swear I heard them scratching up on the wooden rafters. Poor bastards would have to find a new home soon enough. I went up and down the aisles, searching each individual pen for anyone who might've been hiding for whatever reason. The barn had certainly seen its share of human activity. Beer cans, bottles, and stray needles littered the ground. I picked up my pace to avoid staring at the makeshift firing range. I smirked when I found the pyramid of empty paint cans and shuddered when I stumbled across a crusty yellow mattress and imagined the unspeakable acts committed on it, but my search didn't turn up any actual people.

It was time.

I went back to the entrance, barely remembering to dodge the spider-web. Kelly perched herself on the fence that sectioned off the horse pasture, and she yawned as I walked over to her, "Find it?"

"Find what?"

"The thing you wanted to show me. Was it in there?"

"Uh," I said, "Sort of."

She raised an eyebrow and hopped down, "Sort of?"

This was it, my last chance to back out. It'd be easy enough to tell her that she was right the first time, that I just wanted to take her on some sort of adventure, and we could go on with our normal lives. We could write off the trip as dumb fun and not disrupt the status quo.

No. That was the coward's way out. Even if it didn't seem like it at the moment, our friendship was still on the line. Plus, it'd be good for her. If Harry Horse's showed me anything, it's that Rule One was suffocating both of us.

"When I said I wanted to show you something, I meant it more... metaphorically." I rubbed the back of my neck. "The thing I wanted to show you was... well, you."

Her confusion intensified. That sounded much smarter in my head. "Alright look," I said, trying again, "When you're upset, do you ever want to take it out on something?"

My heart sank as her face hardened. She knew exactly where I was going with this. "If you're talking about what happened back at Harry's, it's never gonna happen again."

"No, not like that. Well..." I hesitated, "Sort of like that. What I'm trying to say is that you don't ever get the chance to cut loose, you know? You're always so tense and you deserve to relax, don't you think?"

"What are you saying, Chris?" she narrowed her eyes at me, "What are you *really* saying?"

I had already bungled it so badly that I couldn't possibly recover, but at that point, I was committed. I took a deep breath, "I think you'd feel a lot better if you used your powers to wreck this barn."

She immediately stormed off toward the park entrance. Panicking, I sprinted forward and stood in her path, holding my hands up, "Wait, hear me out."

Without missing a step, she cut around me, "No."

I had to run to even keep pace with her. When she wanted to move quickly, those stilt legs could take her places. Losing my breath, I tossed myself in front of her again, forcing her into a dead stop to avoid colliding with me. I stretched my arms as wide as they would go to obstruct her path, "Where do you think you're going?"

"Home."

She tried ducking around me again, but this time I shuffled to block her. Anyone else could have just pushed me out of the way, but she wouldn't dare. Rule Two was as much for her as it was for me. "And how were you planning on getting there?"

"You're going to drive me."

"Not if you don't at least hear me out."

"Fine. Then I'll just—" the anger in her face drained, replaced by a sudden swell of panic as she patted the pockets of her shorts.

I grinned and held up her phone, "Looking for this?"

"Give it back."

"As soon as you destroy the barn."

"Well, I guess we're never leaving then."

"I can wait."

"Good, 'cause so can I." She made a big point of sulking over to the nearest bench and sitting down, crossing her legs and dramatically looking away. I stayed rooted in place. Her eyes kept flitting back to me.

Within a minute she whipped her head around and pleaded, "Come on, this isn't funny!"

Casually strolling over to her, I tried to keep a calm, almost business-like tone, "I'm not trying to be funny. Destroy the barn and I'll take you home. I bet you can do it in one punch." She surprised me by springing up and lunging for the phone. If she didn't slow down when she came close to touching me, she might've even been able to snatch it, but her faltering gave me the opportunity to put it behind my back.

I probably shouldn't have enjoyed this as much as I did, "Woah, what happened to Rule Two?"

She leaned back, stunned, "You have no right to say anything about any of my rules! I mean, how many times have *you* broken Rule One tonight?"

I shrugged, "You broke it first."

A vein popped out of her neck, and her watery eyes changed color in a flash. I stumbled as she got right in my face, "Chris, if you don't stop right now, I'm never speaking to you again!"

She loomed over me, her breath warming my face. We'd never been that close before. I savored a good, long look at her eyes, since I didn't really get the chance at Harry's. They didn't just change color. They really did glow, shining like brilliant rubies. It'd been way too long since I'd seen them. Still, I couldn't let myself be too amazed. Kelly was one wrong word away from making good on her threat, or maybe even breaking me over her knee. Prodding her would get me nowhere.

"Alright," I said, taking a step back, "Sorry. Didn't mean to make you mad. I'm trying to cheer you up."

She snorted, "You've got a real funny way of doing that."

"I know it doesn't seem like it, but I am. Look, you had a bad day. Like a really shitty, awful day." I took her silence as agreement, "I know when I have a day like that, I can't just sit around and let my anger boil. I need to take it out on something, you know?" I said as I mimed a punch.

"Yeah, and look where that got you."

That jab burned more than it should have. I gritted my teeth and restrained the urge to fire back. "I'm not saying you should take it out on a person. I'm not even saying you should do it all the time. What I am saying is that you should give it a try, just this once. That barn is an eyesore and it's coming down in a month or two anyway. Nobody will miss it, and nobody will see you. You have literally nothing to lose."

She didn't hesitate, "Tell you what, how about you do things your way, and I'll do them my way? Now take me home."

She took off, nearly charging into me. With just a few seconds of walking, she threatened to disappear over the horizon forever if I didn't think of something quick.

"Remember the day we became friends?" I blurted out.

Kelly stopped, but didn't turn around.

"It was sort of like today," I said. "We were both upset, everything sucked, you let your powers slip in front of me and you thought it was the end of the world."

Still, silence. I kept going, "But it worked out, didn't it? We made that dumb snowman and you used your super strength to mount its head on top of that tree. We had a great time."

She gave no recognition that she remembered, or that I was even talking, and my voice started to falter, "I just don't see how this is any different."

I waited for her response.

Waited.

And waited.

And waited.

And when she finally stormed back, I prepared myself for it all to be over, but she blew past me without a word. Confused, I jogged behind her, keeping a reasonable distance out of caution. Empowered by righteous fury, she picked up speed as she broke into a run toward the barn. The earth tremored beneath me, shaking violently each time her feet slammed into the ground, forcing loose shingles to rattle and slide off the barn's roof. I braced myself for impact, plugging my ears with my fingers. Kelly's right hand curled into a fist, and she shifted her weight onto her back foot as she wound up and let loose the wildest, sloppiest punch the world has ever seen.

The crash echoed for miles. I savored every last detail, every crack in every wall that formed before the pressure exploded them, every tiny particle of wood suspended in the air, the subtle surprise growing on Kelly's face as she made her follow through, the small step she took to regain her balance. One punch and the wall disintegrated, shooting a hurricane of shrapnel into the barn's interior. Without the south wall, the rest of the foundation began to collapse. Tiles and then entire blocks of roofing rained down, and the other walls buckled and cracked into large chunks that folded in on themselves. With another crash, the whole structure fell into a heap, shooting a cloud of dust and splinters in all directions. The force of the impact put me flat on my ass, and the mess of sawdust billowed over and through me. I squeezed my eyes shut to protect them.

When everything settled, I opened them back up, and there was Kelly, standing in the wreckage, staring at her hand as she repeatedly clenched and unclenched it. I couldn't see her face.

"Kelly?"

When she looked at me, I had a hard time reading her. Her eyes stayed flooded in red, but the raw anger that sustained them had disappeared. She seemed more confused than anything.

"Are you… are you ready to go?" I said.

"Yeah," she said, betraying no emotion, "Let's go."

We walked side by side, back towards the entrance in silence. After she destroyed the building, I planned on giving her some grandiose speech of encouragement to pump her up even more, but the plan didn't pan out the way I expected it to, so I kept my mouth shut. I don't think I could've felt more idiotic. As if punching a barn in some shithole amusement park was going to fix everything.

After a few minutes, we arrived back at the entrance, at the arch above the box office where the paint flecked away from the words asking us to come again soon. I stood next to the Lenny statue and sighed. I'd have to do some major ass kissing if I ever wanted her to forgive me for this disaster.

"Kelly, I—"

CRASH!

My heart jumped and I whipped around.

Kelly was gone.

Another boom rang out from the concourse of stands. My brain screamed to go run and see, but my legs refused, so I stood there, anchored. Only when a third shockwave thundered over did I sprint back into the park. My eyes darted back and forth between the stands, searching for any signs of devastation. I turned a corner just in time to see her kick a shooting gallery, blowing it to smithereens.

Kelly ignored me. Curiosity, more than anything else, dominated her expression. She moved on from the previous wreckage to the strength testing game next in line. She picked up the mallet, weighing it in her hands before she swung at the metered pole and cracked it cleanly in half. She held onto the hammer, using it to destroy her next targets in one clean blow. That's how she took it at first: slow, measured, reluctant even.

But it didn't last. The raw spectacle started to chip at her armor. A smile here when she tossed a popcorn cart into the sky, a giggle there as a larger restaurant collapsed with a single karate chop. Soon she was entangled in a beautiful dance of destruction, punching, kicking, and laughing as she moved up and down the aisles and systematically took them out, every part of her loose and wild. She acted like a little kid playing make believe, spinning around and yelling out names of attacks. I could've cried when she dropped kicked a hot dog stand into oblivion. I think I peed a little when she picked up a ball from one of the carnival games and threw it in a line, blasting through three different stands like a cannonball and causing each one to fall in succession. In what seemed like no time at all, she leveled the area. I approached her, thinking she was done.

How wrong I was.

She took off at such sudden and incredible speeds I thought she teleported, easily clocking over sixty miles per hour as she sprinted toward the funhouse. I was speechless. Once I was running, I did my best to keep up, but she was way too fast, and halfway there I had to stop and recuperate. After a short rest I continued the pursuit, but when I arrived at the area between the funhouse and the carousel, Kelly was nowhere to be found. I spun around and listened for the sounds of shattered wood and crushed brick to guide me, but all was quiet. Right as I began to worry that I lost her, a thump sprang forth from the funhouse clown's open mouth. I went toward the sound and squinted, trying to see exactly where she might be.

I didn't get more than a few steps when Kelly burst out of a wall like the Kool-Aid Man. She spun on her heel and cracked her neck, placing her hands on her hips as she watched the funhouse come tumbling down. I think I would have actually killed a man for the chance to see what she did in there.

For the first time since we were at the barn, she looked over at me. I had a minor heart attack as she charged in my direction, coming so fast I thought she'd break me in half when we collided, but she skidded to a halt just in time. The debris coating her made her look like a swamp monster, but her goofy smile glowed underneath.

"Money please!" she said with an outstretched hand.

"Huh?"

"I went through the funhouse, didn't I? Pay up!"

My own smile matched hers as her whimsical attitude infected me. I reached in my pocket and pulled out the wad of bills I offered earlier. She snatched the money out of my hand and gestured toward the carousel, "Wanna go for a ride?" she asked.

I found the cleanest looking mount, one of the tigers on the perimeter, and hopped on. This particular carousel had a number of poles with no animals attached, allowing patrons to stand, if they wished. Kelly grabbed one next to me at the platform's edge, and the horrible screech of grinding rust ripped through the air as she pushed and the structure started spinning. Covering my ears didn't alleviate the auditory pain one bit, but the screeching died off as the carousel picked up speed. Kelly ran in circles. If pushing this hundred-ton contraption like a schoolyard merry-go-round strained her at all, she didn't show it. I clung to the tiger for dear life to avoid getting bucked by the centrifugal force, and everything outside began to blur together. On the first few rotations I could pick Lenny's face out amongst the funhouse rubble, but soon enough it dissolved into a blotch of orange that blipped in my vision every second or so. I was on a rollercoaster without a seatbelt, and if I were to let go, the sudden stop would surely break every bone in my body. That made it all the more thrilling.

Kelly pulled herself onto the platform just as it looked like the carousel might start outrunning her. She easily supported herself with one hand, using her other outstretched arm to feel the wind between her fingertips as she leaned off, and her hair flailed behind her like a windsock. I stared right into her brilliant reds and we both started laughing, laughing harder and with more joy than either of us ever felt before. We were on a runaway carousel, and I never wanted it to stop.

We stayed on until the carousel petered out, which

took a long time. Friction could only do so much to combat the inertia of such a massive object moving at high speeds. Unaffected by a weakness as human as dizziness, Kelly jumped off while the carousel was still moving, while I waited on the tiger several minutes after it came to a complete stop. Maintaining my vice grip for so long sapped all the strength from my puny arms. My stomach plotted to revolt against me, and the world wouldn't stop spinning. Before Kelly could charge away to cause more mischief, I held up a hand, panting. She tapped her foot and kept craning her neck toward the rollercoaster as I got on my wobbling feet. Once I was positive that I wasn't going to fall over and vomit, I gave her a thumbs up and waddled over.

Kelly zoomed off, and despite being in no condition to chase her, I managed to stay pretty close. Fast as she may have been, she kept getting sidetracked by new pieces of amusement park to play with. She could've dealt with most of these smaller structures with a simple punch or kick, but Kelly was getting surprisingly creative with her rampage. When we got to the watery grave of the bumper boats she dragged two ashore, tossed one into the air, and used the other to hit it like a baseball before it could touch the ground. She punted a dumpster like a football and sent it soaring into the forest beyond. She stomped on the ground and made a violent tremor that toppled a bunch of signs, and myself, over.

As a result, we arrived at the coaster more or less simultaneously. The cogs started turning in her head as she tapped her forefinger to her lips, sizing the place up. Star-Light deserved an epic send-off, worthy of all the thrills and excitement it gave over the course of its career. I watched with bated breath, eager to see what Kelly could cook up.

Kelly let her attention wander while she puzzled over her next plan of attack. Hit with a bolt of inspiration, the answer came to her when she noticed the overturned train. She trotted over and grabbed the front of the locomotive, dragging it and its tangled cargo to the coaster's entrance. She nudged her head in my direction and said, "You should probably back up."

I obeyed, backpedaling a few steps, but she shook her head, "No, like *really* back up."

My heart pounded harder with anticipation the further back I went. "Keep going…" she said, "A little farther… Okay, you're good!"

The outlines of both the coaster and the Ferris wheel towered over the treetops. Just for that one minute, I wished we came in broad daylight. I could barely see Kelly against the dark mass of the kiddy train. I was worried my view of the grand finale wouldn't be good enough.

But what a finale it was.

The train started to rotate, sweeping out like a tornado from Kelly, the eye of the storm. The vortex picked up speed. Soon enough there wasn't a train car touching the ground as she spun it around and around. The rattling in the caboose gave me the impression that it would fly off any second, but before it had the chance, the trainado started shifting ever so slightly to the right. It inched closer and closer to StarLight, and I prepared for contact. It tore through the wooden coaster's highest hill and shattered the structure into a million pieces. If she stopped there, it still would've been the most beautiful thing I'd ever seen, but she didn't stop there. She kept the train swinging as the coaster fell apart, not slowing even a little as it batted away bars and boards.

Then she let go.

The train flew through the air, arcing over the trees and smacking directly into the Ferris wheel's center. The train brought Leroy's tallest structure down with it. The Ferris wheel toppled like a domino, laid to rest in the woods it overlooked for so long.

I started jumping up and down, grabbing at my hair and nearly tearing it out. Within seconds Kelly came bounding back, and I ran to meet her halfway. We both started flailing about with manic energy, nearly dancing as we tried to out-gush each other about the wondrous events that had just taken place.

"Did you see that!? Did you!?—"

"That was amazing! Just fucking amazing!—"

"That was so much fun!—"

"The train! The fucking train! I can't handle it!—"

"You should've seen me in the funhouse!—"

"How far did you throw that fucker!?—"

"Let's ride the merry-go-round again!—"

"God, when you drop kicked the hot dog stand!—"

"I never could've done this without you!—"

"No, this was all you!—"

We carried on like that all the way back to the entrance, where we stopped dead in our tracks and hushed at once. The decrepit clown sculpture gave us pause. With his kingdom in ashes, he held no power over us. We flashed knowing smiles at one another.

I bowed, and presented the statue with a flourish, "Do the honors."

Kelly waited, taking a final look at the ruin left in her wake, "I have a better idea." She handed me the funhouse money, "Take this and go get as many snacks and drinks as you can. I'll meet you at the high school."

"The high school?"

"Well, yeah. We can't leave poor Lenny here by himself."

Kelly plucked the statue off its base and slung it over her shoulders, and then I understood. "Of course," I said, "The high school. Sure you don't want to ride with me? It's a bit of a hike."

"Oh, I think he's too heavy for the car." She took Lenny around the box office. Without breaking her stride, she kicked the front gate. The chains snapped, flinging the padlock into the woods as the gates flew open, "I can walk."

We split up. Kelly disappeared into the forest, nearly skipping away with the two-ton statue bouncing in her carefree grasp. Meanwhile, I jumped in the Kellywagon and pushed it to the limit down the dirt road, making a hard right towards the closest convenience store, hooting and hollering in victory with the windows rolled down and the radio pumped up. I blew through a red light in my excitement, but Leroy was so devoid of people during the night that I could floor it all the way to the gas station without any consequences.

I couldn't believe it. It worked. It actually worked.

CHAPTER 8

KELLY

WE LAID ON Leroy High's roof, gazing at the stars with a mountain of chips, candy, and soda between us, and Lenny at our backs watching over the empty parking lot like a gargoyle. I cracked open another bag of Onion Funs while Chris tossed his empty can of Dr. Drizzle all the way to the ground. He always said that the off-brand stuff tasted better.

Propping myself up on my elbows, I leaned my head back to get a better look at our new friend, "I think Lenny looks good here."

"Yeah. It suits him," Chris said. As he reached for another can of soda, he caught a glimpse of the state highway running next to the school, and suddenly he looked a little annoyed. He got on his feet, wandering to the edge overlooking the road.

I sat up completely. "What's the matter?"

"Tomorrow's Saturday."

"So?"

"They're going to take Lenny down before anyone sees him."

"Oh." It didn't really bother me, but I'll admit that seeing everyone's face when they came in the next morning would've been a treat. "At least we know. That's what matters, right?"

Gears turned in his head as he peeked over the side, moving around the edge with his hands out like he was trying to find the best way to frame a picture. "Let's move him here. That way any cars that pass will see him from the road."

I yawned as I stood up. Lifting the statue was still easy. Maybe too easy. Chris flinched when I picked it up, and as self-conscious as that made me, it was an important reminder. Even though I had a lot of fun tonight, I couldn't let myself get too carried away. Trying to be gentler, I put the statue down as close to the ledge as I could get it, and turned his monster face to the road.

Chris leaned on Lenny, reaching up to put his hand on the statue's shoulder, "There. Anyone passing through tomorrow won't forget this town anytime soon."

I couldn't help but admire my handiwork, and stood on the other side of Lenny. "Okay, you're right. I like this better. It's like he's waving at them as they go by."

The blackened town spread beneath us and stars glittered above us. As pretty as it was, the guilt creeping in me made it hard to really appreciate. When you sat back and really thought about it, destroying the carnival was a really, *really* stupid move. About a thousand things could've gone wrong. Someone could've been watching us from the woods. Someone could've been in a building we didn't check and got crushed when it came down. Chris could've gotten seriously hurt.

But Chris was right, wasn't he? Everything turned out fine, just like the day we met.

But I was ignoring one small, important detail: I did this on the anniversary of Dad's death.

Or, did I? I mean, it was probably midnight by the time we started… No, don't be stupid. That's splitting hairs and you know it. Dad's spinning in his grave and it was a stupid, selfish insult to his memory either way.

What came over me? Why did I do it? The big smile on Chris's face gave me my answer. I hadn't realized just how much I missed him until now. The real him. My little buddy with grand plans and a taste for adventure. Exploring that amusement park together was like meeting him for the first time in years, like the angry grump who got into fights at school was an evil clone. The real thing finally came back for me.

And I had a lot of fun. I did it because it was fun.

But that was the worst part. That was the slippery slope. All Chris wanted was for me to punch the barn down, but I took it way, *way* further than that. Maybe it turned out fine this time, but what about the next? What about ten years ago? Dad was right. What I had wasn't a toy, and I couldn't afford to keep using it like one, no matter how good it felt.

While all of that stewed in my head, Chris turned back to me and said, "Wouldn't it be great if every night was like this?"

Even if there was a part of me that agreed, I shook my head immediately, "I don't think so."

He sat down, letting his feet dangle over the building, "Come on, admit it. I was right. It felt good to let go for once."

Following his lead, I went around Lenny and slid down next to Chris, so we wouldn't have to lean past the clown to see each other. "I mean, sure," I said, "It did feel good, but it shouldn't have. I wrecked a few old buildings. It's not like I did anything useful."

"Yeah, yeah, great power, great responsibility, whatever. You know what else isn't useful? Actively repressing the thing that makes you special."

A self-deprecating laugh came out of me, "I'm really not special."

"Oh, please. You're the most creative, talented person in this whole town, and that's not even considering the superpowers. But fine, let's say you're right. Maybe you shouldn't use them just to goof off. You're telling me you can't think of a single way to make them useful?"

I instinctively tugged on my hair while my cheeks burned, "I mean... I guess I'd make a good construction worker."

He pinched his forehead and sighed, "You need to think outside the box. Let's say I recorded a video of you at that theme park—" My panic at the thought must've been obvious, because he held out his hand and quickly added, "I didn't, but let's say I did. You could throw that thing on YouTube and everyone in the world would watch that video a hundred times. You'd be a celebrity overnight. You could upload a new video of you doing something crazy every week, monetize them, and be set for life. There'd be a hundred different networks kissing your ass to get you to sign a contract for a TV show. You'd have more money than you'd know what to do with. Hell, you want to do some good? Donate all the cash you make to charity. How's that for useful?"

I bit my lip. That sounded like a great way to get into trouble with the government. Even if it weren't, there were other problems with that plan. "I dunno. If I did that, nobody would ever leave me alone. I can barely handle reading lines for Rich's play; how would I survive as a celebrity?"

Chris leaned back and crossed his arms to think about it. Finally, he cocked his head at me and said, "Wear a mask? You could have a secret identity."

That made me burst out laughing. When Chris looked at me like I was some kinda crazy person, I took a second to calm myself and say, "I'm sorry. It just sounds like you want me to be some kinda superhero."

He stopped himself with his mouth halfway open, furrowing his brow while looking me over.

Oh my gosh, I thought, *he's seriously considering it.* Before he had the chance to say anything, I laughed even harder.

"Well," he said, "Why not?"

"Come on Chris," I said, still giggling, "Don't you think that's kinda silly?"

His expression didn't change. "You've seen every episode of Dragon Ball a dozen times. You don't get to dismiss something for being silly."

"Hey, low blow!" I said, still with a smile on my face.

But he ignored me, mulling things over for a second. "You know what, that's actually a good point. Why do you like that show?"

I probably sounded more defensive than I should've been, "It's not *that* stupid."

He rolled his eyes, "Let me put it another way: why do people like superheroes?"

I thought about it for a second, "Um... because it's all fantasy, right? People can't do that stuff in real life." I started to understand what he was getting at, "Most people, anyway."

"If that were the only reason, I don't think you'd care for Dragon Ball much. There's something about the story or the characters you like, right?"

"It..." I paused, "It feels nice seeing the good guys win, I guess."

He snapped his fingers, "Bingo. We like those stories because the real world fucking sucks. The bad guys get away, innocent people suffer, and most of us can't do a thing about it. But you? You're not most of us. You can change the world if you want to." Chris brushed himself off as he rose back to his feet, "Look Kelly, you can live your life how you want. If you want to keep your powers hidden for the rest of time, there isn't anything I can do to stop you. I'm just saying, don't put yourself in a box because that's the way it's always been. The carnival was the happiest I've seen you in a long time. That happiness doesn't have to end tonight."

Chris wandered over to the snack pile, keeping his back to me while he rooted through it. Was that the first time we ever talked about my condition? Like, really talked about it? I guess he had been pretty good about keeping my secret over the years, so finally seeing his perspective on it was interesting, I guess.

But did he have a point? I didn't know. Chris never gave the consequences of his actions too much thought. He didn't know what it was like having to keep himself under control at all times. Would he still be telling me this if he knew everything that happened? Not even Chris was that reckless, right?

I kept thinking about the last thing he said, about doing things the way I've always done them. I hadn't really thought of it like that before. Dad's been gone for ten years. In all that time I've been trying to live by the same rules, but I'm not the same person. Everything Dad did was to keep people safe, to keep me safe. Would it really be spitting on his memory if I used my condition to keep people safe?

Chris thought I was special. Chris thought I could change the world. I didn't know about that, but I couldn't really argue that I wasn't different. If those differences could help people, even in a small way, was it selfish to pretend I was normal? Or was I just trying to let myself off the hook and give myself an excuse to let go?

Plus, I still didn't really know how I would actually help anyone. In fact, being a superhero sounded like a really stupid idea.

But it was the sweet kind of stupid. Maybe the world needed more of that.

Chris took a big gulp of soda while staring at the stars, and looking at him suddenly made me want to go all in on this insane superhero plan. Because even if I totally failed, even if I was the worst superhero there ever was, it wouldn't have all been just for my sake. There was at least one person I'd be helping. The carnival was the happiest I'd seen Chris in a long time, too.

So, before I had the chance to change my mind, I said, "Okay. I'll do it."

He actually dropped his soda as he whipped around. I had to step around the sticky puddle spreading out on the roof to make my way to him.

"For real?" he said.

I nodded, "I have two conditions." This put him a little on edge, but I kept talking, "I'm not gonna hurt anyone, and nobody is gonna see my face. Otherwise, yeah," I smiled, "Let's be superheroes."

It was like he'd been waiting his whole life for me to say that. His joyful whoop must've echoed across the entire town. He grabbed another soda for himself and surprised me by flinging one my way. Raising his can as high as he could reach, he shouted, "A toast! To Kelly Hatfield! Humanity's last, best hope!"

I hesitated, not wanting to complete my end of the toast. I couldn't help but imagine all the different, horrible shapes his arm would twist into if I put too much strength behind it. But I didn't want to leave him hanging either, and if I was gonna be a superhero, I had to get over some of those old anxieties. I brushed my can against his so softly his hand barely moved. The weak toast didn't make him any less delighted. He downed his entire can and let out a burp almost as loud as his cheering before tossing the empty off the roof. Some soda spilled out the sides of my mouth when I giggled, and when I finished drinking, I closed my eyes and took a breath. If Chris was gonna be my sidekick, I had to get used to him seeing my red eyes, too. Opening them, I let a current of energy rush through and followed his example, unleashing a mega-burp and whipping my can into the night sky. I don't think it came down.

"So, what do we do now?" I asked.

He placed his hands on his hips and stared into the horizon with confidence, "I have no idea."

And you know what? That was okay with me.

CHAPTER 9

CHRIS

"SHIT."

My house cast a towering, oppressive gloom, despite only being one story. Framed by the light emanating from my living room window, Mom's silhouette was visible even from the end of Kelly's driveway. She probably rooted herself to the couch the second she got home, waiting to rain fire on me as soon as I walked in. Times like this made me glad my grandparents moved down south when they retired. The only thing more embarrassing than Mom tearing me a new one was having an audience for it. Unusually for 2 A.M. on a Saturday, Thomas's car was still there, so she must have dealt with him already. He didn't skirt by completely unscathed, thank Christ. Didn't change how deep in the shit I was.

Kelly knew what it meant as well as I did, and shifted uncomfortably in her seat as she said, "I'm sorry."

"Don't be. This is on me."

She sighed, "I guess superheroing is gonna have to wait, huh?"

"No. This is a minor setback. We weren't going to do this in broad daylight anyway."

"We weren't?"

"Of course we weren't. Name one self-respecting superhero who does their work during the day."

She answered almost instantly, "Superman?"

I had nothing to counter that. "Aren't you the one worried about someone seeing you?"

"I mean sure, but I'll be wearing a mask, right? We have school in the morning. I really don't wanna be out too late."

"But that's when crime happens. Justice can't wait for school."

Kelly instantly started giggling, not even attempting to conceal it.

"What?" I said.

She smiled and leaned forward, mumbling in the absolute worst Batman impression I've ever heard, "*Justice* can't wait for school."

"Never do that again." I sighed and ran a hand through my hair. "Look, tomorrow's not a school night. We can at least start training. I'll sneak out my window once my mom is asleep."

"Training?"

"Of course. You don't run a marathon without stretching first, but you shouldn't worry about it. I'll have plenty of time to work out the details. Take tomorrow to relax, and keep an eye on your phone around midnight."

She looked doubtful, "Do you really think your mom is gonna let you keep your phone?"

"Again, don't worry about it. I have my ways."

We popped open the car doors at roughly the same time and stepped out, "Well," I said, "Time to face judgement. See you tomorrow?"

Giving me a solemn nod, she said, "Good luck," and disappeared into her house.

I mulled over a strategy while crossing the distance between our homes, but if there was a way to minimize the damage, I wasn't seeing it. The front door was upon me quicker than I expected, and I couldn't help but sigh. Best to rip the band-aid off and get it over with.

The door creaked open, and my vision didn't have a chance to adjust to the light flooding over me when Mom's arm shot into the air with a snap of her fingers, "Phone."

Squinting to reduce the brightness, I shoved my hand in my pocket and accidentally jingled the Kellywagon's keys while grabbing my phone. Mom leaned over the couch armrest and glared at me with piercing eagle eyes. Thomas and I inherited their color, but not their intensity.

"You didn't even return Mr. Hatfield's keys?" she said.

"Didn't want to wake him up," I grumbled. "It's late."

"I know." She held out her hand and beckoned, "Give."

I dropped both the keys and my phone in it without argument. The fact she was noticeably shorter than me didn't diminish her imposing presence one bit, and her long, black hair cracked like a whip when she stood up, "I'll go over there tomorrow. He already knows not to let you in his house until I say so. Now sit."

And so a familiar scene commenced. Me squarely in the center of our heinously uncomfortable corduroy couch, Mom standing over me with a scowl and crossed arms, the photos on the mantle gazing down at me in judgment. As far as decorations go, my grandparents had kept the house pretty Spartan, but when we moved in, Mom filled every bare space with a photograph. She had so many that she changed them out with the seasons, but there was one constant: a large headshot of Dad's smiling face, just to the left of where Mom stood in front of me. The positioning wasn't accidental: it gave her spiritual backup whenever Thomas and I needed a couch scolding. It was a dirty trick, and the main reason I could never look up during these lectures.

"Well Chris, I hope Kelly had a fun night," she started, "Because that poor girl isn't going to see you for a very long time."

"How long?" I said immediately.

A humorless laugh rose from Mom, "Unbelievable. That's all you have to say for yourself?"

"Well what is it you want to hear? Sorry? Because I'm not even a little. That piece of shit had it coming and I got my ass kicked anyway."

"The least you could do is apologize for not picking up the goddamn phone when I called you."

"It wouldn't have made any difference. You'd already eaten the bullshit Thomas shoveled down your throat."

"For your information, I called *you* first. And if you have a better explanation for what the hell went wrong today, I'm all ears. Because the way your brother made it sound, you pounced on him because he was calling you mean names."

I kept my head down and didn't answer. That was a pithy way of putting it, but not an inaccurate one. Mom leaned forward and pressed me again, "Sound about right?"

"You're acting like I beat him to a pulp. That fucker nearly cracked my skull open. You doing anything about that?"

"That's none of your concern."

"Oh, I think it is. He's the one who keeps starting shit."

That really got her going. "You never learn. You just never learn! For the love of god Chris, you're not a ten-year-old! Just ignore him! Because I've got news for you, if you can't ignore the people who piss you off, if you confront every single person who gives you a hard time, you're going to get yourself in huge trouble one day. In the real world, picking fights is a good way to land your ass in jail."

"Well it isn't the real world, it's high school. And it'd be a whole lot easier to ignore him if he didn't constantly sic his minions on me."

Thomas's voice boomed from the hallway behind me, "Jesus, I don't have minions." He stormed into view, shaking with a fury he'd saved all day for me, "They're called friends. They're what normal people have. Kind of like that ogre you drag around, but not nearly as disgusting."

If I weren't on trial for fighting, I would have decked him then and there. To restrain myself, I dug both hands into the cushions and wrapped my fingers around a fistful of couch, "Kelly's worth more than you and every single hillbilly in that school put together."

Mom gritted her teeth, massaging her temples like she was fending off a migraine, "Thomas, you can have another week for that comment. Now get back in your room!"

But Thomas ignored her and fired back at me, "You know, I was trying to cover your ass today."

"Is that right?" I snorted, "Give me a break."

"Boys!"

"Laugh it up all you want, but you would've been fucked beyond words if Trevor started spreading rumors about you bringing a gun to school. You have any idea how often I have to convince people I'm not crazy like you? You think after what happened at Willow today the principal's gonna take any chances on *you?*" Thomas unclenched his fist over the coffee table in front of us. A small bottle filled to the brim with antidepressants clattered against it and rolled around. Mom's pale face looked about how I felt. "Look what I found in the trash the other day. Maybe if you actually took your pussy pills people wouldn't think you're such a psycho."

That did it. I let go of the couch and sprang to my feet, but before I had the chance to do anything, Mom stepped over to Thomas and smacked him across the face with an open palm. Both of us froze in stunned silence. She'd never hit either of us before. Thomas's hand hovered over his reddened cheek as he stared at her.

She didn't shout. She didn't need to, "Thomas Underwood, if I *ever* catch you talking like that again, you're not leaving this house until you graduate. Understand?" Thomas nodded slowly, his mouth slightly agape. "Good. Go to your room."

As Thomas slinked back down the hall, Mom didn't return to her usual lecturing spot. All the anger in her face was gone when she sat next to me on the couch, and I had to turn away when she started turning the pills over in her hand.

"Chris, look at me." With some reluctance, I obeyed, and suddenly she looked very old. The lines in her face seemed more pronounced than ever. Streaks of gray in her hair looked like highlights. It made me feel guilty, thinking about all the years she's had to put up with us alone.

The last hint of anger in her voice was gone. "Sweetie, show me your arm."

Rolling my eyes to hide my fear, I held my right hand out over the coffee table. Mom reached for it, but I yanked my hoodie's sleeve all the way up before she could, revealing the horizontal slashes scarring nearly every inch of my upper arm. Getting in close and examining it the way a paleontologist might analyze a fossil, with a careful eye and a gentle touch, Mom searched for any fresh cuts that may have appeared since the last time she caught me with the knife. I tried not to sweat. Since I offered it with such little fuss, I was praying that she didn't ask to see anywhere else.

Satisfied, she backed off, and I rolled my sleeve back down like it was nothing at all even though I was screaming on the inside. Mom moved on, pointedly not mentioning my scars any further, "Why aren't you taking your medicine?"

"Don't need it."

All the stray pieces in her head started coming together, and she asked the next obvious question, "So... when you say you're going to see Dr. Wendell, where are you really?"

I shrugged, "With Kelly somewhere."

She thought it over for a second. "Do you want to find another doctor? We can try this practice up in Cleveland one of the girls at the hospital recommended to me."

"No Mom. I don't need a doctor."

"Chris, you're sick. It's like having the flu. These people want you to get better."

"It's not like having the flu. It's nothing. I'm not going to let some shrink charge you an arm and a leg for pills that don't do anything. And they don't want to help, they want to pacify me. You know what that feels like, Mom? You ever have some condescending prick look you in the eye and tell you that you're broken? That they can fix you?"

Mom stopped herself with a deep breath before giving a retort. When she spoke again, there still wasn't any anger. No tears. She stated everything so matter-of-factly. I don't know why, but that bothered me so much more than if she screamed and cried. "Tell you what Chris, I'll make you a deal. We'll let everything slide this time. If you don't think that medicine is helping, you don't have to take it. If you aren't comfortable talking to Dr. Wendell, then you don't have to see her. But, in exchange, you need to find someone you are comfortable with, who you'll actually work with to find something that does help. Because I don't know what to do with you anymore. This is the second time you've gotten suspended this semester alone. Your grades keep getting worse. You disappear for hours at a time and I have no idea where you go. We can't even have dinner in this house without you and Thomas turning it into a warzone. I'm sick of it, Chris. Sick of it all. So consider this your last warning. Either you can make the effort to get better, or you can sit in your room until you graduate."

The stinging in my eyes told me I needed to get out of there. I sprang up from the couch and made for the hallway. Mom didn't follow me or say anything else.

Slamming my bedroom door behind me, I leaned against it and took a few deep breaths, flipped the light on to look for the one thing that helped when I got like this, that kept the panic away. I flung open the drawer in my desk and rummaged through it, looking for the black tube sock where I hid everything. Mom was right to check my arm, but when it came to keeping a secret, I was no amateur. My pocket knife and bandages, along with disinfectant and a pack of handwipes, tumbled out of their hiding place. I removed my hoodie and pants, unraveling the old bandage on my upper thigh to size up the mess of scar tissue on my leg. My more recent wounds had started healing, and I'd been very careful to stay away from my arms.

As I said, I'm no amateur. When I used to take the knife to my arms, I never made any cuts below the elbow. That way I could still wear hoodies in the summer with the sleeves rolled-up and not get too hot while keeping my habit a secret. Not even Kelly knew I did this. Whenever someone questioned why I always wore jeans or hoodies or long sleeve shirts, their suspicion was always easy to deflect. I look stupid in shorts, I get cold easily. I had hundreds of excuses like those.

Only Mom knew. When she first caught me, she obviously freaked out, started checking my arms every single night to get me to stop, made me go talk to assholes with fake voices and fancy degrees who didn't give a shit about me. That's when I moved to my legs, and when the scars on my arm faded into a softer permanence, she began to back off. It wasn't any of her damn business anyway. What I do with my body is my own choice. It's not like I cut myself all the time or anything. I wasn't suicidal. I only needed it on days like the one I just had. It was emotional release, stress relief.

I flipped the tiny edge of the pocket knife open, taking a deep breath while waiting for my hands to stop shaking. Then, finding a clean spot close to my still healing wounds, I jabbed the point into my thigh and instantly, any and all tears building up inside me went away in one sharp explosion of pain. Calmly, focusing only on the hurt, my skin splitting apart as the blade slid across my upper thigh, I sat for a moment and felt the thick coating of blood drip down after pulling it out. Just like that, my problems weren't problems anymore. With something real to focus on, there wasn't any time to cry over ridiculous bullshit. After waiting a second, I plunged the knife back in. The trick was never to leave too many marks in one night. I felt the relief better if I took it slow.

Finally feeling calm, I started to clean my leg. Infection wasn't something I could hide, so I always made sure to clean and properly bandage my wounds to keep that shit from happening. Besides, the extra steps, the sting of the disinfectant, helped give even more clarity. While I patched myself up, my eyes wandered to the picture Kelly gave me the day we met, hanging on the corkboard over my desk and standing out amongst all the other photos and drawings cluttered together in a collage she made for my birthday last year. It reminded me that I had a job to do. No time to waste sulking when I could get a head start on building Kelly's training regimen.

An empty space on the desk marked where my laptop should have been. Obviously, Mom already swept through and put anything that could connect to the internet in her safe, but that was, at worst, a minor setback. Since the safe had a key instead of a combination, a while ago I taught myself to pick the lock, just to see if I could do it. When you're suspended and Mom's too busy working to supervise you, you end up with a lot of time on your hands. Once everyone in the house was asleep, I'd sneak out and grab my laptop to send a message to Kelly giving her the lowdown on the situation, and then do some investigating online. Everything would be fine so long as I remembered to lock it back up before bed.

In the meantime, I ripped off a piece of scrap paper and started brainstorming, jotting down every stray thought about Kelly's powers I had. Where they might come from, other abilities she might not have tapped into, that sort of thing. Before, even Googling this stuff felt like a breach of Rule One, but now I was free. The excitement of it all kept my pen moving, and by the time all the lights in the house went dark, I had a full page of avenues to explore.

When I was sure my family was fast asleep, I made my move, slipped back into my jeans to hide my new bandage, and snuck down the hall in the dark. It occurred to me that doing my research for Kelly, and everything else about this new enterprise, in fact, would be much easier if I'd just taken Mom's deal, but fuck that. I didn't need a shrink, and I certainly didn't need those meds they were hawking. I was fine. If I had to do my work at night, so be it. I wasn't going to sleep anyway.

CHAPTER 10

KELLY

CHRIS WIGGLED OUT of his bedroom window while I got the car ready. Things must've gone worse with his mom than I thought they would, because when I asked him how long he was grounded for, all he said was "Long enough." It looked like we were gonna have to be night owls whether we wanted to or not, but I was excited anyway. Superhero training sounded like a pretty fun way to spend a few hours before school.

We picked the old junkyard for our secret hideout, since it was in a part of town where there weren't any houses and nobody would miss all the old cars we were gonna smash. Whenever someone talked about the junkyard, I always pictured big piles of metal stacked like mountains, but aside from a crusher near the entrance, it looked more like a parking lot for cars that didn't have wheels. We started by doing a quick sweep of the area to make sure there weren't any people around. Again, Chris thought there'd be drug dealers. I don't know why he was so obsessed with drug dealers, but better safe than sorry, I guess? We went up and down the rows of rusty cars and scrap, and when the coast was clear, we decided to make our home base by a school bus with a wrecked front end.

Chris spread the stack of papers in his hands out on an old boat. I leaned over his shoulder to try and get a look at them, but it was too dark to read.

"What's this?" I asked.

Chris flipped his phone's flashlight on and started reorganizing the mess, "Did some research last night."

One of the pages immediately caught my eye, and I took it with a smile. Chris had printed out a list of Sasquatch sightings.

"Looks real important," I said.

Chris narrowed his eyes at me and snatched the paper out of my hands, "It might be," he said, shuffling it back into the pile.

"Are we gonna hunt for Sasquatch? Is that what superheroes do?"

"No. Now shut up. It's time to get to work." He cleared his throat like a businessman preparing to give a talk at a big show, and even though I wanted to dig through his pile and see what other silly things he "researched," I quieted down.

"Alright," he said, "Welcome to your first night of superhero boot camp. By the time you walk out of this junkyard, you're going to be the hero this town so desperately needs. What I have here," he waved the wad of papers around, "Is a simple, three step process to give you all the skills you'll need to keep the streets clean. First," he held up a finger, pacing back and forth as he read out loud, "We're going to figure out what the source of your power is. If we know why you are the way you are, and how exactly your powers work, we'll be able to maximize the effectiveness of your training. Next," he flipped one of his pages over and held up another finger, "We're going to find out what other powers you have. You can hit hard, but for all we know that's just a drop in the ocean, so we'll have to experiment. Finally, when we know exactly what you're capable of, we'll repeat a bunch of exercises to make sure you have perfect control over all your abilities," he stopped and looked up at me, "Any questions?"

"Yes. What does Sasquatch have to do with any of that?"

"Be serious."

"I am serious! I wanna know!"

Running his hand through his hair, Chris sighed, "Look, we'll get to that. First things first," he pulled out a pencil and went back to the top of his packet, "There are a few things I need to know."

I wasn't sure what I had left to tell him. My powers seemed pretty basic. But his official looking stack of papers and harsh eyes told me that Chris was pretty serious about this. My answer came out a little more cautiously then I meant it to, "Like what?"

"Let's talk about your childhood," he said.

I tried my best to sound casual, tried to not grab myself by the arm or yank on my hair or give any kinda hint of being uncomfortable, "I mean, how important can my childhood really be?"

"Pretty damn important if we're going to figure out

what makes you tick. Don't worry, this won't take long. Let's hurry through these questions and get to the fun part."

I sighed, sitting on the front of the boat. This was gonna come up sooner or later, I guess. "Okay. What do you wanna know?"

"You were adopted, right? You know anything about your real parents?"

I shook my head.

"Really? Nothing at all?"

"Nope."

He tapped his pencil against his chin, not seeming too upset. He leaned against the boat as he scribbled something down, "Alright, not that surprising, I suppose. You know where you were adopted from?"

"Nope."

"No foster homes, nothing like that?"

I shook my head again, "I must've been real little. I didn't even know I was adopted for a long time. Grandma and Grandpa told me when I moved in with them."

He raised an eyebrow, "And they didn't tell you where you came from?"

"I mean, they were pretty vague about it, but…" I caught myself twisting my hair between my fingers as I stared at my feet, "I guess I've got a theory."

Chris leaned forward. "Mind sharing?"

"Yes."

"Kelly."

"Okay, fine." My cheeks started burning up. "My dad used to work for a garbage company. I don't know if he drove one of the trucks or if he worked in the offices or something, but if someone found a baby in a dumpster somewhere, he would've known about it. So… yeah."

"You seriously think your dad picked you out of a dumpster."

"Can you think of any other reason Grandma and Grandpa wouldn't wanna tell me where I came from?"

"Maybe you crash landed in some sort of geode from space, and they don't want you to know you're an alien."

I laughed, "Yeah. Maybe Grandpa keeps my *space geode* in the attic in case we need it again."

"Well, why not?" Chris threw a hand towards the sky, "You had to come from somewhere. Space is as good an explanation as any."

"Okay, sure, but why does any of this matter? It's not like knowing where I came from will change anything."

"Sure it would. Imagine if we tracked down your parents and they had powers just like you. Think about everything you could learn from them! Are you seriously trying to tell me you haven't been curious about any of this?"

"I really do my best to not think about it."

Chris clicked his flashlight back on with a sigh, flipping through some pages and muttering, "Just as well. If they really did find you in a dumpster somewhere, then that's a dead end. Dammit, I spent hours slogging through all kinds of crazy-ass paranormal websites. I really hoped you'd have a lead to help make sense of some of this garbage."

Curious to see what he found, I hopped off the boat and creeped over his shoulder again. He went really in depth with it, with pages and pages of stuff about aliens, government conspiracies, religions, even some real science research in there. I had no idea that Chris wanted to know what I was so bad. He'd done such a good job of keeping my secret to himself, but now with this superhero plan, it felt like all his thoughts bubbling under the surface were now exploding out. Honestly, it kinda hurt. Regular old me wasn't good enough.

Right as I was thinking about this, I remembered what we were talking about earlier and swung from "kinda hurt" to "really offended."

"Wait. You think I'm a *Sasquatch?*"

"Of course I don't think you're a Sasquatch!" he said, "I thought maybe Sasquatch was one of you."

"…That's the exact same thing!"

"It's completely different! Look," he handed the paper back to me and pointed at some notes he scribbled in the margins, "Red eyes. Tall, shadowy figure. Uprooted trees. Now you tell me, who does that sound like?"

I said nothing. Maybe I was a Sasquatch after all.

Chris kept going, "I thought maybe if we couldn't find out where you came from, there might at least be other people like you we could find and talk to." He smacked the page and turned to me, "And all these sightings attributed to 'Sasquatch' could easily be one of them."

Huh. I'd never thought about that. I always figured I had to be alone, because if there were tons of… well, tons of me, the world would have to find out about us eventually, right? "Did you find anyone?" I asked.

"Sadly, no. The Sasquatch thing was actually one of the closest matches I got. There was another website that talked about a superman matching your general description but that, uh, that turned out to be Nazi propaganda. If there are other people like you, they don't want to be found."

"That makes sense."

"Looks like we're on our own, at least for now. Since your origins turned out to be a bust, there's only one question left on my list: I want you to try and describe exactly how your powers work. Because whatever's going on obviously has nothing to do with your muscles."

A weight lifted off me, and I breathed easier. He wasn't going to ask about Dad, "Sure. Where do you want me to start?"

"How about your eyes? Any idea why they glow when you Hulk out?"

That phrasing annoyed me a little, but I ignored it, "I'm not really sure why any of this happens, but…" I thought about the best way to explain it to him, and walked over to the school bus, "So, this isn't really a great comparison, but maybe you can think of it like a car engine. When there isn't any gas in it, the car won't go." I put my hand against the bus and leaned on it, "See, it isn't moving. But, if I fill the tank up…" I drew a bit of my energy out and the bus tipped over without an extra push, "See?"

Chris ran over to me and stood on his tiptoes to get in my face, crooking his head around and peering into my eyes. It took everything I had in me to not move away from him. "Got it. Eyes glow, engine on," he said.

When he put his head down to make a mark in his notebook, I used the break in eye contact to step back and get some breathing room, "Right. But like I said, it isn't a great comparison. Sometimes when I'm upset, the car will turn on by itself. And it isn't really like an on and off switch. Like, there's kinda this heat inside me that burns hotter at different times. Like right there, I drew some out and tipped the bus over. If I wanted to, I could get even more and pick it up, and it'd really start bubbling inside me if I wanted to throw it."

Chris rubbed his chin, "Interesting. Tons of cultures believe in some kind of energy manipulation. I'll look into that later, but for now, let's move on to Phase Two."

My heart leaped. Finally. I wanted to throw some cars around, "So what's the plan?"

Chris put down his big stack of research, "Hold on," he said, "I need to rearrange a few things." Curious again, I went and spied over his shoulder one more time. The paper he dug up had two columns: one with a long list of stuff I couldn't make out on the left, and a blank one on the right. He added a few things to the blank column, while going down the other one and underlining parts of the list.

"What's this?"

"This," he said, finished changing it, "Is a list of potential superpowers. I wasn't sure how I wanted to handle your training. My first idea was to test the upper limits of your strength, see what your maximum capacity is, but I never thought of a good way to do that. Then, I had another idea. I made a list of every superpower I could think of. We're going to go down it, one by one, and find out exactly what you can do."

"If you have night vision on there, you can cross it off. I can't see what you wrote," I said. Chris clicked his phone light back on and scribbled something out. I went through the whole thing and it was… um… it sure was interesting.

- Flight
- Super-speed

- Healing factor
- Heat vision
- Hold breath infinitely
- Night vision
- Transformation
- Telepathy
- Mind control/suggestion
- Illusions
- Telekinesis
- Barrier creation
- Pyrokinesis
- Cryokinesis
- Wind control
- Electrical control/resistance
- Acid spit
- Matter manipulation
- Time stop
- Future sight
- Rewind time
- Bouncing
- Phasing
- The power to open portals
- Summoning
- The power to control bees
- Photosynthesis
- Mini-me's
- Grease
- Godzilla breath
- Spider-Man

- Stretch
- Eat
- Ki manipulation?
- Power charge?

He circled heat vision three times. Wanting to have a little fun, I stayed silent and squinted at Chris, letting my energy rise so my eyes would glow. He lifted his head to speak, but jumped back and covered his face when he realized what I was doing, "Jesus! Don't point it at me!"

I laughed, letting myself cool off, "Calm down, I think if I had heat vision I'd know by now."

"You might not! What if you have to consciously divert energy to your eyes or something? Look, we're out here to experiment. Humor me and try blasting the bus from here."

Chris took a few steps back as he held his arm out like a game show host introducing a prize. Not really expecting anything to happen, I squinted again and forced the energy in my body to flare up, but no matter how much I tried, I couldn't make it go anywhere specific. The energy just raged through my body. I was trying to force a forest fire through my pupils.

"No good," I said, careful to not turn while my eyes glowed so he wouldn't freak out, "I can't get it to work."

Thinking about this, Chris scribbled a few notes, "We can always try again later," he said. "We'll start from the top of the list. Let's see if you can fly."

I laughed. I don't think it would've been so funny if Chris wasn't so casual when he said it, like he was asking me if I wanted to get food later.

"What's so funny?" he asked.

The giggling got worse, and when I took another look at his confused face, I made this really gross snort and cracked up. With a stupid smile, I spread my arms out and flapped them like a big, goofy bird, "CAW!"

Scowling, Chris set his notes down, "Quit fucking around."

After stopping my bird impression, I had to brush a thick bundle of hair out of my eyes, "Chris, this is silly. I mean, you put 'the power to control bees' on that list."

He opened his mouth to argue, but double-checked the list before he did. He pressed his lips together and gently scratched it off the page, then tried to sound casual again, "I'm spitballing here. I never said they'd all work."

"But you didn't think about how I'd actually do any of this stuff. Flapping my arms wasn't totally a joke. I don't know how else I'd fly."

"Energy manipulation! That's your shtick! You watch anime where people fly like that all that time!"

"Yeah. *In anime.*"

Chris shook his finger at me, "This right here is your problem. You're always saying I can't. I can't be a superhero because it's silly. I can't have heat vision because I can't get it to work. I can't fly because that only happens in cartoons. Kelly, you don't understand exactly how extraordinary you are. You approach things like you're a nobody, but you're not. You're just not. Your very existence proves everything we think we know about physics and biology and chemistry and, hell, maybe even religion wrong. The super strength *has* to be the tip of the iceberg. That's why we're doing this training in the first place. So you can make the most of that potential." He took a few steps closer to me, and for a moment I thought he was gonna put his hands on my shoulders, so I took a step back to avoid his touch. Instead, he stood there and focused his eyes into a sharp, determined stare, "You can do it. I know you can."

That time, I didn't laugh it off, or make a stupid joke, or argue. I just stared down at him and thought about what he said for a while. Chris was always pretty serious, the kinda guy who doesn't dance around what he thinks or wrap his thoughts in a joke. When he said something, you could count on him to mean it. It made me rethink that hurt feeling I had earlier. Maybe I had it wrong. Maybe it wasn't that he thought I wasn't good enough, but that he wanted me to be the best I could be. That sounds kinda the same I guess, but I dunno. It felt like an important difference.

"Okay," I said, "I'll give it a try."

To keep him safe, I stepped away, scrambling my brain searching for any possible way to fly. I decided to just jump, jump as high as I could and see what happened. Taking a second to get ready, bending my knees and craning my neck skyward, I let my energy burn and flow throughout my body. I wondered how high I could go, if I'd shoot into space or if the planet would crumble under my feet. There was only one way to find out.

I jumped.

The wind roared around me as I left the ground with a thundering crack. Glancing down for just a second, I saw Chris bracing himself and the concrete beneath splitting and fissuring. In seconds he was a speck below me and I turned back to the sky. It didn't feel real. Like my body was still with Chris and this was my soul floating away. Except floating wasn't the right word. I was more like a rocket.

I rose up and up and up, the refreshing cold air seemed to help push me. Soon enough, the top of a cell phone tower blinked below me, and a cloud was almost within my reach. Off in the distance, the lights of the 24-hour truck stop shined, a beacon to help me find my way so high in the sky. A few twinkling lights dawdled along near it, stray cars journeying down the highway. Though it was covered by darkness, the outlet mall wouldn't be too far from them. It was beautiful. I could see the whole town. Hovering in the air for just a second, I thought I'd done it. I thought I'd flown.

Then gravity kicked in.

The world went into slow motion as it tugged me back to the ground, then yanked me all at once. I laughed as I dropped. Sure, I was gonna die, but the view was almost worth it. My life didn't flash before my eyes, but I didn't really mind. There were a lot of things I'd rather not see again. I had so far to fall that I couldn't stay up straight. I tumbled and flailed and the world spun.

My arms flayed out as I slammed onto the roof of a windowless van on the other side of the junkyard. The windshield exploded and the tires popped. It flattened, leaving nothing but a crushed sheet of metal between me and the ground. For a long time, I just laid there in shock. My bones rattled, but the fall didn't hurt me.

"*Kelly!* Fuck fuck FUCK. *Kelly, where are you?*"

Propping myself up, I could just see Chris scrambling through the wreckage of the junkyard. Feeling a little wobbly, I stayed on the ground and cupped my hands over my mouth to shout, "Over here!"

He locked onto my position and sprinted as fast as

his little legs could take him. I laid on the ground while Chris kneeled next to me, "Oh... oh thank god... you're alright... Jesus..."

He took a minute to catch his breath, and when he finally did, I spoke again, "Sorry captain. I wasn't able to do it."

Shaking his head with a smile on his face, he said, "Guess not. But it wasn't a total waste. We got valuable knowledge from that."

"Yeah? Like what?"

Smiling, he offered his hand to help me up, "That you're fucking unbreakable."

Reminding myself that Rule Two was still important, I got to my feet on my own. Chris understood and dropped his hand without saying anything. He just stood and smiled, looking up at me with something like pride in his eyes, or maybe pride isn't the right word. Admiration? It was hard to tell.

But what I do know is that I felt myself smiling.

"Alright," he said, "Let's head back to the boat. I left my list there, and there's a few more powers we should—"

Before he had the chance to finish his sentence, I bent my knees and sprang back into the sky.

This time, I wanted to land on my feet.

CHAPTER 11

CHRIS

THE KELLYWAGON ROCKED and rattled as I pinned the gas pedal to the floor. The old junker couldn't quite muster the strength to bridge 75 miles per hour barreling down the dirt road. It begged me to end its miserable life as the needle danced between 72 and 74 and the exhaust pipe coughed out an endless plume of smoke.

"Come on, come on! Faster, you piece of shit!"

Constantly shifting my focus between the mirror and the speedometer, I almost didn't see the sharp left the road took in the dark. A cloud of dust blasted into the air as I tapped the brakes and jerked the wheel. My tires screeched around the corner and I careened into the other lane as I floored the gas again. The powerslide made the crying rattles of the car even more painful, but I didn't care. Training had made Kelly arrogant, and pleased as I was with this development, sensei needed to put her in her place. Plus, there was money on the line.

The designated goal was straight ahead, just a few more miles. With no curves or obstacles around, I let my attention flit back to the rearview mirror. A storm of dust swirled in the distance.

"Shit. Shit!" I pounded on the steering wheel, as if that would will the thing to go faster, "Come on, you can do it!"

But that was a lie. The storm grew larger and larger and we still had a ways to go. Kelly gained on me within seconds, keeping pace close enough to brush the car with the back of her hand. Illuminated by moonlight, her entire body was playing on fast forward. She flashed a sly grin before bending at the knees and leaping into the air.

"Now you're just showing off," I muttered.

Her shadow landed a good distance down the road, but when she hit the ground, she stumbled and couldn't maintain her ludicrous speed. I had to swerve out of the way to avoid hitting her—though if we did crash, it'd only wreck the car—and outpaced her for a few more seconds. Kelly regained momentum and overtook me almost instantly. She slinked around the driver's side of the car and ran alongside it, her long hair streaming behind her.

I rolled down the window and leaned out. The speed sharpened the freezing wind blustering in my face. I shouted over its roar, "Tuckering out?"

Kelly gave no reply. No taunt, no knowing smile, nothing. Instead, she picked up her pace, blasting forward and kicking up enough dust to block my windshield. I slowed down, coughing as I rolled the window back up. There was no way to win now. When the dust settled, Kelly was a speck on the horizon.

When I finally idled up to the billboard that served as

our finish line, I found Kelly leaning against it with her arms crossed. She made a big show of yawning and checking her non-existent watch. Dancing over to the passenger door, she sang a little song while flinging herself inside.

"Stop," I said.

She sang louder as she buckled in before finally turning to me with a smug smile, "It's not my fault you're a sore loser."

"I only lost because you cheated."

"What!? I did not!"

"Don't think I didn't see you cut across the field. That head start you gave me doesn't mean shit if you don't follow the road, cheater."

Laughing, she said, "You're such a liar! I won fair and square." She then held out a hand, "Pay up!"

"You can pry those twenty bucks from my cold, dead fingers."

Kelly crossed her arms and went into a fake huff as she stole a glance at the clock. 5:30 AM. We still had a few hours to kill before school started. A week passed since we began training, enough time for my suspension to lift.

"Hey," she said, "How about instead of the money, you buy me breakfast? Lucky Dan's is open, and I'm starving."

"An omelet does sound pretty good right now." I put the car back in drive, "Let's roll."

I sped back to the highway, heading for Leroy's only 24-hour restaurant, blissfully unaware of the true nature of the fool's deal I'd just made. We were the first customers in the diner, a chintzy little place with red rubber seats and white tile floors stained with a hint of brown. I'm not sure if the diner pretended it was still the fifties as a stylistic choice, or if it was just that old and "Dan" hadn't bothered to update the décor. As soon as we sat down, Kelly made a big point of ordering exactly 21 dollars worth of food which, considering Lucky Dan's was a cheapo hole in the ground, was a feast fit for a titan. While stoic trucker types filtered in and took their coffee in monk-like silence, Kelly and I were so wired from our race we argued loudly and passionately during the wait about whether or not she'd be able to finish it all. I made another wager, that if she didn't clean all the plates she ordered, she'd have to pay for both our meals, and if she did, I owed her another ten bucks in addition to breakfast. Suffice to say, the clock hadn't struck seven yet and I already had to pay 31 dollars out of pocket for her.

We cleaned our plates with about an hour until school started, so we sat around and enjoyed free coffee refills, shooting the shit as the sun rose over town square. It was nice. Been too long since we'd done something like this. I wanted to savor the moment, but I needed to address one last bit of business.

The booth squeaked underneath me as I leaned forward to whisper, to avoid getting the attention of all the hairy truckers in the diner, "So, I'd say you're about ready."

Kelly cocked her head at me, unsure of why I was being so quiet, "Ready?"

"You know, to get out there and start being a real superhero."

"Oh." Kelly seemed a touch disappointed, but followed my lead by leaning in and whispering, "You think so?"

"Not having second thoughts, are you?"

"No, it's not like that." She sighed, leaning back and slowly tearing a napkin on the table to pieces, "Sorry. I dunno,

I've just had a lot of fun with the training sessions. You know, just me and you and stuff. I'll be kinda sad to see them go."

"Doing actual work will be just as fun. Maybe more so. You get the satisfaction of doing real good on top of the pleasure of smashing stuff."

She still seemed dubious, but checked over her shoulder to make sure the waiter wasn't coming back to us anytime soon before saying, "What'll I be doing? Getting cats out of trees and saving people from burning buildings and stuff?"

Her idea of superheroics was so Christopher Reeve it hurt. "That's what we have the fire department for. You should be helping in a way no else can. Let's say we run into someone getting mugged one night—"

Her face hardened as she sat up straighter, "I already told you, I'm not gonna hurt anybody."

And that was going to make this whole endeavor exponentially more difficult. You can't stop criminals without force. I thought maybe I'd be able to get her to see that, but given her reaction, I knew better than to press this particular issue. I didn't let it discourage me, though. Not when I had a Plan B at the ready.

"Alright, I've got a different angle for you then. We'll focus on stopping crimes before they start, find ways to deter the bad guys so you don't have to beat them up."

Kelly leaned back, tilting her head to the side, "Okay, how do we do that?"

"This works out well because it's going to be hard for us to fit this hero business into our schedules anyway. We're at school all day, and then we have to do homework, and finals are coming up, and we have to sleep, and all sorts of bullshit like that. We're going to be lucky if we can squeeze in three nights a week to go out and do this, and even then there's no guarantee we'll run into something juicy. So, what we do is spend the week with our ears to the ground, pick up on some trouble brewing, and then, when the moment is right, strike. You run in and scare the crooks off with a spectacular display of your powers. The goons will stop what they're doing and flee, and then they'll start spreading rumors about this crazy thing that happened to them. Do this a couple times a month, and bam," coffee splashed out of my mug as I knocked my fist on the table, "you're a local legend. All the thugs in town are going to be too scared to try anything shady if they think you're lurking in the shadows. Leroy's streets stay clean, and you don't have to hurt a soul."

The skepticism on her face was palpable. She said nothing for a moment. Then, finally, smiled and did that horrible Batman impression of hers loud enough for some of the truckers to shift their eyes toward us, "I'll be a symbol. The hero Leroy deserves, but not the one it needs right now."

I ran my hand through my hair and grunted, waiting for everyone to turn around before saying, "Look, mock me all you want, but if it works for Batman, it'll work for you."

"But Chris," she said in her normal voice, "Batman lives in a big city where a lot of crime happens. I don't know if this town needs someone to stop criminals."

"That's the beauty of it. Leroy is easy mode. The crime rate is low, everyone's a bumbling idiot, and rumors spread ridiculously fast. You can get your feet wet before we move on to some real challenges. Unless you want to go all the way to Cleveland and take on hardened criminals day one."

This took her aback, "I didn't realize you wanted to go so big with this."

"Of course. Don't you?"

She didn't answer immediately, twisting her hair the way she always did when deep in thought. "It kinda sounds like you already have something in mind for the first night."

"As a matter of fact, I do. I have it on good authority that Noah Burke is having a huge bonfire this weekend. Your grand debut should be there." Kelly immediately opened her mouth to protest, but I anticipated what she was going to say and cut her off, "Yes, I'm asking you to crash a party. Let me explain why before you write the idea off."

She paused, eyeing me with suspicion, but said nothing. At least she was going to hear me out. I continued, "A small town high school is the perfect place to get an insane rumor like this to spread. You make an impression Friday and you'll be the only thing Leroy talks about for years. Besides, who are the people most likely to cause problems in a town like this?"

She waited for me to continue, either unable to think of an answer or unwilling to play my guessing game. Knowing this would be a dicey proposition from the get go, I decided to minimize the risk by not irritating her and giving it to her straight, "Teenagers, right? Dumbasses our age. Like everyone who's going to be at that party. Sure, most people will be there to just get blitzed and have a good time, nothing worth bringing down the long arm of the law for, but think about it. Of all the kids in our school, who's most likely to be involved in the kind of shit that requires a superhero's attention? The dorks who spend their Friday nights at drama club with Rich? Or the people piling into Noah Burke's backyard to get fucked up?"

"I dunno, until last week, we spent all our Friday nights at Harry Horse's."

"What's that supposed to mean? You think *we're* shady?"

Kelly smiled in a way clearly meant to prod me, "We've been sneaking out to a junkyard at four in the morning almost every night. That's pretty shady."

I rolled my eyes, "Be snarky all you want, you know I have a point. You make an impression on this crowd and they'll be too scared to try anything in this town. You'd cut Leroy's problems in half right then and there."

"Okay, sure, there are probably gonna be a few bad kids there. Why don't we just go after them then? We sorta know who they are already, right? I don't really wanna go out and scare people who didn't do anything."

"Like who?"

She fidgeted with her hands, used a fork to smear around the remnants of maple syrup on her plate, "Um... I mean, didn't Stephanie Dawson have a thirty-year-old boyfriend that went to jail or something? And... I think I've heard some bad stuff about Ed—"

"You think? What bad stuff? Who'd you hear it from?" The waiter interrupted me by coming back and refilling my coffee cup, but I didn't mind at all, because I changed my mind and decided it would be okay to irritate her just a little. The coffee gave me a good way to pepper in a little smugness.

"Do my ears deceive me?" I said, leaning back, "Does Kelly Hatfield want to choose her targets based on *gossip?*"

I stared at her and took a long sip of coffee to punctuate my point. It annoyed her exactly as much as I thought it would. "Okay, okay, I get it. But you still haven't given me a reason why your plan works any better, and I still don't wanna ruin someone's party."

"I'll give you three reasons." I put my mug back on the table with a clang, "One. My plan is extremely low stakes. If we try to bust up some drug deal or something right out of the gate, things could easily go wrong. Hell, you haven't even used your powers in front of anyone but me before. Now, I don't think that's going to be an issue after the training, but if you do freeze up, it'll be in front of a bunch of drunk idiots instead of jumpy dudes with guns."

She mulled it over for a second, "Okay, I do like that. What's reason number two?"

"Reason number two," I said, "is that we can do some recon while we're out. You're right about one thing, we do have a general idea of who the bad guys in our school are, but let's not kid ourselves: we're not in the know with anyone. Any information we have is shit we overheard in the hallway. Even if those rumors are true and not something made up by an asshole, we don't know how the details got twisted or misunderstood as they went around the school. Everyone will have at least a little liquor in them at this party. Lips will be loose. We can do some scouting and possibly get something interesting straight from the source."

"I guess that makes sense. I don't really know how we're gonna do any scouting if the point is for me to be big and loud though."

"You leave that to me," I said, without an actual plan for how to make that work, "Now finally, the last reason my plan is so great is that it'll be fun."

Kelly wasn't impressed.

"What does that mean?"

"We'll be putting on a show!" I said, "You don't have to be worried about ruining the party because you'll be the life of the party. The only people who'll be scared are the people who have a reason to be scared, the bad guys. For everyone else? A superhero crashing their party and doing something impossible isn't scary, it's cool as hell."

Kelly glared at me, "I think you've got a warped sense of what's cool and what's scary, Chris."

Giving that last reason was a mistake. I should've played it safe and closed with the recon. Best to own up to it and try and smooth things over by reemphasizing the point she responded best to, "Alright, fair. I can't guarantee it'll be fun. For you or me or anybody. But being a hero requires taking some risks. And right now, this is the best way to get the most done with the least amount of risk. Unless you can think of a better idea. Seriously, I'm not saying that to be an asshole. This plan lives or dies on you. If you've got a different idea, I want to hear it."

I relaxed my posture and studied her face. Kelly took a long time to answer, continuing to fiddle with her empty dishes as she purposefully avoided looking me in the eye. Only after a few minutes, when she let out a little sigh, did I think I had her. The way she said her last question seemed conciliatory, like if I could answer that, she'd play along, "I dunno, what if someone recognizes me? I mean, we go to school with these people."

I started bouncing in my seat with excitement. Saying it out loud made it seem real, like everything really was coming together, "That's why you're going to have a badass costume."

CHAPTER 12

KELLY

THE THEATRE TEACHER never realized Rich kicked Chris out of the school play, so over two or three lunch periods we pieced together a superhero outfit from the drama club's prop closet. Since Chris was a lot more enthusiastic about it, I mostly let him go through the closet on his own while I sat at a desk and sketched out some original designs. Well, sorta original. I kinda stole them all from Sailor Moon. Lots of white, skirts, ribbons, long gloves and boots, stuff like that. Some of them turned out pretty cute, but there were problems. None of them would cover my face. A masquerade mask would fit with the aesthetic, and for a more average looking person that might be enough for a disguise, but there aren't many girls over six feet tall out there. Definitely no others in Leroy. A dinky mask like that wouldn't protect my identity. The other problem was that I didn't know how to sew, and I'd have to find a way to make these. Maybe Grandma would be willing to help, but I didn't want her asking too many questions, and we wouldn't have enough time to finish it before the party anyway.

None of that really mattered since Chris had more of a "brooding night terror" vibe in mind. We ended up going with the suit he put together, and I had to stop myself from saying that we shouldn't kid ourselves and just buy a Batman costume from the party store. Everything was black and dark and grim and Chris loved it. Black fingerless gloves, black combat boots, black sweat pants, black trench coat, all topped by a black motorcycle helmet with a black visor to hide my face. He said it'd make good camouflage in the night, and he wanted me to cut my hair so it wouldn't hang out of the helmet, but I drew the line there and ended up stuffing the whole long mess of it down the back of my jacket.

I think the most embarrassing part was that it turned out to be the only get-up in the prop closet that actually fit me. The bright spandex and the frilly theatre clothes and the gorilla suit and all the other fun stuff, that was all too small, but the smelly military boots and the musty biker helmet fit just fine. But I tried not to complain; if I wanted something better, I should've taken the time to make one of my designs work. And Chris seemed convinced it was cool, so it could've been worse, I guess. At least somebody believed in it.

So, with the costume all squared away, all we had to do was wait for the day of Noah's party, suit up, and head out once Chris's mom was asleep.

The black tint on my visor made it almost impossible to see in the dead of night, so I hadn't paid much attention to where we were going until we passed by a mansion with a ginormous window lit up. Similarly huge houses popped up along both sides of the road. Each one had acres of land all to itself.

"Wait, Noah lives on Garden Street?" I said.

"According to the address I swiped from Thomas, yes."

"Wow. I didn't think anyone could afford to actually live over here."

"I've heard both his parents are bigshots at Southside Insurance. If that's true, they probably travel a lot, giving Noah plenty of chances to host parties." He glanced nervously at the clock, "I just hope they aren't too drunk to forget you tomorrow morning."

That sounded like the best-case scenario to me. I still wasn't convinced crashing Noah's party was a very superheroic thing to do. For all his talk of rumors and symbols and crime prevention or whatever, deep down I think Chris just wanted to crash a party. I decided to go along with it anyway. Sure, it may not be heroic, but it was harmless. Nobody would get hurt, nobody would know it was me, and... well... maybe it would be fun after all. I'd never been to a party before. At least, not this kinda party.

With his phone in his hand, Chris slowed down and pulled off to the side of the road. "The car will be fine here. If the GPS didn't fuck up, then Noah's is only half a mile ahead. Let's walk the rest of the way so we don't attract any attention. That'll give us time to review the game plan."

We got out of the car and started walking. It's a good thing I always had to slow my pace to stay next to Chris, because with no street lights and almost all the houses completely dark, the visor blinded me. Chris's vague shadow and the loud smack of his footsteps helped guide me a little, but I almost tripped over my own feet every time I took a step. His shoes scratched against the gravel beneath us as he swiveled around to get a better look at me. "You've got some hair hanging out," he said.

"Crap, really? Hold on…"

Taking the helmet off made a world of difference. I saw the annoyance on his face quite clearly as I unbuttoned the top part of my coat and whipped my head around to shake all the hair out. It wasn't really necessary to do that, but I wanted to feel the wind on my face for a second before diving back into the stuffy helmet.

"This is exactly why I said you should get it cut. The minute you start moving it's going to poke out again."

"I'll be out of there before anyone has time to see."

"It's still a problem. Long hair is one of the biggest liabilities in a combat situation."

"Well, I'm not gonna get into any combat situations, and I'm not gonna cut my hair. I like it long." Having finished getting it back under the coat, I snapped the top button back on, but kept the helmet under my arm while we walked.

"Whatever. We've got more important things to go over anyway," he said, "Got your earbuds?"

"Yup!" I slipped the cheap wired headphone into my ear. To stay in contact during the mission, we had to call each other on our phones, so I had mine strapped to my arm with one of those cases joggers used. The microphones in our earbuds had crummy sound quality. And the bad phone service all over Leroy meant it'd probably be hard to hear each other. And if the headphone fell out of my ear there was no way I'd be able to put it back in without taking my helmet off. But we didn't have any money for good headsets and Chris insisted on being, um, "tactical support," so we made do with what we had.

"Good," he said, "Now like you said, this will be a real simple, in and out operation. We go in and scope the place out until we find something you can crush or throw or whatever. Then, wait for an opportune moment. Jump in, give the speech, dazzle them with a spectacular display of your powers and disappear into the night. Any questions?"

I shook my head.

"Then all that's left is for you to recite the speech one more time."

"I don't think that's really necessary," I said.

"Come on, you don't want to fuck up the speech. It's your thesis, your mission statement."

I sighed. The speech Chris told me to memorize was so… well, so Chris. Kinda embarrassed at the thought of repeating it in front of a bunch of people, I started mumbling through it, like going faster would make it less embarrassing, "Listen well, for I'm only going to say this once. For too long, I've endured the cruelty of man, witnessed the dregs of society trample over all that is good, and I've had enough. I am no longer content to watch. I am here to protect the innocent and punish the guilty, I am…" I stopped moving as I realized we had a huge problem, "Uh oh."

"See, good thing we went over it again. The next part—"

"No Chris, I remember the next part, but we never decided on a superhero name!"

"Are you kidding me? I sent you three pages of ideas last night! You didn't even look at them?"

I vaguely remembered getting a text from Chris that morning with some sort of link attached, but the thing is, Chris sends me a lot of stuff in the middle of the night, usually long political essays and professional wrestling videos. I almost never look at any of it since he always tells me about whatever he sent during the ride to school anyway.

"…Sorry."

Running his hands through his hair, Chris trudged forward again, "Great. Looks like we have five minutes to come up with something good. Otherwise, you'll have to cut all that 'remember my name' business out of the speech."

Silently thankful the speech just got shorter, I jumped forward with the first idea I had, "Hey, maybe it isn't so bad that we don't have a name. The whole point of tonight is to get rumors going, right? If they're spreading rumors about me, they're bound to call me *something*. Maybe the town can decide for us."

Chris sighed, "I did consider that," he pondered it for a few seconds before shaking his head, "No. We're leaving your name to chance that way, and names are important. Especially when you're trying to craft a particular image." He started scrolling through his phone, "I have the list here, so let's pull something from it quick. It needs to be mysterious, something that doesn't necessarily describe your powers. Something like… like…" he tapped his index finger on the screen as he found one, "Ghost."

I didn't even laugh. At first.

"Ghost."

"Yeah. Something monosyllabic like that. Maybe we should put a 'the' in front of it. I like that. I can imagine people whispering about being visited by 'The Ghost' in some dark alley under their breath—"

As Chris kept explaining his idea, I tried so, so hard to not laugh. I really did. But his sincerity at how cool he thought it was put me over the edge. I let out a really gross snort trying to hide my giggling, and then it all just broke. Screaming with laughter, they probably heard me all the way over at Noah's house, and any attempt to quiet down totally failed. I had to stop and take a second, "I'm sorry, it's just…" another giggle attack hit me, "Really? *Ghost?*"

Chris tried to hide his embarrassment under a sour face, "If you've got any better ideas, I'm all ears!"

"Is Shadow already taken? How about Reaper? Ooo! Maybe a cool, mysterious animal, like Raven!"

"Alright, dumb suggestion. Got it. Can we move on?"

"Maybe we should put 'Dark' in my name some-where, make it extra mysterious," For dramatic effect, I paused, "*Dark* Ghost. *Dark* Shadow. *Dark*…" I snorted, "*Dark* Raven!"

"I hate you so much."

We went on like that for basically the rest of the way there, and in the end, I think we quietly agreed it'd be best to let the town decide my name after all.

CHAPTER 13

CHRIS

WHILE KELLY BUSTED my balls over the whole Ghost thing, I tried to focus on locating the Burke residence. With all the drunken teens swarming about, I didn't think it'd be too hard, but it did give me an excuse to tune her out. She only ragged on me so much because she didn't have any better ideas.

My shoes weren't particularly well-suited for a long walk on rocks and gravel. As sharp bits and pieces dug into my soles, I began to wish I parked a bit closer, or at least wore thicker boots like Kelly had on. I had the general description of Noah's place, a big house overlooking a hill with a winding driveway, but that described every house on Garden Street. Soon enough we found ourselves standing beneath an ornate arch with the Burke name engraved on it. My vision slithered up the path, first landing on a surprisingly modest one-story building with cars all around it. But the path kept going. The driveway started being lined by hedges until it looped in front of a sleek, three-story house atop a hill in the distance. Light emanated from a window that took up the entire south wall. The paint inside was bright white, with a spiral staircase rising to a balcony overlooking a foyer where nobody was sitting, and though I couldn't see how the room was laid out in much detail, from a distance the TV inside looked bigger than the screens at the movie theater.

"Stop, this is it."

Kelly had to gather herself. "…Are you sure?"

I'll admit, it caught me off guard as well. That palace must have been magnificent in the full view of daylight. Made you wonder what a rich guy like Noah was doing at Leroy High when he could be living the life at some posh boarding school in upstate New York. "Only one way to find out. Put your helmet on and stay low."

The arch was entirely for show; no gate kept us out, so we crouched down and made our way up the hill. I assumed some security system was going ballistic, but since Noah had a party to host, I also assumed nobody would pay attention to it. Staying away from the driveway as we made the uphill climb, I couldn't help but be awed by the first building, which I slowly realized was the garage. My entire house could have fit inside. I tried to find vehicles I recognized from the mob of cars spilling out, but we strayed towards the house to avoid detection on the off chance someone pulled in or out of the driveway.

My legs started to ache. The hill was steeper than I thought and this was an obscene amount of property. I couldn't possibly imagine why anyone needed this much land. They probably had to hire full time landscapers just to mow it. Eventually we made it to the top, and after taking a second to catch my breath, I scanned what appeared to be his kitchen through the window. Sleek, shiny, and well-lit, nobody was inside.

"Do you hear that?" Kelly whispered. And though it took me a second, I did. A thumping, though strangely faint, bass drifted through the air, masking what sounded like shouting. Without another word, we hugged the walls to check the back.

Right as we thought Noah's house couldn't get any more extravagant, we stopped as the backyard of the estate opened before us. An almost cliff-like slope rolled into a massive swimming pool below, its brilliant cerulean glow flashing in and out as a mass of bodies splashed and screamed through the water. A bar, presumably loaded with booze and mounted with the speakers thumping club music, lined the far side of the pool, with an explosion of clothing, beach chairs, and people scattered all around the deck and grass.

Kelly was breathless. The house wasn't blocking the soundwaves raging from the party anymore, so I almost didn't hear her whisper, "Wow."

I had nothing to add.

But I only let myself appreciate the sight for a brief moment. We did, after all, have work to do. My attention wandered back to the house. The patio near us was completely empty, in stark contrast to the pool below. The timing couldn't have been luckier for Noah's party. As soon as the calendar flipped from March to April, a massive heat wave cooked the town, so even late at night it was a solid 70 degrees, just warm enough for someone liquored up to want a swim.

Voices rose over the music, barely audible at first but getting clearer by the second. We were standing right in the open, the glow of the patio lights making us easily visible, but I had no idea if the voices were coming from inside or out.

I jumped behind the corner of the house to hide, hissing to Kelly, "Get back!"

I thought I was going to have to drag her with me. Eventually, she obeyed with a lazy backpedal, keeping her visor pointed at the swimming pool, "Is it too late for us to be friends with Noah?"

"You realize that water is fifty percent piss and vomit."

"Blech. Don't be gross."

"Just saying."

Reasonably confident nobody had seen us, I signaled for Kelly to stay put. She happily obeyed to ogle the pool some more while I poked around the corner to try and identify whose voices I was hearing. Sure enough, two juniors I didn't know were laughing their drunken asses off about something stupid as they stumbled to a glass table on the patio where towels and a change of clothes waited for them. I caught more movement up the hill in my peripheral vision and hid again, not sure how covered we were from this angle.

Venturing down to the pool wasn't a spectacular idea. The whole point was for Kelly to have a cool first appearance. Having the element of surprise was essential. If she got spotted sneaking around—or worse, if I got spotted with her—then in the best-case scenario she'd have to improvise, probably badly, and in the worst-case scenario our cover would be blown. Plus, if the point of this night was to get people talking, perhaps limiting our audience was the best move after all. If Kelly revealed herself in front of everyone, the game would be up. There'd be no room for doubt about what happened here. The police might even get involved. But if a small group of say, three or four isolated people saw her? That'd get possibly conflicting stories spreading throughout the student body. It'd make Kelly more of a legend. Not only that, but staying close to the house meant Kelly could drop from the roof, make her speech, then jump into the sky and disappear, more than dramatic enough to make an impression. She wouldn't even have to smash anything. The people at the bottom of the hill wouldn't be paying attention to what was going on up here, and if they did happen to see her jump, they wouldn't be able to tell exactly what was happening from such a distance. It was almost perfect.

Almost. It would be truly perfect if the group who witnessed her speech were all members of different cliques and varying stages of intoxication, and that depended entirely on who followed the junior guys up here. Wanting to have as much information as possible before making my final plan, I risked exposure by ducking around the house to check the patio once more. A small brunette with shoulder length hair and a black bikini had her back to me as she shared a hearty laugh with the two guys at the table. She turned after chatting for a bit, making her way for the sliding glass door with jelly legs on the brink of collapse.

With her face finally visible, I could identify the girl entering the house as Cassidy Connors, and I don't think we could've asked for a more credible witness. In addition to being the Quiz Bowl MVP, Cassidy was the student council president and locked in an eternal struggle with Drama

Club Nazi for the title of Valedictorian. Not only that, but she also happened to be dating my brother, the captain of the football team. While that proved Cassidy had questionable taste in guys, it also proved she was as high on the social pecking order as she was intelligent. Kelly could drop in front of her as soon as she came back out, and she'd be credible enough for some to believe her, and drunk enough to leave room for doubt.

With the plan set in my mind, I turned to Kelly who, of course, hadn't moved. I clicked my fingers near her ear and she turned to me with a silent start, but before I had the chance to tell her the plan, she said, "I'm getting hot. Do you think anyone would notice me if I took off the costume and went swimming?"

"Will you forget about the pool? Now listen up, we're changing the plan," I waved so she'd poke her head around the corner with me. "We're going to target one person instead of the whole party. Cassidy Connors just went inside. I want you to stand on the roof and wait for her to come back out. When she does, drop in front of her, give the speech, and jump into the sky. Make sure she sees you jump! Don't make her doubt that she witnessed something impossible. If those guys at the table stick around and see it too, great. We have more witnesses. But don't worry about it if they go away. Focus on Cassidy." We ducked back behind the corner and I took a deep breath, "We don't have much time. If you have any questions, now's your chance."

"Are we not gonna do any scouting? I thought we came here for leads."

"Too risky. We don't want to be seen together, and we won't be able to find a good place to eavesdrop without exposing ourselves, not while all the action is down at the pool at least. We'll find another way to get intel. Now, ready?"

She shrugged, "I guess."

With the mask on, I couldn't get much of a read on how she was feeling, so I smiled and gave her some final words of encouragement, "You're going to be awesome. I know it."

Her posture eased up. Even though she didn't say anything, and I couldn't see her face, I knew she appreciated that. She took a step back, keeping her head locked on the roof, and sighed. "Here goes."

Though our week of training gave Kelly much better control over her jump height, she hadn't quite mastered landings yet, and hit the roof with a hard skid. Thankfully, the guys below didn't hear it or pay it any mind. From my position hugging the wall, Kelly was invisible. I could only hope that she was standing on the edge, dramatically waiting for Cassidy. Or, more likely, she was ogling the pool some more. Either way, with everything out of my hands, I waited for the show to begin.

And waited.

And waited.

Kelly still hadn't gone after several minutes. I found myself sweating. Was there really nothing to do but wait? Kelly seemed pretty calm, but her timing was going to be critical; if she froze, we might lose our chance.

Thinking quickly, I pulled out my phone. As the voice in her ear, I could give her as much pep talk as she needed, signal the opportune moment to drop, and feed her lines if she forgot the speech. I jammed my own headphones in and mashed the call button over her name.

CHAPTER 14

KELLY

WE TRAINED FOR this. Nobody will get hurt.

I didn't wanna freeze up and look stupid on my first night. Cassidy could come out any second. I had to be ready to go.

The two boys sitting on the patio got up and headed down the hill, and some of the tension in me went away with a breath I didn't realize I was holding. It'd be less stressful if only one person was watching.

But while I tried to work up the strength, Dad's voice kept creeping into my head: *They'll think you're some kinda monster, Kelly.*

I kept thinking about Cassidy. I had to do a group project with her once. She was really nice to me, way nicer than someone pretty and popular had to be. I tried to imagine how she'd react when I dropped in front of her, when I shot into the sky and the whole world changed before her eyes. When she was scared, was she the kind of person who screamed or froze up? Would she cry? Would anyone else even believe her, or would they start thinking she was some kinda crazy person?

This was wrong. When I told Chris I wasn't going to hurt anyone, I didn't think about what that really meant. I'd been happy to go along with his plan without thinking about any consequences beyond what would happen if I got caught. But there are more ways to hurt people than just punching them. They shouldn't have to deal with the weight of what I was about to do when they were just trying to have a little fun.

Maybe Chris was right. Maybe if people were afraid of me there wouldn't be any crime. Maybe in the long run I'd stop some bad things from happening. But I didn't want people to be afraid of me.

A sudden boom shook my arm. A Japanese girl squealed out the lyrics of my favorite anime song, backed by a thundering chorus of electric guitars and drums. I was so stunned it took me a few seconds to realize my phone was going off. I panicked and fumbled for a way to stop it, but the song kept blaring even when I clicked my headphones to pick up. I clicked the button again and again, but it wouldn't stop no matter how much I mashed it. Scrambling, I rolled my sleeve up to check the phone itself, and my headphone jack slid out, dangling in front of me like a pendulum. It popped out of its socket when I jumped. To make things even worse, the music got much louder without my thick sleeve to hide it. Chris must've finally realized what was going on and hung up.

My face must've gone totally pale. The smart thing to do would be to run, to get out of there without leaning over the side to check if anyone saw me. The noise from the party might've been loud enough to cover it anyway.

I leaned over the side to check if anyone saw me. Cassidy was staring directly at me.

She shrieked and pointed at me, but there was nobody around to see.

Come on, move! Go go go!

My body wouldn't go. I felt like I owed her an explanation, but my lips clamped down to avoid blurting out something stupid. So I just kinda stood around like a statue.

Cassidy turned like she was about to run off to get someone. "Is anyone else seeing this!?"

That got me moving. "Wait! I'm sorry, I'm sorry! I'm not here to cause trouble!"

Cassidy stopped, stumbling a little bit as she squinted at me. She cupped a hand to her ear and shouted, "Whaaaaaaat? I can't hear you!"

Kinda thankful she didn't hear how pathetic that was, I tried to sound more secure as I spoke up.

"I'm not here to cause trouble…" I paused, wondering how I could sound more superhero-y, "…ma'am."

She didn't scream again, but she was still obviously scared, "Who are you? What do you want?"

I didn't really know how to answer that. Chris's speech was out, I'd already ruined that by trying to calm her down. The harder I tried to come up with an explanation that didn't sound stupid, the more I wished I ran off when I had the chance.

Cassidy caught me off guard with another question, the kind that made me wonder how much alcohol she'd had already. She bit her lip and kinda slurred when she said it, but I'm pretty sure she asked, "Are you... are you an alien?"

"Um... no, I'm not—" realizing I should probably disguise my voice, I coughed and tried to lower it more like a man's. I don't think I did a very a good job. "I'm not an alien."

Her confusion seemed genuine, "Then what do you need the space helmet for?"

"Oh, it's not a space helmet, it's—" The more I opened my mouth, the deeper the hole I dug myself in. Should I just go ahead and say I'm a superhero? Eventually I'd have to reveal myself, and I didn't wanna creep around in the shadows anyway, so I guessed it was a good a time as any, "It's for protection. From my enemies. Because I'm a... a knight. Of justice. So have you, um, have you seen any crimes lately?"

I don't think I've ever cringed harder in my life. Cassidy kept staring at me, totally stunned.

Then she started laughing. You'd think that'd make the embarrassment worse, but it wasn't a mean laugh. It was like a little girl's giggle. She swung her head around and shouted down the hill, "*Hey! Hey, did somebody invite a superhero to the party?*" It didn't bother her when nobody answered back. She kept giggling and turned to me, any fear on her face totally gone. "That's—" she hiccupped, "That's what you are, right? A superhero?"

Relief swelled in my chest as I shouted back, "Yes! That's right!"

"Well, let me tell you, Mister Superhero Man. There aren't no crimes here, but there might, miiiiiiiiiiight be a way you can help me."

"Oh! Really?" After a second I realized I'd let my voice go back up, so I did another cough and repeated myself in a bad attempt to sound smooth, "Really. Interesting."

Without thinking, I hopped off the roof and landed on the concrete patio with a loud smack. I only realized my mistake when her jaw dropped. That roof was three stories up. The shock in Cassidy's face slowly turned to delight, "Wowwww! How'd you do *that?*"

"Practice," I quickly said. I put my shaking hands on my hips to look more superheroic, "What seems to be the trouble?"

Before I could do anything, Cassidy lurched forward and wrapped her arms around mine, dragging me down the hill towards the party, "C'mere! He's this way!"

AAAAAAAHHHHHHHHH OH MY GOD WHAT DO YOU THINK YOU'RE DOING GET OFF GET OFF RIGHT NOW THIS ISN'T FUNNY STOP RULE TWO RULE TWO NO NO NO NO NO BAD BAD BAD BAD—

But no matter how much I wanted to, I stopped myself from jerking away. Any sudden movement could rip her in half.

And without anyone helping her keep steady, she was gonna tumble down the hill and break her neck.

And... um... and once I calmed down a bit, it actually felt kinda nice.

Cassidy was really pretty.

I might've had a small crush on her.

Cassidy took one step on the hill and immediately slipped and fell to the ground. If she were holding on to anyone but me, she probably would've dragged them all the way down to the pool with her. Thankfully, she hadn't let go of me. Cassidy laughed and pulled herself up, leaning against me tight in a way that made both my eyes and face glow red.

We took the hill slowly, and Cassidy told me the problem on our way down, "Okay. So. So, you know Noah, right? Wait, this is his party! Of course you know Noah! Okay. So Tommy and Noah have been planning for this party for a long time now, right? His parents aren't home, we're almost done with school, it's gonna be great! Only Tommy and I—Tommy and I and a few other people get here to help him set up, and he's just... he's just pouting! He won't tell us what's wrong or help or do anything! So, we're thinking—we're thinking that maybe, y'know, maybe he's just having one of those days. And once he's done a little bit a drinkin', he'll be fun again! So the party starts, but Noah isn't doing nothing! He isn't drinking or swimming or talking or anything. He just went into the woods and made a fire and let the party at his own house go on without him! So—" She poked me right in the boob and paused. I almost had a heart attack; not just from the unexpected invasion of my personal space. The less about my identity anybody could piece together, the better. I studied her face for any sign that she knew I wasn't a man.

She continued, "So! Masked Man! My job for you, is to cheer Noah up. Can ya do that?"

That seemed like kind of a tall order. All I really knew about Noah was that he was captain of the basketball team and good friends with Thomas. If his friends couldn't make him happy, I didn't see what a weirdo in a bike helmet was gonna do.

But on the other hand, I liked the sound of actually

helping someone much more than what Chris had in mind. And by being in the middle of the party, I could scout for next time like we originally planned.

All I could tell her was the truth, "I mean, I'll do my best. I'm not sure if this is the kinda thing you need a superhero for, though."

"You'll be great!" she said, "Don't even need to find out what's wrong. You just gotta make him not a buzzkill, okay?"

I nodded my head, forgetting that she couldn't see my own smile under the helmet.

Cassidy kept talking as we went farther down the hill, but I sorta wasn't listening. I tried keeping an ear open for any leads as we started to get closer to people, but the music got louder with every step closer to the pool, thumping heavy enough to shake your whole body. It made scouting pretty hard, but I don't know if I would've been able to focus anyway. Everyone's face blended together in the dark, blobs of shadow flailing to the beat with drops of pool water and sweat dripping off them. Large groups raised plastic cups and bottles in the air with shouts and cheers that nobody could hear. Even with my helmet on, the cloud of alcohol breath burned my nostrils. We almost tripped over two people making out in the grass (I *hope* they were just making out). A boy scrambled out of the pool and rushed us, barely missing us when he sprayed puke everywhere mid-run. I froze, keeping Cassidy locked down. He laughed and stumbled to a table with dozens of bottles lined up.

I wanted to go home. But Cassidy was holding on too tight. No way was I gonna make any sudden movements like that, so she dragged me deeper into the party. Things at least got a little easier the closer we got to the pool. The underwater lights revealed faces, and though there were lots of people being rowdy in the water, there were calmer people sitting in chairs around the deck or with their feet dipped in the edge of the pool. Since people could actually see, they started to notice that the student council president was dragging a creepy masked stranger by the arm. Their reactions were pretty evenly split. Most of the guys were laughing and cheering and didn't really question my appearance. The girls were more skeptical. A lot of them shot me dirty looks and seemed kinda uncomfortable. I can't really blame them. One of them even got up and started walking over to us, and I panicked while I tried to think of what to say.

It didn't end up being a problem. With a jerk, Cassidy changed direction and pulled me into the trees that must've marked the edge of the property. The woods did a good job blocking the noise, and the thumping bass died down immediately. The further we went into the grove, the easier it was to hear myself think, and my muscles relaxed.

A clear path between the trees lead to a warm orange glow. A familiar voice shouted in the distance, but it took me a few seconds to figure out what he was saying.

"—I'm not saying it doesn't. But you gotta man the fuck up. You're Noah fucking Burke, the Wolf of Motherfucking Garden Street! Get fucked up. Fuck a girl, hell, fuck two! You could plow your way through every hot girl in town by sunrise if you put your fucking mind to it. Now's your chance to get something better than that stuck up bitch."

Putting the pieces together, I stopped Cassidy and said, "Wait. Did Noah and Annie break up?" I smacked my visor as I went to clasp my hand over my mouth. Stupid. But I was too shocked to not say anything. They'd been dating since freshman year. Honestly, I was kinda expecting Noah to propose to her at graduation. Cassidy didn't seem to catch that hint I dropped about being from Leroy High, or maybe she'd already assumed I was in her class, so I let myself relax.

She looked at me in shock, "What? Is that it? Mask Man, how do y'know that?"

"Just now, whoever Noah's with was telling him to try and find a new girl. He's been feeling down ever since you got here, right? Did you see Annie anywhere?"

She kept shaking her head, "Oh no. No, no, no…" After mumbling to herself for a second, Cassidy suddenly lurched forward again, pulling me down the path. "You gotta do it! You gotta make him feel better? Okay? Okay!?"

You're going too fast. Please let go. This is a terrible idea. I mean, what am I supposed to do? I can't give him advice. I've never even talked to him! We're getting closer. Come on, think of something! God, I'm so—

Soon enough we entered a clearing with a fire and logs arranged like seats around it. Only two people were sitting on them: Noah and Thomas.

We slid to a stop. Cassidy tugged me towards them. "Noah!" she said, "Noah it's alright now, don't worry! Everything's gonna be okay, okay? See? See! I brought you a superhero!"

I stood frozen in fear as Thomas snapped his head toward me. Being near Thomas always made me uncomfortable, but seeing him then gave me the shivers. Maybe it was because he didn't have a shirt on and his muscles made me forget there was no way he could physically hurt me. Maybe it was the beer in his hand and the mean look in his eye. Maybe it was just because I spent a lot of time in his house and felt like he'd see right through me. No matter what it was, I couldn't look at him, even through the mask.

So I faced Noah, but that was maybe even worse. Whenever I passed Noah in the hallway, he always had this warm smile, and his lean, toned body stood tall with just a hint of a slouch, giving him an aura of relaxed confidence. The sandy, wavy hair on his head and the light hazel in his eyes had a sincerity to them, a softness that didn't exist in guys like Thomas and the other football players. There was a reason every girl in the school had a crush on him. Probably more than a few guys, too.

But that wasn't the Noah sitting in front of me. This Noah sunk into his seat, drooped so far forward his back curved into a C-shape. His arms barely kept his chin up, and at any minute it looked like he'd give up and flump to the ground in a heap. He flicked his eyes up to see what was going on, but immediately went back to staring at the dirt. I guess he'd seen weirder things than my costume at these parties. Or maybe he was just too sad to care.

I wanted to help. I really did. But what was I supposed to do? It's not like I had any good advice to give him. Forget having a boyfriend or girlfriend, I'd never even kissed anyone!

While I was searching for something to say that wasn't totally stupid, Thomas's harsh voice broke the silence, "Cass, what the fuck is this?"

Cassidy finally let go of my arm and everything felt lighter. She stumbled over to Thomas, her jelly legs finally giving out as she crawled onto the log next to him, "I already told you Tommy, Mask Man is a superhero! He promised that he could make Noah feel better!"

"The love of his life dumped him. How is a goddamn Power Ranger going to make anything better?"

"He can do… cool tricks! He flipped off the roof and it was sssuuuuper cool!" She flung her arms into what I guess was a superhero pose. It looked more like she was throwing someone a surprise party.

"That's the dumbest thing I've ever heard," he said, "That didn't even happen."

"Shut up! Yes it did!" Cassidy tried to shove Thomas's chest. He didn't budge one bit and she collapsed on him. Another shiver ran down me as Thomas shot me the evil eye, holding her by the shoulders so they could speak face to face.

"Christ, calm down. Why're you yelling?"

"I'm not yelling! You're yelling! And you're being a dick! I just wanted to help, okay? And it's not like—it's not like you're helping either! He doesn't want another girl, idiot. He wants Annie!"

"It's sure as shit better than your idea. Where'd you find this clown anyway? And what the fuck was with you crawling all over him, huh? You trying to hide something from me?"

"No! Mask Man is nice! He just made sure I didn't fall or get puked on or nothin'! Mask Man is nice!"

"You actually expect me to believe that's all?"

"Yeah, 'cause that *is* all! Tommy, what's your problem? You've been acting this way all night! Stop bein' so *jealous!*"

"Maybe if you didn't keep giving me reasons to be jealous—"

While the two of them shouted over each other, I kept my eye on Noah, who shook his head and stood up, quietly slinking away. Finally, an excuse to get out of there. Based on where that fight was going, Thomas might come after me any minute. When I was sure he wasn't looking at me, I slipped away too.

Noah trudged forward in silence, trapped between the shouting behind me and the partying ahead. I stood in the dark and watched him. This was my chance to get out. I hadn't done anything suspicious aside from jumping off his roof in front of Cassidy, and I could make lots of excuses for that. All I had to do was keep a good distance behind him and slip back to the house. But the longer I stayed there, the more I realized that I couldn't just let him sulk away. Not when his friends were doing such a bad job of making him feel better. That wouldn't be very heroic.

…And okay, I may have had a *big* crush on him. I mean, don't get me wrong, I knew there wasn't ever a chance he'd ask me on a date. Noah Burke wasn't going to trade a girl like Annie for a girl like me in a million years. But I liked the idea of him thinking fondly about the mysterious stranger who helped him through a tough time, always wondering who they were without ever realizing it was someone he never gave any thought to all along.

"Wait!"

I'd caught him just before he disappeared, a shadow you could barely see against other shadows. He stopped for a second, shouting back, "I'm not in the mood for jokes. Whoever you are, leave me alone."

Before he had the chance to walk away again, I sprinted up to him, maybe a little too fast, so I could see his face, but I almost immediately wished that I hadn't. There was nothing in his eyes. No anger, no sadness, just exhaustion.

"This isn't supposed to be a joke, I promise! I'm sorry, I just thought... thought that maybe... I dunno, you'd..." Realizing there was no way I could justify my superhero suit without sounding crazy, I took a deep breath and tried to change the subject, "Where are you going?"

Noah dug his hands deeper into his pockets, like he was wondering if it'd even be worth answering me, before saying, "Bed. Enjoy the party."

He turned his back to me again, and for a second I wondered if this time I should let him go. Maybe it'd be best for him to spend some time alone. He obviously didn't wanna host this party. But the more I thought about it, the less I liked that. I don't know about anyone else, but whenever I'm sad and try to go to bed, I can never get to sleep. I always stay up and let whatever's upsetting me run through my head again and again. That doesn't help anything. But was there even something that could help?

His bright blue swimming pool rippled in the space between the trees. I called out to Noah and he stopped again, but didn't turn around as I ran to him. "It's easier to forget the bad stuff when you aren't just sitting around." I tried to sound as warm and friendly as possible, pausing and waiting for him to ask what I meant by that. He didn't say anything. I started stammering before I'd thought of a smarter way to show him what I meant. "So, I dunno, it might help if you go for a swim or something. You know, if you wanna."

Sweat dripped down my forehead. I don't know why I thought that would work.

That feeling got even worse when Noah started moving again.

I messed it up. God, I'm so stupid.

But then he stopped one more time, inviting me to follow with a gentle nudge of his head. It took a second for what that meant to sink in, but once it did, I just barely stopped myself from cheering and rushed to catch up with him.

We walked quietly, for a little bit. It was kinda weird being side by side with someone closer to my own height. I'd gotten used to staring down at the top of Chris's head. The farther we went down the path, the more Thomas and Cassidy's arguing faded and the more the craziness of the party surrounded us. I didn't have much to say, but I figured it'd be less weird if I tried to talk with him before it got too loud.

"Do you mind if I ask what happened?" I said.

Noah's eyes shifted over to me, then tilted his head away like he was deciding whether to bother saying anything. With a little shrug, he gave in, "Nothing dramatic. She pulled me aside after school today and ended it. That's all."

"Oh." I didn't have anything more useful to add, so I mumbled, "Did she say why?"

"We're going off to college pretty soon. Didn't want me holding her back." Noah shrugged again, "Go ahead and tell everyone, I don't care."

I didn't really get what he meant by that last part. I

stood quietly for a moment like maybe he'd explain and I wouldn't have to look stupid by asking.

After a second he sighed. "That's why you're wearing that mask, right? To get gossip? Hate to disappoint you, but my side of the story isn't interesting. I don't really care who knows."

My face started burning up. Even though it wasn't true, something about that accusation made my insides feel gross, "Oh no, no no no, that's not it at all!"

"Why keep it on then?"

I bit my lip. You don't really realize how bad you are at improvising until you're forced to do it, "It's a dare. I don't wanna lose a bet."

"Right."

I almost made more excuses. Almost. But there was nothing I could say that didn't sound shady or dishonest. Someone who actually cared would've taken off the helmet and talked to him for real. But I couldn't do that. Kelly Hatfield would be even worse at this than Mask Man already is.

I wasn't sure what he wanted to hear. So, I said the only honest thing on my mind.

"That was really crappy of her."

Was that stepping out of line? It felt like it was. But I didn't stop myself. If I was going to hide my face, I had nothing to lose by telling him the truth. "I don't know much about breakups, but today seems like the worst possible day to do it. I mean, couldn't she have at least waited? She had to know this was happening tonight, right? I guess it would've been awkward for her to be here if she already made up her mind, but she could've said she was sick and stayed home or something. Let you have one night of fun before breaking your heart, you know? She didn't have to ruin your party. But she did, and that really sucks. I'm sorry. I wish there was something I could do to help."

Noah stopped and stared at me. We were at the edge of the forest now, and the music was so loud again that I don't think I'd even hear him if he spoke. The light from the party ahead made his eyes a little clearer; they seemed like they were shimmering before he jerked his head away and quickened his pace to get ahead of me. Maybe that was progress? I feel like sad is a better place to be than empty.

Anyway, we left the forest and approached the edge of the water. Even with all the drunk people splashing around, the bright lights underneath made it seem so pure and clean. Rows of people crowded around both sides of a volleyball net stretched across the middle of the pool. They tried to bop a white ball back and forth, but most of them were so uncoordinated that it kept plopping into the water every couple seconds.

I did my best not to stare at Noah's abs as he took off his shirt, but I couldn't help myself from sneaking a quick peek. I remembered my phone strapped to my arm right as I was about to jump in. I clumsily rolled up my sleeve to take it out of the case and dropped it in the grass.

Forgetting about Noah and everything I was supposed to do for a wonderful moment, I hopped in and sunk to the bottom. Water rushed into my helmet and the heavy layers of my coat hugged my skin as a gentle coolness brushed my entire body. The water dulled the thumping and the beats rippled around me gently. I wanted to stay down there forever.

But I needed air. I sprang up from underneath and looked around for Noah. He stayed at the pool's edge, shivering as he dipped his big toe in. "I'm not drunk enough for this water."

That wasn't good. I didn't want Noah using that as an excuse to go inside. I had to think of something, fast.

The answer came almost immediately when I noticed a boy splash water at a group of girls with their feet at the edge of the pool. Noah couldn't see the smile under my helmet as I drew my arm back. A little splash never hurt anyone.

A tidal wave shot from my palm with the force of a firehose. The water blasted Noah in the face and swept him off his feet, pushed him backward. I froze as he slammed on the concrete. Everyone in the pool area stopped what they were doing and stared. I overdid it. I knew I'd overdo it somehow.

Swimming towards him, I called out, "Oh my gosh, I'm so sorry! Are you okay?"

Before I made it to the edge, Noah sprang up and charged forward, leaping over my head and landing in the pool with a cannonball that would've blinded me with water if I wasn't wearing a helmet. Noah popped back to the surface with wild bug eyes, yelping from the cold while spinning to try and find me.

"What the f-fuck dude," he said, teeth chattering behind a smile he was trying to hide, "D-dick m-move!" He wound his arm back and splashed me. The helmet's visor kept the water out of my eyes, so it was easy to instantly splash him back. I had to stop myself from giggling as he wound up to make another attack. I was quicker on the draw and blasted him in the face again. I couldn't stop laughing as he made a grumpy face and dove under the water to avoid me and get a better shot. Watching him and following his shadow as he glided below me, I chased him and got ready to counterattack when he came up for air. But Noah was ready for me, and we splashed each other at the exact same time.

A volleyball dropped from the sky and landed right in the middle of our splash war. We stopped and turned our heads towards the sudden shouting and wooping near the volleyball net. One boy's voice managed to rise over the music as he said, "Finally, Moneybags himself is out of hiding! Get over here bitch, serve up!"

Noah shook his head, but he was definitely smiling now, so I couldn't help but feel good... until he glanced back my way and held up the volleyball with a raised eyebrow.

I hesitated. Playing sports was definitely pushing it. I didn't think I could control my powers good enough to hit that ball without popping it.

Besides, not everybody was looking at Noah. Most of them weren't, leaning into each other and whispering. A few people pointed and laughed. For the first time since I got here, everyone's eyes really were on me.

Without saying a word, I paddled back to the pool's edge and pulled myself up, not looking back at the pool as I scrambled up the hill, giving every drunk person tumbling down the hill a lot of space. Yup, it was time to go. Past time.

When I reached the patio again, I took one last look over my shoulder to make sure nobody was still looking at me, ready to follow me to Chris's hiding spot. I almost yelped when I saw Noah striding up the hill, dripping wet and clearly amused through his shivering.

"You know," he said, "someone's always pulling some stupid stunt at these parties and getting the police called on us. Were you here last time? Gabe Heinrichs grabbed my sister's bedsheets and tried to climb on top of the roof. He thought he could parachute into a snowbank."

I maybe overdid my laugh a little bit. "Oh wow. That's crazy. You'd have to be pretty drunk to do something like that… right?"

Noah nodded and smiled, "People say he drank an entire bottle of Jaeger right before he tried it. I feel like that would've killed him, but he did spend the rest of the night puking in the shower, so maybe he can go harder than I give him credit for. Anyway, that's not the point. Point is, I see what you're doing, trying to be funny with the costume. And you know what? It's working. I *am* having fun. So, I just wanted to say thanks. Thanks for getting me off my ass."

My heart fluttered, "It really was the least I could do. Sorry if I annoyed you at all."

He answered with an easy laugh, "Nah, you aren't annoying, but I am wondering who it is under there. Think it's time to take off the helmet?"

I considered it. Aside from my roof jump, which he didn't even see, I hadn't given him any reason to think I was anything other than a normal person… well, aside from the costume itself, I guess, depending on how you define normal. Would it be so bad if he knew who I was?

Then I imagined the disappointment on his face when he found out I was dumpy old Kelly Hatfield. Maybe I shouldn't push my luck when things were going good, "But that'd ruin the mystery. Isn't it more fun if I kept my identity secret?"

He clearly wasn't expecting me to say that. His face twisted and scrunched, and his eyes narrowed like he was trying to rule out everyone I could possibly be. It made me feel strangely guilty, like I was tricking him into being nice by being Mask Man. I thought about taking off my helmet again.

Before I had the chance, Noah broke into laughter, "You're a weird dude, Mask Man, but you're pretty cool too. Whoever you are, you can party with us any time." Noah broke away and headed for the sliding glass door. He turned to me as he gripped the handle, "I'm gonna grab towels. Some beer too. I've got catching up to do. You want one?"

"Oh, oh no. I'm alright. I'll just wait out here."

Noah shrugged, "If you say so," and disappeared into the house.

As the door closed, all my guilty feelings melted away. He thought I was cool. He thought I was cool and he just invited me to a party for real. No, not just *a* party, but *all* his parties. I mean, I couldn't really take him up on it. I don't think I would've gone back into that crowd if you paid me. But still, the idea made me feel like I could float away: Noah thought I was cool enough to party with.

"Maaaaaaask Mannn!"

I turned around just in time to see Cassidy almost fall into me. She wrapped her arms around my waist and gazed into my visor, looking like she was gonna burst into tears any second, "I found you! I founnnnnnd you! You left me all alone and I didn't know if I'd ever find you! That was mean! Mean mean mean *mean!* Don't you leave me ever again, okay?"

"I'm sorry, but I had a good reason! I was hanging out with Noah!"

Her mood totally reversed. Any hint of drunk tears went away as her face shined with enough joy to light up Garden Street. "Wait, really? Is he—" she hiccupped, "That means he's feeling better, right? Right?"

"I dunno about *better.* I think it'll be a little while before he actually feels better. But I think he's gonna try and have some fun, at least for tonight."

Cassidy squeezed me closer to her and nuzzled her head against me, thanking me over and over again. I wasn't really listening to what she was saying though, because it hit me: she was touching me. She was touching me and I wasn't freaking out. I'd come to a party, splashed around the pool with a cute boy who thought I was cool, got offered beer (that I couldn't ever drink obviously, but you know) and got invited to another party. Now a pretty girl was hugging me and I wasn't squirming or feeling anxious or trying to get away.

That warm feeling inside me must be what normal feels like.

CHAPTER 15
CHRIS

WHAT THE ACTUAL fuck did Kelly think she was *doing?*

I'd overheard her rooftop conversation with Cassidy, but the moment Kelly went traipsing into the dark I couldn't do anything but stay behind a bush with my thumb up my ass. She never picked up her phone, never gave any indication of where she was running off to or what the plan was. And when she finally came back, she was soaking wet, awkwardly flirting with the party's host, and getting felt up by the student council president. *What the hell did I miss?*

It's not like I could have followed her. Unlike her, I didn't have the luxury of a mask, and Thomas was still lurking around. The further I ventured into the party, the higher the chance of me running into him, and if that happened, I was dead. While he wouldn't so freely admit to being here, if he gave Mom even the slightest hint that he spotted me out of the house, she was liable to put me in handcuffs to stop me from sneaking out. Kelly's superhero career would meet an early, undignified end if her intel guy couldn't escape his house because he was grounded. I wondered if maybe I should have a sidekick costume for myself. I may not have powers, but that way I could follow her and keep her from going completely off the rails.

Speaking of Thomas, while I applauded Kelly's uncharacteristically bold plan to steal his girl, there'd be hell to pay if she got caught, and I didn't have the faintest goddamn idea how *that* confrontation would go down.

Of course, as soon as that thought crossed my mind, Thomas came stomping up the hill. Instinctively, I ducked behind the house, poking my head out to see him looming over Kelly and Cass. It was crazy how scary he was when he wanted to be. Kelly had half a foot on the guy, but facing down a 'roid raged rhino like him, she withered to a child's size. Cassidy didn't realize anything changed and continued clinging to Kelly.

Thomas didn't shout. He didn't need to. "Alright, you masked moron. Give me one good reason I shouldn't bash your skull in with your own helmet."

Kelly's joints locked up, and she said nothing in response. Just looking at her you could feel the nervous sweat dripping down her. The shift in her body language was subtle, but unmistakable. But that wasn't the worst thing. The worst thing was faint, but visible even from where I was standing. A dull red tinted her black visor.

"Go," I whispered, "Cut your losses. You had your fun, get out of there!"

But it was already over. Kelly was a freezer, not a runner.

Completely helpless from around the corner, I resigned myself to watching this circus play out.

"Let go of my girl, Mask Man. Right now."

Finally understanding what was going on, Cassidy stood upright and turned to her boyfriend. She still didn't let go of Kelly, "Tommy! Why're you picking a fight with Mask Man! He didn't do nothin' wrong!"

"Shut up. I see what's going on here, and I don't want to hear any bullshit. Who is that under there? Mike? Paul? Doesn't matter. You're fucking dead."

Thomas pulled back a clenched fist to prepare for a drunken swing at Kelly. But he wasn't the next person to make a move. It wasn't Kelly either, who had pretty much completely shut down. Cassidy finally let go of Masked Man, and got in Thomas's face.

"Why are you. So. *Paranoid?* We haven't done anything! I don't—I don't even know who he is either! But you know what? You know what Tommy? Fine! If you're so worried about it, maybe he *should* be my new boyfriend!"

Before anyone could stop her or react, Cassidy lurched into Kelly and slid her fingers under the helmet with surprising grace. She popped it off and threw it down the hill. Kelly's hair drooped out like a bundle of limp noodles. Cassidy dived in and planted a wet one right on Kelly's lips.

Kelly's eyes were wider and redder than they'd ever been.

Cassidy finally pulled back to get a good look. After a second, her horrified bug eyes matched Thomas's. She shrieked, literally falling to the ground when she realized who it was she just kissed. Thomas's cruel bellowing echoed through the air.

Somewhere between humiliated and traumatized, Kelly

cupped her hands around the side of her eyes like blinders and frantically searched for the best possible escape route. She stopped for just a moment when her vision crossed a flabbergasted Noah. Right on cue, he'd emerged from the house with towels in one hand and beers in the other.

She mumbled something, I'm pretty sure it was, "You have a very nice house," and sprinted directly for me, leaving the motorcycle helmet behind as proof of her shame.

I ducked around the house before anyone had the chance to spot me. Kelly kicked into high gear when she rounded the corner, shooting down the hill and toward the road at her insane, subsonic top speed. I didn't rush, trying to give her some space.

Sure enough, by the time I got to the Kellywagon I found her leaning against it, mostly calm, but shaken. She startled a bit when I clicked the unlock button and the car's lights blinked, but didn't say anything when I walked into view. It was only when we were both buckled in and driving away from Garden Street that I finally spoke.

"So that was a catastrophe."

"It sure was."

Kelly paused midway through ripping off her sopping wet gloves, worry smeared all over her face, "You don't think—"

"They were drunk. I doubt it."

We left it at that, driving home in the crushing silence of absolute defeat.

CHAPTER 16

KELLY

CHRIS AND I stood in the rain at the bottom of concrete steps leading to a house that was the opposite of Noah's. Noah's house was a beautiful mansion on a hill, with a big yard and every fancy thing a person could want on their property, with no houses near it because the closest neighbors were also mansions.

This house, on the other hand, was a duplex crammed among a hundred similar houses on both sides of the street. Noah's house was open and clean. Even in the middle of the night, the glass on the walls and the white on the outside made it shine like a lighthouse. This house was built with dirty, faded brick. Vines tangled around the stoop, and you could barely see it because the only things lighting up that drizzly night were a dim porchlight and a flickering street lamp a few houses away.

"Um, Chris. Are you sure this is the right place?" I asked for the second time that weekend.

It took him much longer to answer this time, "I'll admit I was expecting like, a library or a church or something." He scrolled through his phone for a few moments before looking up and squinting into the dark, "But this is the right address. Guess there's only one way to find out."

Chris climbed up the stoop to the home of the Paranormal Phenomenon Party, a… group? Event? …Something hosted all the way up in Cleveland that Chris found in his research. I was worried when he texted me first thing in the morning to say he had my "second mission," but when he attached a link to their Facebook page, it didn't seem like such a bad idea. They met on Sunday nights, I wouldn't have to use my powers in front of anybody, I wouldn't have to wear that stupid costume, and there was free food. I mean, I didn't think it would be especially helpful, but then again, I didn't really think anything we did would be especially helpful.

But if this was the kind of house the Paranormal Phenomenon Party met up in, maybe it'd be best if Chris and I just got some fast food on the way home.

Chris hesitated for a second. His fist hovered over the door as he peeked over his shoulder at me. I scurried up the stoop to stand next to him. If this was something shady, it's probably better for me to be near him. He knocked, and it took a long time for the door to open, but we heard thumping get closer and closer. My stomach dropped as the lock unlatched.

I didn't really know what I expected the person opening that door to look like, but I definitely didn't expect a bald man, shorter than Chris, with a long red beard but no mustache, and a camo turtleneck underneath dirty overalls.

"Whatddya want?" he grunted.

I looked over at Chris. His mouth hung open a little bit, and he kept staring at the small man in front of us, blinking and not saying anything. I mean, he was pretty peculiar, but for someone with as many wacky ideas as Chris, I was a little surprised that this man left him speechless.

I finally spoke before things got even more awkward, "Um, hello. Is this the Paranormal Phenomenon Party?"

The man grunted and left the door open as he stepped back into his house. Did I see him nod? I think he wanted us to follow?

A big, stupid smile crept onto Chris's face as he stepped inside. I almost grabbed him by the shirt collar to stop him.

"I think we should go home," I said.

"Are you kidding? You think I'm going to throw away the chance to see what the inside of this clown's house looks like?" He kept going forward, "Besides, if this is some crazy cult, that's exactly the sort of thing we need to put the kibosh on."

I sighed as Chris powered forward, then hurried after him. He was forgetting that we didn't have the costume and everybody would see my face if things went bad, but if I learned anything from Leroy's Landing the other day, it's that he wouldn't listen to a word I said once he got like this. I just had to make sure to stay as close to him as possible.

The inside of the house was barely lit any better than the outside. The man lead us down a cramped hallway with one door leading to a bedroom, and another to a bathroom. Flags of all kinds, American flags, State Flags, political flags, military flags, draped the wooden walls of the hallway. The hot air smelled like cigarettes and had a gross hint of what

I think was a skunk smell. For once, I was glad I'm super skinny. The man looked like he couldn't walk down his own hallway without brushing his wide shoulders against both walls at once. Still, I could feel myself shake. I wanted to go back outside.

I almost ran right into Chris when he stopped halfway down the hall and peered into a glass case. Since there was no getting past without knocking him over or accidentally tearing something off the walls, I stopped and looked in, too. There were lots of military medals, and an old photo labeled "The 23rd Infantry Division" with a buncha army guys posing in front of a jungle.

All I wanted was to break the uncomfortable silence. A little friendly conversation would help convince me that Chris and I weren't walking into something horrible. "So, mister... um..."

It took the man a second to realize I was talking to him, but then he turned around without walking any closer to us, "Nigel."

"So, Mister Nigel," I said, not sure if that was his first or last name, "You were in the army?"

"Three tours in 'Nam."

"So what," Chris said, not looking away from the glass, "You start this club because you saw a Chupacabra in the jungle or something?"

I froze up as the man's eyes narrowed in anger. His footsteps got heavy as he thudded back toward us, knocking some blue flag I didn't recognize down as he stopped in front of Chris. My body hair stood on its ends. This was about to get really bad.

Chris didn't even look at Nigel until he started talking,

"Alright punk, listen up. First off, you know damn well that my wife runs this club for you brats, not me. Second, you can mock me all you want, but don't you dare use that tone talking about the boys who died so your scrawny ass can waste your youth chasing bigfoot. Yeah, I saw things in 'Nam you wouldn't believe, but it wasn't no damned Mothman. I watched my best friend's legs get blown off by machine gun fire, heard his last screams of agony as the medics failed to sew 'em back on. I've had to learn how to get to sleep every night thinking about the Vietcong I cooked myself with those flamethrowers. The day you watch a man's skin blacken and bubble before sloughing off his body, you can make your quips about my brothers in arms. But until then, I suggest you shut your trap. Get me?"

After a second, Chris finally said, "Yes sir."

"Good. Now follow me."

I didn't realize I wasn't breathing until the taste of old cigarettes filled my mouth as soon as Nigel turned around. Chris didn't move, didn't look at me. He was shaking.

"Let's get out of here," I whispered.

Chris still didn't say anything to me. His shoulders shook a little harder, and he made some noise. Was he crying? I wished I could safely put my hand on his shoulder to calm him down. Right when I was thinking of something comforting to say, he made a little snorting noise.

And that's when I realized he wasn't crying, or shaking in fear. Chris was trying not to laugh.

I folded my arms and glared at him, "What is wrong with you? This isn't funny!"

He finally turned around and wiped a tear from his

eye, pursing his lips together to try and quiet his giggling, "Relax. This leprechaun's never been to Vietnam."

"What do you mean? How do you know that?"

"Just look at him. I doubt he's even 40 years old. Anyone old enough to have served in Vietnam wouldn't have a hair on their body that wasn't grey."

"He—" but I cut myself off before I could finish and thought about it. How old were Vietnam veterans, anyway? I didn't really know the answer, but now that he mentioned it, Nigel didn't look that old. "Okay, so what? He was probably in Iraq or something and just gets confused."

"If that dude's done a day of military service in his life, I'll cut off all my fingers and toes. Look at these goddamn medals. Notice anything off? "

I took a closer look at the glass case. Now that he mentioned it, a lot of these medals looked plasticky. Except for a small one in the corner, which was definitely a bottle cap with Christmas ribbon taped to it.

When I didn't say anything, Chris turned towards Nigel and said, "I don't know if he's delusional or running some dumbfuck con or what, but either way I can't wait to meet his wife," before walking down the hallway with an even bigger pep in his step.

All I could think was how it wasn't comforting to know Nigel hadn't actually flamethrowered a person. Because he really, really thinks he did.

I hurried to catch up with Chris and breathed a little easier when we got to the kitchen at the end of the hallway, which maybe was a little too bright, but I was still glad to be in a room with a little bit of space.

Then Nigel opened a door in the back corner of

the room, and I could see stairs leading down to a dim, dirty basement.

"Alright," he said, "The rest of you brats are down there. Hurry up."

I wished Chris gave me a second to prepare myself before flying down the stairs, but I guess I couldn't be too mad at him. He didn't really know that I had a problem with basements. And if anything was going to get me to go down some stinky basement, it was having to be alone with Nigel in a different room.

I took a deep breath and took the first step. I sorta expected it to creak, but it was solid. After that, it was easier to just let gravity take me down the rest of the way. When I stood next to Chris at the bottom, I don't know what was more surprising, the look of the basement or the people in it. Compared to upstairs, it was really cozy. It was still dimly lit, but the light was coming from nice shaded lamps and a huge TV playing a YouTube video of a guy falling down, and instead of military stuff all over the walls, there was Cleveland sports stuff. In the center of the room, there were those couches that meet up with each other to make a half square with three kids our age, or maybe a little younger, all sitting on it. I'm not sure if seeing all these teenagers in Nigel's basement made me more or less afraid of what was happening.

A girl with pink hair leaned back and said, "Yo Nigel, can you pop some—holy crap! Guys, we have new members!"

The girl was so excited she jumped over the back of the couch. A tiny goth girl with lots of black makeup poked her head around, then slowly stood up, making her way behind a fancy looking bar and pulling out a deck of cards.

There was another boy with shoulder length hair. He took one look at us, snorted, and went back to watching the TV.

The pink haired girl ran right up to me. She was pretty short too, and had to bend her neck up to look me in the eye, "Oh wow, you're tall... I mean, nice to meet you! I'm Eliza. What's your name?"

I really wish that wasn't the first thing most people said to me, but I was used to it. "Um, I'm Kelly. Nice to meet you too."

Eliza's eyes lit up when she saw my shirt. "Oh my god, that's so cute! Is that one of those Pokemons?"

I could feel myself blushing, "Yes."

I don't know why I lied to her. It was actually a Moogle from Final Fantasy. I guess I'd feel like a dork saying that.

Maybe I didn't have to worry that much. She pumped her fist and said, "Knew it!"

She didn't explain why that was important, then turned to Chris with the same cheerful smile, "And you are?"

"Chris." He was barely looking at her, searching around the room. "Nigel said his wife ran this club. Where is she?"

Eliza's smile wilted, "Oh, you mean Mrs. Thornwald? Yeah, she does run these meetings, usually. But she... she..."

The long-haired boy finally talked, "Disappeared two weeks ago."

Eliza crossed her arms and glared at him, "We don't know that for sure!"

"You don't take any of her classes. That substitute teacher's psychic wavelengths reveal whispers within the administration. Whispers expressing uncertainty about what to tell the student body regarding Patricia's long leave of absence." He turned his nose up and waved his hand, "That's the price of meddling with dark forces you cannot comprehend."

Eliza stomped over to the boy and got in his face, "Shut up, Fern! You were just as interested in what she had to say about Sasquatch as the rest of us!"

"Of course I was intrigued! But I didn't anticipate the fool woman scurrying to Alaska alone. Had she brought me, maybe I could've restrained the beast. As it is, she's as good as gone."

I felt a little pit in my stomach. Maybe Nigel wasn't actually scary after all. Maybe he just was worried about his wife.

The empty space behind me suddenly filled up, and a voice carried by cigarette smoke blew into my ears, "Eh, she'll turn up."

"ACK!" I couldn't help but jump back.

How long had Nigel been standing there?

He didn't say anything to me as he sidled by, walking up to the bar, "Little witch girl, beer."

The goth girl didn't change her bored face, and spoke in a similarly bored voice, "I suggest you refrain from calling me 'little girl' in the future."

"Whatever. Witch girl. Beer."

She seemed okay with that one and reached under the bar, then handed a bottle to Nigel. He grunted and smacked its top against the counter. The cap flew away and bounced off the wall behind the goth girl before he took a big long gulp. He wiped off some beer that dribbled down his beard and shook his pointer finger at her.

"If I come back down here tonight and find out any of you brats touched my beer," he turned and shook his finger at every single one of us, "I'll make sure every teacher at that fancy pants school rains hellfire on you."

We all stood still as his footsteps thundered away.

Chris, who had been weirdly quiet since we got in the basement, finally spoke up. All of the excitement he had making fun of Nigel disappeared. He was glaring at that Fern boy the way he glared at the kids going to Leroy High, "So you're just a bunch of high schoolers."

"Well, yeah." Eliza seemed a little confused by his question, "Aren't you guys? Come to think of it, I don't think I've seen you two around. Do you go to Grinnsdale?"

Chris's expression didn't change, and he didn't stop glaring at Fern, "No."

Oh boy, if I didn't say anything, Chris was gonna start something. I don't know why he'd rather hang around Nigel. Sure, Fern seemed like kind of a jerk, and that goth girl was a little creepy maybe, but at least Eliza was nice. And didn't think that she melted a person.

"So, um," everyone suddenly looked at me, and I froze up for just a second. "What do you guys do here?"

Eliza got her smile back and rushed over to me, "Oh, all sorts of stuff! Mostly, we research different paranormal phenomena. Mrs. Thornwald started the club to find people to help her look for Bigfoot, but we've all got our own interests." She pulled out her phone and started scrolling through it, "Okay, so I had kind of a weird childhood. I was born on this crazy religious compound." She didn't look up from her phone, and just kept talking like that was a totally normal thing, "And ever since I was a little kid, I'd see weird stuff that I couldn't explain. Check this out."

She turned her phone to me and showed me a picture

of what looked like a dusty old pantry with lots of empty shelves. Chris took the phone, and I peeked over his shoulder to get a better look.

Eliza sounded really excited, "You see it, right?"

"…Yeah," I said, not seeing anything but a dark room. "Um, so what do you think it is?"

Fern caught my attention when he scoffed, "Why intrude on our meeting if you can't even interpret ecto-plasmic signals as clear as that? This is why I've always said that, as a sex, females are lesser in seeing the world beyond the material."

I put my head down to hide my glare. It took a lot of effort for me to bite my lip and not mention that of the four club members we knew about, Fern was the only boy.

Eliza was beaming. Obviously, she'd gotten used to ignoring Fern. "Lulu thinks they're my ancestors trying to tell me something. She says it's hard to get in touch with spirits through a photo, but since I've been seeing them my whole life… I don't know, it's like I'm destined for something big. Is that crazy? Have you guys ever had an experience like that?"

I didn't really wanna answer that question. I guess if we hadn't, why would Chris and I even be here?

"Totally," Chris said, handing her phone back before I could decide what to say, "It was crazy. I put a piece of bread in the toaster the other day, and when it came back up, Jesus was staring at me from inside the toast."

I glared at Chris. His bored face matched the goth girl behind the bar.

"Wow, really?" Eliza said, "That's amazing! Oh, I know! You two should talk to Lulu. I found this club through her.

She's got amazing powers, maybe she can help you figure out what that means."

Eliza pointed at the goth girl. I smiled and sat down on a barstool. Chris could grump all he wanted. This was his idea in the first place, and if there was somebody else with powers, I wanted to know about them.

Lulu said nothing, keeping her head down and shuffling through a deck of cards. She didn't even look up when I cleared my throat.

"So," I finally said, "You have powers?"

She kept shuffling her cards and didn't look at me, "I am a conduit through which the spirits speak. The abilities are not my own. Would you like a reading today?"

"You mean like fortune telling?"

Lulu nodded. "Five dollars."

She held out her hand and stared at me, her bored expression not changing even a little bit since I walked in. I mean, if somebody was able to communicate with spirits, I guess it makes sense that it'd be her. I didn't have any money on me, though. The shorts I liked to wear didn't have pockets, and I left my emergency money out in the car. Right as I was about to tell Lulu sorry, Chris walked up and slapped a five-dollar bill into her hand before crossing his arms.

Lulu nodded again. "The spirits thank you for your generosity." She took a deep breath and placed both her hands on the deck of cards. With a quick flick of her wrist, she drew a single card and pressed it against her forehead, making a low humming noise. Finally, she smacked the card down on the table and opened her eyes.

"The Lovers, upright." She stared directly at me, or

maybe past me? It was really hard to tell with this girl. "You're a lonely person, aren't you?"

That made me sit up a little straighter. Before I realized it, I was nodding, and Lulu gave me a quick nod in return, "Yes, the spirits can see the stress emanating off you. But this loneliness need not be permanent. The paradigm has an opportunity to shift, and soon. Your soulmate will enter your life, but only if you let go of your fears and let them in."

I sat there silently. Could it really be true? That things had a chance to get better? I mean, I was going to college soon, and part of me wanted to hope that it'd be better than middle and high school have been, but I'd tried not to hope too much. That was months away, too. How soon did she mean? I felt my eyes shift over to Eliza, then looked back at Lulu before anyone could notice. Eliza was nice, and pretty, but my soulmate? I mean, she seemed a little weird, but then again I was *very* weird, so maybe it made sense. And she did seem sorta interested in the stuff that I like…

While I was thinking about all that, Chris took a seat at the bar next to me.

"I imagine you want me to read your fate as well?" Lulu said.

"Nah, I'm good. Got any other tricks up your sleeve?"

She waved her hand across the bar, and a few colorful rocks clattered onto the table. I'm pretty sure I heard Chris snicker, but that didn't bother Lulu. "You look pale. These crystals absorb negative energy and promote good health. You can place them in your room or keep them on your person. Ten dollars each."

Chris's bored face matched Lulu's. "Come on, you can do better than that."

"Chris!"

If Chris was annoying Lulu, she didn't show it one bit. "Very well. I'll offer you my priciest service, then. Is there anyone in the Great Beyond you wish to speak with?"

The Great Beyond? Did she mean...

"Like," I said, "you can talk to dead people?"

"Not precisely. I can use my connection to the spirits to channel them through my body. I'll warn you, however, that I can only hold this state for about five minutes. And it will not be cheap."

"How much we talking?" Chris said.

"Twenty dollars."

Chris and I didn't say anything. She couldn't really talk to dead people, could she? No, that's not what she said. If I understood her right, she could let *me* talk to Dad. If she could really do it, then twenty dollars was nothing, right? But maybe it wasn't actually a good idea. Maybe I shouldn't know what Dad would think about this whole superhero thing. But the least I could do is say sorry, right? Could I do that without anyone else in the room? Maybe I could get Lulu's phone number and schedule something alone.

Chris interrupted my thoughts by smacking a twenty-dollar bill on the bar. "Fuck it. Show me what you got."

Lulu nodded. "I'll require a moment to prepare the ritual. And to know the spirit's name, as well as their relationship to you."

I never expected Chris to ask for something like this in a million years, especially since he's been acting like a sourpuss since we came down to the basement. I guess even he couldn't help it. He wasn't much older when he lost his dad than I was.

"Sure," he said, "I want to talk to Vanessa Underwood, my mother."

It took me a minute to realize that wasn't the name I expected to hear, "Wait a minute, what? Chris, your mom—"

He cut me off by holding up his hand, "It's alright, I know. We didn't leave off on good terms. That's why I want to make it right."

His face finally changed. He narrowed his eyes at me, warning me not to challenge this. After thinking about it for a second, I folded my arms and pouted, but didn't say anything. He could prove his stupid point if he wanted to. I just couldn't believe he'd waste his money on something so petty.

Actually, thinking about it a little more, I could. I really, really could.

While Chris and I had our staring contest, Lulu and Eliza cleared a space in the middle of the room and set up what looked like Hannukah candles in a big circle. Fern didn't move from his spot on the couch, but he did look a little more interested in what was going on than before. Lulu finished lighting the candles and pulled a long green stick out of her pocket, which she also lit and put it in front of her before sitting down with her legs crossed. After a few seconds, a faint tinge of matcha drifted over my nose. It was nice for a second, but didn't mix well with the cigarette smoke that hung in the basement air.

"We're ready to begin," she finally said. "Lights."

Eliza ran over the stairway and flicked the lights off, letting us see only the whites of Lulu's eyes and the warm glow of the parts of her face not covered in black makeup. Chris stood in front of her spirit circle with his hands in his pockets.

Lulu took a deep breath, lowered her head, and closed her eyes, "Oh, spirits lingering in the Great Beyond. I entreat you, with what meager power I possess. I call forth the spirit of Vanessa Underwood, taken from us far too soon. I beg of you, inhabit this imperfect shell and let this boy speak with his mother once again! Let what remains unsaid be resolved!"

Suddenly, Lulu groaned. Her arms drooped to her sides as her back twisted into an upside-down U. She groaned a little louder as she shook, and after a second she snapped back up. Her eyes were open, rolled into the back of her head. It was almost creepy.

If I didn't know that Mrs. Underwood was asleep in her own bed.

Lulu's voice boomed with more energy and emotion than I'd heard all night, "Where am I? Chris? Honey, is that you?"

"Yeah mom, it's me. What's up?" Chris looked directly at me while he said that.

"Oh sweetie, I've missed you so much. I can't believe it's really you!"

"It sure is something."

There was an awkward silence. Chris didn't stop staring at me the entire time. I finally had to look away from him, because I felt real stupid for taking Lulu's fortune telling as seriously as I did.

Lulu must've been a little thrown off, too, because the next time she talked, it took her a second to get her ghostly voice back, "What are you... Is there anything in you wanted to say to me in particular?"

"Nah, not really. Just wanted to say hey. Have fun in the Great Beyond or whatever."

Lulu coughed up a big gasp and lurched forward. When she shot back up, her eyes were normal, and looking a lot angrier than they had all night.

"Forgive me," she said, icy, "That connection was particularly difficult to maintain."

"I'm sure it was."

I tried not to make it too obvious, but I looked over at Eliza as she turned the lights back on. Even she was frowning at Chris. Why did he always have to do stuff like this? Either way, it was time to go.

But before I could get a word out, Chris turned to Fern and said, "So what's your deal, then? You a vampire or something?"

Fern glared at him for an uncomfortably long time as Lulu collected her stuff and sulked back over to the bar. Chris didn't look away. The two challenged each other for a moment, and right as I was about to work up the courage to get us out of there, Fern rolled his eyes and dramatically stood up.

"Hmph. I do not usually do this, but just this once, I will humor you, doubter." He went to Chris with an exaggerated strut. Chris's glare turned into a joyful smirk as they stared each other down, only a foot apart. Fern was taller than Chris, but not by much, so he had to kind of puff out his chest to look down on him. "My comrade sells herself short. It is true that she can only use her abilities to commune with otherworldly forces, but that is still far beyond the psychic abilities of the average mortal. I, on the other hand, am a true master of psychokinesis. The world bends to the will of my very mind."

"I bet."

Fern crossed his arms and scoffed with a smile. I think that move is what made me realize he modeled everything he did after anime villains. "Yes, make your japes while you can. You will be in no mood to do so after I have demonstrated a mere fraction of my power."

"Can you skip to your final form and get this over with? I'm getting hungry."

Fern leaned back, his cackled bounced off the walls of the now cramped-feeling basement. "You must think you are quite clever. Rest assured, if I showed you the full extent of my power, everyone in the room would be dead in seconds. But, if you insist, I will give you a demonstration. Behold!"

Fern pulled a spoon out of his coat pocket and brandished it in front of Chris. He clenched his free hand into a fist. As he popped his fingers out like he was shooting an energy blast, the spoon did bend... but you didn't need to be looking too close to notice Fern flicking the wrist holding it at the same time.

Chris tilted his head, "Huh. You know, credit where it's due. If my IQ were about ten points lower, I might have actually fallen for that."

Fern scowled. After spending so much time just watching, Eliza finally got between them, "Okay, we get it. You're making fun of us. Why did you even bother coming tonight?" I felt a pit in my stomach when Eliza glared at me, too. "Because you thought it'd be funny?"

"It is very funny," Chris said, "But no, we do actually

have business with the paranormal. It's just clear that talking to you morons about it would be a monumental waste of time. Even when I saw your Facebook page, I knew there was a decent chance you guys were a bunch of circus clowns, but you managed to disappoint me anyway. You're all small potatoes compared to Nigel. Now *that* dude is a legend."

I didn't think Fern's sneer could get any more hateful, but somehow he managed to do it. "Enlighten me then, if you're such an expert on the paranormal, what makes your experience so much more legitimate than ours?"

"I thought you'd never ask." Chris didn't even look at me as he pointed his thumb over his shoulder in my direction, "She's like a demigod, or something like that."

My blood went cold.

Fern narrowed his eyes at me, "Is she now?"

"Nope!" I said quickly, "No idea what he's talking about!"

"Come on Kelly, no need to hide it. These are very serious paranormal researchers. Your secret's safe with them." He turned back to Fern. The glee in his voice made me even more sick to my stomach, "Seriously, you should see her. It's unreal. The other day she jumped high enough in the air to touch a cloud. We had a race—me in the car, her on foot—and she smoked me even with a ten-minute head start. I watched her toss a train car like a frisbee. Oh, and her eyes glow this badass shade of red when it happens. It's amazing. You could probably learn a thing or two from her."

Fern rolled his eyes, "Your churlish mockery bores me. Anyone trained in the dark arts can tell there is nothing remarkable about this common wench from a mere glance."

"You sound so certain," Chris said, "You sure about that? Or is your power level not as high as you've been letting on?"

I couldn't take it anymore. "Chris! Stop!"

"I suggest you listen to your woman," Fern clenched his fists, "I promise you, it is unwise to cross me."

Chris's grin only got bigger and bigger. "Buddy, I don't need her to take you in a fight."

It looked like the vein in Fern's temple was about to burst out of his head. "Do not say I did not warn you! Farewell, mortal!"

Eliza and I both took a step forward to try and stop the fight before it started. Fern drew his hand back and growled. Chris immediately turned serious as he put his fists up to block his face.

"Behold!" Fern screamed, "My true power!"

His hand shot forward, not as a punch aimed at Chris's face, but cupped like he was choking an invisible person. Chris blinked and put his guard down. Fern's arm quivered as he held it in the air like that.

Then, a second later, Chris grabbed at his hair and screamed. His body crumpled to the ground in a heap. Fern crossed his arms.

Everyone was quiet.

"Chris?"

The energy inside me started building up. I did a bad job steadying my quivering voice, "Chris, this isn't funny! Please, get up!"

CHAPTER 17
CHRIS

THE PINK HAIRED girl shrieked. "Oh my god! Fern, what the hell did you do?"

"Quiet, fool. He is bluffing."

I laid facedown on the floor and didn't move. I had to bite my lower lip hard to stop myself from laughing. Kelly hovered over me. It was nice that she was concerned and all, but I would've hoped that she didn't fall for this after seeing that goth girl's embarrassing display. The jig was almost up, anyway.

"Rise, mortal," that Fern dweeb said, "You deceive only yourself. My ultimate power does not work the way your feeble mind believes it does."

That one did it. I could barely lift my head up I was laughing so hard, but when I finally did, the first thing I saw was Kelly's face. You didn't need telepathy to tell that she was pissed off, but I didn't care. I was having the time of my life.

"Enlighten me, oh wise one," I said, wiping a tear from my eye as I stood up, "What curse has befouled me?"

Fern folded his arms and chuckled like he was Skeletor or something. "I have used my great and terrible power to alter the flow of blood in your body." He smirked and wagged a finger back and forth, "In precisely one hour, blood will pool and clot in your brain's arteries. You will suffer an embolism, and with what little time your conscious mind will have left, you will rue the day you crossed me."

I started wheezing it was so hard to breathe. "Lucky me! I get a whole hour to keep on living. How convenient!"

At this point, even Kelly gave Fern the stink eye, "Okay, I know things got heated, but don't you think that's going overboard?"

Kelly jumped back as he jabbed his finger at her, "Still your tongue! You are on the precipice of disaster yourself for dirtying my presence with this whelp. One wrong word and I will make you suffer the same fate."

She narrowed his eyes at him. Christ, the only thing that could make this evening any better is if she punted this twerp like a football.

I waited a second to see if she'd take the bait before I finally said, "I'll admit, you've defeated me. Everybody else I understand. Goth girl's got a nice grift going, Nigel just needs to be put in an institution, but you? I can't figure out your angle. Do you honestly believe the verbal diarrhea dribbling out of your mouth or do you just have something to prove?"

"Shut up."

I gestured to the girl with the pink hair, "Or what, you

act like Dr. Doom to make Becky here think you're some supreme badass?"

Fern's face turned purple, "*Shut. Up.*"

My heart soared in delight. "Jesus, that *is* it. Damn, love makes people do some dumbass shit. Listen champ, word of advice: you're way overdoing it." I held my hand way above my head, "You're here right now," I crouched and hovered my palm an inch above the floor, "You need to bring it down to here. Don't worry, she'll still believe whatever you say because she's dumber than a bag of bricks—"

"Hey!"

"—And, you get the added bonus of being able to look at yourself in the mirror without cringing so hard you snap your own spine."

Fern just kept screaming. *"Get out!"*

At long last, I turned back to Kelly. It was hard to parse her expression. She probably didn't know how she was supposed to feel about any of this anymore.

"You heard the man," I said, "Time to go." I turned back to the angry crowd of losers and gave a big wave, "So long, my fellow, fearless investigators of the paranormal! You may have been as useful as a car missing three of its tires, and you may have scammed me out of twenty-five bucks, but I'd say tonight was more than worth the price of admission. If your teacher ever comes back, send her our way. I'm sure she's as much of a riot as Nigel."

With that, I went up the stairs, Kelly following closely behind as the crowd below melded into one echoing shout. She leaned over and whispered, "I hope you're proud of yourself."

"Oh, you know I am."

"You didn't have to actually tell them about me!"

"Will you calm down? They thought I was fucking with them. Besides, if they say anything, anyone with a shred of credibility is going to take one look at those bozos and ship them off to the funny farm."

Kelly went silent as we reached the top of the stairs, and since I was looking at her and not where I was going, I ran smack into Nigel's protruding beer belly. "The hell you brats screaming about down there?"

I did what came naturally, which in this case, was stand at attention and salute Nigel while saying, "Captain! It's been an honor serving! Permission to take my leave, sir!"

Nigel snorted, "Yeah yeah, real funny. Get the hell outta my house."

"Sir yes sir!"

I did my best military march out of there. Kelly mumbled some rushed apology and ran to catch up with me outside. As soon as the door closed behind us, our argument started back up.

"Coming here was your idea in the first place!" Kelly said as we walked down the stoop.

"Even I have bad ideas sometimes. I did what I could to make sure it wasn't a *total* waste of time."

She stopped me when we reached the bottom of the stairs and started scolding me about something else, but I wasn't paying attention. In my peripheral vision, Fern loomed through Nigel's front window.

I cut her off, the joy in my heart ringing in my voice, "Holy shit, he's following us!"

Kelly tensed up and whipped around. "Who?"

When I pointed at the window and she saw it was Fern, not Nigel, her muscles relaxed. "Oh. Wait, why?"

"Let's find out." I cupped my hands around my mouth while I called to him, "Hey! We see you! Got something else you want to say?"

Fern disappeared from the window so quickly I thought maybe he could teleport for a second. The door swung open so hard the wood cracked, overpowering the soft drizzle of the rainy night. His voice cracked as he shrieked at us, "Fuck you! Go fuck yourself you little fucking fuck!"

My face hurt from smiling so wide. "Christ on toast, he's *so* mad!"

Kelly stayed quiet as he continued slurring obscenities from the safety of Nigel's porch. Finally, she turned to me and said, "Can we go home now?"

I reached into my pocket and tossed her the keys, "You can wait in the car if you want, I'm going to squeeze every last drop of entertainment out of this jester." Now that he was outside, I didn't need to cup my hands like a megaphone, but I did it for effect anyway, "Dude, you're embarrassing yourself in front of Becky."

That got him riled up again. Kelly and I sat in silence as he threw a tantrum.

He kept babbling, swearing and insulting me, barely coherent, going on, and on.

And on.

"...I kinda can't believe he's still going," Kelly finally whispered.

"No kidding. This guy's a menace. Maybe we should do something about him." I turned to her and mimed clapping my hands, "You know that thing the Hulk does? Where he claps his hands and makes a shockwave?"

"I'm not going to thunderclap him."

"You're no fun."

"That would break all his bones. Sure, he's an annoying jerk, but he doesn't deserve that. Also, we're in a crowded neighborhood."

I thought about this for a second, distracted by Fern's cacophonous music of the night. Even I was impressed now. A lesser opponent would've passed out from the lack of oxygen.

"He tried to turn my brain to mush," I finally said, "He might be the greatest villain we'll ever face."

"I thought the whole reason you're making fun of him was because he can't do that."

"Sure, but think about how easy it would be for him to get his hands on a gun."

That made her think. And while she was thinking, I tuned into what Fern was saying long enough to notice that he'd started going after Kelly.

"And you know what?" He said, clearing a bit of purple from his face with a deep breath, "It's so funny, fucking hilarious, actually, that you think Eliza is out of my league. Look at you! You think you've got any right to say shit to me when your girlfriend is such a disgusting cow? She could break you in half! Try saying shit to me without that bitch protecting you!"

That snapped Kelly out of her thoughts real quick. She scowled at Fern so hard, I thought her eyes would start glowing then and there.

"Is thunderclap on the menu now?" I said.

Kelly didn't take her eyes off Fern as she whispered, "I've got a better idea. Distract him. When I'm in that alleyway, give me some sorta signal. Snap your fingers or something. After we're done, pick me up from the gas station at the end of the street."

It took every ounce of willpower I had to not bounce in place like a child just promised McDonalds, "What are you doing?"

"I'm gonna make him think *you* have powers."

The night just kept getting better and better. I didn't even ask her to elaborate. The surprise was half the fun.

Kelly clenched her fists and whispered one last word of advice to me, "Brace yourself. You're gonna look stupid if you fall over." She took a step forward and shouted back at Fern. "Shut up! I was nothing but nice to all of you! If you two wanna stand out here and scream at each other until somebody calls the police, that's fine by me!" She jerked her head to me and said, "I'll be waiting in the car. Come get me when you're ready to grow up."

Fern and I were both quiet as Kelly stormed down the sidewalk, walking right past the Kellywagon parked on the curb. It was my cue. Whatever she was going to do, she didn't want to be seen.

Not sure what the best option was, I started doing an exaggerated cackle.

"What's so funny?" There was a sickening, rage-fueled smile on his face, "You fucked up big time. Your girlfriend's so pissed off she probably won't peg you for months."

I put a bit more energy into my cackle, tried to make it villainous. I suppose I learned a thing or two about acting from wasting so many Fridays reading from Rich's horrible script. Holding up a hand, I put my belly into it and bent over. There was a secondary purpose to grandstanding like that: it gave me a chance to steal a quick look down the street without drawing Fern's attention to Kelly. A ways down, she checked to make sure the coast was clear before ducking into a dark alley. I was good to go anytime.

But if this was going to be the grand finale for Fern and I's battle of wits, I wanted to savor the moment.

I made a big show of catching my breath. "My dear, dear Fern. You've made my evening oh so amusing until now. But as fun as this has been, I'm afraid I need to put a stop to our little game, once and for all."

He snorted. "Oh yeah?"

Have to admit, now that the shoe was on the other foot and I was doing Fern's schtick, I could see the appeal. I mimicked some of his earlier movements by crossing my arms and wagging a finger, "You see, it didn't matter how many insults you threw my way. Goading an insect like you was simply too much fun. But you crossed the line by bringing Kelly into this."

"How noble of you. Man, you're like two feet tall. You sure you wanna go now that she's not around to save you?"

"Fern, do you know why I was so dedicated to clowning on you all night? Why you and your gang of pathetic frauds get under my skin so much? It's not because I don't believe in the supernatural. No, quite the opposite, actually. It's because I know true power, Fern. And pretenders like you make me sick."

Fern laughed, "Now who's putting on a show for a girl? You trying to trade up?"

It was now or never. I spread my arms out wide to ham

it up one last time, the buildup before the climax, "I won't even pretend to waste my full power on you, worm. When one hour passes, I'll be sitting cozy and warm in my house, alive and well, and you'll be proven a fraud." I planted my feet and pointed at him, partly for the drama, but mostly to brace myself the way Kelly suggested, "You, on the other hand, you're going to be pissing yourself trying to process what you've seen tonight for months." I whipped my hand dramatically above my head, "Once you've seen what I can do with a mere snap of my fingers."

Fern crossed his arms and rolled his eyes, "Oh, this should be good. Go on then, do your magic trick."

I could feel the evil radiating off my smile, "If you insist."

I snapped my fingers.

Nothing happened for a moment.

But only for a moment.

In that second, Fern opened his mouth to talk shit, but when the earth beneath his feet rumbled, he clammed up. The shaking grew stronger and stronger. I stumbled a bit, but I did my damnedest to keep my smug face aimed directly at Fern. The shaking grew violent enough to knock Fern onto his wide-eyed, horrified ass. I stared him down with my evil grin the whole time, standing proudly against the earthquake. Nothing got me to look away, not even when car alarms started going off and a stop sign clanged against the concrete. I had to commit to this.

I only dropped my hand once the rumbling subsided completely. But I didn't relax my shit-eating grin. Neighbors funneled outside to look around. An earthquake in Ohio is, after all, an exceptionally rare thing.

Fern squealed like a hog and tried to scamper back into Nigel's house on all fours. Unfortunately for him, the big boy himself bounded out his front door and bowled right through him. Nigel's grumpy old man eyes had grown crazed. It took me a minute to realize he was brandishing a machete.

"*They're here. The invasion is starting. Inside.*"

Fern stammered unintelligibly and raised a finger toward me.

Nigel snarled, "You *deaf* boy? Get inside *now.*"

Fern didn't need to be told again. He skittered in to meet Eliza and Lulu, who were now gazing bug-eyed at us from the window.

"Goddamned dirty communists!" Nigel flailed his machete around and roared like a bear. "You sons of bitches ready for round two? Come and get me! But if you know what's good for your filthy commie heads, you won't miss this time!"

Despite the fact that there was a very real chance I'd be branded red by Nigel and diced to ribbons by that machete, it took a second for my feet to get moving back to the car. My mind was preoccupied, laughing as hard as I had ever laughed. Fortunately, it didn't take long to remember how to multitask, stumbling to the Kellywagon, wheezing. I hadn't even buckled in before slamming my foot on the gas. In the rearview mirror, Nigel's berserker rage grew distant as more horrified onlookers came out of their houses to see a bald roly-poly flailing with a machete in his front yard.

I whipped the car around a few twists and turns, just in case anybody was following me through the residential area. I had to take extra-long pauses at a few stop signs to stifle more laughter.

Eventually, when I was satisfied that nobody would tail me home, I turned towards a run-down gas station we passed on our way in, and saw Kelly standing near the door.

She got in the car without a word. Neither of us said anything, or even looked at each other, until we reached a red light by the highway entrance.

We turned to each other, and after a second, burst into cackles at the same time.

"What the hell did you do back there?" I said.

"I just stomped on the ground!" She buried her face in her hands like she was embarrassed, but was still giggling, "I can't believe I did that."

"It was awesome. You should've seen that moron's face."

She tried to wave me off, "No, don't look at me."

"I'm looking! I'm looking until you admit that was fun as hell."

"No! That was mean!" Kelly was still laughing as she said that.

"Oh come on, that chucklefuck deserved it."

"Maybe Fern—"

A blaring honk interrupted Kelly. The light had turned green while we were busy shaking off the giggles. I floored the gas and lurched onto the highway.

Kelly took a deep breath to try and calm herself, but right as she began to talk, a few more giggles came out, "Okay, maybe Fern deserved it. But that Eliza girl was nice. I kinda feel bad."

"Get the fuck out of here. You're just saying that because you were crushing on her hard," I said with a smile.

Kelly's face turned bright red, "I was not!"

"Ooooooo," I said in my most nasally voice, "That girl's got neon hair! Just like one of my anime waifus!"

"Shut up! That is *not* what I'm like." Kelly said it with force, but she still kept her dorky smile.

"Nice Pokémon shirt, by the way. That was your tell. When you didn't immediately explain the plot of every single Final Fantasy game, I knew you'd smile and agree to *anything* she said."

Kelly sank in her seat, bright red, laughing harder than ever before. "Even if I didn't think she was cute, I wouldn't want to bore her to death!"

"Don't fight it, insufferable dweebiness is your nature. It's part of your charm, really. How many times have you jumped up my asshole for switching around Piccolo and Cell's names?"

"You mean you've known the difference this entire time?"

"Of *course* I know the difference! I don't think there's anything in your room that doesn't have Piccolo on it. I do it because it makes you so genuinely angry, and that's *always* funny."

She held up the palm of her hand to block out my face. "I'm ignoring you. I really wish I could punch you right now, but I can't, so I'm ignoring you forever."

We spent rest of the hour-long drive home bickering and laughing like that. Another night, another failure, it seemed.

But this was the kind of failure I could get behind.

CHAPTER 18

KELLY

CHRIS AND I didn't talk about the party, or the paranormal club, or superheroing at all, really, the rest of the weekend. Since he was still in trouble with his mom, I didn't even see him again until Monday morning at school, and during the bus ride we had a normal morning chat. Part of me wondered if Chris was gonna let the whole plan quietly drop after how bad the weekend went. I didn't know how I felt about that.

It finally came up when we were having lunch on the wall close to the school's baseball diamond, our usual spot. But it wasn't Chris or me who said anything.

"Hey Kelly, can I borrow you for a sec?"

Nobody was supposed to be outside during lunch hour, so Noah's voice caught us both by surprise. Chris stared at him like a chess player trying to figure out his opponent's next move, but Noah was easygoing as ever, with a relaxed posture and a calm face. It didn't seem like he was there to make fun of me.

I stood up, but couldn't look him in the eye. "Um, sure."

Chris watched us carefully as Noah led me inside. I stayed a few steps behind as we pushed against people heading for the cafeteria in the opposite direction. The sight of us walking together definitely turned a few heads, but for all my jitters about it, Noah acted like nobody would question us being seen together. Maybe he just didn't care. I waited for him to talk, but he seemed to be saving it until we arrived wherever he was taking me. I kept quiet to avoid saying anything stupid.

We ended up in the senior hallway, and Noah drifted over to his locker. With nobody else around, each click of his combination lock made me more and more curious. His broad shoulders blocked the view of his locker, so I didn't see what he had until he turned around, presenting my superhero helmet with an amused smile.

"You left this at my place," he said.

There wasn't any meanness in his voice, but such a physical reminder of my screw ups in his hands made me wanna die. I yanked it from him and whispered thank you. My locker took forever to open, and when I put the helmet on top of the huge junk pile inside, its visor glared back, judging me.

My heart stopped when I turned and stood face to face with Noah. While I wasn't looking, his calm disappeared. He kept fidgeting and squirming in a way that reminded me of... me, really. What was he still doing here? Didn't he want to get away from me, back to his friends as quickly as possible? It almost seemed like he was waiting for me to say something.

"Hey," I said, "I'm real sorry about ruining your party. I was… I don't really know what I was doing."

With a small chuckle, his easy confidence came back to him, "Don't worry about it. Everyone's done some weird shit when they're drunk."

It didn't seem like a great time to mention I wasn't drunk. "I guess. But I dunno, I feel like I ruined other people's nights."

Noah blinked and tried to figure out what I meant by that, "What, you talking about Thomas? Don't mind him. He was just salty because he's been going after Cass for ages. They only got together like, a week ago, so when a certain knight of justice started catching his girlfriend's eye… let me put it this way, Thomas isn't the type of guy to back down from a challenge," he said, winking at me.

My face burned and drooped to the floor.

"Hey, don't be like that," he said with a smile, "Cass is pretty embarrassed too, but she'll get over it. Not your fault she had too much to drink."

Despite everything, I could feel myself smile back, "Are you… are you doing okay?" I said.

Noah showed a glimpse of the loneliness he was bottling up. He quickly brought his shield back with another smile and said he'd be fine. It seemed phonier after he'd dropped it for a second.

"But that's not what I wanted to talk to you about," he continued, "See, I was thinking about it, and Annie made me buy prom tickets way in advance. Since I'm not going with her anymore, I have the extra just laying around. Be a shame if it went to waste. You want to come with?"

I blinked. Did I hear that right? Did I just get asked to prom?

Did *Noah Burke* just ask me to prom?

Not possible. This wasn't real. But there he was, waiting for my answer as casually as he'd asked me. My brain was screaming for me to just say yes, but my lips couldn't form the words. There had to be some kind of mistake.

I stared at him like a dummy for way too long, but that seemed like the reaction Noah expected. "It's cool if you already made plans. It was just an idea I had. I'm not trying to split up you and Chris, or anything like that."

"Huh?" I said, "Oh. Oh no, Chris isn't… I mean, it isn't like that. We aren't…" I took a deep breath. Just say it. This is what you want. "Yes. I'd love to go to prom with you, Noah."

For just a split-second, he looked like he wasn't expecting me to say that. Why? What could possibly make him think I'd say no? Because he thought Chris and I were together? But he asked me anyway, so he couldn't have been that sure. Did part of him think I was a lesbian? Yes, that must've been it. He did see me and Cassidy last night, and I think a lot of the school assumed that anyway, but they were only half-right.

Whatever the reason, he got over it and pulled himself together with an easy nod, "Great. It'd suck to be the only guy without a date. Anyway, I don't want to keep you too long. Just wanted to throw the idea out there. I'll text you later, let you know what the plan is. See you around?"

I nodded my head. That seemed like the safest way to respond.

He put his hands in his pockets as he strolled away like my life hadn't just totally changed. I said nothing, waving like an idiot while I stood in the empty senior hall, still trying to process everything that just happened. All my attempts to ground myself, to remind myself this didn't make me his girlfriend or anything like that, started failing, and I bounced outside singing a cheerful song. I swung the side door wide open without worrying about whether it'd break or not. Not even the overcast sky could bring me down as I nearly skipped back to our spot. It was really happening. I was going to prom with the cutest guy in school.

But when Chris turned his head toward me, I stopped and bottled those good feelings up like it was second nature.

I didn't have to imagine what he'd say if I told him what happened. I already knew it in my soul: *Jesus, you're smarter than this. He's trying to trick you. It couldn't be more obvious. What, his long-term girlfriend dumps him, and of all the girls in the entire school that could replace her, he picks you? Right after the total fiasco at his party? Smells like bullshit to me.*

But I didn't wanna hear about how I was ugly and awkward, how Noah should still be healing from the wounds of a four year relationship, how even if he wasn't there was no way he'd ever ask someone like me to prom when literally any girl he wanted would go with him, how Noah and I had spoken for maybe ten minutes total before Friday night, how I spent every minute of that conversation behind a mask like a crazy person, how he was planning to pull some horrible prank on me once I got there, how even if he weren't I couldn't dance with him and couldn't say why, how even if I could dance I'd look stupid doing it. I didn't wanna hear Chris say any of it, like none of it was true until he did.

I wasn't gonna give him the chance. It was none of his business anyway. He didn't have to know. I practiced a neutral face as I walked along the wall, and when I got close enough to make real eye contact, he seemed more confused than suspicious. That was a good sign.

"What was that all about?" he asked.

Trying to used Noah's laidback attitude as a model, I relaxed my stiff shoulders and dropped to the ground next to Chris. "Oh, he just wanted to give the helmet back." I took a bite of my sandwich to break eye contact.

But it wasn't good enough. All the alarms in his head must've gone off as he narrowed his eyes at me, "Did he now?"

"Yup. I thought it was weird too, but he was actually really nice about it. Maybe we shouldn't use the costume anymore since…" I didn't wanna sound too casual, so I paused and twirled my hair around to add a little embarrassment to my performance, "I mean, you saw what happened. Anyway! We should start planning our next move. I wanna give this another shot."

He kept his eyes narrowed and said nothing, waiting for me to crack, to show some sign that I wasn't telling him the whole truth. But even though Chris could be a little intimidating when he really wanted to be, I didn't let myself show any sign of being uncomfortable. If there was one thing I was good at, it was keeping secrets.

If I waited too long without saying anything, he'd realize I knew he was challenging me, so I perked my voice up and said, "Hey, are you okay? What's the matter?"

Chris stopped himself before replying, really struggling with whether or not to fight me on this. The minute he sighed and brushed his hair out of his eyes I knew I was safe. Although I don't think he totally bought my story, it was enough that we didn't have to talk about it. "Nothing. Just surprised you're ready to get back in the saddle after such disasters two nights in a row," he said.

"I just think we weren't really coming at this the right way. Don't get me wrong, I get what you were going for with the whole Batman thing, but if we're gonna keep doing this, I wanna actually help people. No more intimidation stuff. I wanna be a superhero, not a boogeyman."

Chris thought about it, "That's fair, I suppose, but like you said, this is Leroy. We can't exactly crouch on a rooftop and wait for trouble to show up."

This was true. The concern I had during our conversation at Lucky Dan's didn't really change. By the time we saw something happen on the news, we'd probably be too late. It's not like we had a bat-signal.

We sat in silence for a second. I knew if I didn't take the initiative and come up with something quick, Chris would start asking about Noah again. So I tried to think: How could we figure out where trouble will be before it happens? We could talk to someone, I guess, but who? If we knew any police officers, we could ask them about weird things happening in town, but that would make us look pretty suspicious if Mask Man got involved with every single case. There had to be someone else who could tell us what's going on, someone who had to know everything about Leroy to do their job. Like maybe a reporter?

I sat up straight and checked the time on my phone. We still had twenty minutes of lunch left. Quickly packing the rest of my food up, I stood up and waved for Chris to follow me, "Come on, I have an idea!"

A little shocked at how fast that was, Chris scrambled to get his stuff together as I turned around to head back to the building. The sound of his feet pattering against the grass snuck up on me as I opened the door. "Where are we going?" he asked.

"The library. They've got every issue of the Leroy Gazette in there. We may not be able to predict what's gonna happen, but maybe if we look at what's already happened, we can see some kinda pattern, you know? Or maybe there's a mystery that never got solved for us to look into."

He snorted, "Yeah, if we wanted to find the best bird-watching spots in town, that would be a great idea."

I narrowed my eyes at him. "Well Mister Party Crasher, if you come up with anything better, I'll be happy to listen. Until then," I opened the library door and held it for him, "We're doing this my way."

Not able to argue with that, Chris grumbled as we went inside. Since the teachers didn't allow anyone to bring food in, the room was empty except for the curly-haired librarian, who stopped in the middle of putting a book on a shelf to give Chris the stink eye. He scowled back, and after locking eyes for a few seconds, she went back to organizing the shelf.

The newspapers weren't hard to find. The school district hasn't had any money for new books in a long time, so most of the shelves were empty. To fill some space, the librarian put stacks of recent newspapers on shelves in the back. We headed straight for them, ignoring the rows of computers because we knew it'd take the rest of lunch just to boot them up. I grabbed as many papers as I could and dropped them on the table closest to us, sat down, and got to work.

Both of us worked in silence, quickly scanning papers to see if there was something worth sharing, and tossing them aside when we didn't find anything. I was happy to see Chris so focused, partly because it kept his mind off Noah like I hoped, and partly because I didn't wanna hear him brag about how he knew the newspapers wouldn't be any help. Ads for shops in town took up most of the pages, and from what I could see, most of the stories were innocent stuff like interviews with people in town, weather reports, and announcements for upcoming events at the middle and high schools. No crimes, no calls for help. The few eye-catching stories I did see were all taken from the national news. Nothing really happened in Leroy after all.

I kept my eye on the clock. After ten minutes, as I grabbed my third paper in a row with a birdwatching story on the front page, Chris finally spoke up.

"Ugh," he said, "Football again. Would it kill them to write about the other sports? I'm sick of seeing Thomas's mug on the front page." He flipped the paper around, "It wasn't even in season when they wrote this."

"I think the football team is the only one that does well."

Without looking up from his paper or changing his tone, he said, "What about basketball? I thought you'd be more supportive of your new boyfriend's endeavors."

Pressing my lips together to avoid taking his bait, I stayed quiet and scanned the paper in front of me, pretending to be too focused on something interesting to pay attention. As it turned out, a story on the side of the page gave me the perfect excuse to change the subject. "Look!"

I stretched across the table to hand him the paper. "Someone's horses disappeared in the middle of the night. This might be worth checking into."

Chris shook his head, "Saw how that ended in a different paper. Someone found two horses grazing in Hubbard Park the next day. Dumbass didn't lock up his stable, they got spooked during a storm and ran out. No foul play or horsenapping or whatever." He took a fresh paper from the pile, instantly shooting me an evil grin. "Now *this* is a mystery worth our time."

My heart leapt, and I rushed over to read it over his shoulder, "What? What is it?"

Still smiling, Chris cleared his throat and fluffed the paper before bringing it closer to his face to keep me from seeing, "Beloved Local Landmark Reduced to Rubble: After receiving multiple reports of explosions coming from the old amusement park, police officers were dispatched to Leroy's Landing last night to find—"

"Sssshhhh!" I said, trying not to giggle while I pawed at the paper to block him, "Someone will hear you!

He yanked it away from me, barely keeping himself from laughing, "I think we should frame this." He gave up trying to hold it in, and the two of us giggled so loud the librarian actually shushed us.

Finally calming down, I went back to my seat and took another look at the clock. Three minutes until the bell went off. Knowing Chris would complain about not finding anything, I started thinking of arguments for why we should come back tomorrow while grabbing one last paper, not really expecting much. There was a story about a fire at the apple orchard across the street from Chris's house. I read the whole thing because I only vaguely remembered that night. About two months ago, fire trucks woke me up at four in the morning, and a whole mess of red and orange light flared in the distance while the Carters, the old couple who owned the orchard, stood at the side of the road and talked to the police. Nobody was hurt, but it killed a lot of their trees.

Something seemed off about the last part of the story. In the end, the police determined it started when a stray bolt of lightning struck a tree. I didn't really think about it much at the time, didn't see it as much more than a scary accident, but that was the middle of winter. Would there really have been lightening?

"Hey," I said, "Remember the fire at the Carter orchard?"

"What about it?"

I handed him the article to read and dug back through the pile of newspapers, and found one with the weather predictions for the night of the fire. It called for a clear and cold night, zero percent chance of storms. Folding my current paper to show only the weather report, I handed him that one too, and waited for him to finish.

He looked up, "So what does this mean?"

"I don't know. Doesn't it just seem kinda suspicious?"

Folding his arms, Chris leaned back in his seat and raised an eyebrow. "You think it was arson."

I bit my lip before speaking. "I mean, maybe?"

"How uncharacteristically cynical of you."

"But it could be, couldn't it? Like, Mr. Carter's house gets vandalized a lot, doesn't it? Didn't you tell me one morning a dead raccoon was hanging from one of his trees? I know it's kind of a big jump from that to burning his orchard, but I'm just saying, don't you think it's possible the police got it wrong?"

Chris rubbed his chin, looking back and forth from me to the article. All a sudden, he sat up straight with wide eyes, quickly diving back into the paper. Finally, he smacked it on the table, speaking with a kind of quiet anger, "No, they didn't get it wrong. They just didn't care."

"Huh?" I cocked my head at him, "Of course they cared. Why wouldn't they care?"

Rubbing his temples, Chris craned his neck around me to check on the librarian, who had stopped paying attention to us. A small wiggle from Chris's pointer finger told me to come closer. He leaned in to meet me halfway and whispered, "Don't you remember? A few weeks before the fire, Mrs. Carter announced she was running for State Congress. As a *Democrat*. She managed to make decent waves for a pig fucker district like this before suddenly dropping out. After the fire. And the raccoon. Sounds like some redneck got the idea to intimidate her out of the race."

Something in my stomach turned, like somewhere deep inside I knew this was way over our heads, "But the police—"

"Don't give a shit." he interrupted, "Cops are power-hungry dicks. Of course they're gonna turn a blind eye on the woman who might vote to keep them in check. We may be too late to protect the Carters, but we can get justice for them."

The bell went off, but Chris and I didn't move. We locked eyes, and the righteous determination in his face was the opposite of the queasy concern in mine. We both understood the plan for tonight without saying a word to each other.

CHAPTER 19
CHRIS

SILHOUETTES OF BRANCHES swayed as we darted between rows of apple trees, and a perfect cover of spring leaves shielded us from any headlights that might pass on the road. I never realized how huge the Carter property actually was until I had to run all the way to the far corner where the blaze began. Only when I crossed the edge of the crime scene did I notice how heavy and labored my breathing was. With no moonlight to help us see, masses of shadow rose from the ground in indistinguishable shapes.

Kelly and I snuck out to the Carter orchard at around two in the morning. I made her suit up on the off chance the perpetrators returned, but since we couldn't count on that happening, we set off with the intent of investigating the crime scene, hoping to find a clue the police neglected that would point us in the right direction.

As Kelly emerged from the maze, I flipped my phone's flashlight on and waved it around to scope the area out.

It looked like they were getting ready to build a house. Mounds of unearthed soil were haphazardly piled all around the land. Away from the healthy, blossoming trees, ashen logs were stacked beside an imposing backhoe.

Kelly looked over her shoulder, her helmet not masking her nervousness, "So," she said, lingering in front of the machinery, "What are we looking for again?"

The ash left a smear on my fingers when I brushed them against a log. Rubbing my thumb and index finger together, a sharp irritation filled my nostrils as I sniffed the ash for any trace of gasoline. I blew it out with a sharp sneeze.

"Evidence," I said, coughing, "Anything indicating foul play."

She said nothing. I crouched and shined my light over the dirt to comb through footprints, tire tracks, and treads. To my dismay, the tracks looped around and around until they stopped at the wheel of Mr. Carter's tractor, not a trail to a getaway car. When I stood up, Kelly stayed rooted in place, shifting her weight from one foot to the other, her right arm wrapped around her body.

"Yes?" I said.

She hesitated for just a moment. "Um, Chris? It's been at least a month since the fire. If there was any kind of evidence, I don't think it would still be here."

"Sure it would. Why wouldn't it?"

"Well, Mr. Carter's been working in this area the whole time. I mean, if there were tracks or anything, don't you think they'd be covered up?" She took a few gentle steps over to me, "And if there really was something suspicious, don't you think he would've found it?"

I considered her point while taking a broader look at the property. The shadows of tractors and freshly planted trees punctuated the landscape for what seemed like forever. Even though the fire only took out a fourth of the orchard, that fourth covered an enormous amount of land. Mr. Carter started the process of replanting as soon as he squared away the insurance and the weather permitted it; his farmhands were on the job for almost two weeks now and they *still* hadn't finished. Looking at it that way, the idea of traipsing through every square inch of the ruined orchard searching for the place the fire started—especially when, in all likelihood, some careless worker destroyed whatever evidence the perp left—was batshit insanity.

My attention turned toward the Carter house itself, where a single apple tree, larger than the rest in the maze, shaded the edge of the road and invited customers to stop by. Mr. Carter had to cut a frozen raccoon corpse from its branches. If memory served, that would have happened about two weeks before the fire. Some time ago, but worth investigating nonetheless.

I motioned for Kelly to follow me back toward the road. "Let's check the big tree out front. The culprit might have left something there."

It quickly became apparent we weren't going to find anything. No matter how long I dug around in the dirt, no matter how high in the tree I climbed, I wouldn't find a smoking gun. Making a token effort to search the scene, I gave up after a few minutes and stuck my hands in my pockets. Kelly didn't even bother searching, waiting for me to finish before she spoke.

"Maybe we should try talking to Mr. and Mrs. Carter."

"You out of your mind? They're going to think it was us! What would we even say to them? 'Hey Mrs. C, we're investigating your unsolved arson case. Can you give us a list of everybody who hates you? It would really help.'"

She threw up her hands, "I dunno, it was just an idea! Come on, we're not gonna find anything snooping around."

Since I knew in my heart that was true, I didn't argue with her.

"What if we just kept watch out here?" she said, "We live across the street, so we wouldn't even have to go far. We can catch the criminal red-handed if he comes back to cause trouble."

I sighed, "That won't work. Mrs. Carter already dropped out of the race. Our perp already won. If he's smart, he won't come within a mile of this place again, and if he does, it'll be the first night we call it quits and stay inside. It's not like we can stay up forever." I found myself wandering toward the road, shaking my head, "No, we have to be proactive on this. All we need is something to nudge us in the right direction."

Right as I said that, a pinprick of light blinked on the horizon, quickly growing larger and brighter. For once, Ohio's boring flat landscape made itself useful. I pointed it out to Kelly and whispered, "Hide!"

Hesitating for just a moment to confirm with her own eyes, Kelly moved so quick I couldn't even tell what direction she ran in, like she evaporated. I made a break for the orchard. The vehicle roared forward, giving me barely enough time to dive into a shadow before the headlights hit me. I hit the deck, keeping my head down until the blinding light dimmed and its rattling engine faded into a gentle rhythm in the distance.

When I lifted my eyes, I expected it to be long gone, its taillights a red speck as it barreled to some more important destination. But the piercing red light lingered on our street, swiveled as the car tore down a weed-covered path, a dirt road gone unused for what I thought were many years leading to an abandoned church about half a mile from my house.

This was it. Some benevolent god dropped a lead right into our laps. It made too much sense. The close proximity made the church an ideal spot to dump evidence during a getaway, and since nobody owned it, the criminal had plausible deniability regarding any tools or evidence found inside—after all, that could be *anyone's* gasoline.

Sweat dripped down my forehead. A sudden pang in my gut sent me sprinting out of the trees and across the road. I forced my legs to push themselves faster than my body could handle. The bitter night air stabbed at the exposed skin on my face, like I had to push through an ocean of needles to get the culprit.

The air shifted and a presence took up space next to me. Kelly. Catching up and keeping pace with nothing but a light jog, Kelly said, "Hey, where're you going?"

My elaborate explanation came out as a gasping breath. I didn't feel my lungs struggling to retain air until then, didn't notice my pace dying down as lifting each leg became an arduous process. I slowed myself to a stop. It'd be more tactical to take a sneakier approach, and I needed to save my energy in case we had to chase the bastard. Still catching my breath, I sunk to the ground and waved for Kelly to follow. We were close enough to make out the name of the old Baptist congregation on the rotting sign, gently illuminated by the taillights of what I could now tell was a pickup truck. Crouched down, we snuck closer and closer. The sign was the size of a small car, making it an excellent spot for us to hide and observe the suspect. The coast seeming clear, we dove behind it.

After waiting a second, Kelly whispered, "Chris, what are we doing?"

"We found him."

In my mind, I could see her eyes widening behind the mask, "What? How do you know?"

"There's only one kind of person who sneaks out to abandoned churches at three in the morning."

She stayed silent for the briefest moment. There was no trace of emotion in what she said next. "That's your proof. A hunch."

"It's not just a hunch. Give me another good reason he'd be out at 3 AM."

"Chris, *we're* out at 3 AM!"

"Quiet. Don't blow our cover."

The light of the still running pickup revealed all the finer details of the church. It was an unassuming lair for a terrorist, a plain wooden building with white paint flaking off every board. Its steeple seemed taller than it actually was by virtue of being on a street with nothing but ranch houses; the tip of the cross reached maybe two and a half stories up. There was only one window: a dusty glass circle hanging over a short flight of steps leading to two heavy oak doors, opened wide to reveal nothing but a dark void within. No stained glass to give it color, no crosses on the walls to signify a place of worship, nothing. It was a box, shoddily constructed decades ago and growing more pathetic with age.

Our perpetrator's vehicle made for an even sadder sight. The beaten pickup looked about twice as old as I was, every metal surface coated in rust with duct tape slapped over the cracks in the body. Thinking quickly, I pulled out my phone and snapped a photo of his license plate, and that's when I noticed the bumper stickers: Confederate flags, "Don't Tread on Me," various pro-gun slogans, all the usual shit you'd expect from the kind of asshole who'd burn down someone's livelihood because MAGA. What I didn't see in the truck was a driver.

I took a gamble. Poking my head around the sign's corner, I hoped to catch a glimpse of him and duck back into safety before he could spot me. He finally emerged, and I tried to snap a photo in my mind as I ducked back behind the sign. He fit the profile perfectly. Camo jacket, outrageously hairy chin, grungy greying hair receding far back on his skull, and a sturdy, but not overly muscular build. This was our guy, no question.

Unfortunately, I didn't get the chance to see exactly what he was doing, and I wasn't about to risk getting spotted by popping my head out again. Only the sound of heavy objects shifting in the truck's bed clued me in. There would be silence for minutes at a time once the sound of his thudding feet disappeared. Seems he was making several trips to unload stuff, but he wasn't just dropping things off at the entrance. He was gone far too long for that. But where was he disappearing to? From the outside, the church didn't seem large enough to warrant such long trips.

Finally, after maybe twenty minutes of moving stuff, the heavy slam of the oak doors told me he was finished. His wheels started to spin. The truck swiveled around and blinding headlights took the place of the warm taillights. My muscles tightened up, and both Kelly and I held our breath, waiting, unsure if he spotted us, unsure if his wheels would grind to a halt, unsure if he'd come around the corner and press a gun to our heads.

The truck kept going, leaving us in darkness once again as he tore away from the church as fast as he'd arrived. I waited with bated breath for him to stop at the orchard, but he kept going in the direction he came. Only when he finally disappeared did Kelly exhale.

"Okay," she said, not bothering to whisper anymore, "That was scary."

I barely avoided rolling my eyes. Like there was anything this Bubba could do to her. "He didn't look that tough."

"What do you think he was doing?"

I stood up and cracked my knuckles, nudging toward the church, "That's what we're here to find out."

"Wait," she said as I made my move, "You're not gonna go in, are you?"

I didn't wait, ascending the stairs leading to the imposing wooden doors. "Of course we are."

Kelly inched to the bottom of the stoop, reluctant to follow, "Chris, we can't just break in!"

I stopped, looking down at her and losing patience, "Wasn't this your idea? Weren't you the one convinced that fire was arson?"

"I never said we should break into someone's property! You don't have any proof! Sure, this guy's creepy, but that doesn't mean he's a criminal!"

"First, I doubt this is his property, and second, we're not cops. We can do whatever we want. We're going in to *find* proof, because if we don't, nobody else will bring this asshole to justice."

"Fine, but don't think I'm gonna bust the door down or something. If you wanna break the law, you can do it without me."

I rolled my eyes. Cautiously gripping one of the handles, I quickly pushed and pulled, and much to my surprise, it moved. The weight of the door forced me to summon all my strength. The whole foundation rumbled as I pushed, like one wrong move would bring the house of cards to the ground. But it opened. With only one window for the light of an absent moon to filter through, we stared into nothingness.

Even though she couldn't see it, I scrunched my face into its smuggest possible form as I turned to Kelly. She raised her hand to try and yank on strands of hair hidden behind her helmet. Finding something else to fidget with, she rolled the collar of her jacket between her fingers, "This doesn't feel right."

I sighed. "Look, how about this? I'll go in and explore the place, you stay out here and stand guard. Yell if he comes back, or someone else shows up."

I waited for Kelly to nod in understanding, clicked my phone's flashlight back on, and crossed the threshold.

The light ran to the pulpit at the end of the one-room church, glinting off webs woven between dueling rows of neglected pews. I confidently strode down the aisle, zipping my light around to uncover anything that would confirm my hunch: a can of gasoline, a length of rope, the charred remains of a burnt cross, anything. The edge of my flashlight revealed a book jammed in a pew's shelves. Thinking this was my smoking gun, some sort of manifesto or a book of receipts for everything he used to do the job, I excitedly popped the hardcover out and cracked open a random page, yellowed with age and stained with the stench of rat piss. A row of sheet music and pious lyrics were barely visible in the faded ink.

Hymns. I put the book back where I found it.

The boxes he brought in were nowhere to be found, but I couldn't imagine where he hid them. There weren't doors leading to rooms beyond. The basin used for baptisms, drained when the place stopped being a house of God, seemed my last hope. I went to the end of the aisle and shined my light inside. Nothing.

I grunted and lazed around the altar. Maybe Kelly was right. Maybe there wasn't anything illegal or suspicious going on here. Maybe this abandoned church was a passion project for the guy, like he wanted to repair it and had to come back for something urgent in the middle of the night. He did seem to be in quite the hurry.

Right on the cusp of admitting defeat, something skittered across the floor. Reflexively, I pointed my light at it, and the vague form of a mouse darted over what appeared to be a trapdoor in the back corner. I grinned and walked over to it. The door flipped open with surprising ease, like the hinges had just been used. I stood before a gaping hole with the top rungs of a ladder visible. Of course. He took all his supplies to the basement.

I descended into the pit of evil. The ladder was cold against my fingertips, but clean. No rust, no decay. Unable to hold my phone in my hand, I wished Kelly would come over and shine a light down for me, but I didn't bother calling for her. She always had a weird thing about basements. The ladder didn't take me long to descend, and soon enough my feet had solid concrete beneath them. Pulling out my phone, the first thing my light fell on in the chamber was what appeared to be a generator to my left, with wires attached to bulbs in the ceiling. Wanting the revelation to be suitably dramatic, I pulled the cord.

The generator roared to life. The lights took their time flickering on overhead, but when they did, I got my evidence.

Guns. Everywhere.

Mounted on the walls. Mounted in cabinets.

Pistols. Shotguns. Fully automatic assault rifles.

Boxes of ammo stacked to the ceiling. Scopes and other modifications.

All surrounding me.

It felt like at any moment the barrels would all turn to me on their own and fire.

CHAPTER 20

KELLY

MY HEART POUNDED as I noticed something Chris missed earlier. A long chain piled next to the door, with an open padlock sitting on top.

The church man forgot to lock it.

Seconds later, a pair of headlights rushed towards me, from the same direction the bearded man left.

I immediately shouted for Chris, "Hey, he's coming back!"

No response. What was he doing in there? He had to have heard me; the church wasn't that big. The pickup truck's bright lights blinded me even through the black tint of my visor, and I had to cover my eyes with my sleeve.

I ran into the church, and my heart sank when I saw the light shooting up from the ground. Why did Chris have to go in the basement? Still, there was no way I was leaving him there. I ran to the light and peeked down the hole. Chris had his arm wrapped around the bottom of the ladder like he could barely keep himself standing.

"Chris!" I said, just loud enough for him to hear, "We need to go!"

He stayed frozen, staring at something I couldn't see.

The light behind me shut off with the slam of a truck door. A gruff voice boomed, "*Who's there?*"

With no time to think, I hopped onto the ladder and closed the trapdoor over my head, then dropped next to Chris. I whipped around, anxious to see what had him so worked up. We stood in a small room, no bigger than my bedroom, I think, with concrete walls. A ratty mattress laid in a corner. A generator hummed next to me. Stacks and stacks of canned food rose almost to the ceiling. A single wooden door straight across from us seemed to lead deeper into the basement.

I didn't get it. Yeah, it was definitely weird, but I didn't understand why Chris was acting like a scared little boy, almost like there was a monster I couldn't see, creeping just over my shoulder. He kept shaking and I followed his eyes and found a cabinet stocked with weapons, and once I saw those, I noticed more and more. There were guns on every wall. My hair stood on its ends.

Footsteps thumped above us, and I flipped a switch on the generator to make all the lights go out. If Chris couldn't see the guns, maybe they wouldn't affect him so much. The door was our only hiding place. I reached down to grab him by the hand and guide him myself, but recoiled at the thought of breaking Rule Two. A part of me screamed to just pick him up and wait to explain until we were safe, but I had to stay calm and do this without touching him.

"Chris, I'm gonna get you out, okay? But we need to hide. He's gonna find us!"

I ran over to the door, almost giving us away when I brushed against a tower of cans, but after a little wobbling, they stayed together. I opened the door and found nothing but a cramped space with a toilet inside. My heart sank. There wasn't a whole other room for us to hide in, but at least we'd both fit. Keeping his head down, Chris's shadow darted to me, and once he was in, he slid to the floor with loud, uneven breathing.

I shut us in as quietly as I could. Being in a pitch black, enclosed space made me instinctively press against the door, like this was a punishment to make up for all the years I'd gone without one, but I had to stay calm and keep it together for both of us. Thinking of my locked basement door actually gave me an idea. I turned the knob and gave the door a light push, making sure it only swung in towards us. Raising some energy, I stood firm against it. No matter how hard he tried to open it, he wouldn't be able to push me away. He couldn't get us. All we had to do was wait until he gave up and left us alone.

The layer of wood between us muffled the creaky trapdoor. Chris's breathing got so loud that each time he exhaled, I braced myself for the bearded man's shout. I wished there was a way to comfort him without touching or talking.

Light trickled in through the cracks in the door. The low whine of the overhead lights mixed with the clicking of the rickety generator. Chris let out a small whimper. The repetitive noises must've made the anxiety worse for him. The heavy thud of the bearded man's feet smacking against the concrete signaled a very real threat. He took his time, stepping into a rhythm as he covered every square inch of his room. The seconds that passed while his footsteps came closer and closer to us were the longest of my entire life. I could feel his stare digging into me through the door.

"Now you listen here," he finally said, "'Cause I'm only gonna say this once. I don't know who you are, or what you think you're planning by hiding in there, and I don't much care. I ain't stupid enough to get close. I'm giving you five seconds to get out of my commode and give yourself up."

I wondered if maybe I should just do what he said, say something or open the door to try and minimize the damage. Sure, he couldn't get in, but then what? We were trapped. If a chance to escape came, we wouldn't even know to take it because we couldn't see.

POW.

The explosion of a shotgun made my energy rise, like my body knew it'd need to protect itself before I was conscious of the danger. A cluster of pellets shredded through the door at my back and ripped holes into my clothing; hot metal pressed against my skin and gently bounced off it, clattering harmlessly to the floor after rolling down my spine. Chris shrieked like a terrified animal, burying his face in his knees and slapping his arms over the top of his head for cover.

The man followed his shot with a defined pump of his gun. His voice lowered to a crazed snarl, "You picked the wrong property to trespass, boy. I hate cops and know how to use every single one of these guns."

Our attacker punctuated his sentence with another blast of his shotgun, and once again the pellets came through and bounced off my body. This time, Chris started talking to himself, but everything he said seemed like gibberish. Whether the gunman was getting caught up in the rush of the moment, or he was just sick enough to enjoy the thought of shooting a person over and over, I don't know, but that's exactly what he did. He unloaded shell after shell into the door, getting into a flow of shooting and pumping and shooting and pumping.

The gun's wide spread meant a few shots managed to rip past me, cracking holes in the door to bring more light into the room. I could see Chris swing his head up, but his wild eyes weren't looking at me. He wasn't looking at anything.

"Shoot me!" he screamed.

My eyes widened in horror. He kept screaming at the gunman, *"They need Dad, not me! They don't want me! Please, leave him alone, this is my fault!"*

Although I stood between Chris and the gun like a stone wall, I wasn't protecting him. Not really. Each shot inflicted another wound on Chris, pierced his memories and made the absolute worst moment of his life bleed back out. I was letting the gunman hurt him.

I don't really know how to describe what happened next. I wouldn't say that I snapped. When you snap, you lose control in a big outburst, but the actions I took next were very deliberate. All of a sudden I knew exactly what had to be done. I drew my fist back as I turned around, slamming it into the door with an explosion far more powerful than anything his weapon could do. A flurry of splinters blew towards the gunman, who turned out to be unimpressive in full light. An arm dangling at his side gripped a black combat shotgun, while the other shielded himself from the shards of door flying at him.

"Jesus *fuck!*" he shouted.

I calmly took a step, my hands clenched into fists. The gunman scrambled to level the weapon at me and fire, reacting with the only instinct he had. Every single pellet hit me square in the chest.

It tickled.

With nothing to be afraid of, I kept going, and the gunman's mouth dropped as he fired his last three rounds into me, and though my costume was a tattered mess of bullet holes, not a single shell slowed me down. When I was close enough to feel his breath, he was in too much shock to run away. I snatched the gun from him. To be sure I made my point, I held it out right in front of his face, where he wouldn't be able to look away. Squeezing the gun, a sickening grind echoed as the metal reshaped in my hands like clay.

After crushing the barrel, I let it fall to the ground. The gunman finally let out a cry that showed how pathetic he was without his toys. He tripped trying to run away, screaming, stumbling as he threw himself on the ladder.

I let him go.

Chris. I needed to check on Chris. With the door smashed away and the light coming in, he was clearly visible on the ground, tucked next to the toilet. All sorts of worries flooded back. Did one of the stray pellets hit him when the gunman shot at me? Did he see Chris's face? Leroy was so small. If he filed a police report or, even worse, decided to hunt him down for revenge, he'd be able to find him. Oh god, please let him have been too focused on me to notice him. I'd been so careless, but I had to worry about that later. Chris was the only thing that mattered now.

I shouted his name as I ran to him. He recoiled as he looked up at me with his big puppy eyes, filled with pain and confusion and terror. Sinking to my knees, I leaned forward to get on his eye level and said, "Chris, it's okay! It's okay, I got rid of him! He's gone! You're safe!"

He jerked his head away and whimpered like I was some kind of monster.

Oh god, what's wrong with him?

Then I realized I was still wearing that stupid helmet. I ripped it off and chucked it over my shoulder, shaking the hair out of my eyes. I leaned forward and started tearing up.

"Chris. Chris, look at me. Please be okay."

CHAPTER 21
CHRIS

IT'S NOT SUPPOSED to happen like this. He's supposed to run, not come closer. Go away, you already killed him. Go away. Leave me alone. What are you doing with your face, why are you taking it off. I don't want to know who you really are. Stop talking. Either kill me or leave like you're supposed to—

A wild mess of shining blonde hair appeared with two glittering rubies where eyes should have been. Kelly. If only she'd shown up a little earlier. She could have saved Dad.

She grounded me back in the present moment. The basement, the real world, started to fade in around her. If I looked away from her eyes I knew I'd slip back into the past, so I focused on them even though I could start crying at any second. I wanted her to hold me.

But that very thought filled me with shame. The danger was gone. I didn't need coddling, and it's pathetic that I'd want it for even a second. I ripped my eyes away from her and jumped to my feet, clenching my fists and gritting my teeth to burn away the oncoming tears with anger and defiance.

Kelly didn't get up from the floor. Worry dripped from every pore of her face, "Chris?"

"I'm fine." My voice wavered, and I cleared my throat to make my next statement sound decisive, "Good work. That'll get him to think twice next time he wants to fuck with anyone around here."

I couldn't be sure of that. I didn't know what Kelly did to get rid of him. I didn't know if he was even the culprit. I didn't know if he even existed at all, or if the gunman was something I imagined upon losing my shit. Kelly must have thought I was out of my fucking mind.

"Let's go." I started moving, keeping my eyes to the floor to avoid Kelly's judgement and the sight of all the weapons I may or may not have imagined. A shotgun with a misshapen barrel sent a shudder through me, and I picked up the pace. Did Kelly do that?

Did… did she get shot?

I stole a quick glance behind me. She scooped up the remains of her helmet, which shattered when it hit the wall after she threw it. A smattering of rips and holes ran up and down the back of her jacket like smallpox scars, and when she turned forward, dozens of holes were concentrated on her chest. Like she'd walked away from a firing squad.

I had to force myself to turn around. I didn't want her to say anything. I didn't want to stare at the truth: I was fragile, and she was invincible.

I think I hated her.

My arms still felt weak, but I summoned what little strength remained to climb up the ladder. It wasn't tall. I could do it. But about halfway up my foot slipped, making me look down to correct myself. Kelly waited at the bottom with her arms held out, ready to catch me when I fell.

Scowling, I forced myself to climb faster. I didn't need her to carry me.

CHAPTER 22

KELLY

THE MORNING AFTER, I ate breakfast like any other day. Chris and I took the bus, the way we used to since he was still grounded. We complained about classes like any other day.

Okay. I'm really tall. That guy had to look up to shoot at me, and Chris was on the ground, and he had his face covered, and I was blocking him, and that guy was so shocked he wouldn't think to check if there was someone else in his bathroom. He'd assume I was the only one there. He won't come after Chris, and even if he does, I can stop him.

The bus stopped in front of the railroad tracks like any other day. I caught myself glancing over my shoulder and saw a police car waiting in the back window. At any moment I expected the lights to come on and for him to get out, yank us out of our seats and slam us on the hood of his car while all the freshman and sophomores watched, but after we crossed the tracks, the officer turned the other way at the gas station intersection. Obviously, he needed more evidence. He'd want to talk to the kids at the party about what they'd seen, get Fern's account of what happened at the paranormal club, maybe get another interview with Lorenzo and Francesco. I'd been so careless with my powers. I couldn't stop checking news stories about the Cleveland earthquake, wondering if anybody had gotten hurt when a piece of furniture fell over in their house. Nothing reported but property damage, yet. But somebody who lived alone probably got crushed and nobody found them. I needed to keep checking all the local news sites for at least the next month. I was getting too comfortable in my own skin. I was forgetting why I spent so many years keeping myself in check.

No Kelly, it'll be okay. If the church guy was going to call the police he would've done it as soon as he saw the open door. His first reaction was to try and shoot us. That's not the kind of guy who calls the police when he sees something weird. He won't want them to know about his creepy shelter, and he's got all sorts of guns that probably aren't legal to have, and even if he does call, nobody will believe him. And he didn't see our faces. He can't prove it. We'll be okay.

But as the bus dropped us off, I couldn't get the image of a SWAT team out of my head, swarming the high school, tearing us out of class with guns pointed at us. Or the image of an angry man walking into Leroy High with an assault rifle, going through each and every classroom looking for Chris, pinning him against the wall, demanding to know more about his invincible friend before filling him with bullets.

I hoisted my bag on my shoulder. Right as I stepped

outside, Chris stopped me, "Wait, before we go in, I wanted to talk about what we're going to do next."

I was stunned. How could he possibly be thinking about that? "Can we talk about it at lunch? I don't wanna be late."

Chris said nothing, leading me the opposite way everyone else was walking. Once we were alone at one of the school's side entrances, he lowered his voice, "This will only take a second. We can hash out the details later, but I think we should hit Leroy's drug dealers next."

Leroy's *drug dealers?* Did he already forget last night? When I didn't immediately jump in and tell him what a stupid idea that was, he took that as a sign to keep going, "I walked in on my mom interrogating Thomas this morning—you know Will Kramer? The football player with the Viking beard? A couple days ago he went to the hospital for a heroin overdose and Mom was losing her shit about it. Will's the third person from Leroy High in the past couple months to get fucked up by heroin. Apparently it's a real problem in Podunk towns like this one. If we cut the head off the snake, we can save a ton of lives. Plus—"

I stopped paying attention to what he was saying and just let him talk. It hit me all at once, made things crystal clear: this was insane. If we kept going like this, I was gonna get Chris killed. A few days ago, I had to laugh along and pretend I wasn't horrified when he finally told me about the way Nigel came after him with a machete. The church incident made him believe I was a suit of armor that could shield him from anything. For anyone else, getting shot at by a crazy gunman would be enough to show that we were in over our heads, but Chris didn't care. If things went wrong again, I could take care of it. What would we have to deal with if we went after drug dealers? Knives? Dogs? More guns? I screwed up and let our plans fall apart every time we went out. How many stupid, pointless displays of my power would it take before somebody got really hurt? How many screw ups before he ends up in the hospital? How would I explain to his mom at his funeral that I put him in danger over and over again? All it takes is one mistake. So long as I was doing this stupid superhero thing, Chris would wanna help.

Well, not anymore. Nobody was gonna get hurt because of me ever again. Especially not my little buddy.

Finally, I just came out and said it, "Chris, I think we need to stop."

He groaned, "I *knew* you'd say that! Look, last night was freaky, but you handled it. We're fine. That's no reason to give up so quick."

"That's not it. I don't wanna quit because I'm scared."

That was a lie. I was scared, just not for myself. But how could I tell him that? I knew Chris too well. If I told him the truth, he'd take it personally, like I was accusing him of weighing me down. He'd get mad and spend the rest of the week in a funk, and if it got bad enough, he might even start another fight and get himself expelled with only a month left of school. Whatever explanation I gave needed to be soft. So, I lied.

"Don't get me wrong, I really appreciate you doing this for me, but I dunno, I feel okay now."

His irritation gave way to confusion. We were on the right track.

"I don't understand," he said, "Doing what for you?"

"I mean, back at Leroy's Landing, that's why you wanted me to destroy that barn, right? To make me feel better? And what you kept saying about how I could change the world, that wasn't really true, but you wanted me to feel good about myself, right?" I put on my gentlest smile, "Well, it worked! I've never been better, so we don't really need to do this anymore."

Chris was stunned, "Kelly, this isn't supposed to be a pity party. I meant everything I said."

"No, no, I didn't mean it like that. I just… I dunno, maybe we should quit while we're ahead. Go back to being plain old Chris and Kelly while we still can."

The hurt on his face made me feel guilty. I thought he'd try and fight me more on this. "That's really what you want?" he said.

"I think it's for the best, don't you?"

"No."

Wanting an excuse to end the conversation, I pulled out my phone and saw the clock tick closer to the start of class, "I mean, if I'm wrong, we can always try again, right? But hey, I've gotta go. I have a question I need answered before first period. Catch you later!"

I left him in the lot behind me. That was another lie, but it gave me some time to distance myself from Chris. I didn't check to see if he was following me or how he reacted to the sudden end to our superhero careers. Because if I turned around, I'd start thinking about the joy on his face when I pushed us on the carousel, or the funny way he got flustered when something didn't go exactly the way he planned, or the sun rising while we ate breakfast together, or spending a whole hour-long car ride making fun of Fern, or any of the other fun things we did over the past month. I couldn't let myself miss it. To keep going along with his dangerous ideas because I was having fun wasn't just stupid, it was selfish. I had to be more responsible than that.

It was over. Back to ordinary Chris and Kelly.

CHAPTER 23

CHRIS

THE CLOCK STRUCK 3 AM when I finally made my move. Not only would my family be asleep by that time, but sitting awake in the dark for so long allowed my eyes to adjust. Thomas's room was directly across the hall from mine, so waking Mom shouldn't be an issue. Thing is, our house was old, and the floors had a tendency to creak. I had to approach this carefully. Before our grandparents moved down south, Thomas and I shared a room, but that was so long ago I couldn't remember anything about his sleeping habits. Would he stir with every little noise? Did he have a set time he'd get up and use the bathroom? Was he completely out until his alarm roused him? There were too many unknowns.

At that moment, there was only one thing I knew for sure: Kelly was lying to me. Her decision to quit on me made perfect sense all at once, when the announcements reminded us to get our prom tickets while we still could.

She saw our hero work as a game, a fun thing to do after school, not anything meaningful. Now that a rich prince had descended from on high and invited her to the ball, she had no reason to bother with the ridiculous fantasy I constructed for her. How fortunate, that she'd make some cool friends at the very end of her senior year. Who needs Chris, anyway?

Of course I knew about her and Noah. The only thing stupider than her decision to actually say yes to that piece of shit was her decision to hide it from me, as if I wouldn't find out. It was a big fucking deal. The highest rung on the social ladder going to prom with one of the lowest? After his girlfriend of four goddamn years just dumped him? People were asking me what I knew all week.

Being temporarily relieved of sidekick duty, I redirected my mental energy to investigating the matter. I didn't believe for one second that Noah was so charmed by Kelly's performance at his party that he simply had to invite her to prom. For one, as far as I knew, he hadn't spoken another word to his supposed date since then, and also *fucking come on.* How dumb does Kelly have to be to buy this? To think that Leroy's richest, hottest guy would suddenly fall for the girl with half a foot on him in a Sailor Moon t-shirt, the same girl he and his crowd had spent the last ten years mocking, just because she was nice to him once, was absolute lunacy. No, there was something sinister happening, a plot her trusty sidekick wouldn't allow to come to fruition.

Still being grounded gave me at least one advantage: without the ability to go hang out with Kelly or distract myself with entertainment, I could keep an eye on

Thomas and wait for the perfect opportunity to strike. His phone was as good a place to start as any, and I suspected Thomas was the mastermind anyway. He and Noah were close, and Thomas's douchebag resume was much more robust. Thomas thought Kelly's unmasking at the party was damned hilarious. He likely figured he could squeeze a few more chuckles out of her this way. Even if Thomas wasn't behind this, Noah was the closest thing my brother had to a best friend. They had to be texting about it. He had to have something that definitively proved, in writing, that Noah was tricking her, evidence she couldn't deny no matter how hard she wanted to.

Getting my hands on the thing would be the tricky part. Thomas might as well have gorilla glued his phone to his hand. He only put it down to sleep and to shower, and barging in on him in the shower was *not* an option. Thus, my creeping around at 3 AM.

When I pretended to go to sleep, I had the foresight to leave my door slightly open to minimize the noise when I left, and I'm pleased to say I emerged from my room without a sound. Immediately, I tiptoed to his door and pressed my ear against it. A fan's gentle hum buzzed through the wood and provided a backdrop for the up and down rhythm of Thomas's harsh snoring. Good. There was enough sound to cover my entrance, and an easy way to tell if Thomas woke up.

I turned the knob as gently as possible, took a deep breath, and gave it a light push. It wasn't light enough. The door ricketed and creaked as I opened it just far enough for me to slide my skinny self through.

The snoring stopped. I let go of the knob and jumped

back. Over the roar of his fan, I thought I heard him shuffling in bed. Praying he was too groggy to notice the door, I waited for him to fall back asleep, prepared to rush back in my room on the off chance he got up to shut it, or worse, came out in the hall to see who disturbed him.

My worries went away when the snoring started up again. Not wasting any time, I slithered in Thomas's room, gracefully dodging the piles of dirty clothes littering his floor and arriving at his bedside where, sure enough, the phone resting next to his head served as an alarm clock. With the skill of a pickpocket, I wrapped my fingers around the phone and lifted it without making a sound. My retreat was as silent and efficient as my entrance.

I left the door ajar—I'd need to plant the phone back in his room to avoid suspicion—and paused to see if he stirred. He didn't. So far so good. Just in case Mom woke up to get a glass of water, I retreated to my room so she wouldn't find me playing with Thomas's phone in the middle of the hall. Then, maybe a little too enthusiastically, I dived on my bed and clicked the unlock button.

I had to keep myself from swearing out loud. It needed a four-digit code to unlock. He wasn't a complete dipshit after all. I tapped every number that had even the slightest significance to Thomas. Our birthday. The year we were born. The numbers of some of his favorite sports stars. The year we moved. Mom's birthday. Dad's birthday.

With that last one Thomas's home screen greeted me, a mess of unorganized apps around a New York Giants background, and I couldn't believe my luck. I immediately dived into his text messages, only slightly disheartened to find his contacts all had cutesy nicknames, leaving me unable to identify Noah or anyone else. However, through process of elimination and my knowledge of the social ecosystem, it didn't take me long to deduce who "Moneybag$" was. I opened up their conversations and scrolled through. I couldn't believe my eyes. I'd never seen anything so despicable.

Moneybag$

> AHAHAHAHAHAHAHA
> i CANNOT believe this
> whens the wedding?

Shut up.
You said they were dating.
That she'd probably be going with your brother.

> oh dont you try and blame me
> i had no idea YOU were planning on asking her
> my boy are you okay
> did Annie break your brain?
> you know you can do better

I don't know what I was thinking, alright?
I felt bad for her.
But I'm gonna tell her that Annie and I got
back together.
It's over. Stop riding my ass about it.

> yeah sure you did
> i think you should take her
> way everyone makes it sound
> you were gettin along real well at that party

1. I had no way of knowing that was her
2. I was drunk.

> you were NOT drunk
> come on this will be a great story for your kids
> nasty old bitch broke your heart
> Prince Kelly swept in
> and you saw something in her nobody else
> ever could
> beauty and the beast
> but like reversed

Go fuck yourself.
This isn't funny.

> your right
> its hilarious
> im serious though
> take sasquatch
> itll be funny as fuck
> you don't have a date anyway
> and can you imagine her trying to dance?
> we can get her on prom court and everything
> i bet shell even wear the gimp suit instead of a
> dress if you ask her

Okay, that's kind of a funny thought.
But this is the only prom I'll ever get.

> ditch her when you get there
> we get our entertainment
> you sneak off to dance with whoever you want
> my brother's girl gets taken from right under him

everyone wins

That's a real dick move.
Even if she is gross.

dont be a pussy
shes like autistic i think
wont even know the difference
tell you what ill sweeten the deal
if you actually bring sasquatch to prom
ill give you $200
thats your tickets paid for plus a little extra
even a rich fuck like you can never have
enough cash

You don't have 200 dollars to give.

nevermind where the money is coming from
i can get it to you by friday
come on dude at least think about it
you still have a month to back out

Fine. I'll consider it.
But if I don't have the money by Friday
Or if I change my mind,
I'm telling her that Annie and I got back together.

HAHAHAHAHA YES
this is gonna be awesome
and who knows
if you pregame hard enough
maybe youll trick yourself into thinking shes hot
you know what?

ill double it if you fuck her

Haha I wouldn't do that for two THOUSAND.
Can you imagine? It'd be like having sex with a gorilla.

I wanted to murder him. Both of them. I wanted to grab a knife from the kitchen and slit Thomas's throat while he slept. I wanted to drive to Noah's mansion and burn it to the fucking ground. How dare these heartless bastards try to exploit her like this. It was worse than some prank to embarrass her in front of the whole school. She *was* the joke. They were going to point and laugh at her just for being herself.

With Thomas's phone in my hands, I had the perfect opportunity for vengeance. I wanted to smash his precious phone into pieces. I wanted to send a billion texts and embarrassing photos into the world to destroy his reputation. But nothing seemed good enough. For this, no punishment was too severe.

It came to me at once. Calmly, I walked over to my window and threw it open. I scampered out and, shivering in the cold night air, marched straight toward the Hatfield house with the evidence in hand. This wasn't my vengeance to take.

Kelly had to know, and she had to know now. There was no way I could sit on this knowledge all weekend. Since I was still technically grounded, Mom would be watching me like a hawk the whole time. I'd never get away, and this information was too cruel to casually reveal over a midnight text message. I had to deliver it in person.

I found her window and knocked on it hard enough to wake her. Thomas would finally pay the price for everything he's done over the years. Little did he know, any pain he could dish out, Kelly could return a thousand times harder.

CHAPTER 24

KELLY

I YAWNED AS I opened the window, not fully getting how strange it was to see him outside my window since I was still half-asleep. "Chris?" I said, "What are you doing?"

He said nothing as he pulled himself inside. With groggy footsteps, I went back to my bed and sat down. He cleared his throat while playing with something in his hands. Sitting up as straight as I could, I tried to force myself awake. This had to be important if he came to tell me in the middle of the night himself. He gave no big explanation for what I was about to see, simply tapping the phone before he reached out and said, "You need to see this."

I took it without asking questions, assuming it'd all make sense once I fully woke up. At first, it was like trying to read a foreign language. Then I hit my name. I stopped and reread the message chain from the start all the way to the end.

That woke me up. I scrolled back to the top. Reading one more time confirmed what I always knew but didn't want to admit. Each insult added a little more weight to all the ones before. Sasquatch. Gross. Autistic. Gorilla. They merged together. Everything I ever was and ever would be.

My limbs went limp, and the phone slipped out of my hands. I let it bounce against my bed onto the floor. No energy burned inside me; no tears dripped from my eyes.

"Listen—" Chris started.

But I didn't wanna hear it. I didn't wanna be there. Standing up and staring right past him, I walked out my door, not caring if I woke Grandma and Grandpa up as I blew through the house and went outside, greeting the night covered by nothing but the thin cloth of my pajamas. I didn't wanna talk to Chris or anybody else ever again. Not stopping or hesitating, I walked further into my backyard, towards the woods.

After a few minutes of total silence, completely calm on the outside while I weaved between trees, I arrived at the clearing where Chris and I first met. Fallen logs, the leftovers from my childhood temper tantrums, rotted all around the clearing.

My insides boiled and I tore my throat apart. I punched the tree and the force made a shockwave that carved a path through the woods, pulverizing the trees closest to me and knocking over ones far beyond where I could see in the dark. They fell like dominos, one after the other, and echoed for miles. There was nothing left of the tree I hit.

Drained, my fist fell to my side as I collapsed onto a log and broke down, screaming and crying and unable to breathe from the snot coming from my nose. I hated Chris for finding out about prom and digging up those texts. I hated Thomas for making a game out of my life. I hated Noah for playing along and pretending to be nice to me. I hated Annie for being pretty and popular and the kind of girl Noah likes. I hated Dad for not leaving me in the garbage where I belonged. But most of all, I hated myself. I hated myself for being stupid enough to think anyone could see me as anything other than an unlovable monster.

"Holy shit…"

I whipped around, and found Chris lurking in the shadows, staring at the aftermath of my punch. He *followed* me?

"*Leave me alone!*" I screamed.

"Woah," he took a few steps forward with his hands up, "Take it easy, I want to talk."

"No! You've done enough!"

The confused look on his face made me wanna snap his scrawny little neck. Like he didn't know. I choked back my anger and tried to talk normally, "Was this the first thing you thought when you found out? That nobody would ever wanna go to prom with me? Well you were right! Noah wouldn't ever actually go to prom with me and it was all a big conspiracy to make me look stupid! Happy? Is that all you care about? Being right?"

"No." Chris inched closer, his voice soft and tender, "Kelly, it's not like that at all. What kind of friend would I be if I didn't look out for you?"

"I didn't ask you to look out for me! Do you think I'm stupid, Chris? Do you think the idea that this was all too good to be true never crossed my mind? Do you think—" my thought devolved into wordless, noisy sobbing as I turned my back to him, "I just wanted to believe that someone liked me. Is that wrong? Why couldn't you have just been happy for me? You could've minded your own business and kept your mouth shut and let me think everything was fine!"

Chris paused. "I know you're upset, but you can't be serious."

"I never would've known the difference. I would've gone to prom and had a great time and I would've had no idea everyone was laughing at me!"

"That's not what you want and you know it. I'm sorry it turned out this way Kelly, I really am, but I won't let you live a lie like that." The soft squish of his footsteps against the mud drew him closer to me, "You may not be able to unsee it now, but you can do something better. You can do something about it."

Shock stopped my tear ducts. Slowly, I craned my neck around to him, and saw something sinister in Chris I never noticed before. Something slimy and manipulative, looking at me like a character in a game he could just take control of whenever he wanted. My body went cold. I finally understood. Everything had come together.

"And what, exactly, does that mean, Chris? What exactly do you think I should do about it?" Right as he was about to launch into another one of his disgusting speeches, I cut him off, my voice rising in anger. "I think I know. You want me to show up to prom in a mask, and you want me to trash it, right?"

Chris stopped himself, taking his time to phrase his words very carefully, "They don't know we know yet. I'm just saying, we're in the perfect position to get payback when they aren't expecting it."

"Payback." I rolled the word around in my head, stood up and walked right into his face. He never seemed so tiny until then. "You know, if a certain someone didn't convince me to crash a certain someone else's party in a stupid costume, they never would've come after me. They would've left me alone." I put heavy emphasis on the next part, "*I* wouldn't have to get payback for anything."

Chris glared at me. "You can't pin this on me. If you stuck to the plan, they'd have no idea it was you."

"Right. The plan. Everything was always about *the plan*. What was the plan, again?"

"Look, cut the bullshit. If you have something to say to me, come out and say it."

"I'm saying, Chris, that I don't think the plan was ever about helping people. It wasn't about changing the world, it wasn't about having fun, and it definitely wasn't about making me feel good. I think this was about payback all along. That's why you wanted me to crash Noah's party. Not because of whatever excuse you gave me, but because you knew Thomas would be there. You know you can't beat him in a fight, so you thought you could get me to terrorize him for you. And then, when I said I was through, you thought you could get me back to doing your dirty work by showing me those texts. You don't care about me at all."

Chris struggled to keep an even temper, "That's ridiculous. You're my best friend. I was looking out for you."

"Stop lying to me if you care so much! Admit it! Admit this was all a twisted fucking revenge fantasy from the start!"

Chris clenched his fists and glared at me. "Fine. I'll admit it. That was part of the plan. It wasn't the only part. It wasn't even the main part. But it was part of it."

"You used me."

"Yes I did, and I'd do it again, because you know what? Say what you want about me, but at least when I have problems, I try to do something about them. I'm not the kind of fucking baby who ignores reality when it doesn't suit her delicate fairy tale sensibilities. I'm not the kind of *coward,* who turns her back on her friend while he's getting the shit kicked out of him, *again, and again, and again!"*

"How many of those fights did you start, Chris? Do you wanna know why I really wanted to stop being a superhero? It wasn't because I felt better, it was because of *you.* I didn't wanna be responsible when one of your stupid little plans got you killed. You think you're so smart and tough, but you're pathetic. Your brain doesn't even work right without a bunch of pills you're too stupid to take."

Chris blew up, screaming louder than he ever had, "You want to play that game? You want to talk about pathetic? Look at yourself! Boo fucking hoo, everyone feel sorry for Kelly Hatfield and her godlike power! It's just so goddamn *hard* to be her! Nobody likes you because your powers are the only interesting thing about you! Without them, you're just another worthless hillbilly in a shithole town full of them! *I* wouldn't even be your friend!"

I hit my breaking point. I stepped forward into Chris's space and he realized what was about to happen before I did. The anger disappeared from him as his face went white. He tried to step back and almost dodged in time. I went to shove him and my fingertips barely brushed against his chest.

But that was enough.

A horrible crunch rang through the woods as Chris

shot backward, his body helpless as it blew through the air, landing with another crack as he slammed on the ground. He made no scream or cry of pain as he went limp.

At once the inferno burning in me went out. I covered my mouth with my hands and froze, too scared to face the consequences of my anger up close.

He isn't moving.

Oh god, he isn't moving.

CHAPTER 25

CHRIS

THE FIRST THING I can remember was being strapped down, staring up at a blurry white light. My ringing ears gave way to screaming sirens and the beeping monitor keeping track of my frantically pulsing heart. Someone hovered over me, but in my grogginess I couldn't tell who it was.

"…Kelly?"

As soon as I spoke, pain shot through every last inch of me, like laying on a bed made of a thousand knives while being crushed by an eighteen-wheeler. I couldn't breathe. Panicking and suffocating, I thrashed and whimpered, but the stretcher kept me locked down tight. I wasn't even aware of the mask around my mouth until air rushed through the tube and forced itself down my throat. The cool relief taunted me, fading quickly.

The gentle voice of a kind sounding man briefly took my mind away from the agony, "Hey buddy, how you holding up?"

A bump in the road rocked my bones and twisted the knives. My vision went dark for a moment, and even after it came back, my brain was a swirling mess of noise and light. I needed to make this brief second of lucidity count.

"Where's Kelly?" A neck brace stopped me from surveying the interior of the ambulance.

"It's alright, you don't need to worry about your friend. Now Chris, do you think you can help me with something? What do you remember? Can you tell me what happened?"

"I don't know." I said instantly, unsure if it was a lie. Brief images I couldn't sustain flashed through my mind. The shaking rattle of the earth. The weight of someone's palm crushing my chest. The whiplash when I crashed to a halt after soaring through the air. Red eyes powered by fury. I promised her. I promised I'd keep her secret safe, and I'd already done so much to jeopardize it. Even if it would keep me alive, I couldn't betray her like that. I couldn't point them in her direction.

My head felt lighter. I didn't have much time. "Am I going to die?"

The kind man assured me I wouldn't. That I was going to be just fine. I didn't believe him.

"It's okay if I do. Just not yet. Keep me around for a little longer."

I don't know if he ever responded to that. A monstrous force wrapped around me and dragged me into the black depths of unconsciousness. The last thing I heard was someone shout.

"We're losing him!"

CHAPTER 26

CHRIS

I DIDN'T DIE that night, but for the next 24 hours I wish I had. Fading in and out of various levels of consciousness and lucidity, the only constant was pain. The kind of pain that makes you forget what normal is. The kind of pain where you can't even muster the strength to cry or scream. The kind of pain you can't begin to comprehend until you've had your arm snapped into several pieces.

Since my chest and arm were bad enough, I had to be airlifted to a trauma surgeon all the way over in Cleveland. Even with the hearing protection they gave me, the constant roar of the helicopter displaced me, the mental trauma of the past and the physical anguish of the present playing a deadly tug of war.

After what seemed like hours, we finally landed, and they rushed me from exam room to exam room, breathing machine to breathing machine, operating table to operating table. With my fractured sternum dangerously close to stabbing my own heart and a severe concussion, they couldn't risk putting me under for the surgery, so they had to lock me down for sedation and make do with local anesthetic.

Or maybe they did put me under. I don't know. My memory of that first day in the hospital is nearly non-existent, so all I have to go on is what Mom and the nurses told me. They must have done CAT scans or MRI's at some point to check for permanent brain damage, but I don't know if that was after the surgery (surgeries?) or before it or what. Did they do more than one? The first night or two in the hospital all collapses together, a non-linear mess drawing pieces of previous hospital trips in its grasp.

The surgeon binds the six separated pieces of my radius together with a steel bar. The police ask me to describe the man with the gun. The nurses put me in another machine. They stitch the gash in my skull back together. The psychologist prepares to tell Mom that she's a widow now. They crack open my chest to replace the fragmented bone threatening my heart with metal plates. The whole time I'm at once outside my body and feeling the wrath of every single nerve. Only after the whole ordeal is over does time slip back into linear form, if only because the night after was the most hellish of my entire life, the harsh influx of air from my respirator and the omnipresent pain conspiring to keep me from sleep.

The next day was more of the same. More tests, more pain. The doctor gave me the lowdown on what to expect, as well as the story she was told. Another one of the inexplicable freak earthquakes Ohio's been having for the first time in decades hit while Kelly and I snuck out in the middle of the night, and a tree collapsed on me. The operations went about as smoothly as one could hope. The broken bones in my chest didn't puncture any vital organs, but they were going to keep me on the ventilator for a few more days in case my lungs were bruised. Because I landed on my arm, it bore the brunt of the impact. It would have to stay in a cast for months, and the blunt force trauma damaged the nerves. With extensive physical therapy I'd be able to get most of its function back, but the chances of it ever going back to full strength were low. At least I didn't have much strength to lose.

Finally, though they continued monitoring the after-shocks of my concussion, she was happy to report there weren't any signs of permanent brain damage. I just thought it was a miracle that I was alive and mostly conscious. If my sternum broke in just a slightly different way, it would have punctured my lungs and I'd have died. If I landed directly on my back instead of my arm, my spine would have snapped and I'd have died. If I crashed into a tree, I'd have died. If I'd hit my head a little harder, I'd be a vegetable.

The doctor also had some good news for me: visitors could start coming in. More pain shot through me as I tried to sit up straight. I nodded along with what the doctor said, but disappeared into my own thoughts to plan what I'd say when Kelly walked in. But what could I say? Should I wait for her to say something first? Maybe play it cool, try to smile and do my best to act like everything was normal. Make a few cracks about the way they shaved my head to suture my scalp, or some jokes about how all the metal in my chest basically made me Iron Man. Yeah. That sounded good. She'd laugh and know nothing had changed, that we were still friends. After school she'd come back and bring me my homework, and we'd shoot the shit while she sat down and drew something on my cast. If we had to talk about what happened in the woods, we could do it later. Everything would be fine.

I eased myself back down while the doctor ran to grab her, and the more time went by, the more nervous and uncertain I became.

A shock ran through my system when Mom, not Kelly, rushed in, forcing me in a tight, painful embrace.

"Thank god," she whispered, "My stupid, wonderful, stupid, stupid boy."

Feeling guilty that I'd completely forgotten about her, I didn't groan or protest that she was hurting me with her hug, "It's alright Mom. I'm fine."

"Fine? *Fine?* Chris, look at you! The doctors are saying a *tree* fell on you, for Christ's sake! What the hell were you doing out of the house anyway? Tell me what happened, because I don't know what's going on. An earthquake wakes me up, you're nowhere to be found, and then Kelly shows up on our doorstep saying she needs to call an ambulance for you." Her authoritative mom tone fell away as she whispered, "Do you have any idea how scared I've been? I don't know what I'd do, Chris. I can't lose another one of my boys."

Not really knowing what to say to any of it, I let her keep talking, and after a few seconds, I noticed Mom brought a visitor along with her. My heart soared for a second, but it wasn't Kelly, of course. It was Thomas, sheepishly keeping his distance near the door. Seeing his face

ignited a deep, seething hatred in me. If there was any justice in the world, it'd be him on the breathing machine.

I stared directly at him and said, "Everyone wins."

Confused, Mom released her grip on me. From the
way Thomas cocked his head, I could tell he wasn't getting
it. I removed my breathing mask so he could hear me loud
and clear. Despite hardly being able to remember my own
name, the deep sense of hatred dug his own words from
my memory and rattled them off, "Take sasquatch. It'll be
funny as fuck. Can you imagine her trying to dance? I'll
double it if you fuck her."

Not sure what she was hearing and not believing it,
Mom followed my line of sight to Thomas, who had all
hints of brotherly concern wiped away as he stomped
toward me with murder in his eyes.

Mom stood up and hurried Thomas out the door. He
made no effort to resist. She slammed it behind him and
took a deep breath, her voice shaking and losing what little
stability she had.

"You're just… Can't you just…" she ran her hands
through her hair, "Do you have to do this? Now, of all
times? Can't you just *pretend* to like him? At least while I'm
around? Is it really that hard to be civil to your own brother
for three seconds? Do you have any idea how hard it is to
deal with you two? Do you have *any goddamn idea* how
stressful it is to spend all day at work worrying about what
kind of trouble you two are getting in? Do you even care?
Do you ever think about what you do to me?"

A nurse flew through the door to escort Mom out as
soon as she started screaming, and Mom made no argument or struggle as she went out in tears. Then, the nurse

came back, saying that maybe it'd be best for everyone if I didn't have any more visitors today.

I couldn't believe it. I started yelling and screaming myself, even attempting to throw something at her before realizing the cast around my right hand kept me from doing that. But all my protesting, all my fighting, did nothing but intensify the pain in my chest a thousand-fold. In the end, Kelly wasn't allowed to see me that day.

I blew it. I fucking blew it.

CHAPTER 27

CHRIS

THREE BRUTALLY LONG days came and went. In all that time, Kelly hadn't once come to see me. Hardly anyone came in to see me. Mom was in and out all the time, of course, occasionally bringing Thomas with her. He brought me my schoolbooks and assignments, but otherwise we didn't say a word to each other. Now that he knew I knew, the game was up and not worth mentioning any more.

At first, it was nice having Mom around all the time. Being no longer in panic mode, she wasn't overly doting or condescending, which I appreciated, and talking to her was a much better way of distracting myself than watching Food Network on the tiny TV. But the longer I went without seeing Kelly, the more Mom's company started to grate on me.

By the afternoon of that fourth day, I couldn't take it anymore. I had to call her. Since cell phones apparently screwed with the machines, I had to use the corded one at my bedside. At the very least, the doctor had me off the breathing machine, so my voice wouldn't be muffled by a mask. Once Mom had finally given me some resting time and I was alone, I immediately dialed her number, my heart pounding with every ring, ready to burst from the anticipation of hearing her voice again.

"Hey, this is Kelly!—"

"Kelly! It's Chris! Man, am I happy to—"

"—I can't come to the phone right now, but if you leave a message, I'll call you back!"

I swore under my breath right as the tone went off. Afraid the recording caught that, I stopped myself and cleared my throat. I wondered if I should even leave a voicemail, but the intimidating silence convinced me I should, so I stammered out, "Uh, hey Kelly. It's me. Chris. Just wondering how you've been, I guess. Call me back, alright?"

Cringing at how moronic I sounded, I hung up and thought about immediately calling again, but that would only make me look pathetic. She'd see the message. She'd call me back.

I lasted only forty-five minutes. The whole time I stared at the phone like a child staring at the presents under a Christmas tree before his parents woke up. She never called, and I almost knocked the phone off the table by reaching for it with my casted arm. Despite the pain, I kept forgetting my dominant hand was out of commission. I dialed as fast as my clumsy, uncoordinated fingers could go and held the phone up with my shoulder

"Hey, this is Kelly! I can't come to the phone right now, but if you leave a message, I'll call you back!"

Being more ready, but still disappointed, by the prere-corded message, I cleared my throat and said, "Hey Kelly, it's Chris. Call me back when you get the chance. It's pretty boring being trapped in the hospital like this. Thanks."

Somehow I managed to go a whole hour before dialing her again, but the result was the same. I left another message. After that, the intervals I called her in only got shorter. With my mom and the nurses constantly coming in and out, I tried to make my calls quick. I didn't want Mom to question me. It got to the point where every time one of them stepped out, even for a second, I'd give Kelly another call, leaving her increasingly pathetic and desper-ate messages. This went on for literal hours. I must have called hundreds of times, and I left a message with every single one.

"Kelly, I'm so sorry. I didn't mean it. I didn't mean anything I said. Please talk to me."

Right as I hung up that last one, I noticed that Mom had come in, giving me a concerned look. I said nothing as she took the phone from me.

"What was that all about?" she asked.

At my breaking point, I leaned back and sighed. Maybe Mom would have something useful to say about it.

"Kelly hates me."

"And what could possibly make you say a thing like that?"

"We had a fight. Right before... before I got hurt. She hasn't come in to see me, and I've been trying to get ahold of her, but she won't pick up."

"Calm down. You're overreacting."

"Am I? What other explanation could there possibly be?"

"Sweetie, she's your best friend. Friends fight, it happens. I'm sure she'll be here soon."

"Mom, you don't understand. I said some pretty awful things to her."

"Then you can apologize when she gets here. Now come on, ignore the phone. You're stressing out over nothing when you should be resting."

I didn't try calling again after that. Not because I agreed with Mom, but because I realized I'd already failed. If after fifty voice mails Kelly didn't want to talk to me, she was never going to.

My ribs ached as I dropped back onto my pillow. What was it I said before? That it'd be better for our friendship to go out in a blaze of glory? If only I'd realized exactly how wrong that was.

CHAPTER 28
CHRIS

THE DOCTOR DECIDED to release me after two weeks. Kelly did not visit once during that time.

They wanted me to come back periodically to do some more scans and be certain the concussion didn't do any serious, long-term damage, and I was forbidden from driving or engaging in any kind of physical activity. Once they made that clear, they shoved me out the door with a painkiller prescription, which I immediately threw in the garbage. I tried to minimize my use of them in the hospital so they wouldn't fuck with my head, only taking them when things were truly unbearable. I could take it. The worst was over anyway.

I was allowed to return to my normal life, which meant going back to school the next morning. I didn't mind. In fact, I asked Mom to take me early, under the pretense that I wanted to discuss an assignment with a teacher. This, of course, was bullshit. I didn't do a single one of the assignments Thomas brought me. I just wanted to be the first student, if not the first person, at school. Kelly would have to go to her locker sometime, and if I waited there, she'd have to talk to me.

The sun had barely risen when I arrived, and I planted myself right in front of her locker in the senior hallway. Without the pain meds, there was no way to arrange myself without something hurting. Sitting, standing, leaning, it all dug the knives back in somewhere. In the end, standing up straight seemed to minimize the pain, so I stood on high alert, keeping my gaze focused on the hallway's only entrance. I brought nothing to entertain or distract myself with, standing in front of her locker like a stone guardian, waiting for his master to relieve him of duty.

My unflinching gaze was challenged when I realized exactly how much the white walls reminded me of the hospital. Feeling thirsty all of a sudden, I broke formation to shuffle to the drinking fountain by the library door. Leaning down was awkward and painful with my cast in the way, but I took a big drink while keeping my eye on the other end of the hall. The first person to round the corner was a girl with blonde hair. I sputtered and choked as I cut myself off and started making my way over to her, but it was a false alarm. Hair aside, they looked nothing alike. Not exactly feeling refreshed, but not wanting to make another foolish mistake, I went back to my post.

More people started trickling in. Nobody asked me what I was doing. Most were content to ignore me as usual, though a few gave me funny looks. When Thomas and his goons walked by, even they didn't say anything for once, and I paid no attention to them. Only one person successfully got me to look away, and that was Noah. I'd completely forgotten about him and his role in all this. It gave me half a mind to smash his face in, but I let it go. The moment I started fighting with him would be the moment Kelly walked by. Still, perhaps it was just my imagination, but I could have sworn he hurried out of there faster than usual.

People started to filter out of the hallway long before the warning bell went off. This didn't faze me. Kelly and I almost always arrived at the last possible second. Today would be no different. One by one, the mob of Leroy High's seniors drifted to homeroom. The tardy bell echoed down the empty halls. I didn't move. She was a little late, that's all. Overslept. She'd round the corner at any minute.

Ten minutes ticked by on the clock overhead. I thought I was about to fall asleep where I stood when someone's clopping footsteps snapped me awake. The swell of anxiety turned to hate as Patterson stopped in front of me.

"Chris, I understand you need extra time getting to class due to your injuries, but if you're going to abuse this gesture of goodwill, I will have to inform your other teachers. Get moving. I better not catch you loafing around like this again."

Grunting, I stormed past the crusty old fuck, heading to homeroom without a single book from my locker. If that piece of shit had given me five more minutes, I know she would've showed. But it wasn't really that big a deal. I'd catch her during lunch.

CHAPTER 29

CHRIS

I SLAMMED MY bedroom door, didn't turn on the light as I tossed my bag across the room and flopped on my bed, shooting a burning sensation through my ribs that just added fuel to my anger.

Most of my teachers were kind enough to give me an extension on all those assignments I didn't do, and my English teacher even told me not to worry about them, but Patterson, the dog fucker, stuck to his guns. Since Thomas came by to get them every day, he expected them to be complete when I returned. I got zeros on every one and all at once took another giant leap towards failure. Now if I wanted to graduate, I'd need a perfect score on that final paper, a nigh impossible feat since I pissed off Rich.

But that wasn't the worst of it. I didn't catch Kelly at lunch because she never showed up. So, once I finished eating alone, I went and flagged down one of her teachers, finding out this was the first day all week Kelly had missed.

What a fucking coincidence. She had to have known I was coming back, from my mom or her grandparents or Thomas or *someone*. Well Kelly, I got your message loud and clear. Fuck you too.

Laying on my bed, I could see the Hatfield house from my window. That morning, I'd entertained the idea of walking over there and knocking on the door, to catch her before school started, but at the last second I decided it'd be better to not bother her so early in the morning. Now that school was over, I didn't even want to look at the place. Yanking the blind down, I sat in my desk under the window.

She doesn't come visit me in the hospital, doesn't return my calls, doesn't give me the chance to apologize even though she should be apologizing for nearly breaking my fucking spine, and then doesn't show at school just to avoid me. That's a new level of cowardice. Why was I agonizing so much over getting someone like her back in my life? If anything, her silence was a blessing. I didn't need that bitch. I didn't need anybody.

Hanging above my desk, a picture jumped out at me that had long since faded into the background noise of my room. The drawing Kelly gave me the day we tried to run away together. The first thing I did when I got home that night was tape it to my wall right next to the window, so I'd see it whenever I looked over at her house. Whenever things got hard in those early days, I'd spend a lot of time just staring at the house and thinking about her. It was reassuring to know at least one person cared about me.

Feeling tears coming on, I flung my desk drawer open and fumbled for the only relief I knew. I didn't waste any time cleaning the knife or making sure Mom wouldn't catch me. I fidgeted with the pocket knife until it opened, shook off my pants when I remembered I didn't have a free arm, and plunged it into my leg. I cut my upper thigh, and when the pain started to dull, I cut again. This was a different kind of pain from what had tormented me over the course of the week. This pain was smooth, precise. With one sharp move it cleared my mind and eventually went away. And I didn't cry.

CHAPTER 30
CHRIS

KELLY WASN'T AT school today.

CHAPTER 31

CHRIS

LUNCHTIME BECAME A real ordeal since I stopped going to my normal spot outside. Kelly still hadn't come back to school, but I didn't want to run into her there when she finally did. It only seemed fair. Kelly had been eating outside since before we met. That was her spot. With the natural ecosystem of the cafeteria firmly established, I had to squeeze in the barren corner of a table where a group of burnouts sat. I could leave campus and not have to suffocate in there, but home was too far of a drive to be worth it, I didn't have the money or the inclination to grab fast food every day, and Thomas had complete control of the keys. I had no choice but to stay.

At least the burnouts didn't try to start shit with me. The only one that seemed to notice me at all was a stoner girl who showed up to Noah's party, but she didn't try to talk to me about Kelly's appearance there. That was over a month ago. Ancient news by Leroy High standards.

The cafeteria had a small stage with a table decorated in green, and a poster telling the school that prom tickets were being sold there. Cassidy and one of her student council friends chatted idly behind it. This late in the game, everyone who had any interest in going probably already had tickets, so keeping people up there was just a formality.

However, Cassidy's attention suddenly went stage left, and her face lit up as another student with a microphone in one hand and an envelope in the other approached her.

Cassidy sprung from her seat and rushed to meet the messenger halfway. Seeing her take a second to discuss something gave me the warning to brace myself for the inevitable ear-violating squeal the microphone would make when she turned it on.

Sure enough, Cassidy tensed up as the speakers blasted a horrible screech, but it had the useful side effect of getting the attention of everyone in the cafeteria. All was quiet as she recovered with a chipper bounce in her voice, "Good afternoon, Leroy High! I've got an exciting announcement!" She waved the envelope in the air, "We've counted up all the votes, and inside this envelope are the names of the five lucky ladies on this year's prom court!"

Applause thundered throughout the cafeteria. Voting must have happened while I was in the hospital, not that I really cared about missing this particular beauty pageant. In addition to being a pointless waste of time, everyone already knew who would win: Annie Valentine, Stacy DeLuca, Jenny Wagner, Veronica Brown, and Cassidy herself, with either Annie or Jenny taking home the crown. I went back to my lunch and tried to let their voices fade into the background.

"When I call your name, come and stand where everyone can see you! Now, without further ado…" Slowly, with dramatic emphasis, Cassidy tore open the envelope and bellowed, "Annie Valentine!"

The applause rang louder than before, with people cheering and whistling like a celebrity was taking the stage. I'll admit to scouring for Noah in the crowd just to watch him squirm when she stood up there, but it gave me an interesting thought: what would happen if someone without a date was voted queen? Would they scrounge up a king for her? I suppose I didn't know how prom worked at all.

Cassidy continued down the list, "Jenny Wagner! Stacy DeLuca!" The applause wasn't quite as strong as they took their places onstage. Annie must have been the crowd favorite. I wondered if they even bothered to shuffle the names or if our class president was reading them from most votes to least.

Her cheeks flushed as she paused over the next one, "Oh! Goodness! The next name on my list is… me!" She gave a little curtsy as the applause started up, and took her spot in line next to Stacy, "Thank you everybody!"

I snorted. How conceited do you have to be, acting surprised like that? Even if it wasn't obvious, she had to have known all the names in advance. She was the class president, for Christsake.

Cassidy let the applause go on a little longer than all the others before turning her attention back to the paper. "Okay! The last member of our court is…" The color drained from her face, and after a long pause, the words slipped from her lips without a hint of her previous enthusiasm, "Kelly Hatfield."

No applause accompanied this announcement, only murmurs of confusion from people not in on the joke and fits of laughter from those that were. I nearly choked on my sandwich, causing the eyes of the burnouts to creep over to me. The texts mentioned getting Kelly on the court was part of the plan, but I didn't think they'd be able to rally enough votes to actually do it. Cassidy took a step back and shrunk down, no doubt trying to hide from the jeers of everyone aware of her drunken tryst with Leroy High's least popular girl. The other girls on stage made a face like someone threw a rotting animal at their feet, except, strangely enough, for Annie. She centered a judgmental gaze squarely on her ex-boyfriend, who was swamped by a mob of his basketball players ribbing him and laughing uncontrollably. Noah attempted to laugh along, to enjoy his own joke, but he was obviously aware of Annie watching him. Whether she was disappointed in Noah for acting like a common bully, or merely disgusted that his standards for her replacement sunk so low, I can't say, but it gave me a certain amount of satisfaction to watch him visibly fall even further from the good graces of the girl he was still obviously pining over. Served him right.

The other primary conspirator seemed to be watching me, though he tried to act like he wasn't, and tore his head away when he noticed me looking back. It was almost like Thomas felt guilty about it, like a hint of humanity finally surfaced after so many years of rejecting it. His scrawny little water boy buddy—Trevor, I believe—sat next to him and howled like a baboon, holding his hand up to try and give my brother a high five. Thomas didn't take it.

Kelly obviously wasn't there to take her place in the

lineup. The cafeteria only got louder and more out of control the longer she kept them waiting. Flustered at the ensuing madness, Cassidy leaned into the mic and spoke with a hollow shell of her former enthusiasm, "Come on Kelly, where're you hiding?"

Trevor leaned up and cupped his hands around his mouth, shouting over the crowd, "Yo, anyone check the zoo?"

Without thinking, I dropped my food and got on my feet. I cut directly in front of the lineup to get to Trevor's table on the opposite side of the room. Much of the laughter died down at this sudden move. Thomas pinched his brow and sighed as I got closer, but Trevor was too busy guffawing at his own moronic joke to notice me looming over him.

"What's so funny?" I said.

Trevor wiped a tear from his eye and spun to face me, "You starting shit with me, tough guy?"

"No," I said, keeping a calm, level voice, "That was a legitimate question. I want you to explain exactly what's so funny about any of this." He looked up at me like a particularly dim-witted sloth, like he'd never given the question the slightest bit of thought.

When he went too long without answering, I offered an explanation, "It's because she's so out of place, right? Like putting a chimp in a tux. The natural order of things has been disrupted. Chimps aren't supposed to wear clothes, and Kelly Hatfield could never actually be on prom court, so all we can do is laugh at how ridiculous it is, right?"

Trevor paused, still confused as he nodded his head. I nodded mine in return.

"Right. Only, I don't get why that's so ridiculous. Why shouldn't Kelly be on prom court?" I gestured vaguely in the direction of the stage, "What separates her from one of them? Is it because she's not pretty? Says who? You? I've got some news for you: you're not exactly a prize yourself, so why should she give a shit about what you think? Why should anyone?"

I hadn't raised my voice much, but suddenly I became aware of how silent the cafeteria had become, how all eyes were on me. I didn't care. Putting my good hand on the table, I leaned right into Trevor's face, "If we were voting on anything substantial, if this was anything more than a popularity contest, Kelly would be queen by a fucking landslide. Because you people, you don't know what kind of fire you're playing with. If you knew what she was capable of, you wouldn't have the guts to *ever* mock her for her hair, or her clothes, or her height, or any of that bullshit ever again. If she wanted it, she could *break* you, and there wouldn't be a damn thing *anyone* could do to stop her."

Murmurs started going through the crowd, and I finally turned away from Trevor, raised my voice to address everyone, "But that's not what she wants. We got lucky. You know what she wants? All she ever wanted? She wants people to like her, that's all. But even that's asking for too much, isn't it? Well, joke's on us! When she finally leaves this dump for good, when she finally realizes that she doesn't need to be afraid of bugs like us, everyone will see her for who she is, and they're going to *adore* her! Long after we're dust in the ground, they'll teach our grandkids in school about all the ways she made the world a better place! You'll see! Every news organization in the world will want to interview us, because we had the privilege of growing up with her, and you know what? We'll have to lie through our teeth, because we won't want the world to know that we treated her like *garbage.*"

The cafeteria stayed silent as I took in a panoramic view of everyone, trying my hardest to read them, to see if maybe someone in the crowd felt even a pang of regret.

All at once, the room descended into pandemonium. People were laughing harder than ever before, to the point where a teacher rushed for the mic in Cassidy's hand to try and regain control of the situation. Realizing I didn't have too long until I got dragged off for starting an incident, I appealed to Thomas, who, surprisingly, still wasn't laughing, looking more cautious of me than anything.

"Give me the keys," I said.

He raised in eyebrow, "What do you need them for?"

"Please. Just this once, help me out. You'll have your car back before the end of the day. There is literally no reason for you to say no."

Thomas contemplated this. But slowly, ever so slowly, he handed them over. Having no time to waste on even a thank you, I powered out of the cafeteria and ignored a teacher coming right for me as I tore through the parking lot and strapped myself in the driver's seat of Thomas's car. I gunned it, ignoring the doctor's orders and speeding down the road one handed.

The tight leather of the steering wheel dug into my palm. I locked the gas pedal to the floor, blasting down the road. Realistically, there was no way I could drive to Kelly's house and back before lunch hour ended, but I went with so much speed because I needed to talk to her. I needed to hear her voice again. If that meant being late to English, or ditching the rest of the day, or getting expelled for starting a riot in the cafeteria, then so be it. There were already so many people that hated me. I couldn't let Kelly be one of them.

In record time, I squealed to a stop in the Hatfield driveway, marched to their front door and pounded on it. A stunned Grandpa Hatfield answered, "Chris? What are you doing here? Why aren't you in school?"

"Is Kelly in there?"

A subtle, pained look told me everything I needed to know before he said it. "This isn't a great time. Get back to class before you get in trouble."

He tried to gently close the door on me, and I jammed my foot in there to stop him. "I'm guessing she told you to say that, but please, let me talk to her. I wouldn't be doing this if it wasn't important."

He took a deep breath, ready to gently repeat himself. His wife's voice, echoing from the kitchen, stopped him.

"Chris? Is that you?"

"Yes!" I shouted, "Yes, Mrs. Hatfield, it's me!"

"George, you let that boy in this instant!"

I couldn't tell from the tone of her voice if she was angry with me or not. Regardless, I barely gave poor Grandpa enough time to duck out of my way as I charged through and ran into the kitchen. Grandma Hatfield wheeled herself towards me as fast as her chair would go, and immediately, I knew from the panic shining in her eyes that she was at the end of her rope.

"Oh, thank the lord you're here! You need to talk some sense into her! She'll listen to you!"

Things were worse than I ever imagined. "Where is she? What happened?"

Mrs. Hatfield took a deep breath, trying and failing to stay calm.

"I don't know what to do, Chris. She locked herself in the basement and won't come out."

CHAPTER 32
CHRIS

I WASN'T SURE what I'd find when the basement door creaked open, and the gaping darkness did nothing to lessen my fears. I'd never been down there before, and as far as I knew, neither had Kelly. Keeping my head high, I descended slowly.

Her grandmother gave me the whole story. For the past two weeks, ever since my accident, Kelly hadn't been acting like herself. On the surface she went about her day like normal, went to school and did her homework and all that, but something had changed in her demeanor. She'd grown unusually quiet, only speaking when spoken to and even then, answering with only terse, one-word sentences. Whenever they went in her room, they'd find her sitting in her chair or lying on her bed, glassy-eyed and staring off into space, seemingly doing nothing. Most troubling of all, whenever they offered to drive her up to Cleveland to visit me, she'd brush them off, making excuses at first and eventually just saying that she didn't feel like going. The first day or two, her grandfather tried to rationalize it by saying she was just shaken up by what happened (Grandma Hatfield started getting vague here, never confirming whether or not they knew Kelly was the one behind my accident. It occurred to me that they might not be sure I knew about her powers) and that once she had time to process it, she'd go see me and start acting like her normal self, but things kept getting worse, and by the end of it she might as well have been a zombie shuffling around the house.

Kelly finally cracked three days ago, when her grandmother told her I was getting released from the hospital. The emotion that had been drained from her exploded into a screaming breakdown. All attempts to calm her only fueled the fire. She disappeared into her room, dragging her mattress out with her when she emerged, taking it to the basement and slamming the door behind her.

They found her in the same position every time they checked on her, unmoved with her back to them, on a bare mattress in the middle of the floor. She kept the lights off at all hours of the day, and screamed at anyone who tried to turn them on. Any meals they brought to her went untouched. Knowing this couldn't keep going on, they were preparing to call an ambulance for her... but then I showed up. Grandma Hatfield was convinced I could get through to her where they couldn't.

Making plenty of noise on my way down to avoid surprising her, I didn't know what I planned to say. I couldn't see a thing, and the basement's wretched smell overwhelmed my senses. There was that particular muskiness of old folks with just a twinge of mold, but that was merely an undercurrent to something else choking the room, of the sweat and grease that builds on those who refuse to bathe or change their clothes for days at a time.

Reaching the bottom of the stairs, I could barely make out a chain hanging from the ceiling, presumably attached to a light. I wrapped my fingers around the cold metal. I didn't care if she yelled. I wanted to see her and I wanted her to see me.

A dim light snapped on with a tug of the cord, barely illuminating the cold concrete room. Towers of cardboard boxes lined the walls, looming over the lump on the floor in the center of the room.

The lack of anger in her voice surprised me. The lack of anything in her voice surprised me. "I told you to keep the light off."

"It's me."

As I took a few hesitant steps to get a better look at her, the heap of blankets visibly tightened. Even standing over her, identifying any features other than the mess of her limp, greasy hair was impossible. I imagined this conversation happening in so many different ways, but I wasn't prepared for this. I don't think I could ever have prepared for this. With no idea of how to possibly make it right, I said the first honest thing that came to mind.

"I've missed you."

Kelly pulled the blanket over her head. "Go away."

I knew it. Her grandmother's faith in me was completely misplaced. Kelly hated me. My voice cracked as I sunk to my knees to get on her level, "Kelly, wait! Just... just hear me out, okay? I know I fucked up, I know I'm an awful friend, and I know I've got no right to even be in the same room as you, but please, just listen to me one more time. Once I'm all done, then you can hate me all you want, but just wait until I—"

"I don't hate you."

"You don't?"

The mess of blankets subtly shifted, like she was shaking her head. Just like that, everything I assumed about the situation went out the window. I truly had no clue what was going on in her head. That realization hurt.

"Then... what's this about? What are you doing down here?" I said.

Her answer came without a hint of emotion, "Waiting to starve to death."

"That's not funny."

"It wasn't supposed to be."

"Kelly. Look at me."

She didn't move for a second. Then, she rolled over and pulled the blanket down far enough for her eyes to poke through the strings of her hair. Her shining, beautiful red eyes. I'd never been happier to see them.

But looking at my face destroyed her. Her eyes disappeared behind the blanket she shielded herself with, "Oh god, what did I do to you?"

"It's not that bad," I quickly assured her, "It doesn't even hurt—" I stopped myself. This was no time to lie, no time to try and look like a tough guy, "Okay, it does hurt. But it's not permanent. I'll get better. Now, seriously. Look at me."

Reluctantly, she pulled the covers back down, actually going one further and sitting up to meet me in the eye. In a white, sweat-stained t-shirt, with a colorless face, and red eyes, she was more ghostly than ever. She stayed silent, waiting. Expecting something.

After thinking about it for a second, I shook my head, "You know what? I've done enough talking. I never shut up and listen. Whatever you want to say, you should say it first."

She turned away from me. Her lips trembled and her eyes closed as she prepared herself. "I guess," her voice cracked as she turned back to me, "I guess I should start by saying that I'm sorry. I'm sorry for everything I said, and I'm sorry for hurting you, and…" she got choked up, and took a deep breath to steady herself, "and I'm sorry I didn't come see you in the hospital. I was too scared. If I had it my way, you wouldn't have even got the chance to say goodbye before I did this."

"This? What's this? What are you saying?"

"I already told you. I'm gonna stay down here until I starve to death, and if it turns out I can't die, then I'm just gonna stay away from people forever."

"You don't mean that."

"Yes I do."

"No, you don't. Think about what you're saying. Your grandparents are worried sick about you."

"I already ruined their lives. I can't make things much worse for them."

"What are you talking about? They love you."

"They shouldn't."

"That's ridiculous. Why would you say a thing like that?"

"*Because I'm a murderer, Chris.*"

Her sudden ferocity sucked the words out of me. She lowered her head and sobbed, and I could only stare at her with the kind of shock I hadn't felt since the day she first showed me her powers. I wanted it to be a lie or an exaggeration, but deep down I knew it wasn't, because everything made sense now. I didn't have to ask who or when. The night at the cemetery. Her breakdown after my accident. Ruining her grandparents' lives. Rules One and Two. I thought I was doing her a favor. I thought I was getting her to come out of her shell, but that couldn't be further from the truth.

"Tell me what happened," I finally whispered.

She couldn't bring herself to look me in the eye, "It doesn't matter."

"It does matter." I tried to keep calm. "I don't believe for a second that you killed your father."

"It doesn't matter if you believe it, it's true, okay? He'd still be alive if I just listened to him and stayed in the basement."

"If you *what?*"

She choked back her words for a second. In the end, she couldn't hold it in. She had to get the whole story out to someone after all these years. "That was his punishment for me. Whenever I was bad, whenever I couldn't hold it in, Dad would lock me in the basement. And one day I was really bad and left the house while he was at work. I wasn't supposed to leave. He knew it wasn't safe. So when he caught me playing in the yard, he got so mad and was gonna keep me down there for a whole week and when he went to grab me I... I..."

I didn't need her to finish to understand. I sat there, speechless as she devolved into a storm of anguish. What do you even say to a story like that?

Finally, I did the only thing I could do. I told her the truth she needed to hear. "You were a kid. You were scared and trying to protect yourself."

"*Shut up!*" Anger burned through her veil of tears, "Don't make excuses for me! You don't know what you're talking about! *He* needed protection, not me! He was right about me the whole time! I mean, look at you!" Her anger vanished with another cry of pain, "It happened again. I let it happen again…"

"Alright stop, just stop! He was wrong! You hear me? He was wrong. You've lived a normal life for so long and nobody ever knew you were special. Nobody would have *ever* known if I hadn't fucked it up! I pushed you and pushed you and pushed you until you couldn't take it anymore. You want someone to blame for all of this? Blame me!" My voice started to waver and a thousand needles assaulted my eyes, but I didn't stop, "I've been so jealous of you my whole life, you know that? You have all these amazing powers, but you don't need them or even want them, and that drove me insane because I'm *nothing*. I wake up every morning thinking this is it, this is the day you finally realize you're better off without a fuckup like me."

I was crying. Not a quiet, dignified cry, but a disgusting blubber that rendered my speech incomprehensible. Stunned, Kelly's own tears evaporated as I scooted closer to her beautiful glowing eyes and let everything out. "You know I didn't believe a word I was saying back in the woods, right? You're better than me. You're better than me in every single way and I know it. But I wanted to hurt you so bad. You saw through my bullshit so easily. Everything you said about me was right and I couldn't fucking handle it.

Because deep down, deep down I knew that Kelly Hatfield without her powers is still the sweetest, smartest, bravest person in this shithole town. But me? I'm a disaster. I'm not graduating high school or leaving this town or ever doing anything with my life. You're all I've got, you understand? You can't do this to me." I leaned in and threw my arm around her, stretching my neck up to rest my chin on her shoulder and whisper, "I don't care about your powers anymore. I'll never mention them again." I sobbed, "I just want my friend back."

She said nothing. Her bony frame shivered in my embrace; her arms rigid at her sides.

"Please let go of me," she whispered, "I don't wanna hurt you anymore."

I held her a little tighter.

"I trust you."

My ugly crying filled the room while she sat in silence. Then, slowly, deliberately, she raised her long arms and brushed them against my back, barely touching me. Little by little, she eased into me, pressing me against her. My ribs ached with pain like the pressure was about to crack them all over again, but I smiled through it and refused to let go.

Tears dripped onto my shoulder as she said, "I'm sorry. I'm so sorry."

"No," I said, "I'm sorry."

CHAPTER 33

KELLY

CHRIS QUIETLY LEFT after bringing me back upstairs, knowing that I needed some time to sort things out with Grandma and Grandpa. Through another long talk full of crying and apologies I told them about what really happened to Chris and how I felt like the world would be better off if I was dead, but I didn't say anything about Dad. The truth may not have scared Chris away, but it wasn't his son I killed. Grandma and Grandpa were hurt enough as it was. They demanded I get checked into a hospital, but I begged them not to call, saying I'd be fine and there'd be nothing to worry about anymore.

It wasn't just the thought of being alone in a mental hospital that terrified me, it was what the psychiatrists would learn about me. There was no way to talk about my problems without talking about my powers, and I imagined the doctors doing some kinda test on me and finding something weird, something worth telling the world about. Even if that didn't happen, how long was it before Dad came up? Would they arrest me when they found out what happened? After finally coming up from the basement, after stewing in my own nightmares for three days, I didn't ever wanna be in a dark place like that again.

Eventually, we compromised. They didn't call the hospital, but I had to start talking to a therapist and stay home from school for the rest of the week. They weren't gonna let me out of their sight.

Luckily, they trusted Chris to watch out for me in their place. Grandma even asked him if he wanted to stay the nights on our couch. The lack of privacy didn't bother me, because I didn't want to be alone. Chris tried to convince his mom to let him skip school to stay with me, but he'd already missed so much from his time in the hospital, and with finals coming up, every second of class counted. So, he'd go off to school, and I'd sketch at the kitchen table and talk to Grandma until Chris came back with my homework, and then I'd work on it while we watched TV in my room.

But for all the time we spent together, Chris and I didn't talk much, and when we did, he was careful with what he said, tip-toeing around like I was a bomb ready to go off at any second. It made me feel like I broke something between us, and no matter how hard he tried we weren't gonna be able to fix it.

My first visit with the therapist got scheduled sooner than I thought, the Monday I was going back to school, and my stomach churned with every second it came closer. It got so bad that the night before, I couldn't fall asleep, staring at the ceiling and hearing every little sound in the night, a tree branch scraping against the side of the house, the hum of the air flowing from the vents, the mattress squeaking underneath me as I tossed and turned. At four in the morning I sat up, my eyelids weighed down but the rest of my body still jolting. Without really thinking about it, I slipped out my bedroom door as quietly as I could to avoid making anyone worry, sneaking down the hall to our living room where Chris was. I paused to watch him from a distance, flat on his back with his head propped up by a couple of pillows, not wanting to disturb him but also really wanting to talk to him.

He startled me when he abruptly sat up, quietly groaning in pain, and faced me, "Can't sleep either?"

I shook my head.

He scooted down to make room for me, and I eased myself next to him. I didn't know what to say. Or maybe I did know, and just didn't want to say it, too afraid of making him uncomfortable and mad at me for bringing it up.

After a few seconds I realized he was waiting for me. Taking a deep breath, I said, "Can I ask you something?"

"Of course."

"What's it gonna be like tomorrow? Like, you know, what are they gonna ask me?"

He covered his mouth with his fist, thinking it over, "If she's anything like the shrinks I've had, not much. You'll fill out a couple of forms and she'll rattle off some questions to try and get to know you. Get a general idea of how you're feeling. First session is always low key. Can't imagine it'll take more than an hour."

"That doesn't sound too bad." I felt myself tugging

on my hair. "Do you think... do you think I should tell her everything?"

"Fuck no." He paused and reconsidered, "Well, maybe. I don't know. Definitely not at first. Take a few sessions to feel her out in case she turns out to be a quack. But after that..." he leaned back and sighed, "It's hard to say. Patient confidentiality should apply to you still, since you're not planning to hurt yourself," he lingered on those words, shifting his eyes at me before continuing, "She shouldn't be allowed to say a word, but I don't know if that's the law or just common practice. Plus, you're such a special case that she might blab anyway. You never know if she's the sort of asshole who values a book deal over a patient's well-being." He paused again, "Do you want to tell her?"

"I don't know. Do you think it could help?"

He ran his hand through his hair and sighed, "I'm probably not the best person to ask. I don't trust shrinks, never have. But I also don't want to give you advice that could keep you from getting help. If you think it's safe, then tell her. If she makes you uncomfortable, then get a different one or convince your grandparents you don't need to go. Just... whatever you do, trust your own judgment."

There was that word again. Trust. During those three days in the basement, my power raged without end, burning hotter and hotter with every emotion piling on me. Chris looked right into my red eyes and, knowing exactly what they meant, hugged me. His bones hadn't healed from the last time I broke them, and without any hesitation, he hugged me. He was the first person to do that in... God, I don't even know, maybe ever. He had every reason in the world to stay away, but he held on tight and told me that he trusted me. That one gesture was the last hope I could cling to, that maybe I hadn't broken things forever and eventually we could be normal friends again.

But if that was true, I couldn't keep him at arm's length anymore. I'd have to trust myself as much as he trusted me. No more rules.

I inched closer to him to see how he'd react, to see if he'd recoil from me. My elbow brushed against the hard plaster keeping his arm together and I winced. The guilt was coming back and I thought it would kill me, but Chris didn't feel that way. He smiled and leaned into me. Still afraid he'd shatter, rigid tension kept my body sitting up straight, but Chris's head tilted onto my shoulder. The longer we sat like that, the more gravity kept pulling him into me, the more my shoulders relaxed to try to make him more comfortable.

We kept our conversation going like nothing had changed.

"Is it okay if I ask you another question?" I said, "I mean, this one's a little personal. You don't have to answer if you don't wanna."

"You can ask me anything."

"Okay. So, um, why don't you trust doctors and thera-pists and people like that? You're always skipping out on your appointments and medicine and stuff. Isn't it sup-posed to make you feel better?"

His shoulder raised against me. "Sometimes it does, sometimes it doesn't. I'll be going for a week and everything will be fine, and then all of a sudden I'll have a nightmare or a panic attack or something and I'll throw everything in the trash because nothing I do matters. It's all such a crapshoot and I hate that. And then you have to go tell the shrink what happened and they take this real smug tone with you, like they're talking to a toddler, and that makes it even worse. Like you're so broken and crazy that without their help you wouldn't be able to tie your own shoes. If they're so fucking smart, then how come their treatments don't work?" He shifted to look directly at me with a little bit of guilt, "But I suppose complaining about them babying me is a little hypocritical, isn't it? We don't need to be watching you like this. The fact you came through all that horrible shit as put together as you did proves you're strong. Way stronger than me. You're going to be fine. I know it."

"It's okay," I said, "I'm happy you're here."

It's strange how much more in tune you are with someone when they're touching you. Without looking at his face, I knew that guilty feeling hadn't left him. I could feel it in the tension of his muscles, the pained pause in his breath. The subtle way his neck moved when he swallowed and prepared himself to say something big.

"There's... there's something I want you to see. But," he quivered slightly, and before he even mentioned it, his cast raised slightly into my arm, "But I can't reach it on my own. Not like this."

"Sure. What do you need?"

Another heavy rise and fall from his chest, another swallow to try and prepare himself, his healthy arm reaching across to me. "Lift my sleeve up. All the way to the shoulder."

My body tensed up as I hooked my finger around the end of his long-sleeved pajamas. The old worries of overreacting and hurting him flared up again as my fingertip brushed against his wrist. Gently and carefully, I pulled his sleeve, revealed more and more of his skin, glowing pure white in the moonlight. The closer we got to his shoulder, the more marks and scratches started to show up, and when I was done, I stared quietly at the mess. It looked like he tried to shove his arm through a meat grinder a long time ago.

Chris winced. "So," he said, "That's... I don't know. That's where I'm at."

I stayed silent for just a moment.

"How long have you been doing this?" I said, trying to be gentle.

"Couple of years. Started when I was fourteen. Stopped when I was seventeen. Started again a few months ago." He shifted in my arms. "How fucked up would you think I am if I said I find it soothing?"

I shook my head.

That wasn't what he expected to hear. "What are you thinking then?"

"I dunno. I guess I'm just sad," I said, "Sad you do this to yourself. Sad I never noticed. Sad you didn't tell me until now."

"There's a lot we never told each other."

"Yeah."

Hesitation. His body shifted again, asked without words to lean back and look him in the eye. "Do you think we should make a promise?" he said.

"A promise?"

He held his pinky finger up with a nod of his head, "Promise to stop hiding everything from each other?"

I didn't hesitate. When I locked my pinky with his,

everything felt right. Not just fixed, but better than ever before. "Promise."

"Good. Me too." Chris let go and nestled back into me, the rhythms of his body finally telling me he was happy. I felt the laughter rising in him before I heard it. "You know, when we were kids, I was always upset we never made pinky promises like that."

"Back then I would've tore your finger off."

"Back then? Maybe."

My giggle turned into a big yawn, once I finished I said, "I always wanted to do that kinda stuff too."

I wanted to say more, to keep talking to him all through the night, but my eyelids were so heavy, and with all the nervousness gone there was nothing to keep me awake. Before I knew it, I'd closed them and drifted off to sleep.

The warm morning sun glittered onto my face through our sliding glass door and woke me up. We'd both fallen asleep sitting upright, and Chris was still pressed against me. I couldn't help but greet the day with a big smile. He looked sweeter and calmer than ever before, and I didn't want to ruin that by waking him up before he was ready.

But suddenly something blocked the sunlight, darkening Chris's face. When I looked up, I found Grandpa standing there in his robe, not happy with what he was seeing. My face burned up as I slowly moved away from him. Without me to support him, gravity woke him up. He flailed in surprise and turned his head to me, then to Grandpa.

"You kids better get moving. Got a big day ahead of you." Grandpa said it like nothing was wrong, almost like he wasn't going to say anything about finding us like that.

He turned around, moved a few steps, and stopped, talking casually without looking at us. "Chris, I think it'd be best if you stayed at your own house from now on. Unless you'd like me to break that other arm."

His point made crystal clear, Grandpa went back to the kitchen to make some coffee. Chris and I stayed frozen in place, knowing that if we looked at each other we'd start cracking up. We both managed to hold it in until Grandpa filled his mug and strolled off to another part of the house, his day already ruined. As soon as he was out of sight, we let it all go, looking directly at each other's embarrassed faces and completely losing it. Over breakfast, Chris volunteered to drive me to my appointment. Grandpa responded with a death glare and started to go on about how Chris shouldn't be driving with his cast, but Grandma thought it was such a wonderful idea that she shut him up. We were out the door before we could start laughing again.

For once, I was thankful I didn't have any other friends; nobody poked around with awkward questions and I didn't have to explain where I'd been the past few days, so for the most part, my day went like any other. In classes I had with Chris I'd quietly talk with him, and in ones without him I'd quietly take notes and draw in the back of the room. During lunch, Chris stole one of my cookies when he thought I wasn't looking, and I got my revenge later in the day by drawing an anime girl on his cast when he asked me to make it pretty.

Finding out I was on the prom court was the biggest shock of the day. A girl in fourth period art class told me Chris's speech convinced her to vote me for queen, and that she convinced her friends to do it too. I had to ask what she meant by "Chris's speech," and she told me about how he stood up for me when the whole school was laughing. I was touched, but felt guilty for reasons I didn't really understand. Since she didn't seem to be making fun of us, I politely thanked her and went down to the office after class to tell them I couldn't make it to prom and to take me off the court.

On my way to my last class, I had the chance to corner Noah and tell him I wasn't going with him anymore, but I decided there was no reason to make a fuss over it. It's not like he actually cared.

But I didn't let those reminders of all the bad stuff that happened get me down. At the end of the day, when Chris and I walked out to the sunny parking lot, I couldn't help but smile at the beautiful blue sky. A week is a long time to be cooped up in your house, and I felt pretty good about my first day back in the world.

My smile spread to Chris. He took a moment to enjoy the weather and said, "Feeling good?"

That's when I noticed that he covered my drawing on his cast with a patch of blue duct tape. That made me giggle, "Yeah, I guess I am."

"We've got a couple hours to kill before your appointment," he said, "We should stop by Harry's for a bit."

"Harry's? You don't think we're banned?"

"That'll just make it more thrilling. Besides, I'm going through withdrawal. I never realized how magical Lorenzo's pizza was until I went nearly two months without it."

It didn't take me long to decide. "Lorenzo's pizza *is* pretty magical. I bet he even misses us. Let me call Grandma first. She'll wanna know where we're going."

My phone took a little bit to turn on, and when it did, a voice mail from a phone number a few towns over made my heart sink. This could only be about one thing. Part of me wanted to leave it for later, stick to my promise of not letting the bad stuff get me down. But in the end, I decided to listen. Ignoring it wouldn't make it go away.

The cheerful voice of a familiar middle-aged lady came through the speaker. "Hi Kelly, this is Rose from Sarah's Seams calling to tell you that we've finished your dress. Your grandma made sure it was all paid for, so all you need to do is drop by and pick it up. I think you're going to love how it turned out!"

Disappointment must've been visible on my face as I put the phone down.

"What's up?" Chris said.

I sighed. "If it's not too much trouble, do you think we could go to Harry's another time? I kinda need to go to Medina."

"Medina? What's there?"

"My prom dress."

Chris frowned, "Oh."

"Yeah."

With a shrug, he started off towards the car, "To Medina, I suppose."

We got in, the mood tense and uncomfortable again. Medina was a bigger town about half an hour from Leroy. Chris didn't say anything to me until we were on the highway.

"Can't you call them back and cancel the order?"

"Nope. They don't take refunds. We had it made at this local place because Grandma knows the owner, and they were willing to make my dress a priority as a favor. We couldn't just go pick one out from a store 'cause… well, you know. My body's weird and nothing would fit." I sighed, leaning out and letting my hair fly out the rolled down window. "I feel bad. Grandma wasted a lot of money on this."

"It's not a waste. You'll have something nice to wear when you need it."

"I dunno. The more I think about it, the more I'm worried I asked for something kinda slutty."

"I'm sure it's fine."

We spent most of the drive listening to music. I only piped up every once in a while, to remind Chris how to get to the square. As we found a parking spot by the big gazebo surrounded by lush green grass, I felt weirdly at peace. It was pretty out and we'd already come so far. There had to be some way to enjoy ourselves there.

"Hey," I said as we got out, "Do you wanna try that sushi place they opened down the street? We can get take-out and eat in the gazebo."

"That actually sounds really good. I'll have to stop by the ATM, though. Pretty sure they only take cash."

Both of us were in better spirits as we strolled past all the cute local shops and restaurants. Most places had a table or two out front where people sat and enjoyed some coffee or ice cream. A cool breeze blew through open doors, and colorful drawings on chalkboard easels tempted us to come inside and see what they had in stock. The square in this town was so much friendlier and livelier than Leroy's. There weren't so many boarded windows to sour the atmosphere, and there wasn't a cloud in the sky. Days like this were made for long walks.

When we got to the bank, Chris stepped up to the machine by the front door and lazily tossed his card in, punching in a few numbers on autopilot. I was staring at a pizza place, wondering if it was around last time we were here, so I didn't notice anything was wrong until Chris pounded the machine and muttered, "You're fucking kidding me."

I couldn't keep myself from peeking over his shoulder. He only had $2.55 in his account. Since I was pretty sure I had enough to pay for both of us, I smiled and tried to laugh him off, "Did you spend it all on my breakfast?"

He glared at me with dead seriousness, "No. That was actually the last time I took money out of here. I remember exactly how much I had after that: $202.55." I met his gaze with a cocked head, not really sure what that number was supposed to mean. Helping me out, he sighed and said, "Think about what we're here to do."

It clicked with me all at once.

"No way," I said, "How'd Thomas get your PIN number?"

"No idea, but he's had it for a while now. Sometimes my debit card just disappears and reappears a few days later, and every time I check my account the balance always seems lower, but by such small amounts that I could never prove it. The piece of shit must have thought it'd be a fucking scream to use my money for his sick joke."

"You've gotta tell your mom."

"Are you kidding? It's my word against his. I don't have his phone anymore, and I'm sure he was smart enough to get rid of those texts after I bitched him out in the hospital room. She's never going to believe the bad kid over the one actually going to college." Chris sighed and ran his hand through his hair, "At least this is enough to get a soda."

"Don't be silly," I said, "I've got you."

"You don't have to do that. I'm not that hungry."

"Yes, I do. Now come on, it's sushi time."

Chris opened his mouth to argue again, but stopped after looking me in the eye for just a moment. He sighed before turning back to the machine, withdrawing what little money he had and giving it to me. It was a silly gesture since it wouldn't even be enough to cover the tip, but I didn't fight with him about it and we made our way back towards delicious sushi.

We got a few different kinds of rolls to go and took them back to the square, sitting on the ground for an unplanned picnic. I took off my shoes and happily soaked in the plush grass beneath me while shoveling roll after roll into my mouth. Chris only picked at a couple pieces, not having his full share until I told him about three times I was full, at which point he sheepishly ate the rest. I tried to understand why he fought me so much about such a silly little thing, why he wouldn't let me do something as simple and nice for him as paying for a meal.

But the more I thought about it, the more it started to make sense, and that's when I realized why I felt so guilty when I heard about how he stuck up for me in the cafeteria: Of course he felt like he had to do everything on his own. The people in his life who should be there for him never were.

I thought back to all the times I watched Thomas beat the stuffing out of him, the way I looked the other way when he struggled with his condition, the way I refused to face him after putting him in the hospital. Whenever things got tough for him, I turned my back on him, but whenever things got tough for me, Chris stepped up. When I was crying in the woods, he ran away with me so I wouldn't get lonely. When guilt starting tearing me apart, he found a way for me to blow off steam. When the whole school was laughing at me, he stood in front of them all and shut them up. It's true that he wasn't always being selfless, but no matter how hurtful those things he said in the forest were, they were at least a little true. When I was a coward, he took action. Maybe that led to him picking a few fights he shouldn't… but would he pick those fights if he felt like he had any other option? Of course he was going to be jealous of me. Despite having all the power in the world to stop them, I'd been letting people hurt him nearly his entire life.

I stood up as Chris finished the last of his food, "I'm gonna go grab my dress. I'll meet you back at the car."

He nodded, and I took the few minutes of solitude to try and clear my head, which wasn't so easy on my way to pick up an expensive reminder of his brother's bullying. When I walked in the dressmaker's store, the same lady that took my measurements rushed over and excitedly dragged me to an ice blue dress with a studded black sash tied around the waist, demanding that I try it on and show her how it fit. I wasn't really planning on doing that when we came, but she basically shoved me into a fitting room. Oh well. It wouldn't hurt.

It'd been a little while since I had to wear a dress for something, but as I slipped into it, I could tell it fit right, snug where it had to be but loose enough to be comfortable. Taking a good look at myself in the mirror, I was really wowed by what a good job she did in such a short time. With a skirt that came just to my knees and short sleeves hugging my shoulders, seeing all the skin along my arms and legs made me feel pretty exposed, but I guess when I ordered it, I was still reeling from the confidence boost getting asked to prom gave me. Tossing a few fistfuls of hair back, I thought if I straightened it out, I might actually look okay. Come to think of it, with some gloves and boots, it'd kinda look like one of the superhero outfits I sketched out.

Out of curiosity, I made sure the fitting room door was good and locked before turning back to the mirror. Clenching my fists, I struck a pose out of a manga panel and raised my energy level just high enough for my eyes to glow. It felt right, the bright red of my eyes with my pale blue dress. My legs moved easily enough with the short skirt, and the sleeves would keep the top from falling down if I had to jump around. Throw on some shorts underneath, and I wouldn't actually mind fighting crime in this.

The eyes in my own reflection narrowed to a confident glare. I couldn't believe how cool I looked. Maybe there was still a use for this dress. Maybe Leroy's superhero could come back and protect the person who needed it most.

Feeling good, I got back into my normal clothes, thanked the clerk and returned to the car. Chris was waiting for me in the front seat. I think he expected me to be glum, and chose his words very carefully as I hung the dress up in the back and hopped in next to him.

"Looks nice," he said.

"You know, I think so too."

And that's all we said about it. Chris took a few backroads

out of town, taking the scenic route to the therapist's office. The anxiousness in his face didn't go away though. I tried not to make it too obvious that I was trying to figure out what was up. We stayed quiet until the moment Chris parked in front of a cute blue house that matched the therapist's address.

My fingers wrapped around the car door handle, and I turned to ask him when he'd be back to get me, but he spoke before I had the chance. "So, I was thinking," he said. "We never did go to a single one of those dances. We've been here for four years and didn't attend even one homecoming. So I thought maybe, you know, might be interesting to check it out at least once. They're still selling tickets. You'll be putting that dress to good use, and I could scrounge something together." He shrugged, "Might be interesting."

Once the initial shock of the question wore off, I took a good look at him and understood. He wasn't nervous in the way a boy normally is when he asks a girl to prom, he was nervous because he didn't want me to say yes. If I knew Chris, the thought of being seen at that kind of social event, the thought of dressing up, the thought of dancing, made him wanna puke. He didn't wanna go. He was only asking because he thought it'd make me feel better about what happened. Part of me wanted to say no to save him the trouble.

But part of me kinda wanted to go, too.

I smiled and said, "I'd like that." I shut the door because I knew Chris wouldn't want me to make a big deal about it, turned around, and walked up to the door of the counseling office, not afraid at all.

CHAPTER 34

CHRIS

MY FIRST TRIP to the bathroom that night perfectly summed up the prom experience. In the couple of minutes it took to piss and wash my hands, some kid threw himself into a stall and made enough noise with his asshole to wake the dead. Then, Thomas and his goon squad stumbled in. He removed a flask from his tux, taking a second to threaten me if I ratted them out, and, right as the smell hit, took a shot of god knows what. He passed the flask to one of his minions as I left.

Christ, did I hate prom.

Walking back to the same old cafeteria through the same old hallways filled me with the same miserable feeling Leroy High gave me any other day, only now everything was dimly lit and covered in green construction paper to fit the racist jungle theme. Hosting it off campus wasn't within the school's budget, but surely, they could've done better than giving us just the gym for dancing and the cafeteria for sitting. For some bewildering reason we weren't allowed outside for fresh air, and there wasn't even anything to drink or snack on, the cheap bastards.

But I was doing my best to not be a dick about it. We were here for Kelly's sake, after all. We hadn't moved almost the entire night, camping out just outside the gym doors like cats at the edge of a pond, curious about the fish but unwilling to get their feet wet. Even if the chaperones were successful at keeping the dance from devolving into a sex pit (they were not) neither of us had the courage to actually go in and dance.

All that's to say, returning to our table was the first time I'd gotten an outside look at her all night, and seeing her dressed up and alone was a real gut punch. Kelly had gone all out and the final result was shockingly bold. The dress fit her form perfectly, with the barest hint of sleeves and a skirt not even brushing against her knees emphasizing her slender limbs. Her hair had been tamed after several hours with a straightener and kept in place with a big black headband that matched the sash running along her waist, the perfect smidge of darkness against the cool blue of her dress and eyes. She made me feel like a caveman in comparison. I'd barely scrounged together a white button up with a black tie, not to mention my giant-ass cast and the fact that my hair had only just grown back enough to cover my scarred scalp. But all of her effort was completely wasted. Nobody cared. For all the talk of how funny it would be to have her here, nobody looked surprised or so much as glanced our way. I suppose to them a freak is a freak no matter what. Fuckers.

She flashed a weak smile at me when she realized I

caught her staring off into space, but she wasn't fooling me. She wanted to leave even more than I did, and just didn't want to be the first person to say that.

I sighed, not even bothering to sit down, "This sucks."

She paused and studied my face. I almost had to nod at her to confirm it was okay to admit it.

"…Yeah."

"We don't have to stick around, you know."

It was true. The pain in my bones had become manageable enough that I convinced Mom to let me drive the Kellywagon instead of getting a ride from her. The only thing keeping us at prom was pride.

Kelly still needed a bit of coaxing though. The way she darted her eyes around screamed, "Yes please get me out of here already," but she was too polite to come out and say it.

"But your mom spent so much money on our tickets."

"She doesn't have to know we ditched. It's not that late yet. Movie theater's probably still showing something. Once that's over, it'll be late enough that we can pretend that we stayed."

Kelly instantly sprang up from the hard cafeteria stool without another word. I sighed and lead the way back toward the school entrance. This should have been a relief, but something kept eating at me, a touch of failure building over the evening. This wasn't the way it was supposed to go. Kelly, at least, was supposed to be having a good time.

For a moment I lingered over the entrance to the gym, stared into the dark swirl of bodies and flashing neon lights, felt the awful electronic dance beat reverberate in my muscles. I wondered if I should grab her by the hand and dance awkwardly in the corner by ourselves, away from everyone else. We wouldn't have to touch. It'd be dark and nobody would be able to see us embarrass ourselves.

The longer I stared into the gym, however, the more things started to change. The fast rhythm and hard beat died off. With no music to help them channel their primal urges, the students all waited, anticipating the moment they could begin to move again. The music returned, not with a thundering bass, but with the plucks of an acoustic guitar and a crooning ballad. Everyone got the signal and changed modes. The boys put their hands on the girls' hips and the room started to sway back and forth with a tranquil ease. Honestly, the transformation was stunning to behold.

Kelly must have thought so too. She stood by my side at the doorway's edge, messing up her perfectly straightened hair by twisting the ends between her fingertips.

"You know," she said, "I think maybe I can handle this?"

We stood at the edge, pondering the idea for a silent second. Kelly made the first move, reaching toward me in such a small way that I almost didn't notice it. I reached back, but didn't grab her hand. I didn't want to make any sudden moves, but she surprised me by suddenly leaning over and wrapping her fingers around mine. As awful as this is to admit, I tensed up, anticipating a loud crack and more unbearable pain.

It never came. We met each other's eyes and once we were both sure everything was okay, we stepped into the gym.

She led me into the closest corner, where nobody, not even the other lowest pieces of the totem pole, was dancing. That was fine by me. We were already pushing our luck and I didn't want to be near anyone else.

It only took a few seconds for me to step on her foot.

My face burned up, "Sorry," I whispered.

Kelly chuckled, but not in a cruel way, like she understood. We kept moving back and forth, but soon enough she returned the favor and stomped on my own toes.

I felt her swell with panic, "Oh my gosh, I'm so sorry, are you okay?"

"I'm not *that* fragile," I said, smiling.

She smiled back, and we tried to regain what little rhythm we had. The next time someone stepped on the other's foot—I'm not even sure whose fault it was—we ignored it and tried to keep going. But we kept doing it over and over. Every few seconds one of us was crushing the other's toes. We couldn't keep up the straight faces for much longer, and pretty soon both of us stopped, giggling and leaning on each other like children.

"Are we even supposed to move our feet?" Kelly asked, taking her hand off my shoulder to wipe away a tear.

"I have no idea."

Kelly rooted herself to the ground and drew me even closer. I slid my hand from her hip to her back, entangling it in the tips of her flowing hair. We didn't break eye contact. Everything else fell away. The other students were just shadows, the music nothing more than a vaguely pleasant sound. I could hardly pick out individual lyrics or notes or even place what song we were dancing to. It was only me and Kelly, holding each other. Swaying back and forth. Back and forth. It wasn't weird, or uncomfortable, or embarrassing, or any of that. It was just nice.

The music stopped and we lingered in each other's eyes for a few seconds.

And then another club anthem roared through the speakers. I jolted away from her and went to cover my ears, but with only one hand I was vulnerable to the sound's assault. Kelly pulled me into her. I laid my head on her shoulder until I had adjusted to the music.

"Christ, talk about whiplash." I stepped back, still shaking, "What the fuck is the DJ doing?"

"Come on," she said softly, "let's get out of here."

We were able to escape the gravitational pull of the sex pit without much trouble, and once we were away from the dance floor I was able to fully calm down and look back at Kelly. The satisfaction on her face matched my own. Prom hadn't been a total bust after all, not that we wanted to stay any longer. Plus, aside from watching my brother take bathroom shots, nobody had bothered us all night.

But lo and behold, as Kelly and I arrived at the school entrance, we ran face first into someone coming back inside, an all too familiar girl in a regal red dress matched by a burning face. Cassidy. Her anger dissipated as she and Kelly locked eyes for a fraction of a second before both stared at the floor in embarrassment. I kept my eye on her as Kelly started to make her way outside. Cassidy snuck another look, holding her breath like she was unsure if she should just let us go or not.

But right as Kelly opened the door and was about to leave, Cassidy said, "Hey Kelly."

She stopped and glanced over her shoulder. I tensed up, standing between them with a glare burrowing into Cassidy. A gentle brush on my shoulder pushed me aside as Kelly stood next to me, "H-hey Cassidy. Do you need something?"

"No, not really. I just wanted to tell you that your dress is really pretty."

"Oh." Kelly's weary smile did nothing to hide her blushing. "Um, thanks. So... so is yours."

Not wanting this to drag out, I shifted toward the door without saying anything, hoping Kelly would take the excuse to escape the awkward situation. But Cassidy responded before she had the chance.

"Thanks. But that, that wasn't all that I wanted to say. I... also wanted to tell you I'm sorry. For embarrassing you."

Kelly's face burned with the heat of a thousand suns, "Oh, no. You don't have to apologize. That was all my fault. I shouldn't have been at that party anyway."

Cassidy's fake laughter didn't disguise her shame one bit, "No, I'm not talking about that. I'm talking about prom court. I... thought it was weird when they told me that you didn't want to be on the court. That you weren't coming to the dance. Because I thought Noah... that he... he wouldn't..."

My glare at her intensified, and she took a deep breath when she saw it in her peripheral vision. Just come out and say it. Say the truth.

"I thought Noah was serious when he asked you here tonight. Because you were the only person at that party he was having fun with, you know? But Thomas—" Her lips tightened. Anger returned to burn away her guilt. "That doesn't matter," she finally said with more clarity, "What matters is that I'm sorry. I'm sorry I was part of this. I swear I didn't know. If I did, I never would have announced your name on that stage, I promise."

Kelly blinked a few times, unsure of what to say in return.

But I didn't stick around to see how the rest of this conversation would go down. I quietly slipped out the door. Partly to give Kelly some space—this had nothing to do with me—but mostly out of curiosity. The way Cassidy brought up my brother and then quickly tried to brush him aside seemed suspicious.

Those suspicions were confirmed when the door closed behind me and a horrible retching echoed through the cool night. A figure hunched over in the parking lot gagged and lurched. I stepped closer and my eyes adjusted to the dark just in time to witness my brother's vomit splattering the concrete and peppering his shiny shoes in flecks. Must have pre-gamed harder than intended.

From this pathetic sight, it wasn't difficult to deduce what happened. Thomas, or perhaps one of his idiot friends, let something slip to his girlfriend they weren't supposed to. A crack about Kelly after seeing her at the table, a vague reference to their plan after running into me in the bathroom, whatever. Cassidy, oblivious to Thomas's true nature until this point, dragged him outside and demanded to know what was going on, at which point they got in a fight, one bad enough to compel Cassidy to apologize for something she frankly didn't have much to do with. Thomas, meanwhile, was left to puke on himself in the dark and drunkenly call his (ex?) girlfriend a bitch under his breath over and over.

Thomas bumped into someone's car and swore. Grunting and swinging with the force of a wrecking ball, he struck the hood with a resounding thud. I don't know if he dented it or not, and if it hurt him, he didn't care, didn't notice me as he continued stumbling around.

Seeing him like this wasn't as satisfying as I hoped it would be. If anything, it made me uncomfortable. Almost every interaction between Thomas and I had some sort of anger behind it, but this was something else. This wasn't the macho man routine he used to assert dominance. This was the lashing out of someone deeply wounded, someone who knows he fucked up badly but still can't accept the consequences of his actions. Looking from the outside, a fact I'd long tried to deny became undeniable: We were brothers, more alike than not. All our surface level distinctions—our body types, our hobbies, our social status—washed away to reveal the same frightened little boy underneath. A boy who could only respond to his problems with a fight. I'd been the same way in the hospital, the same way when Kelly confronted me in the woods.

It wasn't a great look.

I took a few tentative steps forward. Our cycle ends here. I had the upper hand, something that didn't happen too often. The urge to rub it in his face was strong, but I pushed it down. If I truly was less of a dick than he was, the innocent brother I always imagined myself to be, this was a chance to start acting like it.

Thomas, meanwhile, continued stumbling forward. He flailed his hands around in his pockets and jingled his keys as they slipped from his fingers to the concrete. He swore again and pawed at them on the ground, springing up and pointing his keys around the lot as he smacked the unlock button over and over again. The headlights of his car flashed and lit up his back. He'd stumbled past it in his drunken stupor. Thomas turned around and made his way toward it.

Sighing, I stepped between Thomas and his car. No way was this happening.

"Come on Thomas, give me the keys. I'll drive you home," I said.

Thomas bared his teeth at me, "Outta the fucking way." He tried to dive around me, but with the liquor hampering his coordination it was a simple matter to continue blocking him.

"I'm not going to tell Mom, if that's what you're thinking. Kelly and I were about to leave anyway. We can drop you off wherever you want and get the car tomorrow morning," I held out my hand slowly, like I was attempting to feed a dangerous animal, "Seriously. Let me drive you home."

My hand stung as Thomas smacked it away, "Think this is funny, huh? Think it's fucking hilarious don't you?"

"No, I don't."

"Liar!" he shouted, "This is what you wanted! That's all you do, try to ruin my fuckin' life. You did it. You finally fuckin' did it. She dumped me. That *bitch* dumped me at prom 'cause of you and your ugly ass girlfriend! You happy? You happy you little piece of shit?"

I bit the inside of my mouth hard enough to draw blood. I had to keep my cool no matter how much I wanted to deck him. I took a deep breath and tried to keep my voice calm, but firm. "You're drunk. Let me drive you home."

"I'm fine, you hear me? Fine! I don't want your help! Outta the goddamn way!"

The pain hit before I even felt Thomas touch me. He

rammed his palm into my chest, now more metal than bone, and I fell backwards. I thought I'd been shot in the heart. It felt almost as intense as the night Kelly destroyed my ribcage. The back of my shirt tore as I slammed into the ground and screamed. The pain wouldn't let me focus on anything else.

But I didn't have time to stay down there. The headlights of Thomas's car blinded my bleary eyes. The vehicle shot backward. He smashed a taillight against a limousine one of the rich kids rented before speeding away.

I acted entirely on instinct. Bursts of pain ran through me as I scrambled to my feet and ran over to Kelly's car. A gentle throb coursed through my body as I floored the gas and chased my brother down the highway.

This stretch of road had no lights, no businesses or street lamps to guide me. Just Thomas's single unbroken taillight, speeding away down a perfectly straight road. It took far too long to catch up. I had to go nearly 30 miles over the speed limit to get to him. He rode the line between lanes, drifting over to the other side and violently overcorrecting every few seconds, almost sliding into the ditch next to us. Lights on the other side of the highway started blinking in and out of my field of view. Any second, harsh blue and red ones would flash and pull one of us aside. If that's what it took to stop this madness, then so be it. Better to sober up in a jail cell then to crash and kill himself, or worse. It was prom night. Someone had to be patrolling the area. Someone had to catch him.

But at the speed we were going, it would only be another ten minutes until we arrived at our house. There was only one major turn. Getting from school to home was nearly a straight shot, and there weren't too many other people out. If Thomas could stay in his lane for just a little bit longer, he could get out of this with nothing more than a lecture from Mom.

He sped up. Like he was trying to keep me from passing. I swore at myself and smacked the steering wheel with my only good hand. I had no idea what I thought I was doing. I tried to formulate some sort of plan to stop him, some way to signal and try and slow him down, but short of rear ending him myself I could think of nothing. I'd taken just about the worst course of action by panicking. By giving chase like this, I'd doomed myself into the role of the observer. Whether this ended with Thomas at home or jail, a hospital or a morgue, I had no control.

Unless I called the police. I could tip off an officer and get them ready to intercept him. My eyes flicked from the road to the bulge in my pocket. I'd need to take my good hand off the wheel while going almost 90 to call.

No. That wasn't an option. He could make it. We were almost there.

A blaring horn and squealing tires wrested my attention back to the road. Thomas was halfway in the oncoming traffic lane. A driver swerved left as Thomas lurched right. The two cars were close enough to kiss. But they didn't crash.

Once I was sure of my place in the road, I took my hands off the wheel and dialed 911, locking the phone between my cheek and shoulder.

Ring.

Thomas had mostly straightened out. He was still going too fast.

Ring.

A sudden twinge of pain coursed through me, but I refused to drop the phone or let go of the wheel.

Ring.

"Come on, come on, pick up!"

Ring.

Thomas only had one brake light. I didn't see the sudden flash of red until the nose of Kelly's car had almost rammed it. Panicking, I slammed on my own brakes. Momentum threw my phone out of the notch in my shoulder mid ring, but I managed to avoid collision.

"*Now you want to watch your speed?*" I screamed.

I had a bigger problem. The phone was nowhere to be found, either down by the pedals or under the seat. I wouldn't be able to find it without stopping.

"Hello?" I shouted loud enough to overpower the engine, "There's a drunk driver on 224! He's almost to the intersection at the gas station! Get out here and stop him before he kills someone!"

It was useless. I had no idea if the phone was connected, if the operator could hear me, or even if they could make it in time. There was nothing they could do. Nothing any of us could do.

The cars kept careening forward until we reached the gas station that marked where we were supposed to turn. Thomas almost missed it, almost barreled straight through the red light, but swerved at a right angle to head for home. I followed him, also not bothering to stop at the red.

Despite everything, I allowed myself to calm down a bit. The road home, though long, was a completely straight shot with other cars unlikely to be around. He could still hit a tree or telephone pole, but more likely he'd just slide into a ditch and be unable to move, a little shaken, but mostly fine. Everything would be alright. There was no reason to panic.

A train whistle echoed through the night.

If Thomas heard the whistle, he didn't react. The car kept charging forward with drunken confidence. My eyes caught a tiny prick of light far to my left. I slowed down, tried to discern if it was moving closer or farther away.

Closer. Definitely closer. I tapped on my brakes to drift to a stop, pushing harder when I realized exactly how fast I was going. I'd left myself plenty of time to stop before the tracks, partially because I'd driven this route so many times and instinctively knew where they were.

If Thomas had that instinct, the liquor dulled it. He didn't stop. The light grew larger and larger until it was a blinding star. The train accelerated at an exponential rate. Thomas must have thought he'd be able to get over the track before it caught up.

The more I slowed, the faster the world moved. I turned on my brights in a desperate attempt to get a better idea of how far Thomas had to go. The earth rumbled as the train whistle roared, accepting Thomas's challenge.

He didn't slow down. It would've been too late even if he did. Because from where I was sitting, now at a complete stop, I saw the whole picture and knew the truth.

He wasn't going to make it.

The train was too fast. It would t-bone Thomas with enough force to topple the tallest building in Leroy.

I didn't look away, didn't close my eyes. I didn't scream or cry or slam on the steering wheel or beg any kind of god to stop this. Only one thought crossed my mind.

It's happening again.

A gust of wind rushed past my window.

No. Not the wind. It had too much weight to it, too much color. And it was moving faster than any wind I'd ever seen.

A tangled blur of blue and yellow appeared in the glow of my headlights. Without slowing down, the figure zipped in front of Thomas's still speeding car. Thomas crashed to a dead stop, and his car rose into the air, front side down, as the windshield shattered and shot a barrage of broken glass at the woman in the blue dress holding it up by its nose, unmoved by the speed. Behind her, with barely enough space to slide a piece of paper between them, the train continued on its course.

Kelly gently laid the car back in the road. She peeked into the broken windshield, made sure that the sudden stop hadn't hurt my brother, and stood tall as she turned toward me. Confidence radiated off her. There was no gangliness to her limbs or hesitance in her posture. She stood proud with her fists clenched, like they were barely holding back the power she could now wield freely.

I flung my door open. Everything went away in that moment. The pain from my fall earlier, the overwhelming noise of the passing train, the panic in my chest, all melted into nothing at the sight of my best friend. I sprinted past Thomas's car and threw myself into her arms, holding her as tight as I could with my one unbroken arm.

I buried my face into her shoulder, unable to look at her or anything else. When the train finally passed us and the caboose blinked out of existence, I whispered, "You made it in time."

Kelly said nothing. Her rapid heartbeat began to slow, her heavy breathing grew light. Eventually, she pulled me closer to her, firm. We stood in each other's arms, in total comfort with each other, for the first time.

The moment couldn't last. An awful howling echoed out of the empty windshield. I let go and spun around. Thomas pointed a finger directly at Kelly from the seat of the ruined car. The front side was crushed together like an accordion; the deflated air bag in his lap and the seat belt digging into his neck spared him from the carnage of hitting Kelly like a brick wall. If he said any actual words, they were coherent only to him.

I turned back to Kelly weighed down by a heavy feeling.

"What are we going to do?" I said.

Kelly shifted back toward the car, "I should probably get him out of the road, huh?"

She placed her hands on what was left of the bumper, and bent down like she was about to pick it up. I rushed over and placed a hand on her shoulder.

"That's not what I mean. What are we going to do about Thomas? He saw you."

She stood up straight, cocking her head at me, "You aren't hurt, are you?"

"No, but—"

"And everyone else is okay? He didn't hit anyone?"

"No."

Kelly turned back around and lifted the two-ton hunk of steel as easily as anyone else would lift an empty cardboard box. Thomas screams got ever louder as his seat belt kept him from tumbling out. She placed him in the ditch and dusted off her hands, "As long as everyone is safe, it doesn't matter."

I sighed and dug my hand in my pocket, "That's a nice thought and all, but we can't leave it at that. Thomas needs an ambulance. Someone has to be accountable for the car. I'm not letting you get exposed because my piece of shit brother got drunk in a bathroom and almost killed himself."

She bit her lip. I know she was trying to act brave because she was doing the right thing, but deep down, she still wanted to keep her existence a secret, "It's like you said. He's already seen me, right? I don't know if there's anything we can do about it now."

No. There had to be a way out of this. I searched the area and almost immediately found my answer. A telephone pole, thick enough to be mistaken for a sturdy tree, stood near the wreckage at the side of the road.

"Alright, take the wreck and ram the front end into the telephone pole. Make it look like he crashed. Then," I made my voice sound as tender as possible, "if you think you can handle it, move him from the driver's seat to the passenger's. I'd do it myself, but…" I sighed, "there's no way I'd be able to. While you're doing that, I better grab my phone. Dropped it in the car."

We broke to our respective tasks with a nod. As I turned and made my way back to the Kellywagon with a brisk walk, Thomas's screaming rang out over the sound of crunching metal. It occurred to me that only a few short months ago, I would have killed to watch Kelly move that thing around, cheered at the sight of her manhandling my brother. Now all I could think about is how annoying Thomas's blubbering was while I dug around in the seats.

It didn't take too long for me to find my phone. The 911 operator was still on the line. I hung up. An officer must have already been on the way, and I didn't want them to overhear what I was about to say to Kelly. We had to move fast. I turned around just in time to see Kelly gently buckle a squirming Thomas in the passenger seat like a baby, and jogged up to her.

"Okay," she said, "So what's the plan?"

"Take your car and go home. Hell, it might even be safer if you went back to prom or the movie theater. You need to get as far away from here as possible." I could tell that she wasn't getting it. I kept going before she could speak. "I called the cops while I was chasing Thomas. They'll be here any second, and when they arrive, they'll find me in the front seat. I'll tell them that I was Thomas's designated driver." He was still going to get busted for underage drinking, and that was fine. Seeing him escape from a near death experience made me a little soft towards my brother, insofar as I didn't want him to go to prison for a DUI. But I was pissed enough to want *some* retribution. "I'll say I lost control of the vehicle trying to avoid a deer. It'll be easy to believe thanks to the cast." I gently rapped my knuckles against it. The worried look on Kelly's face didn't go away.

"Chris, Thomas is panicking real badly. I think he's gonna tell—"

"Who are they going to believe, the drunken asshole spouting nonsense about Wonder Woman, or the brother responsible enough to want him home safe? Thomas might be drunk enough to black out tomorrow if we're lucky, but if not, I'll handle it."

She looked from the car back to me, "Are you sure?"

"I'll be fine. I'm not looking forward to the ambulance ride, and my mom is going to have a heart attack when she hears about this, but that's nothing. Now go on, get out of here before somebody sees you."

She took a deep breath and walked over to me. Without any hesitation, she gave me a gentle hug, "Guess we're not seeing that movie tonight, huh?"

I smiled, "There's always tomorrow."

Kelly smiled back. She looked at me for a second with hesitation, like there was something else that still needed to be said. Whatever it was, she put it out of her mind, simply saying, "See you tomorrow," as she walked back to her car.

In the meantime, I got into the driver's seat. Kelly had popped the door off, so wiggling in wasn't too difficult. Mostly I was just worried about sitting on broken glass. All that was left was dealing with Thomas. I studied his face, watched it twist and contort. He'd finally stopped screaming, at least.

I felt obligated to say something to cushion the blow. When I saw Kelly as a child, it was easy to put the pieces back together, to accept the impossible, but Thomas was an adult, set in his ways and with a naturally closed-minded disposition to boot. This display of power had the potential to shatter his psyche. Now wasn't the time to gloat.

"You don't need to be afraid of her, you know," I said.

Snapping to me, a white-hot rage burned away his fear, "You fucking kidding me? I'm telling the damn cops!"

"There's no way you're going to convince them a teenage girl stopped this car with her bare hands."

"Then... then I'll get a video of her! If you think I'm

just letting this go, you're out of your goddamn mind. People need to know about this… this… this *thing.*"

I sighed, "Alright. Let's say you get a video. Then what? What, exactly, will the police do with her? Put her in a cell? She might go along with it, but only because she's nice like that. The second she gets tired of playing along, she's gone. Nothing can hold her if she doesn't want it to. All you'll do is freak people out. Is that what you really want? Seriously Thomas, she just saved your life. You should be thanking her."

Thomas was screaming bloody murder. Teetering on the precipice of madness, he slammed his fist against the busted dashboard, "Easy for you to say when she's your fucking lapdog. You just want to keep it a secret so you can hide behind your pet monster like a pussy. I'm not gonna let you! I'm telling everyone! I'm telling the whole goddamn world!"

I can't say Thomas didn't know my weak points. Not that provoking me was ever that hard, I suppose. Even now, able to recognize exactly what he was doing, I felt the desire to lash out. The relief at his safety had long since subsided. I couldn't believe he'd do something so colossally stupid over a girl. I couldn't believe that he could stare death in the face and not learn a goddamn thing.

I suppose, deep down, part of me wanted things to be different now, for Thomas to have a new lease on life after coming so close to the brink. Maybe inspire him to be a bit nicer to people, if only because they might hit back with the force of a nuclear warhead. If nothing else, I thought we could come to some sort of understanding.

Maybe I was expecting too much from him. He did

have a lot to process. Maybe once he sobered up, had time to think things over, he'd change, be a little grateful for the second chance Kelly gave him. But I couldn't count on that. At that moment, I had to make myself absolutely clear.

I still wanted to at least try being the bigger man. So I said, with as little anger as possible, "Thomas, if you utter a word about that girl, I'm going to tell the cops who was really driving this car."

That shut him up. Kept him quiet until emergency services arrived, in fact. He did stare at me with uneasy horror almost the entire time, but that didn't matter. What mattered was keeping Kelly's secret safe.

If she was going to protect me, and everyone else, I wanted to return the favor. Even in just a small way.

CHAPTER 35

KELLY

CLOUDS BLOCKED THE moon and kept me from seeing the water's murky surface, but that was okay. It might've even been easier that way. If I couldn't see the water, maybe I wouldn't think so hard about what I was trying to do.

I'd been seeing my therapist every week for about a month. I never did tell her about my powers or Dad, but that didn't mean it wasn't helpful talking to her about my anxieties, my bad self-esteem, all the abuse. There were still days where I felt totally worthless, times when I'd wake up from nightmares where Dad was gonna put me back in the basement, but I started to find ways of fighting back. Mostly, I'd go out in the middle of the night and play around with my powers, sometimes with Chris, mostly by myself. The more I used them, the more comfortable I got with my body, the less reason I'd have to be afraid of Dad's ghost. Once I built a giant tower of wrecked cars in

343

the junkyard and knocked it apart with a punch. Another time, I made a giant cat face in an open field out of trees and big rocks from a nearby park. Sometimes I'd even take out Chris's old superhero training list and try to see if I could make any of those powers work after all, and though I wasn't any closer to shooting lasers out my eyes, there was one thing I'd actually been able to do. Not perfect yet, but it was a start. Since Chris's birthday was June 10th, I hoped to be ready to show him by then.

Graduation day made me more anxious than I thought it would, so later that night, I was gonna try and run across the surface of the park's slimy fishing pond.

Needing a head start, I took my position at the end of the parking lot. With nothing between me and the water, it was a straight shot over to the hill on the opposite side. I'd taken to walking around barefoot whenever I could, mostly because when I started running fast it wore down my shoes. I'd burned through four pairs since we started training. My skin crawled as I imagined my feet touching the dirty pond, or worse, screwing up and plunging into it, but I had to clear my mind, and just run.

Okay. Deep breath. Three... two... one... GO!

I was off. Nervousness kept me from going full speed right away. The rough, concrete parking lot scratched at the soles of my feet as I charged the edge of the pond. When the surface changed to grass and dirt, I shut my eyes and ran faster, and soon enough water splashed my shins as my feet slapped against the pond's surface. Like dashing across a thin sheet of melting ice, the water tried to swallow me up, and I started to sink when my mind got distracted by the weird feeling of it rushing between my toes, but I put one leg in front of the other and kept running faster, only opening my eyes when I felt hard earth beneath my feet a few seconds later. I kept running until I was at the top of the hill. When I looked at the water below, the ripples on the surface were echoes of each footstep.

Wow. I've gotta remember to show Chris. This'll cheer him up.

In our last month of school, Chris did a lot to try and pull himself together, too. With a little encouragement from me, he started seeing his psychiatrist again, and his mood was better for a little while. He seemed to be getting more sleep, and for the rest of his time at Leroy High, he didn't get into any trouble.

But I'm not gonna lie… I was still really worried about him. I think the incident at prom shook him a little more than he thought it would. It was hard to blame him since his brother almost died. Thomas walked away pretty much unhurt. Everyone believed Chris's story, and the judge only gave Thomas a fine. His mom was really mad, but since she didn't know the full story either, the punishment wasn't as harsh as it maybe should've been.

So that was okay, but Thomas started acting weird around us. I think Thomas still resented Chris a little bit for all the trouble he got in. Chris said Thomas never thanked him for covering it all up, never apologized for pushing him down in the parking lot or driving drunk. Thomas couldn't even look at me whenever I passed him. I guess I shouldn't be surprised, but at least, as far as I know, he never said anything about my powers. I could tell Thomas was on Chris's mind more lately because he started telling me stories I'd never heard before, about the games they played as kids and all the trouble they used to get in together in New York. It made me sad. But I guess too much had happened for things to ever be like that again.

I wish his brother was the only thing on his mind, but there was lots for him to worry about. The cast wouldn't come off for another month, and he told me that he hadn't taken painkillers since he left the hospital because he was afraid of getting addicted. Plus, in the last week of school, his mood really tanked, probably because of the big history final hanging over his head. One day he sheepishly asked to see my notes for that class. I wasn't gonna let him tough it out alone, so we spent a few long days writing and rewriting an essay that, when it was all done, I thought Mr. Patterson would love. Chris wasn't so convinced, and the worst of it began after he handed it in, waiting while the anxiety of not knowing if he'd have to repeat a year of high school ate at him.

Chris passed, but only barely. That didn't really make him any happier. Being so sure he was gonna fail, he never sent in an application to the local community college, and even if he had, I could tell he was still comparing himself to both me and his brother, who were gonna be off to big city schools in the fall. Also not helping was the fact that, even though he graduated like the rest of us, Chris's permanent record was so bad the principal barred him from the ceremony. Thomas still got to go despite the alcohol thing, but they wouldn't even let Chris sit in the audience with his family while Thomas got his diploma. Even though it disappointed Grandma and Grandpa, I decided not to go either, asking if we could take Chris out to lunch since his mom made us dinner on prom night. Chris put on a brave face the whole time, acting like he didn't want to waste his time at the ceremony in the first place, but I could see all the hurt bubbling just under the surface, and he tried to disguise statements like "my grandparents only came to see Thomas anyway" as self-deprecating jokes. When I asked him if he wanted to come superpowering with me that night, he said he felt tired, and he should go to bed earlier anyway.

So, sitting around the quiet park at three in the morning, I didn't expect him to call me, but my ringtone broke the peaceful atmosphere. I wasted no time in answering.

"Hey," I said.

"Hey. Sorry, I know you were probably asleep."

"No, it's okay. I'm still out, actually." I wandered over to the water's edge, "What's up?"

The other end of the phone went silent.

"Chris?" I said.

"Sorry. It just sounds dumb, saying it out loud. I… I was having nightmares again."

Immediately, I made my way for the park's exit, "Do you want me to come over?"

"You don't have to do that. If you're in the middle of something—"

"It's okay, I want to," I started jogging toward home, "Be there in a sec."

Hanging up the phone, I took off, cutting through fields and people's backyards for the fastest route home, figuring the night would protect my identity if anyone happened to look out the window. Going this way, what was normally a fifteen-minute drive to that park was only a five-minute run for me.

When I got back to our street, Chris's window was the only light on, and I went directly for it so I wouldn't wake the rest of his family going through the front door. The window was open, waiting for me. Chris was on his bed and still in his pajamas as I climbed through it. He looked more vulnerable than when he fell asleep on my shoulder. I sat next to him. For a moment, neither of us said anything.

Finally, I reached out and touched him on the shoulder. His eyes started to water. Seeing that his words were getting lost somewhere in his throat, I wrapped my arms around his body, brought him close to me. Up and down, his chest rose and fell with a weight he couldn't handle.

"I'm fucking pathetic," he said.

"No, you're not. Now come on, talk to me. Was it about your dad again? Or the train?"

He shook his head with hesitation, "Not this time. This was so much worse." Clearing his throat, he started talking all in one breath, like he was still in the middle of a panic attack, "So, I was in this lake or something. I don't know why, I don't know how I got there, whatever, it's not important. So there was this lake, right? And I decided to go swimming for a while, and at some point I dived under the water. Only when I came back up for air, ice or glass or something froze over the surface. No matter how hard I pounded on it, it wouldn't crack, so water just kept rushing into my lungs and I just kept fucking drowning." He paused, trying his hardest to spit out the next part, "You were there too. You were standing right there on the ice, and all you had to do was look down and you could save me. But you didn't see me, or you were ignoring me, so I screamed and shouted and kept pounding on the ice, but the whole time you looked away and water kept rushing in and at some point I realized I was dreaming but I couldn't wake up so I just kept drowning and praying that at some point either you saved me or I woke up or died or anything to make it stop."

I let him cry as long as he needed to.

When he stopped, he pulled away a little to look me in the eye, "Can you promise me something?"

"Anything."

"When you go off to school, promise me you'll keep in touch. That you'll come back and visit me. Because I'm so afraid, I'm so afraid that you're going to make all kinds of new friends there who are actually smart and talented, and one day you're going to wake up and have forgotten all about me. But I'm going to go fucking crazy here all by myself. My brother won't even be around. I'll just be serving cheeseburgers to assholes day in and day out. So, you have to promise to at least call, alright?"

I didn't answer him right away. Not because that was a promise I couldn't keep. Of course I was gonna stay in touch. But a promise didn't seem like enough. There had to be a way, beyond words, to let Chris know that I cared about him. That he was special to me.

And looking out the open window, I think I had one.

The panic in his face got worse when I let go of him and moved to the window. With a reassuring smile, I climbed out of it and said, "Hey. There's something I've been meaning to show you."

Chris inched his way over, "Where are we going?"

I offered him my hand with a sly smile, "You'll see."

When he took my hand, some of his curiosity and

desire for adventure came out. He groaned a little as he climbed out the window, and groaned a little louder when his feet hit the dirt, wincing with pain as he stretched to close the window above him. I stood on my tippy toes and got it, then stepped into the yard, wanting to make sure I had enough room.

"Okay," I said, "Now close your eyes."

"Why?"

"It's a surprise."

He obeyed and stood up straight. I didn't know if I was quite ready for what I was about to do, but sometimes, you just need to give it a try. This also meant I wouldn't have a birthday surprise for him anymore, but that wasn't a big deal. I still had about a week to figure something out. Chris needed this now, and thinking about it, graduation was a much more fitting time anyway.

Without any warning, I scooped Chris off his feet. Startled, he opened his eyes and cocked his head at me.

"Hey!" I said, "Keep 'em closed!"

He mumbled an apology and closed them again. I took a moment to adjust him so he was as secure in my arms as he could be. After a few seconds he settled in, all snug and cozy.

Before we took off, I craned my neck towards the sky. It was a cool night for June, and that's when it occurred to me that it might be too cold for a normal person where we were going. Maybe I should tell him to go inside and get a jacket. A blast of energy shot through me, and I let the heat pulse through my body.

No, it's okay. I can keep him warm.

Keeping my eyes on the sky, I bent my knees, letting my

energy build and build. Should I have been more scared? Probably. I mean, if I turned out to not be ready after all, Chris would die. Like, actually die. But somehow, I knew in my heart that everything would be okay.

With no point in waiting any longer, I jumped.

CHAPTER 36

CHRIS

IT WAS LIKE being carried into the sky by a rocket on its way to Mars. A thousand tons of force pressured my chest as we shot skyward. My legs dangled off to the side, but the rest of my body felt secure in Kelly's strength, like a tower drop at a theme park going in reverse. The higher we climbed, the more the cold air slashed at me, but the internal engine of Kelly's body generated plenty of heat, so pressing closer to her kept me almost comfortable. Between the sudden shock of being blasted into the sky and the air quickly thinning, breathing came only with difficulty and pain, but I trusted Kelly to make the struggle worthwhile.

Our ascent slowed. When the air around me became denser and damper, I couldn't help myself. I had to open my eyes and see how high up we were. An impenetrable black fog greeted me, with the ground and the sky and even Kelly's face invisible. My eyes involuntarily squeezed shut. She did say to keep them closed.

Slower, slower, we drifted to a complete stop, and panic raced through my heart as we reached the peak. I waited for gravity to drag us back into free fall.

But that didn't happen.

As soon as I realized exactly what was going on, Kelly whispered, "Okay. You can open them."

Larger and closer than it had ever been before, the moon illuminated the sea of clouds beneath her feet, stretching for miles and blocking the town far, far below. As if to prove this was really happening, she floated down and submerged us in the wispy sea. The fog overcame us again, but it seemed less sinister this time, more like the hazy feeling of trying to remember a good dream. After giving me a few seconds to appreciate what the inside of a cloud felt like, she took us back up to the space between the earth and the heavens.

We were flying.

The moon glowed against the teeth of her broad, exposed smile.

"…How?"

"It was easy. All I had to do was flap my arms."

I was too dumbstruck to laugh at her little joke, peering over the side and back into the clouds, "Seriously… this is… holy shit, this is amazing." I looked back at her, "You're amazing."

"Yeah," she said, turning toward the crescent moon, "I guess this is pretty amazing, but it's not all me. We wouldn't be up here without you."

My gut reaction was to protest, but she stopped me, "Chris, I spent my whole life being told over and over again that I was dangerous. That I was the weird, ugly girl who didn't know how to talk to people. My entire life, people have been telling me how worthless I am, and I really believed it. There are times when I still believe it. You're the only one who was different. You made me feel like I mattered. I know you feel bad for pushing me, but if you hadn't, we wouldn't be here right now. So, I dunno, I think it was worth it, don't you?"

We drifted upward, like the wind was the only thing carrying us. Kelly kept talking. "I guess I'm trying to say, the reason I brought you up here is to tell you not to be afraid. I'm not gonna leave you behind. You're too important to me. Yeah, things are gonna be different, and maybe you need a little time to figure stuff out, but I'll have your back while you do. Like you've always had mine. You'll always be my best friend."

I didn't know what to say. In that moment, staring into those red eyes that had me captivated since childhood, I could feel it stronger than I ever had, the understanding that Kelly was more to me than just my best friend, but I was afraid to cross that last barrier between us, afraid of ruining an already uncertain future if the words came out.

Then, she kissed me.

It wasn't dramatic or passionate or even long. She leaned in and gave me a swift peck on the lips, rigidly pulling away almost as soon as we touched. I stared at her in shock.

"I made it weird, didn't I?" she said, her face burning, "We're just gonna pretend that never happened, right?"

I shook my head, sitting up straight as I drew in close enough to feel her breath on my face, "No."

Placing my shaking hand on her cheek, I closed my

eyes and pulled myself back to her lips. We took it slow, nervously. I'd never kissed anyone before, and I don't think Kelly's experience with the class president gave her much to work with. Every once in a while, one of us would pull back to look into the other's eyes, afraid that at any second we'd change our mind and not want each other anymore. But we always did. Eventually, we developed a rhythm, and soon there was nothing to distract us, like the kissing could just go on forever in our own little slice of the world, far away from everyone.

It took us a solid minute to notice we were falling out of the sky.

Kelly yelped and her grip on me loosened. As I slipped out of her grasp and tumbled towards the clouds, I kept my eyes focused on her falling figure above me. She had her eyes closed, muttering something under her breath while she tried to stabilize her energy, or whatever it was that kept her afloat. It filled me with an odd calm. Either Kelly would get it back under control and save me, or I'd fall to my death, and since the situation was completely out of my hands, I might as well have some fun with it. Reaching terminal velocity as I crashed back in the clouds, I flipped and somersaulted and instantly regretted it when it started making me sick. I couldn't see and my brain rattled so much that I wasn't quite sure I was falling down anymore. Somewhere along the way, Kelly had either stopped falling with me or simply had gotten lost in the fog.

Dizzy as I broke through the underside of the clouds, they got smaller and smaller as I fell with my back facing the ground. A few seconds later, another shadow crashed through and hovered for a few seconds before diving in my direction. In the blink of an eye, Kelly swooped down and matched my speed before grabbing me in a bear hug, slowing us to a crawl as she positioned us upright.

Kelly was breathless, "Oh god oh god oh god, are you okay? I'm so sorry, I thought I had it down, but I guess I need more practice. Like I didn't realize how easy it was to get distracted up here. Wait, does your chest hurt? I didn't crush it again when I caught you, did I? How's your arm? I—"

Saying nothing, I reached out and brushed the mess of hair covering her face away and smiled, "Maybe you should concentrate on keeping us airborne."

With a deep sigh of relief, she nodded, punctuating it with one last, quick kiss to my lips, as if to assure me that we would most certainly pick up where we left off. She adjusted her arms to make me more comfortable, and we took a good look at our town below us. Leroy didn't look so bad from up here, with only a smattering of light and the feeling that there was an entire world just beyond our vision, inviting us to come explore it.

Kelly must have been thinking the same thing, "You know," she said, "When I was thinking about what I wanted to do this summer, you know what I realized?"

"What?"

"I've never really been outside Leroy. Grandma and Grandpa don't really go on vacation and, I dunno, I've always wanted to go on some kinda adventure. So, I was thinking, since I can fly and all, maybe I'd take the months before school starts to travel." She paused, "It's gonna get pretty lonely if I go by myself."

My heart started racing. Nothing in the whole world

could have sounded so perfect. "I'll go anywhere you want to take me."

She smiled, "I thought you might say that."

"What are you thinking for the first stop?"

"Well, I wasn't really sure, but now I think I know," she hesitated for just a second, "I've always kinda wanted to see New York. Maybe you could show me where you grew up and stuff. But if you wanna skip it, I totally understand."

Returning to New York was an idea I never considered before. Even though we had family there, I'd more or less filed the city away as a land of ghosts, something that happened to me a long time ago where real people didn't live anymore. Before, the thought of visiting those old ghosts seemed like a nightmare waiting to happen. But now, with enough time and a better grip on my life, it seemed more like healing.

"Yeah," I finally said, "I'm curious to see how it's changed since I've been away. A New York trip's going to take a lot of planning though, even if you can fly. I thought maybe we could start these adventures tonight."

This gave her a start. "Tonight?"

"I'm wide awake, aren't you?"

She pondered this for a second, "Um, okay. What did you have in mind?"

"Let's pick a direction and go until we find something interesting."

Kelly grinned, "That way?" she said, tilting her head to our left.

I nodded in agreement, "That way."

She adjusted her position in the air, keeping me cradled against her as she flipped around to the classic Superman flight pose, belly to the world. We drifted forward like a ship on a calm sea, with just a light breeze pushing the sails. It was relaxing, but I expected our first adventure to have more adrenaline.

"Don't mean to sound critical," I said, "But is this really the fastest you can go?"

Kelly narrowed her eyes at me with a sly smile, and I could feel her body heat rise as she built up energy. We exploded across the sky, accelerating so fast I swear I heard a sonic boom. Despite my attempts to save face, I threw my arm around her neck to steady myself, screaming in terror as we broke the sound barrier. Kelly started cracking up, and eventually, once I had adjusted to the insane speed, my screams turned to laughter too. We laughed together as we left Leroy behind, blazing forward at speeds and heights my fragile body wasn't meant to be at.

But I wasn't scared. Kelly wouldn't let me fall.

ACKNOWLEDGEMENTS

It's been a long, tough road getting this book from first draft to publication, so before I close this out, I wanted to give a few special thanks to the people who made bringing this story to the world possible.

First and foremost, I want to thank my dear friend, and writer of exceptional talent, Alex Lehto-Clark, who served as my wise and just editor on this project. Similarly, I would like to thank Duncan Keller and Hayli Cox, who provided critique and helped me develop the story in its earliest stages into something readable. To Sam Borchart, whom this book is dedicated to, thank you for lighting the initial spark that became this project. It wouldn't exist without all the crazy stories about Medina County you've told me, nor without our long talks in an ice cream shop's dirty parking lot. Finally, thank you to all my friends and family, too numerous to list, who read various drafts of the story and provided their own feedback, all of which was invaluable.

Thank you to all the mentors I've had over the years from Ohio State University and Northern Michigan

University. Particularly to Kathryn Norris, my first creative writing teacher who showed me the ropes of writing a novel from start to finish, and Monica McFawn, my brilliant Thesis Director whose unflinching critique of my work and marketing proved indispensable.

On the production side, a huge thanks to Nicki Gee and Joey Gibbs for giving the book a kick-ass theme song, Shelby Dearth for playing Kelly for the book trailer, and Sean Mekinda for shooting the footage and putting it all together.

For so graciously allowing the Grinnsdale crew to appear in these pages, many thanks to Kangyhun Kim, Sam Grevas, Carleigh Cliff, and Sean Mekinda once again. If only there were room in the book for Kelly to mulch hundreds of rats with her bare hands.

To my wonderful family: Mom, whose aggressive support taught me it wasn't giving up to take matters into my own hands by self-publishing the book. To Savannah, my dear sister. And to Dad, for being the only father on the planet who ever pushed his son towards majoring in English instead of away from it. I wish you were still here to read this.

And finally, a special thanks to you, my lovely reader. I sincerely hope you've enjoyed the book, that the story and characters spoke to you, and that you'll join me in my future endeavors.

ABOUT THE AUTHOR

Jackson Keller is a writer and teacher who is preparing to move to Shizuoka, Japan for his next big adventure. A graduate from The Ohio State University, he furthered his education with an MFA in Fiction from Northern Michigan University. He is one half of *Beating a Dead Horse*, a weekly podcast dedicated to analyzing film. He is currently hard at work on his next project, a documentary series about death and video games called *Grief Quest*, which will begin airing on his *YouTube channel* in Fall 2021.

Made in the USA
Middletown, DE
25 May 2021